$\mathcal{B}$

Praise for D0456397

"The final installment in Worth's CHAIM series ends things with a bang. All the previous CHAIM agents are involved and the book closes with a satisfying finish."
—*RT Book Reviews* on *The Soldier's Mission*

"This is a suspenseful and exciting story about love in all its forms."
—*RT Book Reviews* on *Heart of the Night*

"*Secret Agent Minister,* by Lenora Worth, is a fun and danger-filled treat, with love blossoming along the way."
—*RT Book Reviews*

"This second in the Texas Ranger Justice series solves one mystery as it skillfully advances the ongoing one."
—*RT Book Reviews* on the *New York Times* bestseller, *Body of Evidence*

LENORA WORTH

Assignment: Bodyguard

&

The Soldier's Mission

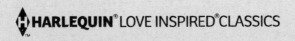

Recycling programs
for this product may
not exist in your area.

First published as Assignment: Bodyguard by Harlequin Books in 2010 and The Soldier's Mission by Harlequin Books in 2010.

ISBN-13: 978-0-373-20855-5

Assignment: Bodyguard & The Soldier's Mission

Copyright © 2017 by Harlequin Books S.A.

The publisher acknowledges the copyright holder of the individual works as follows:

Assignment: Bodyguard
Copyright © 2010 by Lenora H. Nazworth

The Soldier's Mission
Copyright © 2010 by Lenora H. Nazworth

Printed in U.S.A.

CONTENTS

With over seventy books published and millions in print, **Lenora Worth** writes award-winning romance and romantic suspense. Three of her books finaled in the ACFW Carol Awards, and her Love Inspired Suspense novel *Body of Evidence* became a *New York Times* bestseller. Her novella in *Mistletoe Kisses* made her a *USA TODAY* bestselling author. Lenora goes on adventures with her retired husband, Don, and enjoys reading, baking and shopping...especially shoe shopping.

Books by Lenora Worth

Love Inspired Suspense

Men of Millbrook Lake

Her Holiday Protector
Lakeside Peril

Fatal Image
Secret Agent Minister
Deadly Texas Rose
A Face in the Shadows
Heart of the Night
Code of Honor
Risky Reunion
Assignment: Bodyguard
The Soldier's Mission
Body of Evidence
The Diamond Secret

Visit the Author Profile page at Harlequin.com for more titles.

ASSIGNMENT: BODYGUARD

But they lie in wait for their own blood;
they lurk secretly for their own lives.
So are the ways of everyone who is greedy for gain;
it takes away the life of its owners.
—*Proverbs* 1:18–19

To all of my Texas friends, with lots of love.

ONE

"Who is that handsome man wearing the tux?"

Katherine Barton Atkins thanked the waiter for her mineral water with a twist of lime, then glanced around at the woman who'd just asked that question. Red-haired Trudy Pearson had one elegant eyebrow raised in standard cougar mode while she stared across the crowded ballroom.

"Trudy, every man in the room has on a tux," Katherine explained, bemused and just a little morose because of Trudy's need to find a second husband, no matter what.

Some women just couldn't handle being alone, but Katherine was determined not to be one of those. She couldn't fault Trudy for trying, though. They were both widows now. Katherine had married her college sweetheart and Trudy had married an older man whom she'd loved with all her heart. And they'd both lost their husbands within six months of each other. After a year of being a widow, Katherine was trying to get on with her life while Trudy was trying to find a replacement. Katherine kept busy searching for something to fill her empty soul, while Trudy kept busy searching for a younger man because she was so afraid of growing old alone.

"Yes, darlin' Kit," Trudy replied in her sophisticated drawl, "every man in the room has on a tux, but only that man over there by the parlor fern knows how to *wear* one."

Curious, Katherine kept smiling at the people passing by her, then looked in the direction of Trudy's overly interested gaze, her expression shifting from disdain to dismissal as her gaze caught and held that of the man's. She took a sip of her cold water, the elegant bracelet watch Trudy had given her for her last birthday dangling down her arm. "Oh, *that* man wearing the tux. He's my detail."

"Excuse me," Trudy said, almost dropping her sparkling gold evening purse. "Your *detail?* What exactly does that mean? And I want *the details,* all of them. He's positively yummy. And that tuxedo is tailor-made for him and only him."

Kit touched her chignon then looked over at the tall, dark-haired man who was pretending he wasn't looking over at her. "My father thinks I need a bodyguard. I told you about those strange hang-up calls and then the cryptic letters I received. He's just being overly cautious because of this big crowd, I think."

Trudy glanced over at Katherine's father, Gerald Barton, who was standing with his wife, Sally Mae, talking to several other people. "Your daddy doesn't looked worried so why the detail?"

"Oh, he's not worried—*because* of the detail. You know my father hires only the best. And rumor has it this one is top of the line." She didn't want to give her friend the fact sheet on her bodyguard, nor did she tell Trudy about the feeling that someone had been in her house and office. She'd rather not talk about any of that tonight. She'd rather the bodyguard wasn't here in the first place.

But her father was a top-level member of CHAIM, the elite private security organization that worked to protect people the world over. That made him a bit tense and paranoid at times. He'd been worried about her since her husband Jacob had died, but when Katherine happened to mention a few unexplained calls and some of her files being moved and shuffled around, her father had gone into overdrive.

Katherine indulged her father because she knew he meant well, but sometimes his protective nature stifled her. Such as tonight.

"Top of the line is the word, darlin'," Trudy replied, her predatory gaze centered on the man. "He is the very definition of tall, dark and…dangerous."

Katherine couldn't help but laugh at her friend's description, but she tended to agree. At least this time, her father had hired a looker. "Yes, that's him, brought in all the way from London, England. He was handpicked to look out for me tonight. But I'm trying to ignore him."

Trudy's burgundy silk gown rustled as she stepped closer. "British and in a tux. How on earth can you ignore *that*, do tell?" Then she gave Kit a wry smile that held just a trace of condescension. "Oh, let me guess. You can't say anything else about it, right?"

Her friend knew the complications of being the widow of a senator. And Trudy also knew that Katherine's father worked for a mysterious, secretive organization. But Trudy understood discretion and privacy. Besides, it was just too hard to explain right now.

"I'd rather *not* talk about it," Kit said, completely aware that each time she moved an inch the dashing Sir Shane Warwick, known as the Knight, moved an inch with her. Turning away from the agent who worked for the covert Christian organization, she said, "This is a benefit, Trudy. I need to mingle with our patrons and thank them for their generosity toward the Barton Atkins Foundation." She put down the water she'd been nursing and whirled around, her cream-colored evening gown whispering around her legs, her matching high-heeled satin sandals making her feet scream for release. "Now why don't you quit ogling the man and help me greet my guests, okay?"

"Oh, all right," Trudy replied, turning to whisper something to a nearby waiter. Winking at the waiter, she pivoted back to Kit. "But later, you and I are going to have a serious talk. If you're in danger enough to need a handsome guard following you around, I need to know." Then she touched a hand to Kit's arm, her brown eyes turning serious. "I couldn't bear it if—"

"I'm fine," Kit said, wishing her father wasn't so overbearing. "It just goes with the territory."

Gerald Barton was one of the top agents in CHAIM—Christians for Amnesty, Intervention and Missions. And even though her father was supposedly retired, Kit had learned at an early age that a CHAIM agent never really retired. Especially when that agent's only daughter had lost her husband under questionable circumstances and was, herself, constantly receiving threats because of her stand against injustice.

Frustrated with the restrictions on her life, she shook her head then silently chastised herself. Maybe a prayer of thanks would be more appropriate, considering she was loved and held dear by her family and her friends. And she was blessed beyond measure. Which made her quip, "I'd like to forget all of this, just for tonight, okay?"

Trudy nodded, then leaned in. "But, honey, you must be thinking the same thing I'm thinking. They never figured out what happened when Jacob's helicopter went down. That crash might not have been an accident, no matter how hard the authorities tried to do a cover-up."

"You don't have to remind me of that," Kit said, old hurts making her snap in spite of Trudy's concerns. "I think about it every day of my life." And she always hoped that somewhere in her philanthropic travels, she'd find out the truth regarding her husband's death. But no one was willing to delve into that now. It was over and done.

Lord, give me strength and patience, she silently prayed. *And teach me how to get over this deep grief.*

"I'm sorry," Trudy said. She dropped her arm and stood back. "Go do your job. But remember, you promised me you will take some time off for that spa trip we keep talking about. I've found a very secluded retreat out in New Mexico. Just the two of us. We need some downtime."

Kit looked at her watch again, thinking she'd need to make a speech in a few minutes. "That would be good.

I've been so busy planning tonight's event, I think I'm a little overwrought. But, Trudy, thanks for your concern."

Trudy gave her a quick peck on the cheek, her worried look changing to playful as she touched a finger to Kit's pearls, lifting the strand for a second before she let the shimmering strand drop. "Whatever you think about him, that gorgeous man over there can't seem to take his eyes off you, darlin'."

"That's because he's being *paid* to keep his eyes *on* me," Katherine countered.

"And I'm sure he's enjoying his job," Trudy replied as she waltzed away and into the crowd. "Maybe you should enjoy the company."

Kit lifted her head, her hand going up to the single strand of pearls Jacob had given her for their tenth anniversary. They'd gone out to dinner and after they'd come home, he'd unclasped the pearls and hugged her close. They'd been fighting but he'd tried all that night to make up to her. "Promise me you'll wear these every single day."

"I promise," she'd said. That was the last time she'd held him in her arms. Her husband was dead now, and in many ways, so was she. At least she felt dead inside. Her devout mother and former CHAIM operative, Sally Mae, would tell her to never give up hope, to turn to her faith. But how could that help now?

What did it matter if she was receiving death threats for her determined stance? She had work to do and she intended to do it, and no amount of empty threats would stop her. Her work was the only thing holding Kit together these days. Work was her salvation. So with a renewed determination that included ignoring the handsome, dedicated man who'd been shadowing her all night, Katherine put on a convincing smile then moved through the glittering crowd filing into the hotel ballroom, her mind going on autopilot as she played to the hilt the role of hostess.

Head up, shoulders back, and a serene expression. That was the Barton tradition, after all.

He shouldn't have signed up for this. It was never a good idea to be in charge of taking care of a beautiful woman. Never a good idea, but then the Knight was known for taking on the tough cases. This one was killer tough. And so lovely.

Shane Warwick moved through the crowd, his gaze sweeping the room with a cool assessment. The ballroom was long and rectangular with shimmering crystal chandeliers and gleaming mirrored walls, which made it twice as hard to keep up with the subject under surveillance. Glass windows all around the big square room allowed an incredible view of downtown Austin, Texas, and the Colorado River, but Shane didn't have time to look out the windows. If he took his eyes off Katherine Barton Atkins long enough, he could enjoy the view of the State Capitol gleaming brightly off in the distance. But he couldn't look away from her and for more reasons than just this particular assignment required.

The woman was easy on the eyes, as they liked to say here in Texas.

Shane went over the facts, trying to distract himself from getting too involved. Getting involved with beautiful women was his gift and his downfall. Sometimes the job required certain things and sometimes he just fell hard for a pretty face then moved on once the excitement had worn off. He couldn't allow that to happen this time. Mainly because if Shane crossed that line with this woman, her father and his superior, Gerald Barton, would shoot first and ask questions later, as they also liked to say here in Texas.

Back to the facts, he sternly reminded himself.

Katherine "Kit" Barton Atkins, daughter of wealthy CHAIM leader Gerald Barton and his wife, Sally Mae Barton, childless widow of State Senator Jacob Atkins, and CEO of the Barton Atkins Foundation. Old Texas money and all the perks and responsibilities of also inheriting her husband's newly minted money to boot.

According to the information he'd been given, the young widow wasn't a typical socialite. She believed in the causes she worked so hard for, even if it meant she had to attend such stuffy affairs as this one. And even if it meant she had to go out into the field and make her points with photo ops and highly opinionated, impassioned speeches. Plus, she didn't seem to mind getting down and dirty or going into the fray. He'd seen pictures of her holding dying infants in third world countries; he'd seen pictures of her walking through storm-littered villages. And he'd seen an unauthorized shot of her standing in a corner, turned slightly away from the glare of the spotlight, her hand to her face, all alone and wearing exquisite white pearls and a severe black dress, just after they'd buried her husband.

But she hid her grief behind her work and that was why he was here. Her father was very concerned about her. Which made Shane concerned, too, and intent on protecting her. If he could keep the woman in his line of sight.

She moved through the crowd with a grace that reminded Shane of ballerinas and swans and all things lovely. Her whole persona exuded cool, blond elegance. Her evening gown was almost severe in its cut and color—shimmering and sleeveless but with a discreet beaded beige portrait collar and a skirt that flowed all around her in soft, folding wisps of designer-cut silk. And she was wearing what looked like the same pearls she'd worn to her husband's funeral. Other than a pretty glittering watch on her left arm and her wedding band, the pearls were her only decoration. He wondered if she'd chosen this dress and jewelry on purpose—to set her apart from all the standard but predictable black and red formal dresses, festooned with sparkling jewels, fluttering all around her. Or had she just reached into her closet and come up with a winning combination of classic proportions? Either way, it worked for Shane.

Shane had always admired attractive women and he could spot a phony a mile away. Katherine was the real thing. Purebred and gracious, perfectly attired and perfectly serene. She seemed untouchable, unruffled and unconcerned, until she glanced up and straight into his eyes. Then she just looked determined and defiant.

Shane smiled to himself and put on his best game face. Kit was coming to greet him, at last. But she did not appear happy to see him.

"You're becoming a nuisance, Sir Warwick," she said as she walked up to him, a soft smile belying the dare in her pretty green eyes.

"Oh, really?" Shane took her hand and held it to his lips for the briefest of kisses. "And how's that, Mrs. Atkins, since you have yet to even acknowledge me. I was beginning to think I'd lost my touch."

She put a hand to her throat, diamonds twinkling on

her finger. "Where are my manners?" Her smile didn't change, but the expression in her catlike eyes certainly did. "I thought it wasn't proper for a woman to acknowledge the man her father hired to watch out for her, or was I wrong in that assumption?"

Shane adjusted his black tie. "Your father warned me about your attitude. And that you'd spot me the minute I entered the room."

"Did he now?"

"He did indeed. Warned me about a lot of things. And told me not to let you out of my sight." He leaned close and gave her a smile that had reportedly melted feminine hearts all across the globe. "And I must say, I don't mind keeping my eyes on you at all. Your pictures don't do you justice. You are quite beautiful."

She inclined her head, pretending to enjoy being with him, even laughing for the benefit of those standing all around them. "Hmm. Let me see if I can get this straight. A dashing British secret agent in a precision-cut tux and a seemingly interested American woman in an overpriced evening gown. Their eyes meet across the crowded room, they walk toward each other, smiling and cordial...and the rest is written in the stars. Except I know how this ends. I've seen the movie. Your charms won't work on me, Sir Warwick."

Shane laughed out loud then looked into her eyes. She was actually very refreshing. Scary, but refreshing. "Ah, but you forgot the beautiful part."

She touched the pearls at her throat. "Excuse me?"

"The *beautiful* interested woman," he replied, smiling at his own cleverness. "And you *are* beautiful."

She smiled, too. That was a good sign, at least. Then she stopped smiling. "And you forgot the *seemingly* part, you know, as in the *seemingly* interested woman. Only this woman is not interested—so cut the charm, Warwick. I'm on to you and I don't like it one bit that you'd use charisma to try and win me over to allow you to hover around me. Get off my back, and give me some room here. I've got a full evening ahead of me and you're in the way."

Shane Warwick had to heave a surprised breath. There was a bit of fire underneath all that coolness, after all. "Your father also warned me that you'd try to lose me. But that, dear lady, isn't going to happen." There was only one way to handle such a bundle of bemusing contradictions and do his job at the same time, so he took her hand and whirled her out onto the dance floor. "I suggest we make the best of it…and dance."

He was rewarded with a gasp of surprise followed by a tight smile that told him only the most practiced rules of decorum were keeping her from slapping him across the face.

And because of that, Shane grinned down at her and reveled in the way she flowed right into his arms. This waltz might prove either to win her over, or do him in. He'd lay odds on the last scenario. He needed to do some serious praying for patience and control, and that God would allow him to do his duty and protect this woman.

So things would turn out differently this time.

Putting those dark thoughts out of his mind, Shane held her tight, and after taking some time to look into her brightly mad green eyes, he moved his gaze from her pretty face to the other faces in the crowd.

And he wondered the whole time if someone in this VIP crowd had been sent here to murder her.

TWO

Kit breathed in the fresh soapy smell of Shane's rich chocolate-colored hair. This wasn't fair, the way he held her in his arms with an aloof possession. This wasn't fair, the way her heart hurt from missing Jacob so much, the way her heart fluttered to life each time Shane bent his head and held her gaze with icy blue eyes, while he tried to search for all her secrets.

She wished her father hadn't hired this particular man, wished her husband was still alive to dance with her, and wished she could just run away to some quiet island and grieve, really grieve, for all she'd lost the day her husband had died. But a Barton had to be strong; a Barton showed no grief. And so she was expected to carry on. Duty called. And only manners kept her from doing exactly that—up and running out of this room. And away from this man.

"Am I making you uncomfortable?" he asked, his British accent precise and crisp in her ear.

"What do you think?" she shot back, looking up at him. "People are staring." Even her parents had stopped chatting to watch them move around the dance floor.

He dipped his head, his breath tickling against her earlobe. "We could go somewhere more private so we can discuss my concerns for your safety."

"Nice try," she said, lifting away. "But I need to stay here with the people who paid a hefty sum to get in this room tonight, sorry."

He slid a glance around the room. "That's perfectly all right by me, Mrs. Atkins. Less danger in a crowd. But sooner or later, we will need to talk about your father's instructions."

Kit could agree with that, but not right now. "Sooner or later, we'll do that, maybe over a nice cup of tea," she said. "Just not tonight."

Apparently, he didn't like her response. "You are aware that you might be in danger, right?"

"Very aware." But the only danger she could see right now was the man dancing with her. No doubt, it was unwise to be alone with Shane Warwick. So she played her part and carried on until she could figure out what to do next.

"Call me Kit," she said, wondering why she'd decided to give him that liberty. "And I hate crowds, but I can't leave."

He smiled at that. "So you force yourself to do this, anyway? Because you believe in what you do even though events like this are sometimes tedious but necessary."

Surprised that he got her, she nodded. "Yes. I'm a

rather shy, private person but I learned a long time ago I can't live that way. And I won't hide away like a coward, no matter what you and my father think. And no matter how big the crowd, and no matter the situation."

He studied her as they glided around the room. "I'm aware of the crowd, and very much aware of the situation. Heads are turning, whispers are surfacing, but that's not my concern right now."

"Well, it is mine," she replied. "People will talk."

"And you don't want them to, right? So what? The cool, elegant, tragic widow is dancing with a mysterious stranger. And right here in Austin, at that. Scandalous, but maybe exactly what you need right now. People need to think you have a new suitor."

Anger flashed through Kit. Did she seem that sad and pathetic? "I'm not that tragic, thank you. And I have to walk a thin line, to protect the organization I've worked so hard to build through the years, so you can't possibly know what I need."

The intimate look he gave her made her think he might know something about need himself, but right now, he didn't dare voice that—not out loud and to her face. His job was to convince her that she needed him for protection against something she couldn't even see in front of her. Something she didn't want to see. She only wanted to continue her work. And continuing this dance without guilt or worry of scandal might be nice, too, for a change.

He dropped the charm, almost startling her with the lightning fast way he'd changed. "Right now, I know that you need to take *this* situation very seriously. You're in danger and I'm here to keep you out of harm's way."

Kit's heart did a long shudder, fear tickling through

her like a whispering warning for the first time tonight. "Why won't my father discuss this with me, so I can understand?"

"It's too complicated." He watched her for a minute, his icy eyes softening and never leaving her face. "There's been some chatter. Some of the threats you received were becoming very pointed and suggestive. And we've examined your home and office, based on files that have gone missing. It's enough to make Gerald think there's a need to be cautious. That's all you should know."

She lifted her chin. "I get that same line from my father. You know, I might be more willing and cooperative if someone would simply tell me what's going on. How can I be cautious if I don't know what I'm running from?"

"Good point." He looked at her with regret when the music ended. "Why don't we go sit down and I'll try to explain."

She checked her watch. "I have to give a thank-you speech in about fifteen minutes, Mr. Warwick."

"It's Shane," he replied, his smile back in let's pretend mode. "And not to worry on that account. I will be a perfect gentleman at all times and you can escape to give your speech without missing a beat. You have my word on that."

Kit believed him, and to her ultimate aggravation, was almost a little disappointed to cave so easily. Trudy was right about Shane Warwick. He knew how to wear a tuxedo. The man exuded cool, calm, collected and charming. Lethal qualities to tempt a woman who missed the closeness of marriage and a husband. But easing her loneliness wasn't why Shane Warwick was here.

Her powerful father had ordered him to watch over her. And Gerald Barton could pay for the best in everything, including bodyguards. She could rest easy in that assurance at least. Even if she probably wouldn't sleep a wink tonight when she finally made it home.

"We can take that table in the far corner by the orchestra," she told him, her gaze moving through the crowd. "We shouldn't be interrupted there."

"Good," Shane said, his approval telling her they'd also be safer there. "I'll get you settled and fetch us something to drink. Are you hungry?"

"No." She couldn't eat a bite if her life depended on it. Then she remembered why Shane was here. Her life might depend on following his orders, whether she wanted to or not. Dropping her defiance for now, she allowed him to guide her to their table.

The eyes of everyone in the room followed them with clear interest and curious speculation.

Shane set down their drinks and a plate of canapés then pulled out the chair across from her. The vase of red roses on the stark white brocade tablecloth added a sense of drama to their meeting. He'd taken on this job and now he had to do his best to convince the subject at hand that she needed to listen to reason. And, he decided on the spot, he hoped he could make her smile again in the process of getting acquainted with her.

Shane didn't know which part of his task would be the most difficult—keeping her safe or removing her mantle of grief. He hated the look of despair that came into her eyes when she didn't think anyone was watching. But he was paid to observe and paid to pick up on the slightest of nuances.

And right now, as he watched Kit from across the tiny table, he saw a woman who hid her emotions and her fears behind the aura of grace and style and proper grooming.

His mother, British-bred and born, would highly approve of Katherine Atkins. But Lady Samantha wasn't here tonight, thankfully. He didn't need her playing matchmaker while he was on the clock. No, his dear mother was safely ensconced in their country home near London, entertaining a group of pretentious, titled friends who moved in royal circles. And having the time of her life doing it, he imagined.

"You're grinning," Kit said, her exquisite eyebrows lifting like a butterfly's wings. "Is this amusing to you?"

He shook his head. "I was thinking about my mother, actually."

Kit slanted her head. "That's not very complimentary of me, now is it? We're finally alone and you're thinking about your mother?"

He liked her sense of humor. "Trust me, luv, it was a passing thought. I was thinking how she'd love to meet you. She loves all things Texas, so much so that she married a Texan—my father was born and raised near Dallas. We still have property just outside Fort Worth." His smile tipped up into a grin. "And she named me after a movie—that Wyoming western *Shane*. I'm surprised she didn't name me Dallas, but my father loved that particular movie. Watched it all the time."

Kit leaned forward. "Well, I didn't know all of that. But you're so—"

"British?" he asked, following her body language and leaning forward a bit himself. "That I am. My mother's British with a lineage that dates back to Queen Elizabeth—the first Queen Elizabeth, that is." He shrugged. "My parents met on a cruise to Africa, went on safari together and well, as you said earlier, the rest was written in the stars. A true love match."

She lifted away, clearly uncomfortable with any talk of love matches. "Did your father move to England, then?"

"Yes and no. They lived there part of the time and here part of the time by mutual consent, and sometimes they even lived apart by mutual consent, but I attended school in England and spent most of my youth there, per my mother's request."

"And how did your father feel about that?"

"He brought me here during school breaks and the summers so we could hunt and fish and do manly things. Just so I'd have a well-rounded life, you understand."

"I do understand. Texas is so vast, we can all acquire a well-rounded life here. Even an Englishman."

His grin turned impish. "I think my mother would agree with you on that. She did spend a great deal of time in Texas when they were dating. Especially when he was trying to convince her to marry him. She said she almost backed out after meeting his loud, crude, slightly crazy family. But she grew to love them, one and all." He touched a rose petal and watched it fall to the table. "And she loved my father. Their time together wasn't always happy, though. I think they needed their spots of separation."

She frowned. "I thought you said it was a love match."

"I did and it was. But all good things take time and compromise, or as my mother calls it—mutual consent and mutual respect." He looked at her, her eyes, her lips, her long, elegant throat, that enticing strand of perfect pearls. "But some things can be worth the wait."

Kit, following the line of his gaze, toyed with her pearls. "So she didn't give in at first, even though she was in love with him?"

Shane saw the interest in her pretty green eyes. And a bit of sadness. She was a romantic then. "No, he used to say he chased her until she let him catch her. And she used to say that she had him wrapped around her finger, but she just wanted to make sure he sweated a little before she said yes."

"What a charming story."

Shane nodded, took a sip of his drink. "My father, William, died a few years ago. So now, it's hard for Lady Samantha to come to Texas. It reminds her too much of him."

Kit put her elbow on the table then dropped her chin onto her upturned hand, making her look more like a fresh-faced debutante than an attractive, mature woman. "I can certainly understand that feeling. Sometimes, I'd like to get out of this state myself."

Shane noted that. "I'm sorry for your loss. From what I've heard, your husband was a good man."

She blinked, realized she wasn't sitting up properly and just like that, her spine went ramrod straight, no longer touching the back of her chair, while the curtain on her emotions came down with a feminine sigh and an elegant lifting of her chin. "Thank you. Now let's talk about why you're here and what I need to do to make this as unobtrusive as possible."

Shane put his hand on his heart. "Unobtrusive? You want *me* to be unobtrusive?" She didn't need to know that he was an expert at sneaking in and out of most places completely undetected.

She actually laughed and the sound of it flowed over Shane's highly aware nerve endings like delicate bells moving through a warm wind. "What? You've never tried being that way before?"

"Not in my arsenal, I'm afraid. I prefer to operate on the principle of hiding in plain sight. I like to be out there, very visible, but very aware. My plan is to be seen with you a lot, so that the society ladies who love to gossip over lunch at the club or while hitting tennis balls back and forth on the court, will take notice and spread the word. I want us to be seen as an item."

"Your premise being?"

"My premise being that an attached woman is much safer than a single, alone woman." He shrugged. "And besides, it will make my job that much easier."

Her eyes went dark again. "I am single and alone and I've learned to live with that, regardless of making your life easier."

Shane hated himself for making her think along those lines but it was necessary for her safety. "All the more reason to seem involved. My presence could throw off a potential enemy."

"Or invite that enemy to fight to the finish."

"I see you know more about your father's work than you let on."

"Yes, more than I want to know." She pushed at her immaculate upswept white-blond hair. "I don't like living this way. I don't want to walk around in fear."

"You won't have to if I'm with you."

"But how long will this ploy work? Are you prepared

to stay by my side all the time, even when I leave the country?"

His pulse quickened at that. "Especially if you leave the country—make that—if you're *allowed* to leave the country. I have my orders."

"Of course you do. And I like my privacy and my dignity, and I won't be told what I can and can't do. So I don't intend to be part of some facade or deception. It's not right."

"It is right if it means saving your life, Katherine."

She stood up, dismissing him in a shimmer of silk and a whiff of lily-scented perfume. "That's the CHAIM way, isn't it? Always. Might makes right. All for the good fight, the good cause. Do you ever get tired of all the secrecy and the conspiracy?"

Shane almost answered yes to that question. Yes, he did get tired, of war, of the horrors of injustice, of all that he'd seen in his covert travels around the planet, but he'd joined this organization after his father had introduced him to Gerald Barton. They'd both seen something in Shane that he hadn't even seen in himself. A restless need to avenge good people, to help save lives when innocence clashed with evil, when good men had to fight ruthless criminals that no amount of man's law could stop. He'd been trained from birth to hunt, shoot, and fight like a gentleman—at his mother's insistence, but with his father's help, he'd learn how to think like a combination street gang fighter and gunslinger, with purposeful intent and take-no-prisoners determination. And even though he might sometimes have to get down and dirty to do his job, he worked to fight the good fight and he believed in saving lives, not taking them. So he looked up at Katherine Atkins and said nothing.

"Your silence speaks volumes," she said, whirling to leave.

Shane was up and by her side in a flash. "There are some things a lady doesn't need to hear."

She glared up at him, her eyes a sea of unfathomable green. "And there are some things a gentleman should tell a lady. Such as what kind of danger she is in and why? But your loyalty lies with my father and CHAIM, right? So I can't count on you to tell me the truth."

He moved in front of her, blocking her way while those curious gazes all around the room stayed centered on them. They'd make the society columns tomorrow and that would work just fine with their cover. "You can count on me to protect you, to give my life for you if necessary. That is my job."

"Don't you think you're being a bit overly dramatic?"

"Don't you think you could possibly avoid making a scene and listen to reason?"

She looked around, realizing much too late that the room had grown quiet, that the orchestra was on a break. The music had stopped and all eyes were on the two of them.

"This is your fault," she said just as a camera's flash blinded her. "Great, now you've brought out the paparazzi, too. So much for hiding in plain sight."

Shane trained his eyes on the person who'd taken that picture and that's when he saw it. Just a flash in the crowd, a quick bit of action that seemed entirely out of place. There behind the roving photographer, a man dressed as a waiter stood silent and still near an exit on the other side of the orchestra stage, not far from where they were. Shane directed his gaze to the man holding the linen napkin across one arm and saw in that one second, as his gaze locked with the other man's, that the man had a gun trained on Katherine.

In a move that he'd remember later as pure adrenaline, Shane pushed Katherine to the floor behind the table, threw himself down to shield her and screamed at the top of his lungs, "Everyone down. Now!"

A rush of panic hit the room and then bullets started flying all around them. Chaos took over as people either ducked or ran for the nearest exit. But there in the corner behind the protection of a flimsy table, Shane held Katherine's trembling body close to his, his heartbeat racing to match hers, his prayers asking for protection as he tried to get a line on the shooter crouching near the big stage.

Speaking with shouted emphasis into his earpiece, he called for backup, his gaze never leaving the determined shooter. In spite of the shouts, screams and confusion all around them, the man crouched and moved with purposeful intent, weaving between chairs and tables to finish the job.

And Katherine was the target.

"Don't move," he whispered into Katherine's ear. "We're going to get you out of here, just hold on."

Then he reached for the Glock semiautomatic pistol he was carrying in a shoulder holster underneath his tuxedo.

THREE

She couldn't breathe.

Kit twisted, her hands clutching one of the lapels of Shane's tuxedo. He'd shielded her, putting his body between her and the bullets, and now he was trying to peek around the table. He had a sleek, strange-looking gun in his hand. This was real, too real.

"Shane?"

He didn't answer at first. His body tensed, his gaze fixed on someone across the room.

"I'm here," he finally said, giving her a quick look. "Stay down. I'm right here. But Katherine, listen to me, all right?"

"I'm listening," she said, wanting to laugh. He'd tried all night to make her listen but now that she was tossed in a corner like a sack of potatoes—her dress torn, her hair coming undone, and someone hiding in the now-silent room with a gun—she was willing to listen. More than willing. She listened just to hear Shane's breath.

"Kit, could you let go of my jacket?"

Mortified that she was holding on to Shane for dear life, she dropped her white-knuckled hand. "I'm sorry."

"No need to apologize. I want to get a better angle. And I want you to stay behind this table, understand?"

She lifted her head then took her first real breath since he'd pushed her down behind the table. And with that breath, she was back in action herself, her fear turning to a rage that screamed for release. "Shane, I can't stay down here while others are in danger. There are a lot of people in this room besides me. Let me up."

"No, no. I mean it, Kit. You can't—"

"How many?" she asked in a tight whisper.

Shane pushed her back down. "Not now. Stay down."

"How many shooters?" she asked again, her hand now gripping his arm.

He actually appeared shocked. He blinked, looked back at her. "Only one, so far. And if you'll let go of my arm, he won't be around much longer."

"Are you going to kill him right here?"

He watched the still room for movement. "Would you prefer I take him out back and throw him to the hogs?"

"There are no hogs in downtown Austin," she replied, her words growing stronger. "But I know where a mean, old bull lives."

He shot her a worried smile. "You're in shock. It'll pass."

"I am not in shock. I'm mad," she said on a hiss of breath. "And I've got a cramp in my foot."

"Well, I wish that's all you had to worry about, Katherine. Now let go of me and stay down and we'll talk about the mean bull later."

She finally released his arm. "What's the plan?"

"I'm not quite sure," he whispered back. "I'm making it up as I go."

"Some bodyguard you are."

"Yes, right on that." He flipped the table onto its side so fast she didn't even see it fall. A few people down around them gasped but Shane held up a hand to silence them. "Get behind this and stay here. Do not move." And then, in a flash of black, he was rolling away from her and gone.

"Shane?"

He didn't answer. She heard people whispering in fear all around her then glanced up for the first time to find Trudy huddled with a man behind the buffet table—the head of catering of all people. Motioning, Kit held up a thumb toward her friend.

Trudy returned the thumbs-up and shot her a wan smile. Then Kit heard a loud thud, followed by a deep groan. She closed her eyes, praying that Shane wasn't dead. She willed him not to die, not tonight while he was trying to save her. She couldn't bear that kind of guilt, especially after she'd tried so hard to ignore him and discourage him. But Shane was a good man. She could see that now. He had such a nice smile and he had this air of self-assurance that she'd never witnessed in another man. Not even Jacob.

"Jacob," she whispered, her heart breaking with longing, her head down and her hand over her mouth. "Jacob, I need you here. Why did you go away?" She didn't voice her prayer, but heard it clearly in her head.

Dear Lord, I need You to help all of us. Don't let any-one die tonight.

She saw a masculine hand set against a crisp white cuff reaching toward her. The cuff link winked bright and bold and looked like some sort of ancient coat of arms. Katherine blinked, thinking this must all be a dream. But the hand reached down toward her with an impatient shake so she had no choice but to take hold of it. She reached up and felt the man's fingers wrapping around hers, a stirring warmth penetrating the numb-ness that had frozen her entire system. She gazed up and into Shane's crystal blue eyes.

"Come with me," he said, his tone curt and no-nonsense.

Katherine got up but stumbled, her knees refusing to hold her. Then she was swept clear of the floor and into his arms. Wrapping her hands around his neck, she turned away from the few people still hiding in the room and trained her eyes on him. Only him. She heard Shane barking orders, heard her father speaking loudly to the hotel security.

Shane's voice carried through the ballroom. "One shooter, secured. He went down on the right side of the stage, still alive. I'll give a full statement later. I'm get-ting her out of here."

The room sounded with cries and feet rustling and people running across the marble floor. They were all asking rapid-fire questions, men angry and women cry-ing. The music would not start back up now, of course. It had been put silent by a killer's intent.

Katherine heard all of it through the muffled protec-tion of Shane's rock-solid shoulder bearing the weight of her head, but she couldn't face the people and the questions and…she didn't dare ask what had happened to the other man.

"He's still unconscious. But I reckon he won't talk when he does wake up."

Shane looked from Gerald Barton to the two other men sitting in the darkly paneled study. They were back at the CHAIM fortress called Eagle Rock, in the secluded hill country just on the outskirts of Austin.

"He will soon enough," Alfred Anderson said. "The Austin police will see to that."

John Simpson grunted then took a long swig of coffee. "But he might rather be charged, tried and put away for a long time. Because if he speaks, he knows he could die inside prison or out. Smells like a deliberate hit to me."

Gerald got up to stomp around the massive conference room. "At least she's safe here." Then he glanced at Shane. "She is safe here, isn't she, Warwick?"

Shane used to be sure about such things, but tonight, he wasn't so sure. He'd given a detailed statement to the locals and he'd gone over everything with his CHAIM supervisors. But something didn't seem right. His ulcer was shouting a warning with quick spasms of heat. Pulling out a roll of antacid tablets, he chewed one then said, "I have some concerns, sir."

Gerald looked affronted. "C'mon, Knight, you helped rebuild the security system in this place. Kissie and you both said no one can get in here."

"What if someone is *already* in here?" Shane said. "It's happened before."

Gerald nodded. "He's right. Devon Malone almost lost Lydia Cantrell because one of the servants wasn't just here to fold napkins and plan meals. Tried to smother the poor girl with a pillow."

"We've tightened things since then," Alfred said. "My wife made sure of that. She was not happy that we'd let an assassin serve us dinner, let me tell you."

In spite of the image of tiny, spry Lulu Anderson being peeved about a renegade butler, Shane still had his doubts. Something about this whole night didn't make sense.

They'd made sure the hotel ballroom was secure, which meant someone on the inside had set this up. That was the only clear explanation. Or maybe he wasn't *thinking* very clearly since he couldn't stop thinking about Katherine Atkins. Think about the assignment, not the client, he reminded himself. He should have learned from past experiences to stay focused.

And yet, he couldn't get the image out of his mind of Katherine's hand reaching up to take his. Or the feel of her soft skin brushing against his.

"I just want to be sure we're doing the right thing, sir. Another location might be more advisable at this point since we could have been followed. We need to get her away from Austin."

Eagle Rock was Fort Knox—impenetrable and tightly secure, with everything from fingerprint and facial scanners to keypads with state-of-the-art biometric security. Which is why Shane had brought Katherine straight here, rather than take her to her home in Austin. This sprawling ranch-style mansion held eight bedrooms and as many adjoining baths, an industrial size kitchen and a long dining room, a huge den and several smaller offices, not to mention several outbuildings and a private airstrip. Each of those areas could be sealed off from the rest with a flip of a switch. Not exactly a great way to live, but necessary in their line of work.

And usually, CHAIM agents only came here for conferences and training sessions, or to be interrogated when an operation had gone wrong. Which it almost had tonight.

"I didn't do my job tonight," he said, whirling to stare at the three men who, although retired, were still listed as his immediate superiors in a crisis such as this. "I should have been more vigilant."

"Warwick, we've gone over this," Gerald said. "I was there in the room, too, son, and I never saw this coming." His shrug said it all. "We checked everyone who entered that place, especially the hired help. I can't figure how that man got past security with that gun."

"That's just it," Shane said, logic coloring his words. "He didn't. Someone had to give him the gun or put it where he could find it. Someone from the inside."

"Well, thankfully we got the man alive. And you saved my daughter's life," Gerald replied.

"But I was assigned to watch her," Shane said, looking down at his discarded, black bow tie, his mind whirling with images of people running and screaming and a lone gunman standing near an exit door, his sleek gun held with one hand just underneath the shield of his other raised arm. And aimed right toward Katherine Atkins.

"If that camera flash hadn't gone off, she would have died right there beside me."

"But that's the fact, Warwick," John said. "You *were* right there beside her and your quick actions saved her. And a lot more people, too."

Gerald nodded, his fingers thumping on the table. "And that fancy stun gun you carry around put the shooter out cold. Fancy little gadget, that thing. Left a bullet hole in that man's shoulder but kept him alive for questioning."

Well, a Glock .357 with a suppressor wasn't exactly a stun gun, but this was Texas after all. These men were better suited to rifles and shotguns, or maybe six-shooters.

Shane went back over the details. "It was chaos at first, but a lot of the guests did manage to get out of the room. The few who were left stayed behind tables and doors. Thank goodness we only had two wounded and no one dead."

Yet he couldn't get the memories of shattering glass and frightened screams out of his mind. Nor the image of Kit reaching up a hand to take his after he'd felled the crouching shooter, her eyes locking with his when he'd lifted her into his arms and carried her out of the room. He could still smell the scent of lilies on his clothes.

And he still had to wonder if the shooter, who'd also had a silencer on his gun, had been there alone. Or if this had been carefully planned by someone close to Katherine.

"The papers will be all over this tomorrow morning," John warned. "But it can't be helped. The official word will be that someone allegedly came into the room with a gun, but was apprehended and arrested on the scene. It'll be listed as an attempted robbery due to the elite crowd, most of them wearing expensive baubles and carrying big wallets. We don't want any more information than necessary leaking out, especially anything regarding Katherine being the target."

"As far as I know, none of the people there are aware of that," Shane said, not ready to voice what his instincts seemed to be shouting. "And frankly, gentlemen, I didn't stick around to do damage control. My only intent once the shooter was secured was to get Katherine to a safe location."

John Simpson glanced over at Gerald. "And we've put out the word that Katherine and you have been dating, so you've taken her to a secluded location to get over the shock of what happened. That way, the press can leave her alone. We hope. The official statement should be in the papers and on the news tomorrow."

"That's our best cover," Shane agreed. And that's exactly what he'd planned to insinuate to the public— that they were an item. Well, the best laid plans of mice and men...

"You did the right thing, bringing her here," Gerald said. "You have my gratitude."

"I'd like to check on her," Shane said, wondering if he'd be dismissed or watched himself. These three men were some of the original five-man team that had started CHAIM all those years ago, halfway around the globe while they'd all served their country in Vietnam and later, other areas of the world. They were still a force to be reckoned with. "If I may have your permission, Gerald."

Gerald gave him a mean-hard stare, but nodded. "Her mama's in there with her right now. And trust me, son, you don't want Sally Mae getting her dander up again tonight. She was in a real tear about her daughter almost getting shot, let me tell you. I should have sicced her on that gunman. She'd get some answers."

"I do believe she would have, sir."

Gerald ran a hand over his silver hair. "Better give them some time together before you go knocking on any doors."

"Duly noted," Shane said, his smile tired. Sally Mae had nearly taken down the house earlier, demanding to see her daughter, and she didn't care if it hair-lipped the governor. Frightful woman she was when she was in a tizzy. "I'll be out on the back patio then."

He took his leave, knowing they'd want to discuss this latest development in private. He'd get his orders soon enough. But right now, he needed some time to digest all that had taken place. And he needed to find a way to make sure an incident such as this never happened again. Because that shooter had been a hired expert. Hired from someone high up and able to afford an assassin. Shane couldn't get the notion out of his head that maybe that same someone had been in the crowd tonight.

He had to get Kit to safety. And that meant away from Austin and away from Eagle Rock. He knew how to hide a person. And besides, he knew exactly which room they'd whisked Kit off to earlier and he wasn't above breaking into that room to make sure she was safe.

She might not ever feel safe again. In spite of having a warm bath and putting on a soft cotton tunic, matching pants and a cashmere robe someone had handed her a few minutes ago, Kit felt cold and clammy. But she held herself tightly together because she refused to shiver in fear.

"Honey, why don't you lie down?"

Kit turned from the drape-covered, bulletproof window to find her mother hovering near the brocade sofa of the cozy sitting room just off the bedroom. "I'm not sleepy, Mother."

"I could give you something," Sally Mae Barton said, reaching into her purse. "I have a sedative."

"I'm not taking a pill either," Kit said. "I just want to go to my own home. When can I leave Eagle Rock?"

"Oh, now, honey, I don't know about that. Your daddy is in a real pickle about what happened. I can't say when you'll be able to leave."

"You can't be serious," Kit said, pacing in front of the fireplace. It was late summer and humid even at this hour, but she thought about building a fire. Only, someone would rush to stop her. Too many people were hovering around her tonight, stifling her with well-meaning concern. She just wanted to get away from it all.

She thought of Shane and wondered where he was. Had they sent him away? No, her father wouldn't do that. He liked Shane and trusted him or he wouldn't have brought him here. Shane had done everything in his power to help her, and she owed him her life. He'd saved a lot of people's lives tonight.

"I want to see Shane," she announced to her mother.

Sally Mae lifted a slender hand through her dark hair. "I don't think that's wise, darlin'. It's late and he's in with the others right now. You just need to rest."

Kit wasn't about to rest. "Mother, I can't sleep. I'm too keyed up. And I'd like to talk to the man who put his life on the line in order to save mine tonight."

Sally Mae stood to her five-feet-two-inch height. "You can't do that, Katherine."

Katherine wasn't having any of that. Her mother might have been a CHAIM operative in her heyday, but she wasn't going to bully Kit with that superior attitude. "Mother, I want to see Shane and if I have to scream at the top of my lungs and sound every alarm in this stucco and brick fortress, I'll do it. I've had about enough for one night."

"I'll go see if I can find him," Sally Mae said, her tone even-keeled. "But only if you promise to rest after you see him."

Kit nodded, waving a hand. "That's a deal."

Sally Mae looked doubtful. "Do you want me to get Lulu or Rita in here to sit with you? They're both in their rooms but I have them on standby."

"No, I'm fine," Katherine replied, thinking her mother's friends would put her in a chair and give her a facial to soothe her frayed nerves. She didn't want a facial. She wanted to see Shane. "Honestly, Mother, I'll be fine."

She watched as her mother hurried out of the room still wearing her teal blue ball gown and matching kitten-heeled pumps. Kit loved her mother, but Sally Mae was just as protective as her father. They only cared about her welfare, she knew. And she appreciated and respected both of them.

"But right now, I just need—"

"You rang?" a voice called from the bathroom.

"Shane?" She rushed across the soft carpet and into the wide, open bath, her heart doing a strange little dance. "How'd you—"

"Trade secret," he said, pointing to the wide, square window over the garden tub. "I broke in."

"But the alarms didn't go off."

"Of course not," he said, adjusting his jacket. "I helped develop the security system in this place last time they updated it. Even Kissie herself said I did a good job." He checked the window. "I simply went to the main frame and reset the timers back long enough to allow me to enter the building in an unconventional way." He looked at his gold watch. "They'll reset in about…three seconds."

Kit heard a soft beep, beep coming from the monitor on the wall. "And what if my father notices?"

"He won't. I only did it for this wing of the house. And I knew the exact time when the live feed to the security room switches cameras. Plus, your mother won't allow any visual monitors in your bath. That would be an invasion of privacy."

He stopped talking and looked at her, his tone going soft as his crystal-shot gaze swept over her. "I had to see you." He lifted a finger toward her face to push a strand of hair off her cheek. "I like your hair down."

Kit lowered her head, suddenly feeling the need to burst into tears. But she held herself in check, figuring all of these strange, electric emotions were due to the scare of almost being shot. She wouldn't fall apart, not tonight. And not in front of him. "I'm okay. I just sent Mother to find you."

"I heard you from my spot in the shrubbery. And I'm here."

Before she could say anything, he took her hands in his. "Are you all right?"

She nodded, the warmth and strength of his fingers bringing the life back to her limbs. She allowed her gaze to wander away from his eyes for just a minute. He'd lost the bowtie and now his shirt was opened at the throat. Even rumpled and fatigued, he was still a striking man. Katherine decided she'd better focus on his face. But that didn't help matters. His expression held an edge of anticipation capped off with weariness. And guilt.

"I'm okay, really, I am," she said. "Is my friend Trudy Pearson okay? They wouldn't let me check on her."

"I saw her, yes. She was a bit shaken but she's fine. She went home, but only after I promised her you were safe. I'm pretty sure her new friend—the hotel employee she befriended while under fire—was going to escort her to be sure."

Katherine smiled at that. Leave it to Trudy to find a date even in the face of attempted murder. "Good. I'm glad."

"Katherine, why did you want to see me? Did you remember something or see something tonight that I need to know?"

She stared up at him, seeing the solid concern in his eyes. "Oh, no. I mean, I can't remember anything that would help. I… I just wanted to thank you, for saving my life."

He leaned close, his eyes flaring as his gaze held hers, the sincerity in his words endearing him to her. "It was my duty and my honor."

"It's not over yet, is it?"

"No, I'm afraid not."

"Where do we go from here?" she asked, gripping his hands to ward off the trembles moving through her body.

"I'm working on that. The shooter is in the hospital and under police custody but he's still unconscious. Our people and the police have gotten statements from all the eyewitnesses, but no one has come forward yet with any solid explanations or motives." He leaned close then, his words a whisper in her ear. "And I'm not so sure you're safe, even here."

Shocked, she pulled back. "You can't be serious."

His touch moved up her arms, protective and intimate. "I think you're still in danger."

"But this is Eagle Rock. I've always felt safe here."

"Things have changed," he retorted, his eyes locking with hers, one hand going to his stomach as if he were in pain. "I've got a bad feeling."

"So what do you suggest?"

"I have a plan, if you're willing to trust me." Holding her shoulders again, he leaned forward and asked, "How would you like to run away with me?"

FOUR

Katherine opened her mouth but her words only came out in a whisper. "What do you mean?"

"As I said, I'm not so sure you're safe in Austin, even here at Eagle Rock. Devon's wife Lydia was attacked here a couple of years ago, before they were married. They were on the run and came here to hide."

"I remember. Mother told me their story. Devon had a target on his back and Lydia got caught in the cross-fire. And it involved Eli Trudeau's grandfather Pierre Savoy."

"Yes, because his grandfather—the Peacemaker and one of the founding members of CHAIM—wanted them both dead so he planted someone on the inside to do the job, or at least to kill Lydia."

"You don't think—?"

"I'm not paid to just think. I'm paid to act. Someone

smuggled a weapon into that room tonight in spite of our best security measures. It had to be someone above suspicion but with easy access to the event. And that means the same person could also reach you here. So as I said, I have a plan but your father and his cronies won't like it. Are you interested?"

Katherine looked around at the place where she'd always come for extended visits growing up. While the Andersons lived here year round and took care of the compound, Eagle Rock was like her second home. She'd spent so much time here and never once had she questioned her safety.

Until now.

Should she trust the CHAIM system or the man who'd broken into this room to make sure she was all right? The same man who'd saved her life tonight?

"How can I be sure of anything?" she asked.

"You can't. Nor can I. I usually rely on my experience and my training, my instincts and…a lot of prayer."

"I've been praying since this happened. I'm hoping God will give me understanding until we can find out why this is happening to me."

"That's my job," he said, "if you're willing to trust me and let me do that job."

She looked up at Shane, her hands trembling again. He took her hand in his, waiting for her answer.

"What did you have in mind?" she finally asked.

He leaned down to whisper in her ear. "Well, first, we have to break out of Eagle Rock. And after that, well, we'll be on our own until I can do some digging and put all the pieces together. But Kit, I can't do this if you don't feel…if you aren't sure."

She didn't know if it was because she was in shock or

just tired of fighting, but she shook her head, her blood pulsing back to life. "I'm not sure."

He looked disappointed, but he nodded understanding. "Then we'll go to plan B."

"And what is that?"

He gave her a soft grin. "I'll just have to take you hostage."

"You're not serious."

"No. But it's tempting."

"But won't we be in even more danger out there?"

"Not where I'm going," he said. He rubbed his stomach. "I can't shake this feeling."

She faced him, her world tumbling and crashing much too fast. She wasn't used to this. She liked stability and structure and calendars and committees. Those things kept her on track and helped her to focus on helping others. But how could she be a good steward if she was putting everyone in danger?

The room was still and hushed, but Shane didn't push her. The silence didn't seem to faze him. She supposed he was used to silence.

Finally, she swallowed, pushing away the solid wall of fear. "I didn't say I wouldn't do it. I don't think I have any choice. I didn't take these threats seriously before, but if that man was after me then my presence at that gala put others in danger. Maybe it would be best if you and I did leave."

He lowered his head. "Is that a yes?"

Her prayers lifted with each heartbeat. "Yes."

He gave her a quick peck on the cheek. "Okay, we're going to have to act very quickly and I need you to do exactly as I say. Are you up to it?"

"I want my life back," she said. "And Shane, I think

my father hired the right man to make that happen, regardless of *how* you make it happen."

He took her hand in his and kissed it, then bowed deep. "At your service, Madame. Now let's get you into some decent traveling clothes. And pack a bag. We'll be gone for a while."

Katherine hurried to change, her mind whirling with a renewed awareness. Her trembling had shifted to nervous energy, but she couldn't decide if she was running away from danger or using that as an excuse to run right into Shane Warwick's waiting arms.

Kit's mind raced with worry and anticipation, her prayers scattered. Worry that she was making a drastic mistake and anticipation that she would finally be free of the yoke of propriety that had held her since she was presented as Cotillion Queen back during her college years.

"How are you coming in there?" Shane asked from the sitting room, his pacing making her even more nervous.

Kit put on her watch and her pearls—silly but necessary for her sanity. "I'm almost ready."

Was she? Kit knew how to pack a light travel bag. She usually kept things packed and ready to go at home, since she sometimes had to travel at a moment's notice. But here at Eagle Rock, things were different. Her mother and Lulu Anderson kept clothes here in various sizes for all the wives of the CHAIM agents—maybe because Sally Mae instinctively knew her friends might have to leave quickly? But Kit was so confused, she could only stare at the huge walk-in closet full of feminine things. What to take?

Black, she decided. A lady could never go wrong with black, even when she was on the run from someone who obviously wanted her dead. Trying to keep her head with a little bit of humor, she grabbed a slinky black travel set—pants and a matching lightweight duster. That would work on the run, wouldn't it? After adding a few other things, she grabbed an overnight bag from a shelf then stood still, the enormity of her situation making her numb.

She whirled to find Shane staring at her from the doorway. "Don't analyze your wardrobe, Katherine. We have no time for that."

She lifted her chin. "What do you suggest then for someone who's got a target on her back?"

With a grunt and just a bit of sympathy in his eyes, he gently pushed her aside and started grabbing at garments. "Jeans—they're sturdy and fit in anywhere. Some T-shirts and jackets and good walking shoes."

She watched as he selected various items and tossed them in the open bag she'd found in the closet. But he held her cell phone out then dropped it in his pocket. "There. You'll make a statement, I'm sure. And you'll live to buy more clothes."

"Can you guarantee that?" she asked, smarting from his obvious impatience and his misunderstanding of her hesitation. "Can you promise me that my presence won't get someone else killed?"

He zipped the bag. "I can assure you that while you're in my care, *you* won't get killed."

While you're in my care.

His words, spoken in a low, gravelly voice, flowed through her like a gentle rain. Not "While I'm trying to protect you." Not "While I'm trying to keep you alive."

But "While you're in my care." And not a promise, but an assurance. Was there a difference?

The man had a way of saying things.

"I'm ready," she said, sending up one last prayer for hope and guidance.

They made it to the door just before it burst open.

Sally Mae Barton saw the overnight bag, and shook her head. "Oh, no. You are not taking my daughter out of here."

"Mother—"

Sally Mae pointed at Kit. "You can't leave. Your daddy will blow his top. He wants you here where he can keep an eye on you."

Shane stepped forward, his stance at once protective and formidable. "I want to get her out of here because I don't believe she's safe here, Mrs. Barton."

Sally Mae looked affronted, her tiny fist clenched at her side, her head held high. "This is Eagle Rock, Mr. Warwick. It's a fortress."

"It's designed to be such," Shane said, nodding his head. "But I have reason to believe your daughter might not be completely protected."

"And I won't put all of you in danger," Kit added, hoping her mother would listen to reason. "If Shane isolates me, then I won't have to worry about everyone else."

Sally Mae shut the door then put her hands on her hips. "Are you telling me you think someone on the inside is behind this? We've been through that already with Devon and Lydia, remember? And with Eli and Gena. That was definitely an inside job from one of our top operatives. But he's dead and gone and I thought it was over. Mercy, when will it end?"

Shane touched a hand to her arm. "I'm not saying that. I don't believe this threat is coming from within CHAIM ranks. We've pretty much wiped that problem clean. But I do worry that someone from the outside knows Katherine is here. And that's why I think it best to take her to an undisclosed location where few people are—the fewer people involved the better."

Sally Mae's shrewd gaze passed over his face. "You're one of the best, I'll give you that. But you can't take her out of here without discussing this with my husband."

Shane let out a breath. "You know that will only delay things. I don't have time to listen to a lecture or to go over strategy by committee. My gut is telling me to get your daughter to safety immediately and worry about the details later."

"But—"

"Mother, I'm not a prisoner here," Kit said, using her best assertive voice. "I can leave on my own or you can let the man you hired to protect me do his job. And you can try trusting me. I won't be responsible for someone doing harm to anyone inside Eagle Rock or out."

Sally Mae clutched at her gold rope necklace. "I declare, I don't know about you young folks. We had a way of doing things back in the day, but now…"

"Now threats can come from many sources," Shane said, glancing over at Katherine. "If I can get her to a safe location, I can do some digging and get to the bottom of this. Starting with Jacob's death and working from there."

Sally Mae gasped. "Are you saying there was more to that? I knew it. I tried to tell your daddy—" She stopped, her expression thoughtful. Finally she said, "Okay, what's the plan?"

Kit heard Shane's exhaled breath. Had he been planning to take her hostage as he'd suggested earlier if her mother refused to cooperate?

"The first order of business is a means of getting us out of here," Shane said. "We need a car."

Sally Mae nodded. "I can help with that. We've got plenty of vehicles around here. Meet me in the garage in about five minutes." She turned to Kit. "Are you sure, honey?"

Kit didn't want to lie to her mother. She wasn't sure but she couldn't risk getting all of them killed. "I don't have any other choice right now, Mother. It's best if I distance myself from all of you—to protect you."

"And what about you?" Sally Mae asked.

"Shane will take care of me."

Sally Mae turned toward the door then whirled toward Shane. "You listen to me, and listen good. If anything happens to my daughter…well, you just remember I was once a CHAIM agent myself and I still know a few surefire ways of dealing with those who fail me— or make me mad."

Shane's eyes widened. "I understand, Mrs. Barton. And you have my word I will protect her with my very life."

"That's mighty reassuring," her mother replied with all of the serenity and sweetness of someone at a country club luncheon. "Now, about that car…"

"A yellow Miata?"

Shane stared down at the toy car sitting in front of him, not sure he could get his legs to fit in the tiny thing, let alone his entire body. Even with the top down, he didn't see how he could be comfortable, but he didn't dare put the top down tonight.

Sally Mae shoved the keys at him. "Look, it's the only one I can spare right now. It's little, it's fast and it's bulletproof. Even the hard top, which I suggest you don't let down. You'd be like low-hanging fruit with the top down. And it gets good gas mileage." She shrugged. "What more could you want?"

"A real car," Shane said on a snort. "This is like a go-cart on steroids."

"Take it or leave it," Sally Mae replied. "The SUVs all have the standard CHAIM GPS tracking." She lifted her eyebrows. "Which means—"

"That your husband could track us, I know, I know," Shane interrupted. "And you're sure this car isn't bugged?"

"No, it is not," Sally Mae replied, her indignation showing in the flash in her eyes. "It has a GPS system, of course. But that's just so I can find where I'm going when I'm shopping or lunching, you know. Woman-type stuff. I like my privacy and my husband knows I can dislodge any tracking system in about five minutes, anyway. So he indulges me now and then."

"By allowing you to drive around in a bright yellow car that looks like a bumblebee?" Shane asked.

"Hey, it's cute and it's fast—I had the engine re-worked to make it a little quicker," she replied. "And you're wasting time."

"You're right," Shane said, looking over at Kit. "Get in."

Sally Mae patted the little car. "Oh, and just so you know, it does have an emergency button. That red one on the dash. Hit that and you'll get a secure satellite line right back to Eagle Rock. Or you can request a secure line to signal any other agent by code."

"Good to know," Shane said, impressed with Sally Mae's steel magnolia calm. He handed her Kit's cell. "We won't need this. She's to have no contact with anyone for the next few days, understand?"

Kit didn't like that. "No contact? But I have obligations, calls to return. Everyone will be wondering where I am."

"We'll take care of all that, honey," her mother replied, holding the phone up in the air.

Kit had remained quiet while her mother and Shane discussed their mode of transportation. But now, he saw the apprehension in her eyes. "Katherine?"

"I'm ready," she said, turning to her mother. "I love you."

Sally Mae pulled her daughter into her tiny arms, hugging Kit close with a mother's fierce protection. "I'll stall your daddy. He'll be madder than a hornet but it won't be the first time I've made him mad." She looked at Shane, her expression bordering on murder to him while she said such sweet words to her child. "I love you, honey, and I expect all of this to be over real soon. You have my prayers."

Shane interpreted that look to mean "And I expect you to keep her safe or you will have to answer to me, Mister."

He nodded to Sally Mae and she silently accepted that nod as his promise. Then she stood back to look up at Katherine. "This life isn't for sissies, that's for sure. We've tried to do good over the years but sometimes bad catches up to us. It's warfare, honey. Always. But we have to fight the good fight, no matter what."

Katherine kissed her mother again then slipped with lady-like agility into the low car, leaving Shane to shove her designer overnight bag into the small trunk.

"Thank you, Mrs. Barton," he said as he opened the door. "I won't forget your help."

Sally Mae waved a hand in dismissal. "You can thank me by finding out who's behind this and bringing my daughter home safely. Now I'll open the gate and then I have some explaining to do to my husband."

"Of course," Shane said, praying that he could deliver on his promises.

Then he forced himself into the tiny space behind the wheel, cranked the little car and listened to the purring motor for a few seconds before he shifted gears and took off into the night.

"Where are we going?" Kit asked after they cleared the gates of the sprawling complex and hit the main highway.

Shane didn't want to talk about it. The less she knew, the safer she'd be. But he understood her need for answers. "Remember the ranch I mentioned near Fort Worth? My father's ranch? Mine now."

"You're taking me there?"

He nodded. "It's big and vast. And secluded. The isolation will give me time to focus on research and give you time to unwind so you can answer some specific questions for me."

"About my husband?"

He'd have to remember she was a very smart woman.

"Yes, that and other things. Something, someone that can trigger memories that might give us some clues."

"Jacob and I met in college. I fell for him instantly. He was smart, ambitious and he believed in all the causes I wanted to support. It was as if he'd been hand-picked to find me. I decided God had put him in my life for a purpose."

"So you left school and became his wife?"

"Yes. My senior year. Jacob wanted us to be married right away. I always wanted to go back and get my degree, but you know how that goes."

"You got busy with your life and then Jacob practiced law and moved up the ladder in politics."

"Yes. We both had connections, so we used that clout to get him elected. He was a very smart man and people listened to him, believed in him. He was good for Texas."

Shane kept his eyes on the road. "Tell me about your life before Jacob."

She smiled at that, memories darting through her mind like a child running through a field. "I had a good life. My parents loved me, loved God and taught me to always do the right thing. I wanted to serve others. Not in a Mother Teresa way, of course. But I wanted to do what I could to help people. After I married Jacob, I had that chance. The foundation supports several global charities."

"Such as?"

She saw the spark of interest in his eyes. "Shane, the foundation is solid. And clean."

"Such as?" he asked again, never skipping a beat.

"We do work with orphans in the Middle East. We support a school down in a remote village in Mexico.

We work with school children here in Texas to improve grade scores and prevent dropout rates from going up. And we've started a new program on environmental issues."

He glanced in the rearview mirror. "I have the list of your board of directors. I might need to glance over that again with you, see if any one name stands out."

"Most of our board members are pillars of society."

"That doesn't mean they're perfect, luv."

"I can't see anyone on our board wanting to harm me."

"We have to keep digging."

When he looked in the mirror a second time, then checked the side mirrors, Kit grew uneasy. "Is something wrong?"

"Maybe," he said, his brow furrowing. "I think someone is following us." She tried to turn, but he grabbed her shoulder. "Don't look back."

Thinking they'd had a brief reprieve, she said, "What are we going to do?"

Shane checked the mirrors again then smiled. "We're going to put your mother's adorable little car to the test. We're going to outrun them, of course."

And then he hit the gas and blasted the little car off so quickly, Kit had to hold on to the dashboard. "I guess taking this car wasn't very smart, was it?"

"It's all right," he replied. "It's bulletproof remember?"

Kit nodded, but she wondered if that would help them now. She wasn't sure if anything could help them at this point. She leaned her head back against the tiny black leather headrest, dread gripping her.

Shane exited the road and waited. When the other

car kept to the main road, he patted her hand. "False alarm, but I'm going to take the back road, just in case."

Watching him shift into reverse, she said, "So you think whoever this is might be from my husband's past?"

"It's a good place to start. If that helicopter crash wasn't an accident, then someone deliberately set out to kill Jacob. And now they're coming after you. Which means they think you know something or have something that they don't want you to have."

"But it's been a whole year since my husband died and I can't imagine what they think I know."

"They probably watched you for a few months to find clues and when you did nothing, they went into action. Or your recent activities, something you did or said, inadvertently tipped them off, got their attention. They'd dig into your daily life and routine so they could form a plan based on your activities. Some of the threats you received were more in the form of intimate questions, coming from various quarters. People were being a bit too pushy in asking about your personal history. Then you started receiving those pointed phone calls and obvious intrusions in your office and possibly your home, so they must have found something to scare them into a bold attempt."

"Oh, well, that explains why they waited until I was inside a packed ballroom with all kinds of civic leaders and prominent people from all over Texas, right?"

He touched a hand to hers. "They might have had more than one target tonight, Katherine. First, you. Then…who knows. That's why it's imperative we find out what's going on."

She pulled her hand away, shock slicing across the

shadows over her face. "It's worse than I imagined. You mean they could *still* come after my parents, my friends, and my staff?"

"I can't be sure, but yes. Removing you from the situation could bring them out of hiding, at least."

"And cause someone else to become the target? No!" She thrashed around, grabbing at his arm. "Shane, turn this car around now!"

He held her off with one hand while he steered the car with the other. "It's not like that. It's complicated."

"Complicated?" Her laughter was tinged with disbelief. "You can say that again. First, you tell me I'm the one in danger and now, after you force me to leave with you, you're telling me others might still be targets, too? How can I trust anything you say to me?"

Shane let go of her and focused on the road. "Can you trust that *you* are my number one priority? Can you trust that getting you away from Eagle Rock was the first line of defense?"

She shook her head. "But my parents?"

"They will be safe. Your father knows how to deal with this sort of thing. And your mother seems very capable of taking care of herself, too."

That bit of levity seemed to calm her a bit. She pushed at her hair then stared out the window. "What about all the others? Who's going to protect them?"

"Already taken care of," he said. "Your father and I agreed immediately after the shooting that we'd need to put people on those closest to you. Your staff is being watched and so are your closest friends."

"Including Trudy?"

"Especially Trudy," he replied, his tone never belying the fact that Katherine's best friend was a person of interest in this entire case.

FIVE

Dawn was rising in a burst of orange and yellow pastels behind them when Shane pulled the little car off the main highway and onto a clay road that trailed around a low valley surrounded by wooded hills. "We're almost there."

Kit glanced over at him, wondering how she'd gone from a glittering charity ball in the heart of the city to being on the run in a Miata with an Englishman she didn't even know. "You weren't kidding when you said it was off the beaten path."

His brow wrinkled into a grim frown. "Purposely so. My father liked his privacy. This place is secluded and hard to find. And I like it that way, too."

Kit looked toward the beamed gate where a tiny sign was the only indication that they'd reached the ranch. "*Rancho solo del Roble*. Lonely Oak Ranch." Had he brought her to the end of the earth?

Shane hit a button on his fancy phone and waited for the gates to swing open. Then he pointed up the long lane.

"Lonely Oak," he said, showing Kit the towering old live oak that greeted them as they came around the curve in the open field. The scarred, aged tree branched out with mushroom-shaped symmetry like a welcoming shelter toward the sky. "That tree has been here for over three hundred years. It's my compass toward home."

She filed that away in her good-to-know mental notebook, along with all the prayers she'd gone over in her head tonight. So the formidable, world-weary Sir Shane Warwick did have a home. And in the middle of the Lone Star state, of all places. "You come here a lot then?"

"As often as I can, between assignments. This place keeps me grounded. It's a good place for prayer and contemplation. It's so different from the stuffy old rooms at Warwick Hall—which used to be called something else until my mother married my father and they inherited the place. My father's ego couldn't allow it to be called anything but Warwick, of course."

Kit heard the hint of resentment in Shane's voice. "Were you close to your father?"

He nodded but kept the frown. "As close as a father and son can be, I suspect. We had our clashes, of course. I attended all the right schools in England but my father insisted I come here for my real education. I learned a lot about life on this old ranch. And then, he introduced me to your father and his…er…friends."

"You mean, your father suggested you join the ranks of CHAIM?"

"Strongly suggested," he shot back. "And I have to

admit, I was hooked from the first orientation seminar. I wanted to serve God and help other human beings. Plus, I get to play with all sorts of cool gadgets."

"And how's that working for you so far?"

He smiled at that, his gaze lingering on her. "It has its moments."

Kit viewed the rolling hills as they neared the ranch house, her gaze taking in more oaks as well as elm trees and a pecan grove. Off in a far pasture, massive long-horns strolled over the grassy fields. She could picture Shane here sitting on a big horse, galloping through the pastures. But that image made him a paradox.

"You were caught between two worlds and now you're caught in a dark, secret world."

"Yes, I was caught," he replied, apparently choosing to ignore her pointed comment about his current occupation. "A proper young Englishman who knew the decorum of having royal blood flowing in my veins—my mother saw to that—and the youth yearning to break free and just live my life. And my father taught me that, in more ways than I wanted to know, I'm afraid. CHAIM has taught me the rest."

Kit watched his face, saw so many flickering emotions etched there in the crinkles at his eyes, in the tanned slashes of his jaw. What had he seen or done in the name of CHAIM? And did she dare tell him she'd had those same conflicting emotions about breaking free and just becoming herself? Probably not. Not now at least.

He slowed the car and downshifted. "We're almost there."

Kit dropped her dark thoughts and looked up to find a sprawling two-storied Spanish type stucco ranch house similar to Eagle Rock sitting atop a tree-shaded hill. But where Eagle Rock was all modern sophistication, this house seemed set in another time. Obviously, it had been built long ago and updated through the years. Beyond the house and stables a creek bed gurgled through the pasture.

"The house is stunning," she said. "And the creek is beautiful."

"That creek flows toward the Brazo River," Shane explained. "Plenty of good bass fishing. We have longhorns in the pastures and whitetail deer roaming the meadows at dusk. Plus lots of other creatures."

Kit shuddered involuntarily at that, her reasons for being here once again front and center in her mind. "Under normal circumstances, I think I'd love this place. But we're not here for a vacation."

"No, we're not," he said, shifting the car forward. Driving around toward the back of the house, he looked over at her. "First things first. You need to rest." As if sensing her trepidation about being here with him in such a secluded place, he added, "We have a staff of three—very loyal and very trustworthy. And my grandmother lives here year-round."

Kit's shock registered in her words. "Your grandmother? You have a grandmother?"

"Yes, and as I said, she lives here as part of the staff but she doesn't have to work as hard as the rest of us, of course. So you have an *abuela*. That should make you feel better about things."

"She's your grandmother, not mine," Kit countered with a soft smile. "What if she doesn't like having me here?"

"Abuela?" He laughed, his eyes crinkling. "She loves everyone. And she'll spoil you, too."

"So she's your father's mother?"

"Something like that. She's not his biological mother, but she raised him from a young age after my real grandmother died. So that makes her as close to a grandmother as I can have. My grandparents are long dead—on both sides."

Kit was beginning to understand why he was a nomad, a man who couldn't settle down. "I see. So you 'adopt' people, so to speak?"

He brought the car up to a big garage attached to a long, covered gallery toward the main house. A big pickup and a couple of off-road vehicles were parked inside. "I suppose I do. I have a lot of good friends all over the world."

But he hadn't mentioned anyone in particular, such as a special woman in his life. Had he ever brought another woman here, she wondered? She almost asked then decided against it. She wasn't here as a special friend. She was here because someone was after her.

But Kit did wonder if she'd be counted among his friends once this was all over. She could see that Shane was a loyal, devout person. He'd do his job, no matter the cost. But at the end of his assignment, would he disappear back into that dark, murky world that being a CHAIM operative demanded? Would she ever see him again?

Remembering the way she'd reached up and taken his hand last night, she wondered why she held that hope so high. The man was her hired bodyguard. Nothing more—no matter how he made her heart lurch and shift in the same way he'd made this sweet little car purr through the dark night. He'd managed to bring them here in less than the three hours it normally took from Austin to hit the Fort Worth city limits about fifty miles behind them. He might also manage to move with swift expertise into her heart, too. If she let him.

She couldn't depend on a man who could be packed and ready to move on in thirty minutes. She didn't even want to depend on any man right now. She still missed her husband. And prayed she'd one day be able to let Jacob go.

"Kit?"

She looked up from her silent prayers to find Shane's crystal blue eyes centered on her. "What?"

"Let's get you inside. You're exhausted."

She didn't argue with him on that point. She was numb with a bone-deep tiredness that made it hard to lift out of the low-seated car.

So Shane came around and lifted her up, his arms holding her waist for just a few seconds too long before he turned and got her bag out of the trunk. "Come on. Let's get you settled."

Kit doubted she'd ever be settled again.

Abuela Silvia clicked and clucked over Kit like a mother hen while Shane made a few calls on his se-cure cell phone and then instructed the staff regarding their houseguest.

"Mrs. Atkins is under my protection, so be aware of that and follow proper protocol. She is to be given every consideration," he said in both English and Spanish, his tone gentle but assertive. "Make her comfortable and let her rest for as long as she needs today."

Abuela Silvia nodded, waving an aged hand in the

air toward her grandson, Ricardo. "Go, go. Back to work now."

Ricardo did as his grandmother asked, while his mother Nina just smiled over at Kit. "It's good to have you with us, Mrs. Atkins. I'll show you to your room."

"Let me have a look at things first, Nina," Shane said, hurrying ahead of them toward the gleaming wrought-iron and wood staircase that dominated one corner of the tiled entryway. "Just as a precaution," he said to Kit, his hand on her back.

Kit didn't respond. She looked drained and disoriented. And how could he blame the woman? She'd been snatched away in the night, taken from the people she loved and brought to this beautiful but desolate place for her own protection. She was in shock.

Shane went into the big bedroom located in the middle of the top floor, his hands touching on vases and lamps, his eyes scanning the walls for any signs of unseen visitors. This ranch was his haven, his safe retreat. He knew in his heart no one had been here but he had to be sure. He'd do an entire sweep of the house later, run a few scans on the computerized security system. That would make him feel better. He felt sure they hadn't been followed and he'd taken every precaution to make sure no one had tailed them. And still he worried.

He turned to find Kit and Nina standing at the doorway, silent and watchful. Nina was used to this but even though Kit had grown up with this type of paranoia, she didn't need to worry about it right now.

"I think things are fine," he said to Nina. "Will you help Mrs. Atkins get ready for a nap?"

"Of course." The dark-haired woman who'd lost her

husband to the war in the Middle East took Kit by the arm. "Let me show you where everything is, ma'am."

"It's Kit," Kit replied with a soft smile.

Always with the impeccable manners, Shane noticed. Even when she was dead-tired on her feet.

"I'll leave you to it then," he said to Nina, but his eyes held Kit's. "If you need me, use the phone by your bed and hit Operator. It works like an intercom throughout the house."

She nodded, her eyes holding his. Eyes full of questions and doubts, eyes too beautiful to be so sad and unsure. "Thank you."

Shane hoped she'd sleep. She needed rest.

And he needed to sit down and figure out where to begin in trying to find out who wanted her dead.

Shane wasted no time getting down to business. After some strong coffee and a ham biscuit Abuela Silvia insisted he eat, he went into his study at the back of the house and clicked on his laptop. Then he put in a call to Kissie Pierre in New Orleans. The longtime CHAIM operative was the go-to girl for digging up information no one else could find. While Kissie ran a halfway house for troubled teens and managed a coffeehouse on the premises of the old French Quarter mansion where she lived, she also continued to work behind the scenes for CHAIM.

"Shane Warwick. What a surprise," Kissie said, her throaty chuckle making Shane think of warm gumbo and buttered cornbread. "I've heard some chatter about you, Knight."

"I'm sure you have," Shane responded, his own smile belying his concern. "What did you hear?"

"That you brought down some assassin right in the middle of a posh Austin charity ball then somehow managed to take Katherine Barton Atkins right out of the gates of Eagle Rock with Gerald Barton in the house."

"A bit overblown, but accurate," Shane said, pinching his nose with two fingers. "What's the real word?"

He could hear her shuffling papers. Then he heard computer keys singing. "The official word—in the papers and on the news—a would-be burglar tried to rob some of your clients' rich friends during a fundraiser party at a big downtown hotel. As the story goes, an unknown security officer hired by the Barton Atkins Foundation brought the burglar down without killing him or hurting a single guest. You're a hero. An unknown hero since the press can't seem to locate you."

"And the authorities have been briefed to keep it that way," Shane replied. "Hopefully, it will die down and I can get on with finding out who's trying to harm our beautiful subject."

"Yes, the cover is that Mrs. Atkins is in seclusion for her own protection—just until the authorities can clear her to return to her duties within the organization. Reports indicate she was scheduled for some big mission trip to Mexico in a month or so."

Shane's antenna went up on that one. "Dig into that a bit more, will you, luv? And in the meantime, I'll get back to my job here."

"And have you figured out that job yet? Or did you just decide to spend some downtime with a beautiful blonde?"

Shane admired Kissie's no-nonsense attitude. She was street smart and full of soul. But she believed in

CHAIM and she worked hard to keep kids off the streets of New Orleans, so he could deal with her wry sense of humor.

"I'm about to get started on that very thing—the job that is. The beautiful blonde is resting right now."

Kissie whistled low. "You know, Knight, you don't do so great with pretty women. They tend to make you lose your focus. Maybe I should take over this case."

The teasing in her words didn't hide the bit of warning in her tone. Kissie was ever the moral compass of the whole CHAIM team but she sure had him pegged. "Are you suggesting I'll let a beautiful Austin widow go to my head, dear Kissie?"

"You've been known to fall fast and hard before, yeah."

"But Kissie, you know you have my heart," he retorted, hoping to deflect her warnings and the memories they brought up. "I'll be on my best behavior, I can assure you. Gerald Barton would have me tarred and feathered if I dared make a move on his lovely daughter."

"You can count on that, anyway," Kissie replied. "The man is spitting mad, especially since you've blocked all of his alerts and refuse to report in. Yep, you sure got it bad."

"I know exactly what I'm doing," Shane replied, calm in spite of Kissie's dire warnings. "She wasn't safe there. And you can put that in the report that I'm sure you'll send directly to Mr. Barton when you're finished with me."

"I'm just saying," Kissie replied. "But enough with your love life or this death wish you seem to have. What do you need from me?"

"A bit of research for starters. The initial threats started about two months ago—just some odd email inquiries and too many questions regarding her travel schedule—from sources her organization couldn't identify. Then she got some strange phone calls, threatening her and warning her to stick close to home. I need to set up a timeline of all of Mrs. Atkins' activities beginning the year before her husband died and leading up to the present. Her travels abroad, all the organizations she's worked for or served on as a board member and any new contacts she made in the past few months, that sort of thing. Especially anything you can find on her upcoming trip to Mexico."

"Her life history," Kissie said, already tapping her fingers on the keyboard. "Give me a little time. I'll post it when it's ready."

"Thank you," Shane said. "And in the meantime, I'll do a search of any radical groups in Texas—for starters. I'm thinking someone didn't approve of State Senator Jacob Atkins. If I can find something, some indiscretion in his past, I might be able to trace that back to why someone is trying to kill his widow."

"Got it," Kissie said. "I'll see if I stumble on anything on this end."

"Thanks again," Shane said. "You have my heart."

"And you have a way with words, even if I don't believe anything you say," Kissie replied. "You'll hear from me soon."

"Oh, Kissie, before you go—who's playing in the coffeehouse tonight?"

She laughed at that. "Still love your jazz, Warwick?"

"I do," he said, "but I like my country songs, too."

"Then you'd love this gig tonight. Southern style

blues—a bit of country and a bit of Mississippi Delta with a little gospel thrown in for good measure."

"Ah, wish I could be there."

"Come on down when you get done with this case. I'll have 'em back in just for you."

"I might take you up on that offer."

Shane cleared the phone screen then stared at the computer, wondering where he should start. Did he dare go through the CHAIM archives to see if Katherine's father had past dealings with his son-in-law, Jacob Atkins? Couldn't hurt. By his way of thinking, everyone around Katherine Barton Atkins was suspect right now.

Especially those closest to her.

SIX

Kit woke abruptly to find the sun setting behind the hills to the west. Disoriented, she sat up and glanced around the big comfortable room, remembering she wasn't in her lonely house back in Austin. Nor was she at Eagle Rock in the bedroom where they always put their charges—the cause of the month—she thought bitterly.

"Now I'm one of those," she said out loud, her voice croaking and raw. All of her life, she'd known and understood that her father was involved in a highly secretive security company that helped Christians in their time of need. But she'd never dreamed she'd be on the run and in need of the exclusive services CHAIM offered to people. Which brought to mind—was this coincidence or was she a target because of her father's line of work?

Deciding she didn't have the energy to consider the answer to that nagging question, she thought about Shane and how solicitous he'd been to her. Just one more thing she had to adjust to—Shane Warwick in her life. She certainly never imagined she'd be holed up in a beautiful old Spanish-style mansion somewhere west of Fort Worth with a British operative called The Knight, a man who personified all of the stereotypes she'd read about in books or watched on the movie screen.

Personified, yes. Outshined completely, double yes. The real live man she'd been forced to rely on was much better than any fictional character or screen star. Shane had immediately taken control of a scary situation last night. He'd not only saved her; he'd also saved everyone in that room. And for that she'd be forever thankful.

Sir Shane Warwick was the real deal. A real life security expert and spy who'd signed on to protect her. And he was also an interesting, intriguing man who moved through several different worlds with grace and assurance. She had yet to see him ruffled or distracted. That gave her a feeling of security in spite of her worries.

Lifting her hands then letting them fall by her side, she looked up at the intricate gold-etched arched ceiling over the bed. "Couldn't you have sent a different man, maybe someone with a paunch and a balding head?"

If she weren't so terrified, she'd have to laugh out loud. But nothing about this was funny.

Katherine got up and wobbled around the room. She was sore from her head to her toes, probably from tense muscles and holding on for dear life for the last twenty-four hours. "Just breathe," she told herself as she wandered around in constant prayer, her hand touching on the wrought iron of the bedposts, her gaze taking in the beautiful portrait over the marble fireplace of a dark-haired *senorita* astride a great white horse. "Exquisite," she whispered, thinking Sir Shane Warwick wouldn't accept anything less.

And yet even if he had been knighted by the queen, he seemed a simple man, a simple man who knew how to dress and how to use a weapon, she mused as she went into the adjourning bathroom and almost wept with delight over the beautiful soaking tub and rain-forest-like shower.

After washing her face, she turned to find a set of clothes laid out on a pretty brocade chair near a large closet. Noting that the jeans and sweater were her own—or ones she'd taken from Eagle Rock, Katherine went about freshening up—a long shower followed by a bit of makeup. Then she stopped and said a few more prayers, part of her usual morning ritual.

Fully dressed, she realized she was starving. The kitchen. She'd find her way to the kitchen and make herself a good strong cup of coffee and a grilled cheese.

She made it out into the hallway before she was stopped with two strong hands on her arm.

"What are you doing?"

Katherine looked up to find Shane staring down at her, his expression shadowed, his eyes blazing hot.

"Hello to you, too," she said, her breath hitching in her throat. Did he have to appear so sinister and so concerned all in one fell swoop? And he was just as dashing in jeans, a button-down shirt and boots as in a tuxedo.

He stepped back, surveying her as if she were some sort of interloper, until his eyes went soft and steely blue. "Did you rest?"

"I did. I must have slept all day, since the sun's going down and my stomach is growling for dinner."

"Good. I was on my way to check on you. Dinner is ready."

Katherine wondered just how many times he'd checked on her during the day. Knowing him, she figured he'd been sitting out here by her door for hours.

"Then I'm right on time, aren't I?" she asked, her smile hiding the unease that had settled on her like a yoke and refused to let go. "What are we having?"

"Spicy lime chicken, I believe," he said, turning to guide her toward the stairs. Then he leaned close. "Don't leave your room again without notifying me first, okay?"

Katherine stopped at the top of the stairs, a mural along the stairway of a courtyard lush with forest green ferns and rich pink bougainvillea blossoms acting as a backdrop to his reprimand. "Am I a prisoner here, Shane?"

His gaze swept her in that way that left her slightly dazed. "No, you're under my protection. And that means I need to know where you are twenty-four/seven. All you have to do is pick up the phone and alert either the staff or me each time you leave your room."

"If I'm safe here, then why the need for all this?" she asked, knowing the answer before he grabbed her arm to halt her.

"You're safe for now," he said, his eyes glazed with aggravation. "But someone is after you, Katherine. We have to take every precaution."

"Isn't that why you brought me here?"

He held her there on the stairs, his expression at once

hostile and hopeful. "Yes. This place is so off the beaten path, I doubt anyone can find us. But—"

"But these people, whoever they are, might be able to do just that, right?" Yanking her hand away, she took off down the stairs. "Maybe I should have stayed at Eagle Rock."

"Maybe you should have," he said after her, taking the stairs at a run to catch up with her. "Do you want me to take you back?"

She whirled in the dining room. "What? We just got here."

"But if you're not pleased with the accommodations…"

Not sure if she'd truly offended him or he was just testing her to make sure she understood how things had to be, she went straight to the Rococo buffet table and helped herself to a steaming cup of coffee from the silver urn. "The accommodations are beautiful and your staff is very considerate. But your boorish way of bossing me around is irritating. Especially when I just woke up."

Shane stomped to the buffet and poured a glass of water then drank the whole thing down. "Excuse me for trying to keep you alive."

That statement halted her and caused Ricardo, who'd just entered the arched doorway from the kitchen with a steaming bowl of rice, to whirl and exit the same way he'd entered.

Katherine turned to glare at Shane across the long room. She started to speak but shut her mouth. Then she took a long sip of her coffee and closed her eyes for a minute. When she opened them, she smiled serenely at him. "I'm sorry. This is difficult, Shane. You've done everything possible to help me and I'm being a brat. Please bear with me and let me get adjusted. I think I just needed some caffeine."

He lowered his head, his gaze following her as she sniffed at the food spread out on the buffet. "I understand. You're not used to being closed off from the world."

"No, I'm not," she said, motioning toward the spicy-smelling chicken. "Can we eat while we talk?"

"Of course." Shane followed her along the buffet, taking meat and vegetables onto his plate with aggravated efficiency. He waited for her to sit, then took his seat across from her at the long table. "I apologize for my testiness. I've been poring over documents all afternoon."

Kit sat down, flipped her linen napkin open then began to cut her chicken into little bite-size pieces. "Documents about me?"

Ricardo made another effort to deliver the rest of their dinner, entering with his head down and his stride full of purpose. After he placed the dishes on the buffet, Shane nodded to the boy then waved a hand for him to leave the room.

His frown answered Kit's question however. Then he asked another one. "You travel a great deal, don't you?"

She sent a glowering look right back at him. "That's part of my job at the foundation. I don't like sitting back while others do all the work."

"You've put yourself on the line, traveling to some of the most dangerous spots on earth."

"Unfortunately, those spots are also the most needy."

He took a long sip of iced tea. "That puts you in a

very compromising position—your face is all over the Internet and in every major newspaper in the world."

"My face gets me the publicity I need to fund my causes, Shane."

"And also makes you an easy target for criminals."

She dropped her fork. "Did you find something?"

He sat back against the studded burgundy leather seat of the high-backed mahogany chair. "Oh, yes. I found out everything I'd ever want to know about Katherine Barton Atkins. You've had dealings with so many heads of state, it makes my brain fuzzy."

Trying to picture this brooding man with a fuzzy brain made her smile inside. But she didn't dare smile at him right now. She needed to be as cooperative as possible.

"So what do we do now?" she asked, ready to get down to business.

After connecting some of the dots that made up her busy, highly public life, Shane wondered that himself. "We wait." He chewed his own chicken, the taste of fresh jalapeños complementing the tangy lime in the juicy, tender chicken. His ulcer would protest this later. "I've done some research, sent out some feelers."

"Regarding?"

Regarding a few of the trips she'd taken over the last months and the one she planned to take later this fall. But he wouldn't tell her that. Nor would he tell her that he was a bit concerned that her friend Trudy Pearson seemed to have gone underground, too, since the authorities in Austin couldn't reach her for further questioning. Maybe Trudy was still frightened after last night's shoot-out. That was reasonable, but his burning stomach made him wonder.

"Regarding your life," he said to Kit. "I need to piece things together. And now that you're rested, maybe you can help. Let's start with your upcoming trip to Mexico. Why were you going there?"

"You mean, why *am* I going there? I fully intend to make that trip. We're taking medical supplies to a remote village and we're going to help finish building the clinic several organizations have been working on for over two years now. "Our trip will be the last one. We'll hold a large celebration there once we're finished."

"Very high profile."

"Yes, to get the much-needed attention of leaders in both of our countries."

"Did your husband ever go down there with you?"

She seemed wary then nodded. "A couple of times, yes."

"And did he ever conduct any other business while there?"

"No, why would he? He helped us. He volunteered as much as he could—when he wasn't on the phone with his staff back home. And speaking of that, I should alert my staff," she said, her hand steady on her water glass. "They'll be worried."

"Already done. They understand you're a bit traumatized by what happened last night. We have the weekend to tidy this up before people start asking questions."

"My cell phone—"

"Has been taken away for your own protection. Your staff has been advised to make no calls for now. And we're monitoring all incoming calls."

"And my parents?"

"Know you're safe with me."

"How did my father take our quick exit?"

"Not very well." He had to grin at that even though she'd managed to steer the conversation away from her husband and Mexico. "I called in earlier and…let's just say he wasn't very appreciative of my tactic, but he's a bit calmer now that he knows my purpose. Still, I think I'm in hot water."

"Well then, welcome to my world," she said, holding up her glass in salute. "I've been in trouble with that man for most of my life."

Shane could only image how a father such as Gerald Barton would do anything to protect his only child. And perhaps smother her to the point of exhaustion, too. "Does your father have a forgiving nature?"

Her chuckle rattled with dryness. "He wasn't exactly thrilled when I left college to marry Jacob."

Antennas went off inside Shane's brain. He'd read about that, too. Seen the elaborate wedding pictures. She made a lovely bride. And the whole union had read like a perfect power match, something all Texans with old money lived for. "Oh, why is that? Wanted you to have a degree to fall back on?"

She crinkled her nose. "It wasn't the degree. He didn't want me to marry Jacob Atkins." Her words were so full of bitterness that it seemed to shock even her. She actually blushed, looking flustered for a few seconds before she regained that regal control, her hand grasping at her pearls. "It doesn't really matter now, though, does it?"

Shane needed to know more because it might matter a whole lot. He'd never picked up on any disapproval in all the news reports. But then, everyone would have been on their best behavior for the press. "So your father didn't approve of your husband? Interesting." Even more interesting that Gerald hadn't shared this bit of information. But then, it was a family matter and private.

She looked up at him, her eyes turning wary again. "It's hard to explain but I can assure you, it's nothing sinister. They disagreed on some of the issues regarding an oil-and-gas merger between Barton Industries and the company Jacob worked for at the time. He was the attorney in charge of the merger. But they worked it out between them and after we got married, they became close. Jacob and I had a few good years together, in spite of everything."

Shane didn't press her to explain that "in spite of everything" ending since he hadn't found anything incriminating regarding her father's dealings with Jacob. But he would have to revisit the merger she just mentioned. He watched as she shut back down, her expression going soft and uniform, trained. And he imagined she'd practiced just such a stance many times with her parents and with the press. Maybe with her husband.

And then a new thought occurred to him.

What was Katherine Atkins hiding from the world?

An hour later, Shane took her out into the secluded courtyard between the house and the garage. Katherine noticed more intricate wrought iron out here on the gates and woven into the heavy stucco walls surrounding the tiled floor of the enclosed patio. A tiered water fountain gurgled in the center, its colorful mosaic tiles shimmering like jewels in the moonlight.

"This looks like the mural by the stairs," she said, glad to have a safe topic to discuss. Glad to be away from the ever-increasing unease of her thoughts and her memories.

"It's the same," Shane replied, handing her another cup of coffee to go with the dark chocolate truffles Nina had left on the buffet. "My mother painted the mural based on this courtyard. She loved it here. Still does."

"It is peaceful," Kit said, taking a deep breath. "And, Shane, I do feel safe here."

"Good." He sounded relieved. They sat silently for a few minutes then he said, "You know I'll protect you."

She ignored the little currents shooting throughout her system like fireflies, chalking them up to the luscious chocolates. "It's your job."

"Yes, but it's also an honor to be trusted enough to help you, even if your father wants my head on a platter."

She sipped her coffee and stared at the water spilling over the fountain, watching as a few stray flower blossoms floated across the bubbling waves. "My father is overprotective. He never liked any of the men I dated, so why would he completely trust the man he hired to protect me?"

"Especially when that man went against the CHAIM handbook and broke every rule ever droned into his thick skull."

"There is that," she retorted, holding her cup to keep her hands from shaking. Why did being alone with Shane Warwick make her feel as inadequate and inexperienced as a shy schoolgirl? It seemed she'd forgotten how to carry on a polite, civil conversation.

"You mentioned that your father didn't like Jacob at first? I can't see that he wouldn't. Jacob Atkins had impeccable credentials—an upstanding family heritage that came from old Texas oil money, a law degree from a prominent university and a sharp, business-centered mind. I'm surprised your father didn't tag Jacob to work for CHAIM."

Katherine understood why she'd been so keyed up and it had nothing to do with how handsome Shane Warwick was or how his silver-blue eyes held hers. Now she understood. He was fishing for answers, the kind she couldn't give him.

"You're interrogating me, aren't you? You really do think Jacob's death has something to do with these people who are after me? What are you insinuating, Shane?"

"Nothing at all. I told you I needed to ask you some questions. It's the only way I can build a case and find out who's after you."

"But are you building a case to help me, or you trying to establish a case against my husband?" Tired and frightened, she set her coffee down on a nearby table then stood up. "Did my father put you up to accusing my husband of some sort of wrongdoing? Did he? He never believed in Jacob, never."

She stopped, realizing she'd said more than she wanted. She'd given him way too much ammunition already.

"I'm tired. I'm going back to my room now."

But Shane was there, holding her arm, forcing her around to look at him. "Your father never suggested that, Katherine. But I have to tell you, everyone is suspect. Everyone you know, everyone you love, anyone and everyone you've ever done business with or associated with. So you might as well search your mind and get ready for the real interrogation. Because as soon as we go inside, I have another thick file to read over—a file all about the people in your life. And I hope I'll find something inside that file that might give me a clue as to what's going on now."

He took her by the arm, half guiding, half dragging her toward the open doors into the house. "So get used to being interrogated. And keep in mind, it's part of the job."

"That's obvious," she said, anger clouding her logic. "And we all know you'll do that job in order to please my powerful father, no matter how much it might hurt me, right?"

She watched as he gritted his teeth then nodded. "If it means keeping you alive, yes, that's exactly what I'll do. And you'll just have to get over that." Then he tugged her close, his face inches from her own. "But make no mistake, this isn't about pleasing your father. There is much more going on here."

His eyes moved over her face, settling on her lips.

Katherine lost the ability to breathe. She was about to give him a choice retort just to stop herself from doing something crazy such as kissing him, when they heard a rustling in the bushes at the back of the courtyard. A rustling that sent chills down Katherine's spine and caused Shane to push her toward the doors with a hiss of warning. "Inside now. And stay there."

She watched, her heart caught in her throat, as he pulled a gun out of the waistband of his jeans and headed back out into the night. Watched and wished she hadn't been so flippant about her situation or his job.

SEVEN

Shane carefully opened the well-oiled gate and worked his way around the perimeters of the courtyard walls, his eyes adjusting in the moonlight enough to make out shapes and shadows. The motion detectors were on and gleaming bright out into the night, but he couldn't see anyone out there. Leaning against the still-warm mellowed stucco, he didn't dare breathe as he willed himself to be invisible.

He listened, praying Katherine would stay inside and out of the way. His gun by his side and ready, he moved again, taking each footstep in slow motion until he reached the back corner of the long wall. Stopping underneath a bent mesquite tree, he listened.

The night was as still as a ghost town, the wind quiet and sparse, the air dry and heavy with shadows. Then he heard it again, a soft rustling about five feet away.

Without hesitation, he whirled around the corner, his gun raised, his eyes focused. Then he let out a breath of relief.

An armadillo.

Shane stared down the wobbling uncomely creature, a wry smile on his face. "You don't know how close you came to death, little fellow." Picking up a rock, he threw it toward the thick-shelled animal, watching as the armadillo scurried away into the surrounding pastureland.

After making sure the armadillo was the only thing lurking about behind the house, Shane checked the garage and the outbuildings. Everything seemed intact. No sign of human footprints, no sign of tire tracks or any other sort of tracks. No markings of a horse and rider nearby either.

Was he imagining trouble? His spicy dinner hissed its way through his stomach, burning him with a reminder that only added to his apprehension. Hurrying back to the house, he prayed he'd find Katherine and the others safe.

Katherine stood huddled with Ricardo, Nina and Silvia in the dark kitchen. Ricardo had a shotgun slung over his right shoulder, ready to do battle.

"All clear," Shane said on a sigh of relief. "Our nocturnal visitor was only a lowly armadillo on the prowl."

"Thank goodness," Nina said, shaking her head. "Miss Katherine was terrified."

"We all were," Silvia added, eying her grandson. "This one had to be a big man and get his gun." She kissed Ricardo on the cheek, causing the teenager to groan.

"Sorry for the scare," Shane said, his eyes on Katherine. "But we have to be careful."

Ricardo stood up straight. "Want me to patrol tonight, Shane?"

"No, not necessary," Shane said, a hand on the boy's arm. "You have time enough to learn all the CHAIM maneuvers. No need to worry your mother about that now."

Nina gave Shane an appreciative nod. "I agree." Then she turned to her son. "I know you'd do your best to protect us but you're still so young. You'll get your chance in a few more years."

Ricardo's dark eyes lit up even if he did look disappointed. "Yes, *Madre*. I know, I know."

Shane sent them all back to their quarters then looked at Katherine. "Are you all right?"

"I'm fine. I was just concerned for your safety."

His smile turned tipsy. "You were worried about me?"

"Of course." She shrugged prettily. "If something happens to you, I'm stuck here. What would I do? I couldn't bear endangering Ricardo and his family."

Disappointed that she wouldn't pine away for him, Shane motioned toward the big den. "Let's go and sit down so we can talk." After he'd seated her on a high-backed leather chair, he said, "You will immediately call your father if anything happens to me. He'll send someone or come for you himself. Understand?"

"Yes." She studied him for a few seconds. "I can't stay hidden away here forever, Shane. So let's get on with this. I'll tell you anything you want to know."

Surprised at this turn, he said, "That armadillo must have really shaken you."

She shot him a harsh glare. "It wasn't the armadillo.

It was the thought that it could have been a human being out there, ready to kill me. Or worse, shoot you."

Shane saw it all there on her face. Katherine wasn't the kind of woman to watch others suffer, especially if they were doing it for her sake. She'd try to end this as quickly as possible so she could get back to her life, but more importantly, to protect everyone else around her. And possibly, to distance herself from any further closeness to him. That could make her a bit too reckless.

Trying to lighten the mood, he leaned forward. "So you *were* worried about me."

Her haughty expression didn't quite make it to her troubled eyes. "Yes, I was worried about you. I told you I didn't want you to get killed on my behalf. Satisfied?"

He put a hand to his heart. "Touched."

She leaned forward, too. "Don't be flippant about this, Shane. I might not like being here, but I certainly do appreciate how you've put yourself on the line for me."

"Accepted," he said, not daring to push this particular issue right now. Nor would he mention how close he'd come to kissing her out there in the courtyard. That wouldn't do, not tonight. Maybe not ever. She had to feel the same things he'd been feeling, but they were both avoiding the obvious. This attraction couldn't go anywhere for many reasons.

"Let's get down to business then," he said, taking her to his office at the back of the house.

"Okay." She took the chair across from his desk and sat straight up, as if facing an executioner. "What do you want to know?"

Shane had read through most of the early reports Kissie had emailed him with the promise of more to come. He'd printed the pages out so he could memorize what he needed to know and then destroy them. And he'd highlighted some points to go over with Katherine.

Shuffling through the papers, he said, "Your husband was a state senator for two years."

"Yes. He'd planned on running again." She shrugged. "He'd talked about running for governor on down the road."

"High aspirations."

She looked down at her folded hands, apparently not so thrilled about being first lady of Texas. "He lived and breathed politics. I think that's why he turned my father down about joining up with CHAIM. His heart wasn't in this kind of work. Of course, I didn't want him to join. We both felt we could serve better if he went into politics and I ran the foundation."

He registered the sadness on her face. This business was hard on families, but her storybook life might have been hard on her. To the point that she was hiding more than a widow's loneliness. "But he supported your father's efforts?"

Her gaze locked with Shane's. "Yes, and why would you even ask that?"

"Oh, no particular reason. But some of these news articles indicate they were at odds on some of the issues of this great state. You said they had some differences early on when you started dating Jacob. Your father didn't always agree with your husband's voting record in the Senate. Even after you became Jacob's wife."

Kit lowered her eyes, staring down at her joined hands. "They did like to argue politics, true. But it was always with respect. They agreed to disagree."

She was hiding something there. Shane could tell

by the way she lowered her eyes and looked away. But he didn't press her for more information on that. "Did your husband ever talk to you about any other business associates?"

"We talked about a lot of things. We attended certain functions on his behalf many times. But we also attended functions to promote the Barton Atkins Foundation. We always needed extra funding."

"And you knew at all times where that funding was coming from, how it was being provided?"

"Of course I did. I still do. Jacob had to be careful that his campaign contributions never overlapped our fundraising dollars and vice versa for me. Because of all our holdings, we kept meticulous records for that very purpose. What are you suggesting?"

"I'm not suggesting anything. I'm just asking the proper questions. We have to check every avenue. Some of your husband's holdings are a bit convoluted."

Her pupils dilated, irises a brilliant green, throwing him completely off. Was she trying to protect her husband, or did Shane just make her uncomfortable?

"My foundation is solid and completely transparent. I have good people in place to make sure of that, some of them specifically chosen with my father's help in order to safeguard our funding."

So, she was protecting her foundation. From her husband, maybe, or from her husband's questionable activities. Interesting.

"Did your husband ever suggest patrons or donors?"

"Of course he did. I can't believe you're targeting the foundation this way."

"I'm not targeting anyone, Katherine. Just let me finish."

She shifted, crossed her legs then stared at him. "Go on."

He could tell she was uncomfortable. What was she trying so hard to hide? Was she protecting her husband or someone else close to her? Or was he just imagining things?

"Your husband had a lot of holdings—oil and gas mostly. Did he ever deal in any type of government contracts or deal with other countries?"

"No. I mean, not after he became a senator."

"But what if there was something on the side, some sort of deal under the table?"

Katherine stood up, her hands fisted on the table. "I don't understand why you keep going back to Jacob. The man is dead, Shane. And that death was thoroughly investigated and deemed a tragic accident. The authorities didn't find anything suspicious about his business or his associates. Try looking somewhere else, please."

"I know how to dig into places the authorities might not," he said, hating the hurt in her eyes. "Jacob might have been a decent, honest man but even a good man can get caught up in a bad situation."

She reached up her right hand to clutch her pearls. "Not Jacob. He went by the book."

"Okay then. Let's talk about your friends. How long have you known Trudy Pearson?"

She looked shocked and annoyed but she answered the question. "Since grade school. We've had our share of differences, but she's my best friend."

"And she also lost her husband—just a few months before you lost Jacob."

"Yes, and we've helped each other through that."

"Her husband died of a heart attack?"

"Yes, completely natural causes."

He filed that for more research. "And you and she are still close?"

"Yes, obviously. She helps me with the foundation. She's one of our biggest donors and a regular volunteer around the office. Very devoted."

"I can see that from her generous contributions."

"So she's clear, right? Surely you don't think—"

Shane didn't want to say anything more about Trudy Pearson right now. "As far as I can see, yes, your friend is clear."

"You don't sound so sure."

He didn't dare tell Katherine that her best friend couldn't be located. But Trudy had left the hotel last night with that catering manager, who also couldn't be found. "I can't be sure about anything at this point."

"No, I suppose not." She let out a sigh. "Is this really necessary, to ask about and suspect the people I care about the most?"

"I'm afraid so. The more people we can eliminate the better off we'll be. And we have to start with those closest to you and work our way from there."

"So you've done background checks on everyone who knows me, right? And what have you found?"

This was tricky, trying to question her without giving anything away. "So far, so good. But we have a lot of ground to cover still. Are you tired?"

"No. I could make us some more coffee and find more of that chocolate Nina left for us."

"More chocolate?" He laughed out loud. "For someone with such a slender figure, you sure can pack away the food."

"I'm a Texas girl. We like to eat."

"You must have good genes."

"More like, a fast metabolism. I'm usually too busy to eat most days. I'm sure I'll gain a few pounds before this is over. I'm a stress eater."

"I see. Maybe we can go for a ride tomorrow, if everything looks safe. Take the horses out. I find a good long ride relieves stress for me."

And on horseback, he could look for anything out of the ordinary.

"That might be nice. Do you have a lot of horses here?"

"About a half dozen. Ricardo is great with them. And Nina and Silvia both are excellent horsewomen. When I'm not here, they pretty much run the place."

"What about Nina's husband? How did he die?"

"He was in the army. He died in the Middle East."

"That's tough. So you offered them a home?"

Shane sat back, his hands on his knees. "It was more like they gave me a home. After my parents began living separate lives, my father only brought me here to hunt or fish, to practice my shooting capabilities with every type of weapon known to man. I did a lot of my CHAIM training right here with some of the senior members, under my father's watchful eye. But at the end of the day, I could always find *Abuela* Silvia in the kitchen, waiting to talk to me. She taught me about Christ, about church, about family. I watched her with Nina and later, young Ricardo and after Nina's husband died, I invited them to live here permanently and help me with the place. I've always wished I had that kind of close-knit family."

"Maybe you still can one day."

He looked across at her, his gaze locking with hers as

the image of her in a wedding gown floated through his mind. "Maybe so. It's not easy, but when I think about how happy Devon and Lydia are now—"

"Devon Malone? He's retired from CHAIM, right?"

"Yes, after almost getting himself killed. But he and Lydia are so in love."

"My father brags about them all the time. He seems to adore Lydia."

"She is truly a woman of strong faith."

"And I hear even Eli Trudeau has settled down with Devon's sister Gena."

"That was a surprise. And now they're raising Eli's son Scotty and Eli is always bragging about having more children someday." Shane lifted up in his chair. "All very nice, but some of us aren't meant for that kind of domestic bliss."

Her smile shifted into a frown. "I thought I'd have that. I wanted children but it just never happened."

Shane got an image of her holding a baby in her arms. It was such a beautiful torment, he had to clear his throat. "I'm sorry. You'd make a wonderful mother. You've shown that with your humanitarian efforts."

A flush of heat seared her face. "I'll go make that coffee now."

Shane watched her go, aware that they were dancing around so many questions neither of them could ask. Or answer for that matter. He didn't want to probe into her past. He wanted to hold her close and ask her about the here and now and the future.

And in spite of his declaration to the contrary about domesticity, he wouldn't mind at all being a part of that future. But right now, he had to make sure she lived to have a tomorrow. So he sat staring at the reports in front of him, wondering when he'd hit on something that triggered a clue, his mind drifting from the job at hand to the sounds of a woman making coffee in the kitchen. Nice, domestic sounds. Homey and pleasant, peaceful and contented.

He could get used to that—having her in his home, in his life. He'd never before thought he would want that. He'd purposely stayed away from a lifetime commitment because of the nature of his work. That, and the shining example of living separately his parents had shown him made Shane a little gun-shy on matters of the heart.

His thoughts strayed ahead to kissing her and holding her and going on long rides through the hills with her.

He was so lost in that pleasant daydream, he forgot the reason he was sitting here.

Until he heard Katherine scream, followed by a crash in the kitchen.

EIGHT

Shane rushed into the kitchen with his weapon raised.

"Katherine?"

The kitchen was empty.

He'd protected many people in his lifetime. He'd been on security details in some of the roughest places on earth. But he'd never felt this kind of heart-shattering fear before, a fierce protective fear for the woman he was trying to guard. It tore through him, rendering him helpless. Until he remembered her beautiful smile.

"Katherine, answer me?"

"I'm here," she said, her voice barely above a whisper. "In the pantry."

He whirled toward the partially open door to the walk-in pantry just off the kitchen. Rushing toward that door, Shane yanked it open then pulled her into his arms. "What happened?"

Katherine clung to him for a minute then stepped back to wipe at her face. "I… I thought I saw someone in the window."

Shane pulled her behind him, switching off lights before he pivoted toward the long row of windows lining the kitchen. "Are you sure?"

She shook her head. "No, not really. I was standing by the sink and…the way the moonlight shot across the backyard… I thought I saw someone standing out there looking at me."

Shane absorbed that information then went into action. "Can you describe them?"

She took in a long breath then lifted her head toward him. "Shane, it looked like Jacob."

"Jacob? Your dead husband?"

"Yes," she said, putting her hands to her face. "That can't be possible. He's dead. I know he's dead. But it looked so much like him. That's why I screamed. I thought I was seeing a ghost."

Shane didn't believe in ghosts. "Listen to me," he said, holding her close again. "I have to go out and investigate."

"No!" She held him tight. "Don't go out there. They might kill you."

"Kit, I have to take a look." He lifted her away. "I want you to go to the back of the house and get Nina, okay? Stay there with her and Ricardo until I come back in."

"I'd rather go with you," she said, holding on to his shirt. "I need to see who that is out there."

"You can't. You'd only distract me. Let me walk around, see if they're still out there or if they left any tracks."

She looked doubtful, but she nodded her head, determination taking the place of her anxiety. "I'll give you ten minutes then I'm coming to find you, Shane." She stood back then turned toward the gun cabinet in the big den. "I know how to use several weapons."

Shane could tell she wouldn't back down so he hurried her into the den and found a Smith & Wesson .38 revolver. "Can you shoot this?"

She glanced at the gun then back at him. "Yes, I can."

He handed her five copper-tipped bullets and then whirled toward the door. "Go and find Nina and Ricardo. And don't use that unless you absolutely have no other choice."

She nodded and took off down the hallway.

Her courage brought the beat back into Shane's heart. He had a feeling Katherine was much stronger than everyone around her realized. And that only added to his growing fears and concerns for her.

Kit knocked on the sitting room door of Nina's apartment on the left wing of the big house and waited, the warmth of the loaded revolver giving her strength.

Nina opened the door, took one look at the pistol then pulled Kit into the room. "What's going on?"

"I thought I saw a prowler," Kit explained. "Shane went to look, and he gave me this." She held the gun down.

"I see," Nina said, motioning toward a floral couch. "Come on in, Miss Katherine. You can wait here with me."

"Where are your mother and Ricardo?"

"*Madre* is asleep in her room." Nina pointed toward

a small hallway. "And Ricardo is watching television in his room."

"Let's check on them," Kit suggested, her gut instinct telling her this wasn't over yet. She'd seen a human standing outside that window. A man who looked remarkably like Jacob—or at least someone who'd disguised himself as her late husband.

Nina gave her a worried look and led the way into the bedrooms. *Abuela* Silvia was fast asleep in her bed. Nina opened the door to Ricardo's room and gasped.

"He's not here!" She glanced around then pointed to his bed. "He left his cell phone here."

"Are you sure he was here?" Kit asked, dread coursing throughout her system.

"Yes." Nina went to the windows. "He's been known to sneak out during the night though. That boy is always wanting to be like Shane. Trying to protect us." She whirled to face Kit. "Do you think you saw *him* out the window?"

Kit didn't think Ricardo had purposely dressed up like Jacob to scare her. At least she hoped not. "No, no. This was a man, but it wasn't Ricardo. I screamed out when I saw him and he ran. Do you think Ricardo heard my screams and went outside?"

"He might have. I didn't hear anything," Nina said. "But I was listening to my iPod earlier. I barely heard your knock at the door." She looked around the empty room. "We need to find my son."

"Let's go," Kit said, wondering what they could do. Praying that Ricardo wouldn't get caught in the line of fire, or worse, she hurried with Nina toward the hallway leading back to the kitchen and garage. "We'll have to be careful. If someone is still out there, we could get hurt."

"Or Shane could mistake us for one of them," Nina said. Then she pulled out a cell phone. "I think we'd better call him and warn him that Ricardo isn't in his room."

"Good idea," Kit said as she slowly opened the heavy wooden door leading to the catwalk and the garage.

Nina listened then said, "Shane's not answering his phone. And I used the code we always use for alerts."

"That can't be good," Kit whispered. "Stay with me, Nina."

Nina held to the back of Kit's shirt, her lips moving in prayer as they crept along the hedges until they reached the corner of the big garage. "We can't go out there. Shane's not answering and that either means he's in trouble or he can't pick up. I have to make sure you're safe."

"I know," Kit replied. "But we have to do something. I can't leave him out there alone. And we have to find Ricardo, too. Let's stay together."

Nina clicked open her phone again. "Maybe I can send a text to Shane."

Kit waited while Nina punched at the keys, the sounds of the night putting her on edge. Every rustle, every gust of wind caused her skin to bristle. Where was Shane? Where was Ricardo? And who was doing this to her?

"No answer from him yet," Nina said, her tone full of apprehension. "I just hope wherever Shane is, he has my son with him. Ricardo knows not to leave when things are dangerous out there."

Kit interpreted that to mean whenever Shane was

working on a case. Did he bring a lot of people here? She couldn't think about that right now. She just wanted to know he was safe and that Ricardo was okay, too. Holding the loaded gun down, she whispered to Nina. "You stay here. I'm going around to the front of the house."

"Are you sure?" Nina said, her breath rushed. "Shane won't be happy if I let something happen to you."

"I'll take full responsibility for my actions," Kit replied. "I can't stand around waiting."

She didn't have to wait. In the next seconds, they heard the pop of gunfire somewhere off in the distance.

Nina screamed and grabbed Kit. "We need to stay in the house."

But Kit was already running toward the garage. Hitting a button on the wall, she waited until the big doors opened. "I'm not going on foot. I'm taking my mother's bulletproof car." Grabbing the keys from the box on the wall, she turned back to Nina. "Get inside, get a gun and wait for me. I'm going to find Shane."

Shane glanced over at the boy holding the gun. "Ricardo, are you all right?"

"*Sí.*" Ricardo glanced over at Shane. "I messed things up, didn't I?"

Shane did a visual of the surrounding hills and trees, the buzz of his silenced cell telling him Nina was trying to locate him. But right now, they were penned in. He couldn't give Nina a signal until he got a handle on the situation. Praying that they were dealing with a lone intruder, he turned back to Ricardo.

"You didn't mess up," Shane said on a gush of a whisper. "You shouldn't have left the house, but now that you're here, we'll make the best of it. We've got him cornered and it's two to one. The odds are in our favor. Thanks for coming to help." Grabbing his cell, he texted a message to Nina.

"Sit tight. Ricardo OK. Keep Kit inside."

Ricardo's dark eyes flashed in the moonlight. "I had to help. I heard her scream and then when I came around the corner, I saw him running."

Shane didn't know whether to send up a prayer of thanks for boys who sneaked out of the house behind their mothers' backs, or to give Ricardo a serious reprimand for leaving the house with a gun. "I'm glad you heard Kit and I'm glad you saw the prowler. But you'll have some explaining to do with your mother— about being out here with your gun on patrol. You went against my orders."

"I wanted to help," Ricardo replied. "And if I hadn't been out here, he might have gotten away."

"True," Shane replied, admiring the boy's fortitude. "Describe him to me again."

"He's tall with dark blond hair," Ricardo said. "And he has a gun."

"Yes, we can vouch for that based on the shots he just fired at us," Shane retorted, his sarcasm passing right by Ricardo's nervous energy. He'd also managed to get a brief look at the man. And Kit had been right; the man looked remarkably like her late husband based on the pictures Shane had seen of Jacob Atkins. Someone had gone to a lot of trouble to scare Katherine.

"What's the plan?" Ricardo asked, his rifle aimed toward the darkness in front of them.

Shane glanced around. They'd managed to hide behind an old bale of hay but the prowler was still out there. "We wait for a few minutes," he replied. "He'll make another move any minute now."

"How do you know that?"

"Because he has to get out of here before morning. And I can wait all night if I have to. If he's found here, he knows what will happen to him." Shane would take pleasure in questioning this impersonator.

Ricardo stared out into the night. "I'm so ready to learn, Shane. Why do I have to wait until after college?"

Shane and Ricardo had had this discussion before and now was not a very good time to go over the details again. But the boy needed to understand the commitment he was about to make. "Because you can't become a CHAIM agent until you're over twenty-one and you have your degree and good and proper training. You know the rules."

"I think the rules are *estúpido*," Ricardo said, his Hispanic heritage kicking in with each accented word. "I'm ready now."

"You're too young," Shane replied, remembering how he felt when he was a teenager. "It will come in due time." Then he leaned forward. "And right now, we need to focus on that shadow slinking across the pasture. That's not a longhorn. That's a human."

Ricardo looked through the scope of his rifle. "It's him. He's making a move just like you said. I can get a clean shot."

Shane held a hand against the boy's trigger finger. "Don't do anything, Ricardo. Do not shoot that gun. That's an order."

Ricardo frowned but he nodded and kept the gun

trained on the shadowy figure moving through the grass and trees.

Shane lifted his own weapon, waiting for the right moment. He didn't want to kill the interloper, just hurt him enough to make him talk.

But before Shane could position himself to get in a good shot, he heard a motor revving near the house. And then he looked up to see a sliver of bright yellow glowing in the moonlight as Sally Mae Barton's little sportscar zoomed past them.

"That was Miss Katherine," Ricardo said, his voice squeaky with shock. "What's she doing? Look, she's headed toward that man!"

"So I see," Shane replied, his nerves going into a jangling warning even while his phone hummed a message he didn't have to read.

Nina hadn't been able to keep Kit inside.

There was nothing more dangerous than a headstrong woman who was just a tad ticked off. Then he turned to Ricardo. "I need you to cover me. I have to get to that man before she does. Don't move from this spot and don't shoot to kill. Just rattle him a bit to keep him from hitting me or that car. It's supposed to be bulletproof, but I don't want to take any chances."

Ricardo nodded. "Is she gonna run him down?"

"Something like that, it appears," Shane said, gritting his teeth at the sound of gears shifting. This was not good. He should have never left the infuriating woman alone.

Kit was building up enough speed to flatten that intruder. That is, if the man didn't shoot her first.

NINE

She didn't want to do this.

Katherine had never deliberately tried to kill another human being but right now she didn't have any choice. Someone wanted to either scare her to death or make her come out of hiding.

"Congratulations," she said as she shifted gears. "You managed to do both."

Seeing the figure out in the pasture, she turned the little car around and headed straight toward where the surprised visitor was now hulking behind a lone cottonwood tree. What would Shane do in this situation? Maybe bump the man enough to knock the wind out of him? After all, if she mowed the man down and killed him, they might not get any answers. And she had to have answers. She was a logical, methodical person.

She liked things in order. She needed answers and she needed to understand.

She watched the shadow up ahead, speeding along, building up steam with each shift of the gears when she saw another shadow out of the corner of her eye. Shane!

Then she heard gunshots. Worried that he'd been hit, she rammed the little car into Reverse and did a one-eighty toward Shane. Slamming on brakes, she opened the passenger door and shouted, "Get in!"

He was ready and waiting. Shane slid in and gave her a harried glance. "Fancy meeting you here."

"What now?" Kit asked, adrenaline making her hands shake. "I can still get to him."

Shane put a hand on hers over the gearshift. "Yes, I have no doubt you could do that. But Ricardo is out there, too. You don't want to run over Nina's only child, do you?"

Her heart clanked and rumbled like a rig pumping oil. "No, of course not. But we can't let him get away. I want to find out who he is and who sent him."

"Of course you do." Shane held her hand steady. "Ricardo has the man cornered behind those trees. And we're going to fall back on the old-fashioned way of getting to him."

"How?"

"We're going to rustle him up. Pretend he's a lost calf, so to speak. We circle back around and force him out of hiding. Can you do that, or do I need to drive?"

"I can do it," Kit said, relief replacing her need to hurt the man. She felt immensely better now that Shane was with her, but she was determined enough to take care of this culprit on her own if she had to. "I can do that."

Shane let go of her hand. "Okay then. Let's rodeo."

Kit didn't need any further instructions. She put the car into first and hit the gas, circling around the big moonlit pasture. "Where's Ricardo?"

"Behind that old bale of hay near the outbuilding to the west," Shane retorted. "He's holding off the intruder until he sees us coming over the north ridge."

"Got it." She maneuvered the purring car toward the copse of small trees and shrubs where the big cottonwood stood like a dark giant. "He went inside there."

"Yes, he's behind the cottonwood. He has nowhere else to hide."

"Okay. What do I need to do?"

Shane gave her an appreciative look then said, "Just head into the thicket. And watch for stumps or brush. We don't need to crash and we don't want to get shot. We just want to flush him out."

She stopped the car, revved the motor for a minute then hit first gear and plunged across the dry grass toward the bramble surrounding the cottonwood. "He's going to regret scaring me."

"I do believe he will at that," Shane replied. Then he put down the window on his side and leaned out, his gun pointed toward the trees.

It all happened in a matter of minutes, but in Shane's mind it seemed to drag on and on. Kit expertly drove the little car toward the cottonwood, bullets pelting all around them. She never blinked, she never wavered. In fact, he would always remember her face as being completely serene and completely determined, almost calm, as she "herded" the lone man hiding behind the tree out into the open.

Shane saw all of this in his mind even as he trained his weapon on the figure suddenly zigzagging in front of them. The man hurried away, the moonlight pinpointing him in the middle of the dipping terraces and hills.

And then, firing behind himself, the man practically ran right into the barrel of Ricardo's twelve-gauge shotgun. Ricardo, disobeying orders to stay hidden, pushed at the man with his gun, causing him to panic and drop his own weapon.

Kit centered the headlights on the two of them then slammed on the brakes. "We've got him."

"Yes, we do." Shane said a prayer and held his breath, hoping the boy wouldn't pull the trigger. Ricardo did not. He simply stood very still and held the gun trained on the man's chest.

And then he shouted, "Down on your knees."

The man, winded and tired and more than a little dazed, held up his gun and dropped it on the ground as he fell to his knees, all the while glancing behind him to make sure the little car didn't run him down.

Kit had stopped the sports car in a spray of dust and dirt just inches from the man's dark tennis shoes. Yanking her door open, she said, "Now we can find out why he's here."

Shane let out a deeply held breath. "Yes, I believe that will do, luv. Turn off the motor, please."

She looked reluctant, but she did as he asked. Then she got out of the car, her revolver held with both hands as she walked slowly toward the man.

Shane was right behind her, his own gun on the ready. Kit had done a marvelous job of staying cool under pressure but now the woman was at the boiling point. Shane prayed she'd stay calm and let him do the talking.

She looked so pristine, holding that gun like a true cowgirl ready for a shoot-out. Rather cute, if he didn't think about the circumstances.

Adorable. Kit Atkins was a brave, adorable, formidable woman who didn't back down.

Until she came face to face with the man in front of her. Then she gasped and her hands went limp by her side. Shane caught the revolver before it hit the ground.

She couldn't believe what she was seeing.

"Jacob, is that you?"

The man grunted and held his head down.

Kit stepped forward, her hand reaching out into the night air. "Jacob, answer me, please?"

Shane moved between her and the man. "Sir, you're trespassing and you've given all of us quite a time tonight. You'd better start talking now, or things could get much worse for you."

The intruder finally looked up at them, his gaze shifting from Kit to Shane in a jittery dance. "I... I can't talk. They'll kill me."

Kit snapped out of her shock at the sound of his voice. "You're not my husband."

Then she let loose, grabbing the man by his black shirt, her fist hammering into his chest. "Tell me who you are, right now!"

Shane pulled her away then took over where she'd left off, lifting the man back to a standing position and fisting the man's shirt with his hands. "You'd better listen to her. She is not one to be trifled with. And while you're at it, take off that ridiculous disguise and tell us your name."

"Tim. Timothy Williams." The man slowly lifted the thick wig off his head to reveal dark, stringy hair. After dropping the wig to the ground, he tugged at the moustache over his lips. "Sorry, lady. They just told me to scare you and then to run."

"Well, you did," Kit said, sick to her stomach. "And now I'm not scared, I'm angry. Is this some awful joke?"

"I don't know," the twitching man said. "They offered me a lot of money, told me how to get past security and…they told me to make sure you saw me and then to leave this somewhere." He held up a cell phone. "I was going to put it by the back door when you spotted me." He nodded toward Ricardo. "But when I saw him coming around the corner with a gun, I panicked and ran."

Shane took the cell phone the man pushed toward Kit. "Why a phone?"

Timothy shrugged and twitched some more. "I think they want to give you a message."

"So that's it?" Kit asked, thinking her life had turned into one of those weird crime scenes she'd see occasionally on the evening news. This man was either scared to death or needing his next fix, from the looks of him. "We just wait for a phone call." She turned to Shane. "What do you think?"

Shane looked over the disposal phone. "It looks like one of those cheap pay-as-you-go phones. Not traceable. But that could be a disguise, too. We'll just have to wait and see who calls us." He shot her a warning look. "In the meantime, Timothy and I need to have a little chat so we can get to know each other."

He yanked Timothy by the collar, bringing the kid nose to nose. "Come with me."

"Don't call the locals," Timothy hollered. "I'm on probation for distribution of illegal drugs. They'll send me back to prison."

Kit was right on his heels, anger fueling her need for answers. "Well, you should have thought about that before you took this job."

The man shook his head then glanced up at her. "They offered me a lot of money, lady. I was gonna use it to get a new start." Then he shifted, his old boots stomping against the hard ground. "And they threatened me, said they'd make things look bad for me if I didn't cooperate."

Kit stepped so close to the man, Shane feared she was about to wring his scrawny neck. "Well, you can double that for me. If you don't tell us everything you know, I will make you pay in every way imaginable. I can promise you that."

Shane noted how little Timmy cowered underneath that feminine declaration. "I'm sorry, lady, okay?"

"Don't worry, luv," Shane said to Kit as he pushed the man toward the house, Ricardo helping him to guard the culprit. "We'll have some answers before sunrise, I can promise you that."

"Good," she said. "And I hope whoever gave him that phone will call soon. I'd really like to talk to them, too."

"Just be patient," Shane said. "Do you feel up to driving the car back to the house?"

Kit nodded. "I'll be fine. Unless I decide to finish him off right here and now."

"Now, darlin', take a deep breath and drive the car

back slowly, very slowly so I can keep an eye on you while I walk Timothy home," Shane said, his gaze moving over the jumpy man in front of him. "I think our friend Tim here has had enough excitement for one night."

"Don't let her behind that wheel again," Timothy said, glancing over his shoulder. "She's crazy."

"Not crazy," Shane said, pushing hard on the man's backbone for emphasis. "Just really, really mad that you played such a despicable trick on her. And she won't forget it, not for a long time." He glanced over at Kit, his eyes holding hers in a plea. "That's why she needs a quiet drive—to calm her nerves." He motioned toward Ricardo. "Ride with her, will you?"

Timothy looked sick to his stomach. And Shane feared that underneath her anger, Kit was very close to the same.

Two hours later, Timothy Williams still wouldn't tell them anything other than some "rich-looking stranger" approached him in a bar about twenty miles up the road and asked him if he'd like to make some spending money.

"I said sure," Timothy told them, his beady eyes full of woe each time he glanced up at Shane in the big, shadowy office at the back of the house. "He took me to this hotel room and showed me the file he had on me. That dude knew everything about me, good and bad. He offered me ten thousand dollars and told me if I didn't do exactly as he said, he'd get me thrown back into prison on some trumped-up charge. Said he'd make sure they found drugs in my apartment."

"What else can you tell us?" Shane asked, his patience wearing very thin.

"That's it, man," Timothy insisted. "He gave me the instructions. Put on the wig and mustache and go to this place out in the middle of nowhere. Gave me the exact location but I got lost anyway. Told me to find the woman, scare her then leave the phone by the back door where you'd be sure to find it. Never seen a place so hard to find, especially the way he had me come in on the other side of the river. Just got lucky, seeing her at the kitchen window. I was gonna drop the phone and get out of here."

"Describe this man to me one more time," Shane said, glancing over at where Kit sat nursing a cup of strong coffee. She was quiet, too quiet. And she looked exhausted, her usually vivid green eyes slanting down in a forest-like darkness.

"I told you, man. He was tall with reddish-brown hair cut close to his head. He wore a fancy suit and didn't even break a sweat, even when he was telling me exactly what might happen to me if I messed up." He shrugged, bent his head down. "And now, I've done that. I was supposed to report back to him—"

He stopped, his Adam's apple bobbing as he lowered his eyes, his gaze shuttered again.

Shane grabbed him, yanking him up and out of the chair. "Where and when?"

Timothy shook his head. "No, man. I can't tell you. He'll kill me."

"And I'll kill you if you don't," Shane said, his deadly tone full of a calm intent. He'd had enough for one night.

Timothy's fear palpitated throughout his skinny frame, causing him to tremble. "I can't do that. He's dangerous. He made it clear what would happen to me—"

"Perhaps *I* haven't made *myself* clear then," Shane said, his hand still on Timothy's torn, dirty shirt. "I can do just as much damage to your good name, my friend. And I can make things much worse than your mysterious employer ever promised you." He leaned close, so close he could smell the fear radiating off Timothy's scrawny body. "I know this place, far away, where we send people who don't cooperate with us. You'd disappear, Timmy. You'd cease existing all together. You won't die but you'll certainly wish you could." He stood back, his gaze moving from Timothy to Katherine, hoping she'd believe his exaggerated threats. "You don't realize what you've done or with whom you're dealing. This woman's father will come after you and make you suffer, just as she told you earlier."

Katherine sat there, her eyes centered on Timothy Williams, her expression bordering on murderous. But she didn't threaten the man and she didn't speak up as Shane had expected, which scared him more than he was willing to admit. What was she thinking? What was she planning?

Deciding he'd talk to her later, he looked down at Timothy. "I'm going to give you one more chance to tell me the truth, Mr. Williams. If you aren't completely honest with me, things are going to go from bad to worse for you in a very short time."

Timothy looked up at Shane, terror in his dark eyes. "He said—"

The disposable phone lying on Shane's desk rang.

And before Shane could grab it and take the call, Katherine had it up to her ear, every muscle in her face strained and tense as she spoke into the receiver.

So that was what she'd been waiting for.

"Hello?" she said, her tone full of tremors.

Shane held his breath as he watched her face go pale.

TEN

Kit gripped the phone so hard her knuckle bones protested. "Trudy?"

"It's me, suga'," Trudy said, her voice sounding faraway and strained.

Kit couldn't tell if her friend was laughing or crying. "Are you all right?"

"I've been better," Trudy said. "How about you?"

"I'm fine," Kit said, her gaze locking with Shane's. "Trudy, why are you calling me on this phone?"

Trudy let out a long, shuddering sob. "No one would let me talk to you. You're not answering your phone. I've left messages with your staff at your office and at home. Your daddy wouldn't even talk to me."

"They were all told not to take any calls," Katherine explained, her mind whirling with fear and concern. "I'm all right. But how did you get this phone number?"

"They gave it to me," Trudy replied. "Told me I had to talk to you, make you understand."

Kit motioned to Shane. "Understand what?"

Shane dumped Timothy Williams in the chair and whispered, "Don't make a move or you'll die right here." Then he hurried around the desk to Katherine. "What's going on?"

She mouthed, "I don't know." Then turning her attention back to Trudy, she said, "Trudy, tell me what's wrong. Tell me why you're involved in this."

"They...they have me, Kit," Trudy said. "They took me right out of my bed a few hours after the attack at the gala. They're upset that you didn't die that night so now they want you to come to them. Just to talk."

"They? Who? Talk about what?"

"I don't know—something to do with Mexico, I think. I don't even know where I am. It's dark and they only come in to bring me food. I'm in some big house or some sort of building. I know that from all the stairs I had to go up to get to this room. I—"

Trudy stopped talking then Kit heard a quick noise that sounded like a pop. "Trudy? Are you there?"

"I'm here," Trudy replied, her voice weaker now. "Sorry about that. I said too much. My keeper had to remind me to stick to the script."

Katherine's heart pumped so hard it hurt to breathe. "What do you mean?"

"Kit, I've been kidnapped. They're trying to get to you through me. They want you to come out of hiding and talk to them or...well...they're threatening to kill me. But I'm not scared of these bullies."

Katherine heard another whacking sound, followed by a moan. "Trudy?"

It took a few seconds before Trudy responded. "That's all I can say, except—don't do it. They know where you are, so get out of there and don't come near these people. We'll talk later. Gotta go."

Kit heard Trudy's high-pitched scream then the connection was lost. Staring down at the ugly black phone, she put her hand to her mouth. "They have Trudy. Somebody kidnapped her and they're holding her. I think they've been beating her. Shane?"

He pulled her into his arms, his hand resting on her hair. "What else did she say?"

Katherine glanced over his shoulder at Timothy. "She said they want me to come out of hiding and talk to them." Her panicked gaze held his. "Something about Mexico."

Why did Mexico keep popping up on the radar?

Shane pulled back to stare down at her. "Or?"

She wiped at her eyes. "They'll kill Trudy if I don't do it. She said they were angry that they didn't kill me the other night and now they're threatening her unless I come to them and talk. She told me not to do what they wanted, but I have to. We have to help her."

She hit keys on the phone. "There's a number. I have to call it back."

"No, don't. They'll have it blocked," Shane said, taking the phone from her. "I'll have to analyze it more and try to do a reverse trace. But without the number that might be impossible. But if you call them back, they can verify Trudy was talking to you. They'll keep her alive. She's the link to you."

Kit couldn't live with that. The thought of Trudy being held and tortured made her dizzy with nausea. "So we just wait?"

"It's okay," Shane said, his eyes a calculating blue. "First things first, luv." He pointed to the man in the chair. "We get this one to tell us where he was supposed to meet up with his friend and then we go from there. Maybe we can track them back to Trudy."

Katherine pulled away to stare up at him. "It might be too late by then. We don't have time. They obviously know I'm here with you since they sent him here."

"Yes, but maybe they sent him to *make sure* you were here," Shane said. "Why send him just to scare you and bring you a phone? They sent an assassin to kill you the other night. Why didn't they come in and try to take you?"

"No one could reach me," she tried to explain. "My father wouldn't take Trudy's calls. They must have grabbed her immediately after the attack, hoping she'd be able to talk to me or get to me. And now they know I'm here but they're afraid to show their faces." She shot another boiling look at the man in the chair. "So they sent him instead to do their dirty work."

Shane glared at Timothy Williams then turned back to Kit. "We're monitoring all incoming calls to your father's location, so we might be able to pinpoint something there. Any wrong word could put you in even more danger now that they've verified you're here."

"So you'll cut me off from my best friend, let her suffer just to protect me. I won't do that. I can't."

She saw his expression change. It was so quick she almost missed it, but Katherine saw the cautious way he went blank, saw the look of doubt in his eyes.

A sick feeling pooled inside her stomach, making her feel queasy. "You don't still think Trudy had something to do with all of this?"

"I can't rule out anyone, Kit. And now it looks as if she's right in the thick of things. Someone found out I brought you here."

"But it couldn't have been Trudy. She didn't know where you were taking me that night."

"But your parents trust her. They might have inadvertently said something to tip her off. She might have caved and given out a clue. Maybe that's why our friend here showed up tonight. Someone knew how to get to you."

"But she said my parents weren't taking her calls. How could they tell her anything when *they* didn't even know where you were taking me?"

"True, that doesn't make sense but neither does the fact that they tried to kill you and now they just want to talk to you. Someone figured out where you are. Somehow. They might have managed to get a tracker on your mother's car before we even arrived at Eagle Rock. She did say she takes that car out a lot."

Frantic, Kit shook her head. "We can worry about that later. Shane, if they're trying to force information out of Trudy, we need to find her right now!"

Pulling away, she pushed past Shane and lunged for Timothy Williams. Grabbing him by the arm, she said, "You'd better tell me where you're supposed to meet this man, do you understand? They have my best friend and they'll kill her. Tell me now, do you hear me?"

Shane managed to pull her off before she could claw the man's eyes out, but that didn't stop Katherine from taking action. Lifting away from Shane, she said, "I'm okay. I'm fine. Just get some answers out of him." Giving the man one last scalding look, she turned back to

Shane. "Make him talk. I can't stand to be in the same room with him anymore."

Then, the black phone tucked in one fisted hand, she turned and left the room, intent on taking her mother's car and going back to Austin. They wanted her to come to them? Well, then, that's what she'd do.

And she prayed she'd get there in time to save Trudy.

Shane's gut was burning with all the fire of a tree hit by lightning.

Ulcers. That's what he had to show for with this job.

And now was not a good time for ulcers to flare up. He had a bad feeling that Kit wasn't going upstairs to retire for the night. And he had a bad feeling that Timothy Williams wasn't going to give up the goods without a fight.

But the worst of his feelings kept coming back to Mexico. What was going on there? And did this attack have anything to do with Kit's upcoming trip? Mexico was full of dangerous drug cartels and corrupt people in authority. What had Katherine gotten herself caught up in?

Which crisis to handle first?

Turning to Timothy, Shane decided he'd deal with him after he kept Katherine from doing something foolish. He needed to get that phone from her.

"Okay, my friend. I need to take care of some business. So I want you to sit tight, as they say here in America, and wait for me."

He buzzed Nina and told her to bring rope and a gun. Then he stared down at the shivering man in the chair. "Someone will be in shortly to watch you. And while you're sitting here, think really long and hard about your options. Your mysterious benefactor isn't here to protect you and as I said before, I can make you disappear. You'll have to decide which way you want to handle this."

Timothy turned a sickly white-pale. "Man, don't do this. Don't hold me here. He's waiting for me."

Shane leaned close. "He wants her to come out of hiding. We know that now because they're holding her friend and they forced her to make the call. You did complete your mission but now because you failed to report back you've become expendable. He sent you here so he could stay in hiding and protect his identity. Your identity doesn't matter anymore. Do you actually think he'll let you live now?"

"You don't get it, do you?" Timothy shouted. "He's gonna kill her, too. He sent me instead of coming here himself because he wants to talk to her first but he can't reveal his face. The man who hired me isn't the main man. He was just the hired help, like me. But the big shot behind all of this wants to flush her out—and you, too. She has something they need."

Shane leaned down, a hand on each of the chair arms. "Go on."

Timothy held up his hands, palms out. "I don't know what it is. Nobody's bothered to share that with me and they told me not to use that phone for anything—just make sure she got it. They gave me the wig and mustache and showed me this picture of her dead husband. Said to make it look good to shake her up. They knew you'd come running and find the phone. But I messed up and now I need to get back to the meeting point and explain."

"Oh, you won't have an opportunity to explain. They are going to kill you and leave you at my doorstep."

Timothy's expression turned petulant. Then he made a plea. "If I help you, can you help me?"

Shane let out a derisive chuckle. "There is no help for any of us, Timothy. We're all in a fine mess here."

Timothy was sweating now, grasping for tidbits of information as reality set in and his last fix wore off. "Look, whatever it is he's got on your woman, he thinks it's worth killing her—after he finds it. He needs to get her to talk, but after that things look bad. That's all I know, I swear."

His words sent a chill rushing down Shane's backbone.

"You need to tell me where you were supposed to meet him, do you understand?"

Timothy shook his head. "I can't be sure. I don't know except he was going to pick me up out on the same road where he dropped me—that old stagecoach road that runs in front of your property—that long dirt lane. Said he'd pick me up around dawn and then he'd pay me the rest of my money and drop me off at the bus station. That's it, honest. I just want to go to the road and wait."

Shane's burning gut told him differently. Timmy might be lying to protect himself from a very dangerous man. Shane could become dangerous, could end this right now. He had to find Katherine, but he also needed someone to knock some sense into this idiot's head. And he wouldn't put Nina and her family at risk by asking them to do it.

"I need backup," he said to himself. They were no longer safe here. Then he looked over at Timmy. "I hate to do this, but I'm going to have to call in someone I can trust to watch out for you and…persuade you to remember more. You won't be meeting up with anyone out on the road at sunup. But I will. And if you're lying to me, my friend will take care of you, one way or another." And his friend could offer protection while Shane planned their next move.

Tim glared at him, his eyes wide with fear. "You're making a big mistake."

"We'll see." Shane dialed a number he hadn't used in a long time and prayed his fellow teammate would be there. It rang several times then he heard a loud, snarling grunt.

"This better be good."

The voice rasped over the wire, making Shane wonder if he'd chosen wisely. Top command would tell him to leave the Warrior out of this. Too much, too soon.

Well, the top command wasn't here. "Paco, is that you, my friend?"

"Who wants to know?"

"Now don't be coy," Shane said, hoping Luke "Paco" Martinez would be in a good frame of mind. "I need help and I need it rather quickly. How soon can you be in Texas?"

Another grunt then a sigh. "Tell me some Scripture."

Shane smiled in spite of the fire pit in his belly and recited the last verse of Job, Chapter 21, hoping Paco would pick up the code for his location at the remote ranch. "The counsel of the wicked is far from me."

"How soon do you need me, brother?"

"Yesterday," Shane said, breathing a sigh of relief. "I have a man here who can't seem to remember who sent him to terrorize our client. Think you could help him recall?"

"I'm on my way."

And that was all the confirmation he needed from the Warrior. If anyone could make Timmy give up the goods, it would be Paco Martinez. The man had ice water running through his veins and he wasn't the sociable, small-talk type. Paco liked to get down to business right away.

"You're in for a real treat," Shane told Timmy. "I picked the best of the best to come and sit with you—a war hero who misses the fight, so to speak. But until my friend arrives, I'll have my staff bring you some breakfast. And they'll be watching you until your keeper gets here."

After a knock at the door, he got up, grabbed his gun and turned to stare down at Williams. He let Nina and Ricardo in, watching as Ricardo set a plate of food down then securely tied Timmy's hands. "Nina will feed you. Don't try anything stupid." He nodded to Ricardo. The boy leveled his infamous shotgun on the prisoner. "Oh, and Timmy, they both know how to use every weapon we have in this place. Don't tease them now, you understand?"

He left with the sound of Timmy's whining demands echoing inside his head. Shane didn't have time to worry about Timmy's comfort, however.

He had to get to Katherine before she bolted and went out to fix this mess on her own.

The phone had rung again. "Trudy? Trudy, is that you?"

Someone had been there, listening. But they didn't say a word. Then the connection had ended once again.

Kit looked down the long hallway, the dark shards of a cloudy night streaming through the many windows to remind her she didn't have much time. She had to get out of here before Shane tried to stop her.

Her overnight bag in her hand, she made her way down the stairs, her sneakers barely brushing against the polished wood of the steps. Glancing around the back hallway, she knew Silvia was still asleep. And Nina and Ricardo were probably in the kitchen having a heart to heart about the boy's bold and courageous acts last night.

Wishing she could thank Ricardo again for helping them capture Timothy Williams, Kit kept her eyes straight ahead. She only had to make it to the back door leading to the garage and her mother's car.

No one was in the back hallway, so she carefully opened the door and looked out into the murky shadows. The clouds parted to show an angry crescent moon lifting across the foothills, hovering over the trees like a sinister smile.

Such a beautiful night in spite of the fitful clouds. Nothing about it indicated that she'd had to chase a crazy man all over the big, sloping pasture or that they could have all been killed if that man's misguided bullets had hit any of them.

Thankful that Shane's office was secluded toward the back of the house, she opened the smaller back garage door then the big one that enclosed the garage from the other side, using the code she'd learned from watching Shane and Nina.

Then she was inside, the bright yellow car waiting like a beacon to help her make her escape. Taking a long, calming breath, she inhaled in relief and clicked on the remote key pad to unlock the little car.

And felt that now-familiar hand reaching out to touch hers. Kit turned to find Shane staring down at her, his eyes as rich and full of clouds as the conflicted late night sky.

"Going somewhere, Katherine?"

ELEVEN

Shane could see the stubborn all over her face.

"I'm going home," she said, pulling her hand away. "I have to help Trudy."

"We're going to help Trudy," he said, blocking her way into the car. "But not like this. You can't walk into their trap, Katherine. They know you're here now."

"Oh, and what am I supposed to do then? Just sit around here waiting for them to come after me again? If this has something to do with my trip to Mexico maybe I can talk to them and make sense of this."

"These are not sensible people, Katherine. I can still protect you here."

"I wasn't protected last night. That man walked right up to the kitchen window."

Shane couldn't find a retort for that. She was right. In spite of all his security measures, someone had breached the perimeters of his property. "I'm sorry," he said, hoping she'd be reasonable. "I plan to rectify that. I've called in reinforcements."

She shook her head, causing her shimmering hair to fall around her face. "You can bring an army here and it won't matter. I can't stay here, knowing they have my best friend, knowing they took her to get to me. Can't you understand that?" She waited but apparently didn't like his silence. "Oh, right. You actually suspect she might somehow be involved in all of this."

"She could be," he said, wondering how much he should tell her in order to keep her here. Her friend Trudy had married into old Texas money and since her husband's death she'd made some questionable investments, dealing with some unsavory people. He couldn't put his finger on it yet, but something didn't sit well with all of Trudy's after-hours soirees. And the fact that Trudy had been the one on the other end of that phone line. Shane didn't know what was nagging at him, some memory, something he'd processed that refused to come to the surface. But each time he thought of Trudy Pearson, his gut started burning.

Katherine fumed a response. "Do you have proof of anything? Do you know things about the woman *I've* known since grade school?"

"I told you, we're investigating every possible avenue."

"Right and that's supposed to make me feel better about them holding her and slapping her around? I don't think so. If you don't let me go right now, Shane, I'll find another way. If I have to bust Timothy loose to help me, I'll do it. You can't hold me here against my will."

Shane knew when he'd been bested. She'd gone from

ladylike charm to getting down and dirty. He opted to change the subject. "Do you still have the phone?"

She watched his face, probably looking for signs of weakness or treachery. "I do. They wanted me to have it, so now it's mine. And you're not going to take it from me."

"I wasn't planning on taking it from you," he said, grabbing her bag. "But I do need to analyze it and try to locate where it was purchased. I might be able to figure things out if I can trace the serial number."

"I don't have time for you to do that. And I need it in case they call me back."

Shane considered that. It would be nearly impossible to trace a disposable phone but he could at least try. But they'd probably send her another message soon. He'd want to listen in on that. First, he had to take care of the beautiful woman trying to get away from him. "Let's go then."

Her shock was priceless. "Go where?"

"You want to leave, then we leave. I promised your father I wouldn't let you out of my sight and I promised your mother I'd take care of you. That means if you leave then I go with you. Besides, they know you're here now. They might send their own reinforcements if you don't do as they ask."

He tried to look relaxed, as if they were about to go on a weekend trip. Then he glanced toward the skies. "I'd hoped to ride out to the road on horseback at dawn to see if I could track anyone else. Timmy said a man was supposed to pick him up at dawn out just off the main road. I have every reason to doubt him but I'd like to test that theory at least. If we could get to that person, we'd have a connection that might quickly lead us to Trudy."

Wariness settled in her green eyes, making them go dark. "Okay, I have to admit I wondered why they didn't just come here and try to take me. Why all the games?"

Shane debated whether to tell her everything. Maybe putting the hard facts out there would stop her.

"They obviously want you alive now, darling. Very much alive. They've located you and now they've verified that through the phone. They want to make you come to them so they won't blow their cover after the gala fiasco. But I can't let you go out there all on your own to face them. Once they get what they want from you, they'll kill you. And if you can't give them what they want because you don't have anything or you don't know anything, they will certainly kill you anyway. I have no doubt of that."

"Just like they'll kill Trudy if I don't help her."

"She's safe for now. She's their bargaining chip." He touched a hand to her cheek. "If you can give me a few hours, we could take some horses and ride out to watch the road. That way, I'd know you're safe and we could wait for the next call. And I assure you there will be a next call."

"Why wouldn't you set up a trace somehow?"

"A trace won't work on this type of cheap, pay-as-you-go phone. These people know what they're doing and they probably bought several phones at once. Next time they call you, they'll just switch to a different one, with a different return number. Then they'll throw them away as they go so we can't trace them."

"They've already called again," she said, guilt coloring her expression.

"Why didn't you tell me that right away? What did they say?"

She looked down, her shoulders shifting. "Nothing. I asked for Trudy and I heard someone there, but they wouldn't respond."

"Then you verified to them that you truly were the person Trudy spoke to the first time. That's what they needed to know for now. And I'm sure they have an elaborate system in place to respond to you without being detected. They'll kill Timmy, not help him get away. That's why I need to get up to the main road and meet whoever was coming for him. That's the next link in the chain. And that will better serve us than you rushing off without any forethought to find your friend."

She glanced at the car, longing and aggravation centered in her eyes. "What if it's too late? What if they'd already killed her now that they've located me?"

Shane put his hands on her shoulders. "I've called in people to help, luv. My fellow team member Paco Martinez is on his way here to take over with Timmy's care and feeding. We can only hold him for so long before we have to turn him over to the authorities. And I've alerted your father to the situation with your friend. He's putting men on it right now. Don't you think that makes more sense than trying to take off on your own? And don't you know me well enough to realize I would do anything in my power to help another human, especially a defenseless woman who might be in danger?"

She stared up at him, her eyes turning a forest green, all misty and lush. Then she reached up and wrapped her arms around his neck. "I have to learn to trust you."

Shane was so astonished at her words and so aware of her there in his arms, he had to search hard for his next breath. "And I have to remember to tell you everything right up front from now on." He pulled her close, his words touching on her sweet-smelling hair. "Especially if I get this kind of reaction."

Realizing she was still holding him, she stood back into a less intimate stance, proper decorum back in full force. "Ready?"

She'd managed to surprise him yet again. "Uh, I think. With you, luv, I'm pretty much ready for anything. But apparently, never quite prepared."

She gave him a stern look. "Now that I know someone cares about Trudy, I can take care of the rest. Let's go on that horseback ride out to the road."

"Are you sure?"

She looked doubtful for a second but she lifted that defiant chin and put on her best showtime face. "Yes." She dropped the phone into the pocket of her jeans.

"Right, then." He took her bag and put it on a nearby shelf. "I'll alert Nina and then we'll go get prepared to saddle up."

"And what about the man you left chained to a chair in your office?"

"Ricardo and Nina are entertaining our guest for now. I told you I called in help. I've asked a highly qualified team member to come here and take care of that little bit of trouble. And to handle any other surprise guests who might follow. So that leaves us to go about our business."

"And what will this highly qualified team member do?"

He guided her toward the path just past the garage leading to the stables. "You don't need to worry about that."

"Oh, I see. You think I can't handle it. What happened to being upfront with me about everything?"

"I'd rather not give you the details on that particular subject." Rapping his fingers against his jeans, he said, "Look, Paco has his own methods for getting information out of people. The man is an uncelebrated war hero and he's a bit rough around the edges. He can be scary to some."

"I don't scare easily."

"I can clearly see that."

"Can you? Can you really see me, Shane?"

She studied him, her cool green eyes assessing him with a clarity that left Shane feeling stripped of all the facades he so carefully used. For once in his life, he wanted to let go of the secrecy and the facades and take her into his arms and kiss her silly. But he didn't do that.

Not yet.

He did, however, adhere to the new "up-front" rule. "Oh, yes, my dear, I see you very clearly. And you take my breath away."

Her smile wasn't quite happy. "Always the debonair charmer. I just hope you didn't charm me into making the wrong decision about this."

"I'm telling the truth," he replied, his fear of how she made him feel topping any tactics Paco could bring. Or the fact that she'd figured him out so completely.

"I'll have to take your word on that," she said as she purposely strolled into the stable. "Let's go track a bad man."

Shane sent up a prayer of thanks then punched some numbers into his phone. "Mr. Barton, sir. I'm still with Katherine, but we had a breach of security. The Warrior is on his way. And I've convinced Katherine we need to remain at this location for now. I'll give you a full update later. Katherine is secure, but she's had word from Trudy. Once we finish clearing up a few matters, we'll relocate to another safe house, and I'll explain more thoroughly."

That caused Katherine to wrinkle her lovely brow and frown at him. And caused her father to launch into a tirade that wasn't nearly so lovely.

"Warwick, I thought I could trust you on this. How in the world? This is dangerous. Too dangerous. I don't like you taking her all over the infernal country. It's risky, especially with Trudy missing, too. Where is she?"

"All we know is that she's safe for now. Have you been able to find out anything on her, sir?"

"Nope, and I've got several men on it. It's as if the woman has disappeared off the face of the earth. You let me know the minute you hear from her again. I'll keep you posted if I hear from her."

Shane decided not to share any more information with Katherine's father. It would only worry her even more. "Yes, sir. And I'll keep Katherine safe until we can decide our next move." Gerald Barton didn't need the details, and Shane couldn't explain Trudy's strange behaviour.

"I'll give you one more chance, Warwick, and if that doesn't work, you'd better bring my daughter home. This hiding out in the hills is just too dangerous. Where are you, anyway?"

He held the phone away, letting Katherine's father shout himself out. "Yes, sir, I realize that. It's dangerous but your daughter wanted to leave by herself to go and find her friend. She's very worried. I've convinced her to let others handle that matter. I won't let any harm come to her but it's too risky to leave our location right now. And I'd rather not say where that is."

Gerald Barton let out a loud grunt. "Just like her mama, always taking matters into her own hands. I tell you, I didn't like it when my wife snuck y'all out of here and I don't like it now. Not one bit."

Shane listened, heard a long sigh then Gerald said, "So what's your plan, anyway?"

"I'll get back to you on that, sir." He glanced over at Katherine, spoke reassuring words into the phone again then ended the call, not quite sure about the plan at all. Or if he'd have a job or not whenever this was over. "Your father sends his best, luv."

Katherine sent him a slight nod then walked to a gorgeous mare named Peaches and began saddling her with expert precision.

Watching her, Shane called the house and explained the situation to Nina. "Paco Martinez is flying in from Arizona. His code name is the Warrior. He should be here by mid-morning to take custody of our visitor. He has full access to security measures, understand? You can trust Paco with your life so do whatever he tells you to do. And he'll keep young Ricardo under his wing, too." Then he told her he'd be out of range for a couple of hours and explained that Katherine would be with him.

Shane dropped the sleek phone into his pocket. "Well now that I've reassured everyone that you're safe and I have things under control, we have a couple of hours before we're off to see if we can find our pickup man. We'll take the long way around."

By the time they made it to the main road, taking the path that meandered through the stream to avoid leaving too many tracks, the sun was giving a valiant try of coming over the distant foothills. But the low dark clouds surrounding it didn't bode well.

"We might have missed him," Shane said, his gray stallion Hercules snorting in the bluish-pink dawn. "We'll leave the horses here, though, and walk the rest of the way."

"Why didn't you just drive us up here?" she asked, her tone low.

"In that shouting yellow car? I think not."

"You have other vehicles made for off-road. We're out in the open now."

He couldn't argue that point. "I was afraid you'd take off in a car or a Rhino or a four-wheeler for that matter. Or run yet another criminal down."

"I might have done all of that."

"This way, we have a getaway plan and we can hide in places a vehicle can't get into."

She nodded at that. "Makes sense in a cowboy kind of way."

He motioned to her to follow him into some thick bramble by the back entrance, a few miles from the main gate. "This is the way our Timmy entered. He left enough evidence to spook a bull." He pointed to some cut fence markings and footprints. "See that broken bramble. He must have come through right through over there."

She eyed the trampled leaves and torn branches. "I thought this place was solid and secure."

Shane glanced around, making sure they were alone. "I don't have heavy security on the backside of the property because this is rough country—overgrown with trees and bramble, full of snakes, the occasional bear, coyotes, and not many markers. Easy to get lost. Only a fool would venture through here."

"Well, that just about describes him."

Shane put a finger to his lips. "Let's go settle down by the fence." Then he stopped and tugged her close. "I only brought you with me to keep an eye on you. Don't do anything—just watch and wait."

She gave him a long, hard stare. "I'll try."

"I mean it, Katherine. If something should happen to me, you run as fast as your pretty legs can carry you back to Peaches and Hercules. And you get on that mare and ride for home. Hercules will know to follow—or lead if need be. Do you understand?"

"Got it. Ride for home."

Shane's stomach sizzled and singed. He popped an antacid tablet. "Did you pack that revolver?"

"Of course I did," she said. Then she pulled the gun out from the back of her sweater. "Just in case."

Shane was afraid to think about what she might do. "Don't use that gun, Katherine." Then he changed that to "Use it to protect yourself if you must."

"Don't worry about me," she said. "Let's just get this man."

They crept through the bramble, hiding behind shrubs and bushes until they were near the gap in the heavy wire fence. Shane patted a spot underneath an aged elm tree, making sure no unwelcome creatures waited for them. "Sit."

Katherine sat down beside him then looked up at the sky. "Shane, I think it's going to—"

Rain.

The first fat drops hit them, sending a chilling wetness down Shane's back. He scooted her closer to the trunk of the tree, hoping the thick branches would serve as protection. "Great. Just great."

Then the sky opened up into a real downpour. He put his arm around Katherine, pulling her close. "Sorry."

She looked up at him, her gaze locking with his just as a big clap of thunder rattled behind them. Shane saw the lightning crashing across the sky then heard another round of thunder, but that couldn't match the pounding inside his ears.

Katherine must have felt it, too, this roaring of awareness and attraction. She leaned close, a sigh escaping her parted lips. Shane held her, saw the acceptance in her eyes, took that same acceptance into his heart. There would be no turning back now. None at all. But for once, he didn't want to turn back.

And that's when he gave in and leaned over to kiss her.

But that was also when they heard a motor revving just around the curve in the road.

A big vehicle was headed toward them.

TWELVE

Shane pushed Kit down, the sound of thunder above them warring with the engine of the big truck moving slowly up the muddy dirt lane. His pulse had quickened for another reason. It was showtime.

"We have company, darling," he said, his heart still recovering from kissing her. "Stay down."

She looked up at him, her expression full of surprise, but he couldn't be sure if that surprise stemmed from the situation or the fact that he'd broken all protocol and fallen for her. They'd deal with that later.

The rain would give them a measure of cover, he thought as he crouched behind the big elm tree, lush shoots sprouting around him near its wrinkled trunk. And the tree would act as a cover of sorts. "Let's get a look."

"Be careful," Kit said behind him, her words as strong and sure as her kiss had been just a minute ago.

He carried that thought with him as he crept to the fence line and squinted into the storm. "One. A lone driver. That's good for us." Studying the surrounding woods, Shane prayed no one else had come along for the ride. "And from the description Timmy gave me, it looks like our man."

He had to stop that lone driver and keep him alive to give them information, so he pulled out the pistol he'd brought along for this purpose, covering it with the tail of his damp shirt.

"What are you going to do?" Kit asked, her hand on his back as she crouched beside him.

"I'm going to blow out both of the front tires of that truck then I'm going to grab the driver."

"Oh, all right. Good luck with that."

He glanced over his shoulder at her. "And you have a better plan?"

"Let me act as decoy. If he sees me here, he'll think he has what he came for."

"No. Absolutely not. I won't put you at risk."

"I won't be at risk. You said they want me alive. He wouldn't dare do anything to me."

The lady had a point. But so much could go wrong. "Not a good idea, luv."

"What if I just poke my head out and he spots me? I'll hide and then you can take over from there. I'll cover you—I have my own gun, remember?" She waited a delicate beat then added, "Shane, we're running out of time."

Shane didn't like this. But he figured she'd jump up and follow him out onto the road if he didn't involve her in the plan. Katherine Atkins liked to be involved in things. This much he knew.

The rain stopped as quickly as it had started, but the sky didn't look finished. The storm would move back in. He needed to end this now.

"All right," he said on a winded hiss as the truck came closer. "Just stand up and wave. Then duck down and don't move until you see me again."

"Yes, sir." She pushed at her hair, ever the glamour girl. "I'll only be a minute."

Shane's heart stopped beating for that tiny minute. He watched her, watched the truck, watched the driver, and motioned to her. "I'm going through the fence. Stay here."

Kit played it to the hilt, lifting up, the wind and rain pushing at her glistening wet curls. Then she waved both hands in the air in a motion that immediately got the driver's attention. The big truck slid to a grinding halt and the driver stepped out.

And right into Shane's gun aimed at the back of his head.

Kit sank down in the bushes, her gun trained on the driver as Shane pushed the man back toward the truck and began questioning him. "Who's with you?"

"No one." The well-dressed red-haired man held up his hands. "I got lost out here. Got off the main road and wound up here. What's this all about, Mister?"

"Don't lie to me," Shane said, nudging the man back against the big fender. "Show your weapons. And do it very carefully, one hiding place at a time."

"I told you, I got lost," the man repeated, rolling his eyes in frustration. "If I'm trespassing, I apologize." He looked over Shane's shoulder. "It's mighty lonesome out here."

"Stop the small talk." Shane put the gun to the man's heart. "I can always shoot you then frisk you, of course."

"All right. Okay." The man reluctantly did as Shane asked, revealing a pistol and a pocket knife. "I always carry a weapon. For personal protection."

"Throw your *personal protection* in the grass," Shane demanded.

The stranger did that, too, then glanced into the trees. "I thought I saw a woman in there, waving at me. Y'all need some help here?"

"As a matter of fact, we do," Shane replied, the gun still centered on the man's big chest. "We need you to take a message back to whoever sent you here. We have Timmy in custody and we will not let him go until *we* get some answers. If we don't get those answers, we'll turn him over to the local sheriff and let the great state of Texas do its own digging. But I'm guessing your boss wouldn't like that, now would he? *Or she?*"

The man's bushy bronzed-colored eyebrows lifted. "I don't know what you're talking about, Mister. I told you I got off the main road and couldn't find my way back. What's going on here? Who are you looking for?"

"Let me see your identification," Shane said, motioning to the man's coat pocket. "And be very careful about reaching for it."

The stranger let out a string of curses, then slowly pulled out a wallet and handed it to Shane.

"Walter Rogers, private detective. From Austin, Texas. Imagine that. You're a disgrace to your industry, Mr. Rogers. And you won't have a P.I. license after this."

Kit couldn't wait any longer. She hurried through the broken fence and rushed up behind Shane, her revolver pointed toward the surprised captive. "Where is Trudy Pearson?"

Shane moved an inch, shielding her from the man. "Go back and stay there," he said over his shoulder, his tone brooking no argument. "And be a dove and put the gun down."

But Katherine wasn't listening. She nosed closer. "No. I won't hide like a coward. This man knows something and he's going to tell us, right?"

Shane lowered his head in frustration. "I was working on that part, darling."

The man seemed a bit amused, which only made Kit even madder. Waving the gun, she asked, "Where is she?"

"She'll soon be out of the picture," the man said, grinning. "And you will be too, if you don't cooperate and come back to Austin with me."

Kit went for him, but Shane blocked her with a strong arm around her waist. "Patience, luv." He pushed the gun into the man's gut. "You've not only given us some very concrete information but you've upset her so I suggest you answer her. She knows how to use that revolver."

Then he whispered to Katherine, "We have our guns on him, now don't we? So no need to do anything rash."

She didn't care about that right now. She just wanted to tear this man's eyes out. "You won't get away."

"You do have me cornered," the man replied, laughing over at Shane. "Big gun aimed at my heart and big-shot woman to protect." Then he lifted one hand. "But *we* have even more big guns."

And then two more men stepped out of the trees on the other side of the road.

Kit gasped, but kept her weapon aimed steadily toward the man by the truck. She wouldn't go down without a good fight.

Shane leaned close to her, his eyes on the other men. "Careful. They do have big guns. And since you insisted on coming to the party, you'd better do exactly as I say."

Kit really should have done what Shane had told her to do. *Stayed hidden.* But she thought with mutinous relief, if she'd stayed behind, she'd have been forced to ride back to the ranch alone. While these thugs loaded Shane onto the truck.

After a few minutes of a tense standoff where the two thugs advanced toward Shane and her, Rogers had finally told Shane that if they didn't throw down their weapons, he'd signal the sharpshooters waiting on a nearby hill. To kill the woman first.

So reluctantly, Shane had dropped his gun and motioned for her to do the same. And now they were on the back of the truck, getting wet while the two newcomers held them captive.

At least this way, she was here with him. And that meant these creeps couldn't use yet another person she cared about as a bargaining chip to get to her.

Then, in spite of the rain coming down on them, in spite of the two big men holding guns on them, in spite of it all, she realized she did care about Shane. A lot. And he'd kissed her back there underneath that tree in a way that told her he might just feel the same.

"Shane?" she whispered now, her mouth hardly moving.

Shane shot a covert smile toward the two solemn

henchmen sitting on the truck with them. "Yes, my dear."

"I'm not sorry. I wouldn't have let them take you anyway. Not without me. I'd have come after you."

"That brings me a great deal of comfort, Kit," he replied, his own lips tightly drawn. "But the thing is, now I have to worry about keeping you alive."

"We can worry about each other," she said back.

She wanted to add more, much more to her declaration but one of the men grunted and pointed his nasty looking semiautomatic rifle toward them. "No talking."

Shane gave the man a serene smile. "So sorry. Did we bother you with our chatter?"

"Hey, I said no talking and I mean it. I'll put a gag on *her* if you say another word. And I'll take pleasure in doing it."

The look he sent Katherine made her shiver even while she stared him down. The look Shane shot her gave her courage, however.

Shane nodded to the man, his expression bordering on brutal even while he smiled.

"Sir, can I ask you something?" Katherine said in her best feminine voice, her eyes wide with an exaggerated concern.

The big man pushed at his wet, balding head, his fat fingers dragging through a few strands of oily hair. "What?"

"Where are we going?"

"Nice try, lady."

"It's a fair question, don't you think?"

At her sweet question, Shane poked her then gave her a warning glare.

"Your friend thinks you need to pipe down, honey,"

the other man said. "You'll find out where we're going soon enough."

And she did. They were taking the road back to the ranch house. She glanced over at Shane, her brow lifting in a question mark.

He sent her yet another warning look then glanced at their guards. He quickly mouthed "Wait."

She heard the message, looked up to make sure the Brothers Grimm hadn't seen it then told herself to relax and let Shane handle this. Only she couldn't relax. So she started looking for ways to end this without getting herself or Shane shot, hoping Shane was doing the same on his side of the big, roaring truck.

He was.

The way Shane figured it, they would take them back to the house, kill him and probably everyone else, including their own mule Timmy, then take Katherine to the person who was waiting for all of this to happen.

And right now, Shane couldn't be sure if that person was a man or a woman.

His fired-up gut told him their nemesis could very well be a woman. Maybe even Kit's own best friend, Trudy Pearson.

What a dilemma. How could he convince Katherine that she might be in danger from a woman she'd trusted for so long? He'd have to worry about that little problem later. Right now, Shane had to figure out how to knock both these men off the truck and overtake the driver without getting Katherine killed in the process.

He had several things in his favor. One, the truck was wet and slick from the continuing rain. Traction would be at a minimum. Two, these two didn't look as sharp as they pretended to be. They looked downright confused and dazed, as if they hadn't signed up to hurt a woman. Three, they had left the horses grazing freely but Hercules would sense something was wrong and hopefully hightail it for home with the loyal Peaches following him. That would alert Nina and Paco that something was up. And four, if he could make Katherine understand his intentions, she just might save herself by helping him out a bit.

So he sat silent, calculating the distance to the house, calculating the distance and energy it would take for him to butt the bigger of the two off the side of the truck and grab the other one's gun at the same time and turn it on both the fallen men and the driver. He'd have to work fast and make sure he didn't get shot. If that happened, they'd finish him off and take Katherine away immediately.

Then he remembered the deep rut in the road about two miles from the main gate. Watching the bored men sitting on each side of the wide truck bed, Shane touched a finger to Katherine's arm but stared straight ahead. She took the hint and did the same, motioning back to him. He held her hand in his, tapped three times and prayed she'd get the message that on the count of three he aimed to get this fight started. When she glanced up he shifted his head toward the man on his side then looked over toward the muddy ditch.

She seemed to understand. She circled a finger in his palm, spelling out a number and letters that seemed to say "On 3? Got it."

The touch of her fingers tickling his skin, Shane wrote back "Y-e-s."

Then he waited, watching for the familiar turns on

the muddy dirt road. Once he was sure they were approaching the dip that would be a full-blown mudhole by now with all the rain, he sent Katherine a quick glance, followed by a curt nod.

He stared straight ahead, waiting for the moment he could make his move. When he saw the road changing and recognized the curve, he winked at Katherine and tapped her palm again.

She took a long breath and gave him a covert lifting of her eyebrows, her hand squeezing his.

Shane looked up at the man nearest him, leaned up to stare past the man and shouted, "Did you see that?"

The man turned at about the same time the truck dipped to go through the mudhole and that's when Shane head-butted him in his midsection, making sure to grab the man's rifle before the poor soul tumbled over the truck's side. Before he could turn toward the now-surprised other guard, however, Katherine managed to use the shift in the truck to rise up enough to give the man a big shove, her deep grunt indicating how much energy she used to do so.

He went over the side, losing his gun as he joined his shocked buddy in the mud. Katherine held on to the side of the truck, her breath heaving as they watched the confused man give a valiant try to reaching for his soaked weapon. Shane shot him and ended that quest. Then even as the driver brought the truck to a halt in the middle of the big mudhole, Shane pumped a bullet into the first man who'd fallen into the mud.

"Stay down," he shouted at Katherine as he whirled toward the driver who was trying to emerge from the truck.

But Shane didn't get a chance to take down the

driver. Another shot rang out from the nearby woods and the driver fell out the door face first into the mud.

It was over. The silence of the countryside screamed relief even as the echoes of the last gunshot vibrated through the trees. But where were the other sharpshooters the men had mentioned? And how many of them were there?

"Katherine?"

"I'm all right," she said, her hand reaching for his.

"Stay there," he said, lifting her hand to kiss her fingers then pushing her back down.

Shane realized the rain had ended. And he realized they were alive, but they were not alone. He heard a motor revving up.

"More?" Katherine asked from her spot in the bottom of the wet truck. "They said they had others posted on the hills, right?"

"I hope not," Shane said, squinting toward the overbearing noise. "I don't have enough ammunition to hold them off." Lifting her up, he said, "Let's get in the truck. We'll try to outrun them somehow."

He quickly lifted Kit over the side of the truck then pushed her toward the open door of the cab.

"Shane?" She pointed up the lane.

A man on a massive, shiny black motorcycle flew down the road toward them, coming from the direction of the ranch. A man on Shane's very own massive, shiny black motorcycle.

And he had a big gun, too.

THIRTEEN

Shane kept Kit there behind the truck door. "Hold on."

"But he's coming right at us," she shouted over the roar of the growling motorcycle.

"Yes, and just in time, too," Shane said, a grin splitting his face.

Thinking he'd somehow lost touch with reality, Katherine stared at Shane then looked at the approaching monster bike. "Shane, what's going on?"

Shane didn't answer. Instead, he dragged her around the truck and waited for the man to pull the sleek machine up next to them, the big tires spewing out a whirl of mud and wet rocks.

Shocked, Katherine instinctively moved closer to Shane while the man on the motorcycle lifted off, his weapon still intact, looked around at the carnage, then nodded to Shane. "Guess you didn't need my help out here after all, Knight."

Shane actually chuckled out loud. "We managed to take care of this mess," he said. "But why aren't you at the house interrogating our friend?"

"Been there, took care of that," the man said, his black eyes moving over Katherine with a keen appraisal. "Oh, by the way, I borrowed your bike. Is this the client?"

Shane pulled Katherine to his side. "Yes. Katherine Barton Atkins, I'd like you to meet Luke 'Paco' Martinez, better known as the Warrior."

Katherine looked from Shane to the big man standing in front of her. Everything about the Warrior shouted darkness. His hair was the color of midnight dark chocolate. His eyes weren't very far behind, almost onyx. Even his skin was bronzed to a rich deep tan that looked as chiseled as a rock face and just about as hard and impenetrable. He held the heavy, nasty-looking rifle with an arm that rippled with firm muscles, his stance as fierce and determined as any ancient warrior she'd ever seen in books and on the big screen.

"Hello, Mr. Martinez," she said, her voice just above a squeak, or so it seemed to her ringing ears. "Thanks for coming."

"My job," the man replied, walking around the truck to check on the two unconscious men in the mud. "One's dead and one's still breathing," he reported back in a growling voice. Then he went to the ditch and checked the unconscious driver. "He's a goner, too."

"Had to be done," Shane replied. He turned to Katherine. "Paco is a trained sniper."

Paco watched her face as if to say "Does that scare you, lady?"

A chill went down Katherine's back. She could very

well see that with her own eyes. "Again, thank you," she said, thinking how strange to be thanking someone for killing another human being. Her answer apparently worked. The man stopped glaring at her.

Paco looked from her back to Shane. "Hey, I took care of two other shooters, in case you were wondering," he said, his tone all business. "Found them on my way in, hovering up on that north ridge." He pointed off toward the curve leading to the main gate. "Probably planned to take you out then once they had the woman, move on into the house and finish off everyone there. But they're all trussed up and waiting for the authorities. Had to talk myself out of shooting 'em."

Katherine gulped a breath, hearing him describe in such a monotone, matter-of-fact way how things might have ended up here. She said a quick prayer of thanks, her stomach roiling in sick waves, the heaviness of death all around her.

"I owe you yet again, my friend," Shane said, shaking Paco's big hand. "And our young Timmy?"

"Timmy can get pretty chatty when he sets his mind to it," Paco replied, his face as blank as a slab of marble. "I got some stuff we might be able to use. He's still kinda tied up, waiting for you."

"Let's get this cleaned up," Shane said, turning grim and serious. "We'll discuss this at the house."

Paco nodded, the movement curt and without an inch of waste. "Take her on back. I'll deal with this."

Shane looked at Katherine. "Good idea. She's too exposed out here in the open."

Paco didn't respond. He simply went over to the still-alive man and frisked him with the agility of a magician.

Then he did the same with the two dead men. "Go," he finally said to Shane, a sleek phone in one hand.

Shane urged Katherine ahead of him. "We'll have to walk. The truck is evidence." He turned to face his friend again. "How'd you know to come, Paco?"

Paco stood up, grunted. "Hercules. He came galloping up to the house and whinnied. Had a cute little mare with him. It was annoying. Figured that stallion wouldn't shut up until I did something." He pointed toward the big bike. "Found this out in the stables and tracked y'all to the fence line. Saw a lot of muddy tracks all along the road, did some snooping around. That's when I spotted the snipers up on the ridge."

Shane nodded. "So you arrived undetected, interrogated Timmy, then tracked the sharpshooters first and came here and found us."

"Something like that." Paco sent Katherine a hard look then turned away. "I came in through the river."

"He doesn't discuss his methods," Shane whispered as he helped Katherine along the road.

"I don't want to know anyway," she said, all sorts of horrible images running through her head. But she couldn't help but turn and watch as Paco Martinez made fast work of securing the bodies. "What…what will become of the ones who survived?"

Shane glanced around. "Paco will call the authorities, explain the situation, and get the injured man medical attention right away. The other two will have some explaining to do."

"And the dead?"

"Will be identified, sent home and hopefully given a proper burial."

"Just like that. Two men dead and it's all so cut-and-dried?"

He watched her face, probably waiting for some sort of feminine hysteria to kick in. But she didn't give him any theatrics. She was too numb and tired to care if all of the CHAIM agents were trained to read body language.

"It's never cut-and-dried, Kit. Those men came here to kill my entire staff and me, and probably young Timmy, too. They wanted to take you. And they nearly succeeded. I should never have taken you out there with me."

"But if you hadn't, you might be dead right now and they would have found everyone inside the house anyway."

He didn't respond to that. He kept on walking, his gaze darting here and there. While Katherine tried to imagine what she would have done if they had killed him.

"They'll go over this truck for prints, anything that might help us."

"Thank you," she finally said, aware that he was trying to maintain his professionalism to block the real issues here. "You've saved me yet again." She gave him a questioning stare. "You'll be taking me back to Austin now, right? So we can find Trudy?"

Shane slowly guided her through the ruts and mud. "I can't take you back there yet. It's too dangerous. And it might be too late."

The implication of his words hit her full force. "You mean, too late for Trudy. They did say if I didn't come out of hiding, they'd kill her."

"Yes, they did say that. But we can't base anything

on such threats. And you are my first concern. They're waiting to hear from their man and…he won't ever talk again."

"So you're just going to keep me here and let them kill Trudy?"

He looked straight ahead. "As I said, you are my first priority."

Kit was so mad she seriously thought about making a run for the highway. But then she wouldn't be able to strangle Shane Warwick. Yes, he'd saved her life, but he'd also manipulated her into believing he would help Trudy.

"Shane?"

"Remember, I have people looking for your friend already. No need for you to get involved in that right now."

She did remember that, and she remembered hugging him tight and telling him she'd have to learn to trust him. But still, she couldn't help but be furious that he refused to take her home.

"You tricked me. You said you needed to talk to that driver to find out more information. And now he's dead."

"No, I did not trick you. I did what I had to do to keep you safe."

"But we didn't find out anything more than we already knew. I want to go to Austin."

He sent her an indulgent look, which only infuriated her further. "They don't have her in Austin."

"Oh, so you know where they're holding her even though you never got that information out of any of those men back there?"

"No, but I can lay odds it's not in Austin. Too obvious."

Well, she hadn't considered that but because she was still angry with him and everyone else involved in this, she wanted to fight a bit more. "Shouldn't we start there and see?"

"First things first," he said, his tone so patently patient, she wanted to scream. "We get all of this cleared up with the local authorities, we get you to a new location, then we try to find out about that little black phone. Meantime, Paco has worked on our little Timmy and he'll give me a full report. And we still have the authorities in Austin holding the shooter in custody. He won't be going anywhere for a while since he tried to shoot up a room full of people and we have hundreds of witnesses. The people who sent him have to stay well hidden for now. That's why they sent Timmy here.

"Timmy, bless him, is too stupid to do more than whine out a few hints however. They probably made sure he was completely confused and unreliable in the memory department and they put a huge fear in his heart, so he might not have given Paco much to work with. We'll have to turn him over to the local authorities and explain he was trespassing and that he threatened us with a weapon. That should hold him in a secure spot for a long time. So that leaves your friend Trudy."

"How will we find her?"

"I'm working on that." He hurried along, constantly checking the trees and pastures. "Kit, please understand me. I had no choice but to kill those men. If they'd accomplished what they came to do, you'd be headed to a fate I can't even begin to describe. It was the only way. They obviously put some sort of GPS tracker on that phone they had Timmy hand deliver so we don't have much time. We have to find out how they found us in the first place then we have to move you. Do you trust me to do that?"

"I'm trying," she said, some of her anger dissipating in view of his fierce protectiveness and that sure fate he'd saved her from. "I'm worried about Trudy. She shouldn't have to pay for my problems."

"We'll find her," he said, his hand touching hers for a brief second.

Kit watched his face, wondering how the man never managed to break a sweat. His dark hair was sleek and crisp, as fresh as dark coffee in spite of being damp. His eyes, so crystalline and challenging, held no hint of all the turmoil surrounding them. And even in a dirty button-down casual shirt, jeans and expensive cowboy boots now caked in mud, he still exuded the markings of a man born to wear a tuxedo.

While she on the other hand felt aged and frazzled, tired and ragged, in her own filthy short-sleeved sweater and damp old blue jeans, her hair falling out of the loose clip she'd tried to secure it with earlier. Kit supposed it didn't matter very much what one wore on the run, but…she couldn't help remembering the feeling of being all dressed up and in Shane's arms, before all the terror began.

If she survived this, would she ever get that chance again? Did she want that? To be in his arms, dancing?

And what did it matter now? She was supposed to be mad at the man, not daydreaming about dancing with him. But she realized she was misdirecting this anger toward the one person who was on her side— Shane Warwick. She'd just witnessed the kind of violence that made her sick to her stomach. She should be praying for Trudy's safe return and praying for those poor men back there, dead or alive. So she did say her prayers and she included *this* infuriating man in those prayers. How could she be mad at him for doing the best he could to protect her?

Dear Lord, help me to remember all the good in this man. Such as his kiss and his honor.

"What are you thinking over there?" he asked, as if he knew her thoughts.

She didn't dare tell him the whole truth. "Nothing. Prayers for everyone involved in this and just remembering my life before. It seems like a dream now."

"Why don't you tell me about it?" he asked, smiling over at her as they approached the open gate to the main house. Seeing her distress, he said, "Paco left the gate open for us. Now, back to your life before?"

"I've told you a lot about my past already. Are you hoping maybe I'll give you some more hints?"

"Well, there is that to consider, luv. But I'd really like to hear about your life, because, work aside, I'd like to know more about you."

She stretched, gazing out at the dark morning sky. "I might bore you, although my life has been anything but normal lately."

"You, my love, could never bore me."

The way he said that made her body turn all soft, made her heart flutter like a trapped bird. She knew the endearment was second nature to such a charmer, that he probably hadn't even realized he'd said it. And yet, his words lingered over her like a soft shield, making her feel safe and secure. Why had she been so angry earlier? She had no reason to blame all of this on Shane. Maybe her anger was misplaced to protect her battered heart.

She glanced over at him, her whole being softening to him yet again. He made her feel as if they could get through anything together. He gave her hope and showed her how to trust again. And she knew in her heart she was finally ready to talk to him about her life up until now. Even the parts she'd never talked about to anyone.

He held her back when they reached the house. After searching the yard and looking around, he said, "I want to hear everything about you, Kit, and not because I'm fishing for information. I want to know about your life because I like hearing about *you*. You're an amazing woman."

She glanced around, her gaze taking in the beautiful old house and the surrounding land. The rain dripped in a slow cadence off the tiled roof, making her wish they could curl up together on the couch and really talk. "But you have things to take care of right now."

"Yes, I do," he said, his hand reaching up to touch her disheveled hair. "Let me get to the task at hand while you freshen up and get some rest." Then he leaned close, a soft smile covering his face. "I'll make a deal with you. I'll tell you everything I can find out about Trudy and these people who are after you and you can tell me everything about you and your life."

Kit basked in the radiance of his beautiful eyes, letting the warmth of his nearness hold her for one brief blissful moment. She wanted to kiss him again. "Shane—"

"Not now, luv." He touched a finger to her nose. "Not now. Too much between us." His finger moved with a featherlike caress across her cheekbone. "Later, my dear Kit. Later, we will get to know each other on a proper date. I promise. Just a brief interlude before we go back into the fray. Or if not, then definitely after."

Kit would hold him to that promise. If they could even hope to have a proper date now or after this was over. "I'll be there," she said in a whisper.

He smiled, kissed her cheek and said, "And maybe you can wear that lovely dress you had on the other night."

"No," she said. "I don't want to wear that dress ever again. But I will dress up."

"I don't care what you wear, just so I can know you're safe once and for all."

And with that, he gave her a peck on the cheek. "Now inside with you. I'll go in with you and check to make sure everyone is safe and accounted for then I'll have to do a walkabout around the property."

His cell rang. Still watching her, he touched the screen to answer. "Warwick." Listening, he kept his eyes on her.

Kit turned toward the house, her mind humming with all sorts of contradictory thoughts about the man who both frightened and endeared her. But she had to wonder where this relationship would go once the threat of evil was behind them.

Before she could form another thought, Shane grabbed her and put a finger to his lips, pulling her back toward the garage, his whisper near her ear. "We've got more trouble. The Warrior didn't make the kill shot on the driver. Someone else did. He found casings that don't match any of our weapons. And he thinks whoever did it might be in the house waiting for us."

FOURTEEN

Kit inhaled a haggard breath. "No. No, Shane. What about Nina and—"

He silenced her with a shake of his head. "We have to get in there and find out."

Kit tried to block the horrible images running through her head. If something had happened to Shane's family here—the people he loved—she'd never forgive herself. "Let's go."

"Don't make a sound, no matter what you see or hear," he told her, his hand holding tightly to her while he shielded her body with his. He had his gun back, but she'd left hers behind after those men had taken them.

Slowly, with hardly a sound, Shane clicked open the back door leading into the kitchen. Pushing Kit behind him, he whirled with his gun drawn, his gaze moving with computer-like efficiency across the room. "Clear," he said, motioning for her to stay behind him.

Kit looked around, shock expelling in every rapid breath. "They've ransacked your house."

"Yes, I can see that," Shane whispered as they skirted around broken dishes and open cabinet doors.

Kit followed him through the first level of the house as they entered room after room. And in each room, drawers had been opened, contents spilled out, books had been thrown off shelves and pictures ripped from the walls. They finally made it to the back of the house where Shane's office door stood open. "Stay back," he said, pushing her to the side as he pivoted into the room.

Kit didn't know whether to look or not. A heavy dread held her down, clutching her in a grip of sheer terror. And when Shane emerged from the room, his expression grim and dark, she knew that dread was right on target. "What?" she asked, her hand grabbing his arm.

"Timmy is dead," he whispered, shaking his head. "One shot through the forehead. And the office is a mess."

Kit gasped and put a hand to her mouth. "Oh, no. Oh, no." Then she touched his shirt. "Where is everyone else?"

"I don't know," Shane whispered, a hand on her arm. "But they know the rules. They should have managed to hide."

"How can we find them?"

He didn't answer. Pulling his phone out, he touched the screen and put the phone to his ear, waiting. Then he breathed a sigh of relief. "Nina, where are you?"

Kit's heart pulsed into overdrive. Nina was safe and hopefully that meant that Ricardo and Silvia were, too.

"Stay put," Shane replied. "I'm going to make sure the house is secure."

At her questioning look, he said, "Ricardo was guarding Timmy when he heard the intruder. He decided to protect his family—smart move. They managed to get out of the house and hide out in the barn. We have a safe room out there under the floor for tornadoes and other dangers. We've rarely had to use it, but thank goodness Nina thought about it today."

A safe room. Kit shuddered again, chills warring with heat throughout her body. She imagined that's where she'd be stuffed if Shane thought it would protect her. She followed him up the stairs, her thoughts on the dead man downstairs. It was all too much, just too much. She didn't think she could make it up the stairs. Every ounce of energy she had left seemed to drain right out of her system.

Shane turned, sensing her hesitation. "Kit?"

"I'm dizzy," she said, grabbing the railing. "Just go. I'll wait here."

"No." He pulled her close, his gaze locking with hers, his eyes soft and gentle. "Don't give up on me now. You're safe. You're alive."

She held her head down, her hands gripping the railing. "But for how long? And how many more have to die in order for you to save me?"

"Kit, look at me."

She lifted her head and saw the concern in his eyes. This was different from the first night she'd met him. Today, his concern was soaked in some other emotion that matched what she was feeling in her heart. "I'll be okay. It's just so horrible. And senseless. It makes me so mad I can't function!"

He held a hand to her chin. "I'm going to get you out of this, I promise."

"But so many people are dead." Her eyes burned with the hysteria she'd held at bay for days now. "Dead, Shane, because of me, because of something they think I have, or some kind of information they want me to give them. And I don't know what they want. I don't know anything and I don't have anything."

"C'mon," he said, tugging her close. "Just hang on until I can make sure we're alone."

She managed a deep, calming breath, his strength, his warmth, helping her to get her bearings again. Clutching her pearls like a lifeline, she said, "I'm all right." But she wondered if she'd ever be all right again. What did these people want from her?

Dear God, please help us. Please help Shane find out the truth.

They checked every room in the house and found no one. The culprit had accomplished his main objective and now he was long gone. The intruder hadn't found anything but he'd done his best to destroy the whole house.

Shane called Paco to give him an update. "I think one of them got away."

Kit had to wonder when the next one would show up.

"You were right," she said after Shane called Nina to tell her it was safe. "They killed Timmy just as you said they would."

Shane nodded, his expression grim. "Yes, not only did they kill him but they took out their own man there on the road. He'd compromised them with that little run-in with us."

"But they had us. They could have taken me."

"Instead, they tried to bring us back to the house," Shane replied, his confusion measured against the calm in his eyes. "Someone instructed that sniper to finish off the last man standing, which means Paco missed a man when he subdued the two on the ridge. Why didn't the last man try to take out Paco or us when he killed his own man?"

"Do you think he panicked?"

"Possibly," he replied as they made it back to the kitchen. "Or maybe his superiors thought we had evidence here at the house. That would mean one of them came here after Paco left, killed Timmy and searched the office." He ran a hand through his hair. "The plan was for Timmy to meet the driver at the designated location and when he didn't show, they knew things had gone bad. So they took out Timmy and the driver after we'd already shot the other two. That eliminates any witnesses."

"Except us."

"Someone set out to kill you but now they want you very much alive, luv."

Kit shuddered again, her eyes going wide. "But they let you live, too, Shane."

"Yes, they did." He gave her a level look. "Which means they need both of us alive now. Just until they have what they want. Based on what they did to this place, they must think you've told me something very incriminating." Then he tugged her close, his expression hard. "But you haven't now, have you?"

* * *

Kit sat by the window in the big den, her mind reeling with Shane's earlier question. Did he actually think she was keeping information from him?

After helping Nina and Ricardo straighten what they could of the messy house, she'd been waiting here with Silvia for two hours and now it was growing dark outside. In spite of Silvia's stoic comments here and there and the bright security lights surrounding the house, each shifting shadow made her shiver. She'd been jittery all day long. No, she'd been jittery since that night at the gala. And she had to wonder what Shane and Paco were discussing behind the closed door of his office.

Closing her eyes to the memory of the coroner coming to remove Timmy's body, she wondered what Shane had told the big, burly Texas Ranger who'd shown up to get a statement from all of them. While she understood CHAIM had operatives in all sorts of law enforcement quarters, she also knew those operatives were trained to stay inside the law and to always call in the proper authorities for assistance on any mission. Still, it was never wise to mess with a Ranger. But whatever they'd discussed in Shane's office, the man had tipped his hat and left without getting a statement from her. Did elite private security spies trump everything as a means to an end? Or had her name and status allowed her a reprieve from any further interrogations?

And when would Shane ever come out of that office and talk to her?

Earlier, after they'd made sure Nina and the others were safe, Shane escorted her to her door. After checking the room and clearing up some of the spilled contents of the dressers and closet, he'd told her to rest.

"But—"

"We'll discuss everything later."

His brusque manner of dismissing her had left Kit confused and angry. Had he suspected her all along of harboring some sort of information that could solve this?

As if I wouldn't tell him that right away, if I had anything to tell.

She got up and paced around the room, eyeing the many books she'd helped return to the long shelf across one wall. When her gaze hit on an old Bible, Kit pulled it off the shelf and sank into a leather chair. Leafing through the pages, she hoped to gain some comfort from the Scriptures.

"Read it out loud, *querida,*" Silvia said.

"But select capable men from all the people—men who fear God, trustworthy men who hate dishonest gain—and appoint them as officials over thousands, hundreds, fifties and tens." The verse from Exodus seemed to leap off the page at Kit.

Silvia nodded her approval. "Shane is such a man."

Shane was such a man. He was trustworthy and he hated dishonest gain, but he was also a trained operative who went after criminals with a vigilante force. Did that make all the death surrounding her tonight right? Was all of this justified in order to save her from some sort of evil?

And Jacob. He'd been trustworthy once. But something had happened to her husband. Had Jacob done something for dishonest gain? Had he used her trips to Mexico to hide something else? Had she blocked something out along with the pain of his death? And the pain of his rejection?

Tears pricking her eyes, Kit went back to reading the Bible, hoping God's word would trigger some sort of distant memory that could unlock the puzzle she'd somehow become involved in. She stopped in Proverbs this time, chapter 16, verse 11—"The Lord demands accurate scales and balances; he sets the standards for fairness."

Balances. Fairness.

Silvia stopped her knitting. "Good over evil, always."

Kit's heart pounded a heavy beat. Memories of Jacob behind the closed door of his office, just as Shane was now, came into her mind with kaleidoscope clarity. His voice had risen in anger as he told the person on the other end of the line that the balance wasn't adding up.

Balance of what?

Jacob had never discussed his work with her, other than in general terms. She learned more at dinner parties about his commitment to Texas and his many holdings than she did during dinner when it was just the two of them.

Dropping the Bible on the table by her chair, Kit put a hand to her pearls. Maybe she *had* been hiding the truth from Shane…and from herself. She and Jacob had drifted apart over the years but she'd refused to face that. She'd wanted children while he kept coming up with excuses to wait. She'd wanted a more simple life while he thrived on the spotlight. Jacob demanded power, status and wealth while Kit tried so very hard not to make any demands on her husband. She'd buried herself in the foundation, hoping to help other children since she didn't have any of her own.

And she'd wanted her husband to come home on time and be with her when she knew in her heart he'd been spending time with another woman. Yet she'd never been able to prove her suspicions. Jacob had been good at hiding his indiscretions.

That was why he'd given her these pearls and taken her out to dinner. He'd tried to pacify her, to assure her she was the only woman in his life and that maybe it was time to start that family they talked about. And she'd believed him because she thought that was the only way she could keep him. Talk about standing by her man. She'd tried so hard.

Had he been lying to her even then?

"Kit?"

She turned, startled by her thoughts and by the man standing in the doorway staring at her with fathomless blue eyes. "Yes?"

Abuela Silvia gathered her things and silently left the room. Her sitter had been dismissed, Kit thought.

Shane came into the room and sat down across from her. "Are you all right?"

"Not really," she said, her confusion and pain making her words sharp. "I've been waiting here all evening." Sickening, how familiar that statement sounded. She'd certainly said that enough to her husband.

Shane, however, was not her husband. Not even close. "I'm sorry. I thought you'd still be resting."

"I did rest. And then I helped put this house back to order and I had dinner with Nina and Silvia. We need to talk, Shane."

"I know that," he said, rubbing his hand down his neck. "Paco thinks someone close to you managed to find out where you were located—some sort of tracking device maybe. We can't figure how or where they planted it. I checked your mother's car and it's clean.

This place isn't even on the map and I was careful that we weren't being followed the other night."

"What else did he find out from Timmy?"

A dark wariness colored his gaze. "Mexico, again, luv. Timmy remembered hearing the man speaking on the phone about some sort of demands from someone in Mexico."

"I don't know what that could mean," she replied, hoping he'd believe her. "I only went down there on humanitarian trips, Shane. That's the truth."

"But your husband went with you on occasion."

"Yes, yes, he did. I can't speak for him."

"We'll start at the beginning again. Maybe we can find a clue if we both think back."

Kit saw the fatigue pulling at his face. "Where's Mr. Martinez now?"

"Checking the premises. The man never sleeps. And when he does, it's usually out under the stars."

Glad to have another subject to discuss for a brief minute, she said, "He's…interesting."

"That's a good word for it, yes." Shane put his hands down on his knees, his eyes holding hers. "Paco has Native American blood running through his veins. His great-grandfather was Apache. He comes from a family of soldiers and he can track anything that moves. He fights down and dirty, but he's terrified of any sort of intimate relationship with a woman. That's why he's so good at his job. He stays focused."

Kit felt the sting of that implication. "And you're not able to focus? Because you seem to thrive on relationships with women?"

He gave her a hard stare that moved through a shadow of emotions—empathy, need, longing, understanding and finally, regret. "I've had a lot of bad relationships with women, and yes, it does tend to become a distraction." He lowered his gaze. "Sometimes that kind of distraction can turn out tragically."

"Who was she?" Katherine asked, determined to learn more about him, too.

He pushed into the chair. "It was early on in my career. A spoiled college student. Her father was a diplomat. Two of us were assigned to escort her on a foreign tour. But I got distracted by her charms and she betrayed my trust. A tragic lesson well learned."

"I'm sorry," Katherine said. It was obvious that incident had colored his whole life. "But you stayed with CHAIM."

"Yes, after some intense training in Ireland—and to prove myself. Sometimes I think they assign me to beautiful women as a test." He leaned up. "And I don't intend to fail that test, Kit. Not with you."

"Am I now a distraction? Because you're attracted to me and yet you think I'm hiding something from you?"

His body jolted, his eyes going dark. "I lost someone I cared about because I let my heart get ahead of my focus. I wasn't as experienced then. I am experienced now—in both combat and in matters of the heart. I'm here to protect you. End of discussion."

Shocked, she saw it all there at last. He wasn't such a player after all. He was terrified of giving himself over to his feelings. "Are you afraid you'll fail again, Shane?"

He ignored that last question. "Are you hiding something?"

How like him to answer all of her questions with one of his own. "Is this an interrogation?"

He sank back in the chair. "No. I don't want to interrogate you. But Paco and I have gone over every bit of information we could find on you and your husband—thankfully I destroyed most of it and the rest is locked up in a secure cabinet—and downloaded to my phone—so our intruders didn't get to it. Everything looks clean. But looks can be deceiving, even on paper. I'm beginning to think you actually *don't* know the whole truth."

She swallowed back the choking dread in her throat. "Maybe I didn't want to see the whole truth."

He watched as she fidgeted with her pearls then moved her hand over her gold bracelet watch. "Would you like to talk about it? We did agree to do that, remember?"

"I remember. And if I'm honest with you, will you be honest with me?"

His dark eyebrows shot up. "About what?"

She leaned forward, her fingers touching together. "I want to know everything good or bad you've found regarding my husband. I need to know the truth, so I can move on with my life. That is if I live to see another day. But I also need you to trust me, show me that you believe in me. So be honest with me. Don't hold anything back. I can't take that again, ever."

He was up and out of the chair in an instant, pulling her close to stare down at her. "Oh, you'll live another day, darling. You'll live a lifetime. I intend to see to that. And whatever happened between you and your husband won't happen between us. Because I would never neglect nor betray a woman like you."

So he did know some of her secrets after all.

And she needed to know some of his. "Is there something happening between us?"

"In spite of my best intentions otherwise, I do believe so."

"This person you cared about—it was the young woman?"

His smile betrayed the truth. "No, it was another CHAIM agent—a fellow rookie. The woman I thought I loved turned out to be a ruthless killer—an extremist with misguided intentions. She took his life to punish me. And I made sure she paid dearly for it."

Kit held a hand to her mouth. "That's not what I expected." Then she lifted her gaze to his, honesty her only weapon. "I'm not that woman, Shane. I'm just the widow of a powerful man who stopped loving me long before he died."

The expression in his eyes changed, went dark. "And I'm just the man who's beginning to care about you too much."

"What are you going to do about it?"

"For starters, this."

He reached for her and kissed her long and hard, with a tenderness that left her breathless and confused. Then he lifted his head, his eyes bright with longing. "And in spite of my intentions otherwise, I want to keep kissing you until I figure it out."

Kit pulled away, her pulse doing a rapid dance. "You don't trust me and yet, you just kissed me. You said yourself you've been down this road before."

"No, never *this* road. Never feeling the way I do with you." His eyes traced a path over her face. "There's a big difference between a kiss and a deep, abiding trust, luv. Trust makes things that much sweeter."

She stepped back. "So your kiss means nothing even

though you say you've never felt like this before? Is it a means to get me to relax and talk?"

He tugged her back again, one hand around her waist. "Kissing you, dear Kit, means more than I can say. And that's what scares me the most."

"Then stop kissing me and let me tell you the story of my marriage."

He moved a hand down her hair, his fingers touching on her pearls. "The real story?"

"Yes," she said, closing her eyes to the gentleness of his touch dancing over her skin. "But not the story of secrets and shady dealings. The real story of how our marriage was falling apart, piece by piece, and how I let it happen. Maybe in doing so, we can find out the truth about who's trying to kill me, and then you'll see that I have nothing to hide. Except a broken heart."

FIFTEEN

Shane sat there in the quiet, dark room, listening to the beautiful woman sitting across from him as she poured her heart out. It wasn't easy, listening to someone's deep, dark secrets, watching the slash of pain expressed with each word, each memory. But sometimes, with this job, it came with the territory. Devon Malone would know how to counsel Kit right now. Devon was a minister in every sense of the word. The man had always been a minister first and a special operative second. It was in Devon's blood to help those who needed counseling and solace.

It was in Shane's blood to make the bad guys suffer. That was his mode of operation. Get in. Get the bad guys. Maybe fall for a pretty face. And move to the next assignment. He'd known going in that protecting a beautiful woman would be his downfall, but he usually handled the situation with a light touch. And Kit was so right; it wasn't as if he hadn't been here before.

Only this time, with this particular woman, was different. She was different. She was real. Real in her faith, real in her devotion to her charitable works and real in her sense of loyalty to those she loved.

This time he'd fallen hard. So hard that he intended to get to the bottom of things with this bizarre case so he could be with the woman free and clear. And maybe forever.

"I loved him so much," she said now, her green eyes as deep and rich as the ferns growing underneath the cottonwood trees out on the stream. "I wanted to be the best wife possible." She shrugged, the movement causing her shimmering hair to shift over the soft blue scarf covering her shoulders. "It was a matter of pride and propriety, you see. I'm a Barton, after all. Everything had to be perfect—at least on the surface. And we had the perfect marriage—the success, the looks, the big house in the exclusive neighborhood, the same seats on a front pew each Sunday. We were the 'it' couple for many years."

She stopped, her hands wrung together in her lap. "He did go on several trips with me and he seemed genuinely interested in my work at the foundation."

"When you were down in Mexico, did he disappear sometimes? Go off by himself?"

"Yes." She lowered her head. "I had my suspicions, but it has nothing to do with business deals. I didn't question him. I was too glad to have him there with me."

"And then?"

"And then, the power and control overtook the love and the vows we made to each other. Jacob had high aspirations while I wanted to have a family. We argued a lot. He didn't come home on time. He hated going to church and only attended so he'd be seen as a fine, upstanding man. Sometimes, he'd stay in town in the apartment he rented near the capital." She looked up then and straight into Shane's eyes. "And I'm pretty sure he didn't always stay there alone."

"He was unfaithful?"

She nodded and lowered her head, her obvious disgust and shame breaking Shane's heart. "I could never be sure. But a woman always knows these things, doesn't she?"

Shane couldn't answer that question. But he had his own suspicions regarding Jacob Atkins's less than stellar reputation. When he remembered all the women he'd thought he loved and left, he felt that same intense shame, too. "What made you think your husband was having an affair?"

She laughed, a curt little shattering laugh. "Oh, there were a hundred clues. His late nights away from me. His excuses for staying in the city. The way he'd sit staring off into space at the breakfast table or take phone calls in another room. The way he'd lavish me with gifts and promise me one day we'd have that family I wanted."

She reached up, twisting her pearls around her finger, her wedding ring shining with diamonds. "He gave me these pearls the last time I saw him. I had accused him earlier that week of deliberately pulling away from me because he had someone else, so he came home early and we had a wonderful dinner. He swore to me he'd never do anything to hurt me and that he loved me. Then he made me promise I'd always wear these pearls, for him." Her smile was full of pain. "But he never actually told me the truth. Jacob had a way of spinning things, a way of making me think I was all wrong, that I'd imagined everything."

Letting go of the pearls, she shook her head. "I honestly think that's why I kept denying I was in danger after he died. I wanted to keep the image of our perfect marriage intact in spite of the ugly letters and strange phone calls I started receiving. Even dead, my husband messed with my head to the point that I couldn't make coherent decisions regarding my own safety. How pathetic is that?"

Shane refrained from taking her in his arms. He needed to take his own advice and focus on this case. Those letters and phone calls were the reason he'd been called in the first place. Every threat had to be taken seriously.

But right now, he needed to reassure her. "You are a good and decent woman, Katherine. You wanted to honor your marriage vows. And you wanted to do right in the world. There is nothing pathetic in that. I'd say it's very admirable."

"Admirable?" She hissed through a tight breath. "Admirable to let your husband lie to you over and over, to sit in church together with smiles on our faces knowing we were the worst kind of hypocrites? Admirable to ignore the whispers, the signs, the well-meaning suggestions of friends? But I refused to listen. I refused to accept the truth. And now, I think my denial has brought this on me. If I'd demanded answers, if I'd asked questions when he was still alive, I might have saved not only myself but my husband, too. Maybe he would have talked to me, asked for my help. But he didn't. He couldn't, because Jacob never included me in his business decisions or his life, for that matter." Her eyes caught Shane's in a tormented light. "Trudy tried to tell me, but I wouldn't even listen to my best friend."

Shane's pulse bumped through his system like a warning beeper going into high alert mode. "Trudy knew about Jacob's affair?"

"She hinted at it, yes."

"When was this?"

Shocked, Kit frowned at him. "Right after her husband died. I went to see her, hoping to comfort her and when the conversation turned to Jacob, she told me I couldn't trust him. So we argued. I can't even remember half of what we said to each other except that she envied Jacob and me and told me I needed to quit taking him for granted. She said if I wanted to save my marriage, I'd better start paying more attention to my husband."

"But you obviously made up with her, reconciled things."

"Yes, we forgave each other when Jacob died. She came to the funeral and we sat and cried together. We're closer now than we've ever been." She held up her wrist, dangling her bracelet watch at him. "She took me out to dinner for my birthday and gave me this watch."

Shane's pulse went into a flatline. "When is your birthday, luv?"

"It was a little over a month ago," she replied, her frown increasing. "Why do you ask?"

Shane got up and grabbed her wrist. "I need to see that watch."

Without waiting for her to take it off, he managed to loosen the clasp and pull the delicate gold bracelet off her slender arm. Then he turned the watch over. "I'll need to take the back off it, if you don't mind."

"Of course I mind," she said, shooting up and out of her chair. "I'm trying to tell you what I've been through and you're worried about this watch?"

He nodded then took her hand in his. "Yes, I'm very much worried about this watch. Because I think your friend Trudy put a GPS tracking chip in your birthday gift."

The look on Katherine's face moved from a confused frown to shocking, all-consuming anger. "You can't be serious!"

Shane held the watch in the air as if it were a snake. "Deadly serious. It explains everything. That's apparently how she kept tabs on you. And that's how she knew you were here with me. She probably panicked after the shooting since no one would tell her where you were. But she had this to locate you. And then she somehow managed to come up with a plan to find you. It's elaborate and hard to believe, but it was a plan to draw you out. She's pretending to be kidnapped, to bring you back."

Katherine stood behind her chair, holding on to it so hard her knuckles looked as if they'd crack. "They're *holding* her hostage, or did you forget that? Why do you insist on thinking the worst of her? You said you'd be honest with me but you haven't been at all. What do you think you know about Trudy Pearson, Shane?"

Before he could answer, Paco came bolting into the room. "Shane, the cell's ringing. And we can't get a trace. Kissie tried every way possible to break the encryption but we haven't managed yet."

He threw Shane the cheap black phone that had started this whole new chain of events. Shane had passed it to Paco earlier so Paco could coordinate things with Kissie to see if they might have a chance of tracing it. But he'd given Paco orders to bring the phone to him if they got any incoming calls.

Shane stared down at the phone then handed it to Kit. "I think your best friend wants to talk to you, luv. Try to get as much information as possible from her. And please don't mention that we might be on to her."

Kit shot Shane a pointed look as she took the phone then tugged away when he tried to listen in. His frown shouted disapproval but his ridiculous conclusions made her want to knock him silly. She'd deal with that later. Right now, she wanted to hear Trudy's voice and know that her friend was safe. "Trudy? Where are you?"

A male voice rasped across the wire. "Oh, she's about six feet under right about now."

"What?" Kit's heart accelerated so rapidly, she reached for a chair to hold her up. "What are you saying? Where is Trudy? Put her on the phone right now!"

"Trudy can't come to the phone, ever again. You didn't follow our directions," the voice replied. "People are dead because of you. Including your feisty little red-headed friend."

"No. No." Kit looked around at Shane, anger merging with a deep dread throughout her system. Turning away from his questioning gaze, she screamed into the phone. "I want to talk to her!"

"Too late for Trudy. But if you listen to us and do not repeat our conversation, you might get to live after you give us the information we need. If you don't listen we will find someone else to take your place. For example, your parents are such a lovely couple. We see them in church every Sunday and we have it on good authority that they are no longer holed up at Eagle Rock. And you have several college students working for you this summer. We know where they all go to school and we know some of them stay at your lovely home in Austin while they intern. One of them could go missing." He paused then growled, "Or we could just take out Shane Warwick and end it all. Without his protection, you'd be easy to find. Are you ready to meet with us, Mrs. Atkins? Just answer yes or no, please."

Kit swallowed the bile rising to her throat. Could they be lying to her to draw her out? She couldn't take that chance. "Yes, I understand."

"I'll be in touch in a few hours. For the well-being of all involved, don't repeat this to your bodyguard."

The connection was lost, the phone line silent. "Hello?" Nothing. She frantically tried dialing the number back but no ring tones echoed through the line.

Finally, she turned to Shane, tears of rage forcing their way down her face, her whole body shuddering with grief and anger. "I hope you're satisfied."

"Katherine?"

Still gripping the phone, she lunged at Shane, her fist balled up like jagged barbed wire as she pounded his chest. "She's dead! Dead. They killed her! You wouldn't let me help her and now they've killed her." She glared up at him, her body shutting down with each beat of her pulse, her mind going numb with a death-like fusion of pain and despair as everything that had happened over the last few days finally and completely caught up with her.

Shane grabbed her wrist, holding her hands away as he watched her face, his eyes burning a raw, white-hot crystal. "What did they say? Was it a man or a woman?"

"A man," she replied, her control just beyond snapping. "He said Trudy was dead and if I didn't cooperate, I'd soon be too." She stopped, calculating how much to tell him. She wouldn't reveal anything to Shane because Shane couldn't help her. "They killed her while we sat here, waiting. We did nothing. You told me you had people looking for her and yet, you didn't stop this, Shane. And now she's dead."

He gave her a pleading look. "We do have someone on this. You should have let me listen in. This could be a trick." He reached for Katherine again, remorse turning his blues eyes to a muted gray. "I'm sorry."

Katherine pushed at him, freeing her hands from his with a twisted tug. "You're sorry? That's all you can say? You just stood there and accused her of keeping tabs on me and being a part of this horror and she's dead. Dead. And you're sorry." Her hands at her side, she said, "You've failed again, Warwick. But this time, I'm the one who's lost someone I love."

Shane stepped out of his calm. And she was glad. Although she hated the hurt fusing through his eyes, she wanted him to feel the same gut-wrenching numbness that had her paralyzed.

"They might be lying to you," he said, his tone urgent, his gaze shattered. "They want to scare you out of hiding."

"They tried that, remember? They put Trudy on the phone even while they were abusing her. And you held me here anyway."

"I had no choice, Katherine. They sent people here to capture you. I had to stop them."

"Well, you did. You stopped them from harming me but Trudy didn't have a protector, did she?"

She whirled to leave, her only thought of getting

away from him and the dormant longing and need he'd awakened in her. But her grief overpowered that need right now. Then she pivoted at the door. "I'm sorry, too. Sorry that I ever trusted you or listened to you." She pointed a finger in the air toward him, sobs choking her. "And I will never forgive you for this. Never."

Then she ran all the way upstairs to her room and slammed the door shut.

Shane held her watch in his hands, the warmth of her skin still lingering on the gold, the chill of her parting words still lingering on his heart. She hated him now, blamed him for this. And maybe she had a right to blame him.

Paco, who had a way of sinking into the shadows of a room, cleared his throat from behind a chair. "I tried every way to set up a trace, man. We ran out of time."

Shane put his hands on his hips. "She refused to let us listen in. But I'm sure she's been threatened again." He lifted the glistening watch. "I need you to take this apart. Look for anything that could be a GPS chip."

Paco stepped into the light and took the watch. "I'm on it."

Shane watched him leave then held on to his own chair. Had he been wrong all along? Was Trudy Pearson just an innocent bystander, collateral damage in a case that seemed to twist and change right before his eyes?

Wondering if he could have prevented this, he thought back on everything. No. He knew something wasn't right with Trudy. He'd watched her the night of the gala, making her rounds, working the crowd. It was his business to watch anyone who happened to be close to Katherine. And that night, Trudy had seemed too close, too observant, and too keen on Katherine's every move. At the time, Shane had chalked it up to their being such good friends and the fact that Trudy was helping Katherine with the festivities. But after reviewing all the information on Trudy Pearson, he'd ramped up the apprehension a notch on this woman. That apprehension had only increased when no one within the ranks of CHAIM had been able to locate Trudy.

What had he seen that night?

Thinking back, he remembered Katherine had ordered a sparkling water. They'd chatted, glancing his way. He remembered the way Katherine had only given him a passing glance while Trudy's gaze had stayed on him a long time.

Shane closed his eyes, reliving that moment in his mind, his stomach burning with an urgent fire. The waiter had handed Katherine her water and then he'd winked at Trudy. She'd leaned close to whisper something in his ear before she turned around to continue her conversation with Katherine.

The waiter!

Shane's pulse came back alive with such a quickening he had to inhale a breath. And then the whole picture came into his head, full-blown and crystal clear. The waiter. The same waiter who'd stood behind the stage with a gun aimed on Katherine. He'd changed his look, combed his hair differently and added a mustache but it was the same man.

Shane had to be sure. He quickly called Kissie, asking her to compare the surveillance video the hotel had downloaded to CHAIM. "See if you can get a match on the waiter who served Mrs. Atkins and her friend Trudy." He described Trudy and an estimation of the time. "Compare that image to the one we have of the shooter."

Kissie went to work on that while Shane tried to get his own visual on the events of that night.

He kept his eyes closed, going over each detail with a renewed emphasis. In his mind he could see the waiter with the gun hidden underneath a linen napkin, could see the man's intense gaze as he searched the room and spotted Katherine. Shane remembered pushing Katherine to the floor and shouting for everyone to get down. He'd watched the crowd, his gaze locking on the man who'd planned to quietly make the silenced shot then get away undetected. But after Shane had spotted him, the shooter had crouched down and moved with purposeful intent through the frightened, shocked crowd. Everyone had fallen down behind chairs and tables, hiding after the first shot had missed Katherine.

Except for one person.

Trudy Pearson hadn't ducked down at first. She'd just stood there behind the refreshment table, staring out into the crowd.

Until the caterer had tugged her down beside him.

Shane opened his eyes, the truth staring him in the face. He'd wondered time and again why they'd tried to kill Katherine that night but had gone to great lengths since then to keep her alive until they had her.

And now he knew the reason.

Trudy Pearson had been in on the hit that night. But now she was fighting to capture Katherine, not kill her.

Had she believed she'd be able to find something on Katherine that night, in that room?

The gunman had missed Katherine then turned toward Trudy Pearson for guidance and when he failed to do the job, someone else had come for both of them. She'd called here, trying to get Katherine to help, maybe hoping to redeem herself somehow, too? Or to save herself by sacrificing Katherine? What did the two of them know?

Or rather, what did Trudy know?

Whatever it was, she could be dead now because of it.

He stared down at his desk, the papers blurring before his eyes as he remembered Katherine's parting words to him, remembered the venom in her gaze, the hurt in her voice.

She'd never forgive him for this.

And he'd never forgive himself. He had failed again.

Because of his actions, Katherine's best friend might now be dead. And whoever had killed her would surely come after Katherine with a renewed vengeance.

Then another image came into his mind. One of Katherine rushing out of this room with the cell still in her hand.

Shane looked out into the dark hallway then sprang into action. He had to get that cell phone away from Katherine before they called again. And this time, he'd do the listening.

SIXTEEN

Katherine slowly backed the little Miata out of the garage, turning off the automatic head lights until she could make it to the gate. Glancing in the rearview mirror, she was glad to see no one had noticed she'd left. Since she knew the garage code, she hoped the security system wouldn't even register she'd opened it. And she'd taken one of the remote controls to the main gate, too.

Not proud of having to stoop to theft to escape, she told herself she was doing this for the good of everyone involved. These people obviously wanted something from her and now she was going to give it to them, one way or another, and on her own terms. She had the phone on the seat in case they called again. And she had the revolver Paco had recovered from the road tucked safely in her bag.

So why were her palms so sweaty she could barely control the steering wheel?

Well, for starters, she was leaving Shane behind and his solid presence had made her feel safe over the last week or so. But Kit couldn't get past her anger or her grief. She wasn't ready to admit all the other feelings Shane brought out in her. And she might be going to a fate worse than she could imagine but she had to do this to stop the violence. She couldn't live like this anymore. These people were ruthless but she didn't have a choice. They wanted her and they were willing to kill others to get to her. She only prayed she could talk to them and hopefully help them find what they needed then somehow get away alive.

They'd killed Trudy.

They'd try to kill her, too.

And for what? Katherine didn't know anything. Didn't want to know anything. But her dead husband had obviously become mixed up in something criminal and now she was paying dearly for that. At least this way, she could find out the truth that so many people seemed to want to hide from her. And she'd start by going back to her office to do some research on the documentation they'd saved regarding her work in Mexico. That had to be the key. Either someone close to her had a criminal connection in Mexico and somehow thought Kit knew about it, or her husband had done something against the law and they needed to destroy the evidence and get rid of her, too.

She made it to the gate. Pushing buttons on the tiny remote, Kit waited for the big gates to slide back so she could get through. She'd have to find her way back to the main road without the help of the GPS system. Hopefully, she'd be well on her way before anyone alerted Shane.

Praying that Shane and the others back at the house wouldn't notice she was missing for a while, she shifted gears and hurried the eager little sports car along the curving lane. When she passed the spot where the road dipped into what was left of the mud hole, Kit couldn't stop the shivers coursing through her body.

No trace remained of what had happened here earlier. The big truck had been moved and all signs of the shootout had disappeared. Feeling as if she'd lived two lifetimes in the last few days, Kit carefully drove around the deep ruts and hurried out to the main road.

Shane had just left Paco busy working on the watch and was on his way to find Katherine when he heard the beep and knew instantly what had happened. He raced through the house, his gaze locking on the entry code by the back door. Usually the code read green if the house was secure. But right now it was reading red. And then it blinked green again.

He rushed out the door and watched as the garage light also went from red to green. Then he heard the doors to the other side sliding down.

Someone had left the premises in a vehicle.

Pulling out his phone, he called Paco. "We have a problem. I think the subject is on the run. In a yellow sports car."

"And you never saw that coming?"

Shane hated Paco's deadpan way of cutting to the chase. "I never thought she'd try this, no."

"Go after her. I've got everything else covered. Oh, and Warwick, I found a tiny GPS chip in the watch. The signal was weak but I disabled it anyway."

Shane's stomach muscles tightened in dread. "Try to jam the censors on the gate. Maybe we can stop her."

"I'm on it."

Shane hopped into his truck and peeled rubber as soon as the garage doors were clear. He prayed, asking God to protect Katherine. Surely she wasn't going to meet these people on her own. That would be like writing her death sentence. Why would she do such a thing? Maybe to show him she didn't need his services anymore, since he'd failed her? Pushing that aside, he reasoned they'd probably threatened someone else close to her, using Trudy's murder as collateral.

His heart ripped at his rib cage at the thought. Katherine would do anything to stop this, to protect those around her. She'd lost Trudy so now she had some sort of death wish that could only lead to tragedy.

And Shane couldn't let that happen.

Not to the woman he loved.

Kit looked straight ahead, the muted lights dotting the city causing her eyes to glaze over. Exhaustion tugged at her, making her lids droop. She'd been on the road for over three hours and no one had tried to call on that infernal phone. And the man had said he'd call back in a couple of hours.

Her skin crawled with energy and her nerves twisted like tumbleweed. She wanted to cry for the death of her friend, but no tears would come. Maybe because Kit was burning with such a rage of fire, everything inside her burst into flames with each thought.

Soon she'd be in her office in downtown Austin. She'd pushed the little car to the limits and only refueled at the last possible minute, circling around and back to the gas station to make sure she wasn't being followed.

Remembering how Shane had driven the little car too fast to get her to safety at his ranch and done the same thing when he'd stopped for gas, Kit shook her head to block out that memory, her guilt at running away eating at her almost as much as her feelings for Shane.

Dear God, I know he's trying to help me but at what cost? What price for my salvation, Lord?

Her thoughts fluttered to the memory of his kiss. Had she ever been kissed that way before? Kit tried to remember Jacob's kisses but she had to block those bitter memories, too. The last time he'd kissed her was the night he'd given her the pearls and in her heart, she'd known his touch was full of betrayal.

Oh, Lord, help me. I feel so sick, so tired. Why did I ignore the truth? Why, Lord? Help me to understand.

The phone on the seat buzzed to life with a shrill jingling, causing Kit to gasp. Her hands shook as she gripped the steering wheel with one hand while she grabbed for the phone with the other one. She was a block from her office so she pulled off onto a side street.

"Hello?"

"Mrs. Atkins, so good to hear your voice."

"What do you want?"

"We want to talk to you. Ask you a few questions."

"I want to talk to you, too. So we can end this."

"Where are you?"

Katherine almost blurted it out but then decided to give them a taste of their own medicine by being cryptic. "I'm not on the ranch anymore. I'm close to Austin."

"And are you alone?"

"Yes."

"Very good."

"Where do you want to meet me?"

"There's an old warehouse on the river. Be there in one hour." He gave her the address. "And Mrs. Atkins, if Shane Warwick shows up, we'll kill him before we discuss anything with you, do you understand?"

"Yes. He won't be there."

The phone went silent in her hand. Leaning against the steering wheel, she took a breath then wiped at her eyes.

Kit was shaking so hard, she had trouble finding the entryway to the parking garage of her office. Very few cars were parked here this time of night—another warning for her to be careful. After what seemed like hours, she finally pulled into her assigned spot then changed her mind and parked one floor up, all the while watching for any cars moving toward her.

Stopping the little car, she took a deep breath, her hands gripping the steering wheel as if it were a lifeline. She glanced around to make sure she was alone then sat silent for a minute, leaning her head against the wheel, her prayers scattered and choppy as she asked God to protect her, to comfort her, and most of all, to keep Shane away from her for just a little while longer.

He was two car lengths behind her and gaining when she pulled over on the deserted downtown street.

Shane downshifted and stopped in the street as he watched the bright little butterfly of a car parking up ahead. Careful to stay out of her sight, he slipped the truck into a nearby open parking lot and shut off the headlights. He'd found her on the interstate and stayed with her, watching her gas up and admiring the tricks of the trade she'd obviously learned from her father and from watching Shane, no doubt. But being careful wouldn't stop these criminals from harming her. Only he could do that.

His phone rang, startling him. Praying it was Katherine, he answered it, his eyes on the car ahead. "Warwick."

"Brother, I've got some news," Paco said, his voice low and strained. "Kissie reported back—got a match on the waiter and the shooter. Same man. We've sent the information to the Austin police. And based on our suspicions about Trudy Pearson, we were able to get a definite on how and when she bought the phones. Got 'em the day after the gala shooting—from several different discount stores all over the city."

"Good," Shane said, gritting his teeth. "Maybe the Austin police can get the shooter to talk since the evidence is building. Make sure they know about the phones."

"Yep on the phones. And let's hope the shooter spills it. The lone survivor from this morning's shoot-out died at the county hospital about an hour ago. And I'm thinking it wasn't from his gunshot wound."

"Someone got to him?"

"Let's just say things looked suspicious, according to my sources."

Shane hit the steering wheel. "Any good news, Paco?"

"Yeah. But it won't make you smile. After talking to some of the subject's interns and aides, Kissie managed to dig up some pictures from one of the subject's trips to Mexico. And she found something very interesting."

"Oh, what's that?" Shane asked, making sure Katherine hadn't spotted him. He held his breath when he saw her slumped over the steering wheel.

"Seems Kissie found a picture of Senator Atkins with a woman in the lobby of a Mexico City hotel where some of the foundation's staff members were staying. And she wasn't his wife."

Shane kept his eyes on Katherine. She lifted her head and wiped at her eyes and his gut clinched. "We suspected as much," he said into the phone.

"Yeah, but we never expected the other woman to be Trudy Pearson."

"Trudy? You have proof that she's the woman in the picture?"

"Kissie's compared photos. It's her all right."

"She did go on a few of the mission trips with our subject. Maybe the subject was nearby?"

"Negative on that. Not in this particular shot. The intern who gave it to Kissie did so under duress after being interrogated by Mr. Barton himself. Was told by the senator to destroy the picture but said intern saved it, just in case."

"Are they in a compromising position?"

"No, but they look mighty cozy."

The tiny yellow car pulled back out onto the empty street. "Got to go. Good work, Paco."

"Later."

Shane waited until he saw Katherine turn the corner into the parking lot to her office building, then he parked the truck and started out on foot toward the building.

Telling herself security cameras were on her and she'd be safe because of that, Katherine rode the elevator to the fifth floor and breathed a sigh of relief when no one was waiting for her in the hallway. Hurrying to her office, she slid her key card into the slot and quickly locked the door behind her. Then she hurried to her files and began searching for any information she could find on her last trip to Mexico as well as the one planned for next month.

But everything regarding Mexico had disappeared.

She sat down at her desk, a single light on as she read through reams of paper and searched the computer files, too. Where were her files on Mexico? What if Jacob had some sort of secret files she didn't know about?

Maybe her donor list would give her a clue, since they had to keep accurate records on each donation. Hitting computer keys, she tried to pull up the list but couldn't find it. After several attempts, she knew the reason why.

The file had been deleted. It was gone.

And she couldn't find the hard copy in any of the folders on her desk or in the file cabinet.

Someone had swiped her donor file and all the information regarding the project in Mexico.

Kit got up to look around, hoping maybe the files had been moved for her protection or for the privacy of her clients. But that didn't make any sense either—unless her father had taken the files to help her out by protecting her patrons.

Finally, tired and frustrated, Kit glanced at the time on the computer screen. She'd have to hurry to make the meeting at the warehouse. And she still didn't have any more information than when she'd arrived, nothing to plead her case with these people who wanted to talk to her so badly. And no time to get to Jacob's files.

Sending up a prayer for guidance and protection, Kit turned off the lights and shut the door of her office. When she turned around, a strong arm grabbed her from behind while a big hand went over her mouth.

Then a familiar voice rasped into her ear, "Don't move and don't make a sound."

SEVENTEEN

Katherine twisted in his arms, adrenaline and terror abating as she realized Shane was holding her. His hand gently held her arm and his clean country scent surrounded her. And yet, she wasn't ready to forgive and forget.

"Listen to me," he said, his mouth pressed to her ear. "We're not alone."

She gulped back the fear threatening to overtake her. Moving her head again, she tried to speak.

"I'm going to remove my hand but you can't say anything. We have to get out of here, now."

She nodded. He kissed her temple then lifted his hand away. "Just do as I say."

She should have done that all along. She should have listened to Shane and stayed with Shane. Now she'd brought him right into even more danger. Maybe she could get away from him if she acted angry. Then she pointed to her purse and mouthed "gun."

"Forget that for now."

He urged her forward toward the stairs, a finger to his lips. Slowly, carefully, he opened the door to the stairwell, his gun at the ready. When he saw that it was safe, he shielded her with his body as they made their way to the next floor. Glancing both ways, he finally turned to her and pulled her into his arms. "Don't ever leave me again."

Katherine fell against him then pulled back. "Let me go, Shane. You're no longer needed."

"I don't care," he said. "*I* need to be here."

His lips on hers cut off her attempt to sway him and took her breath and her anger away. It was enough for now that he was with her and she was back in his arms. It was enough, but her worries for him, coupled with the hurt of losing her friend, overruled her love for him. Later, when she knew he was safe she'd tell Shane the truth.

She loved him. And she'd do anything in her power to protect him. But beyond that, her mind blurred into a haze of pain. Because she could never have a life with the man who caused her best friend to die.

He loved her and he'd do anything in his power to protect her, Shane thought as he tiptoed with Kit down the stairwell. But she was still hurt and angry. He didn't think they'd ever get past that. But right now, he had to get her past the people who wanted to do her harm.

Just a few feet to the next exit and the parking garage but he wasn't certain of the big garage's security measures so he planned to take her out the same freight door he'd entered. They might have a chance once they'd made it out to the street.

"Who's following us?" she whispered when they stopped.

"Two men, dressed in black and carrying impressive weapons." Shane put a finger to her mouth. "We'll talk later."

His cell vibrated, then beeped the ASAP code. Paco with an urgent update. Guiding Kit to a dark hallway near the doors of the freight entrance, he pointed to the cell. "I need to check this."

It was a text:

"Urgent. K broke into encrypted files. T and J Petro-stolen oil from remote Mexican pipeline near village where subject mission work continues. TJ shell corporation owned by Pearson Industries. T and J is acronym— Trudy and Jacob. Selling stolen oil to unsuspecting U.S. refineries—with help from drug cartel—money missing. Someone found out—not happy. Careful, brother. 'Everything that is hidden or secret will eventually be brought to light and made plain to all.'"

Shane hissed a breath after reading the verse from Luke. This was big and deep and far-reaching and someone wanted to keep it secret and hidden. They'd never let Katherine live if they thought she knew about this. Siphoning off oil from a Mexican pipeline to ship into the United States and sell? Working with a drug cartel?

"Let's go," he told her as he tugged her through the freight doors.

"No. Not until you tell me what's going on."

The first bullet hit two inches from Shane's head.

And the next one hit him in the left shoulder, knocking him to the ground.

Shane's left arm filled with a burning fire of pain. He struggled to stay conscious, Katherine's screams echoing inside his head.

Katherine bit at the rag they'd stuffed in her mouth, fibers of twisted material gagging her as the silent scream shouted inside her head. They'd blindfolded her so she had no way of knowing if Shane was alive or dead.

He hadn't answered when she'd called out his name right before they'd tackled her and put a gag on her mouth.

Please, God, let him be alive. Please, God.

That prayer kept her going, kept her from passing out or going hysterical. They were taking her somewhere in some sort of big truck. The gears shifted and groaned each time they stopped and started. Where was Shane?

She tried to twist her tied hands, hoping to free herself but a foot on her leg halted her. "Don't move."

Katherine sank back against what felt like packing blankets, praying that if she did as they asked, they'd spare Shane. Or was he already dead?

When the truck finally ground to a halt, she felt a strange sort of relief. At least now maybe she'd come face to face with her tormenters and get this over with, one way or another.

Shane groaned, a lit fuse of agony racing through his arm as he was lifted and dragged into a dark, damp room and dumped onto a pile of cold, dirty plastic. Looking through the slits of his closed eyes, he got around the haze of pain enough to see Katherine, tied up and gagged, being shoved onto a chair. She lifted her head, the dark blindfold unable to hide her fear or her anger. He prayed she'd think carefully about how to handle this. He prayed she wouldn't do anything rash.

He recognized the setup. Interrogation and torture.

His first instinct was to scream so loud they'd turn from her and put all their attention on him. But then, they'd probably finish him off and move back to her. He was expendable at this point. She was not—at least not until they'd tried every means possible to get information from her.

So he closed his eyes against that disturbing image, dropped his head and thanked God for the small blessing—and deadly mistake on the part of their tormentors—of not being gagged, tied and blindfolded as she had been. The only reason they'd brought him here was to make sure he died a slow death right in front of their eyes, or to make Katherine suffer as she watched him die. He didn't plan to oblige them, however. He wasn't going to die tonight. And neither was Katherine.

Katherine continued to take deep, calming breaths. Her father had taught her this when she was young and she'd had nightmares. "Just breathe, baby. Breathe and let God's love shield you from any monsters in your dreams." Her father would pat her hand then hold it tightly in his, the warmth of his strong grip making her feel safe and loved. "God will be with you, Kit, no matter what life throws at you."

Focusing on her daddy's words and his face as he'd tucked her back in and sat by her bed until she drifted off to sleep again, Kit asked God to shield her in his love and grace right now. And she asked the same for Shane.

She only prayed that wherever Shane was, he still had breath left in his body. Please, Shane. Stay alive.

Wishing she'd told him there on the stairwell that she loved him, Katherine pushed at the tears piercing her eyes. She listened to the movements around her. Chairs dragged across the concrete floor. Voices whispered in anger. Somewhere in the distance, she heard thunder rumbling. She thought she heard a woman's voice echoing across the air.

The fishy smell of the river assaulted her from an open window or door nearby. She could hear the slight flapping of some sort of curtains and feel the wind hitting her hot skin. They must have brought her to the warehouse they'd told her to meet them at—the deserted warehouse where no one would find her.

Get your bearings and get a plan, she told herself. Focus, Kit. Focus and listen. Find an opportunity, any opportunity.

Shane squinted, opening one eye enough to see that he was being loosely guarded by one man while the other stood staring down at Katherine. If he could make himself stay still and keep pretending to be unconscious, he might be able to save Kit. And if he could hit the right app on his phone screen, he could alert Paco to send help. He'd have to move very slowly but he thought he could find enough strength to take out the man guarding him. And maybe gain a weapon in the process.

Maybe.

Sweat moved in a slow, wet crawl down his spine and

his arm throbbed and oozed blood, but he gritted his teeth against the pain and waited impatiently for someone to make a move. They were waiting on the big dog.

And it didn't take long for that person to show up. Shane heard the tap, tap of footsteps and surmised this was not a man. But then, this was no surprise to him. He had a feeling he knew exactly who'd just entered the dirty, dark warehouse.

"Take the blindfold and gag off her."

Kit gasped at the sound of that voice, her stare clashing into Trudy Pearson's the minute the blindfold was lifted away from her face. Shock kept her from speaking once the disgusting gag was gone, but a heated rage coursed through her body, giving her renewed determination. Shane had been right all along. And she might not ever get the chance to tell him how sorry she was for not believing him.

"Hello, Katherine." Trudy smiled sweetly, looking fresh and very much alive in her designer jeans and lightweight cream linen jacket, her chic black ankle boots tapping on the concrete floor. "What's wrong? You look like you've seen a ghost."

Katherine watched Trudy smiling over at the henchman holding a gun close to Katherine's temple—the head of catering from the hotel—and thought about spitting on her. Instead, she braced herself and decided she didn't need to use proper manners tonight but she wouldn't give Trudy any satisfaction by stooping to her level either. "I think I've had my fill of ghosts, Trudy. Yours and Jacob's. Why don't you tell me what's going on."

Trudy leaned down, giving Katherine a harsh glare.

"You're too stubborn for your own good, Kit. Why did you have to run off with Shane Warwick? It's so unseemly for someone as uptight as you, after all. Besides, we both know you can't keep a man happy."

Katherine ignored that jab and cut her gaze across the dark room, her heart leaping when she saw a still figure lying on a pile of plastic sheeting a few yards away. "Shane was protecting me. Doing his job."

Trudy glanced over to the man on the floor. "Yes and he did such a good job, I was beginning to think I'd never find you again. But here we all are, together at last. Your protector is either going to bleed to death or get himself shot again right in front of your eyes. I haven't decided which yet." She grinned. "Of course, if you tell me what I need to know, I might let him live for a little while. After you're gone, of course."

Katherine's stomach churned but she held her head up. She didn't want to give in to Trudy's demands, but she didn't have a choice. "What is it that you think I know? Is it worth all the trouble you've gone to or the lives you'd taken?"

"I think so," Trudy replied, her cold eyes burning with a heated intensity. She motioned to her caterer-kidnapper friend. "Pull me up a chair. This is a long story."

Shane listened, not daring to breathe, as Trudy Pearson promised to end the mystery and tell what had to be a fascinating if not twisted tale. He listened, his right hand inching toward his pocket, only to discover his cell phone was gone. No help there other than the alert he'd sent to the CHAIM satellite earlier when he'd been tracking Kit. Meantime, he'd have to do this the old-fashioned way, with sheer will and a determination to keep Katherine alive.

He prayed for a solid armor of Christ. He'd need every inch of the protection to get through this night. But for now, he could only wait for the right opportunity while he listened to Trudy's confession.

Fortunately, his guard seemed as interested as Shane. The man hadn't glanced his way since Trudy had entered the room and he was now sprawled across a chair, his gun relaxed at his side. And the man he now recognized as the catering manager who'd taken Trudy home the night of the gala was all ears, too. She must have promised them something big.

"I do owe you an explanation," Trudy said through a smirk. "This started before either of our husbands died. You know how these things go. I got bored when Gus was away on business."

Kit took in that bit of information with a shake of her head. "So you decided to amuse yourself with my husband?"

Trudy made a face. "It wasn't that hard, darling. You sure didn't give him much attention."

Kit leaned forward, straining against the ties. "I trusted you, Trudy. I told you all my fears regarding my marriage. I tried to give Jacob love and support. But it was never enough. Never."

"Apparently not," Trudy replied. "He liked my way better."

Shane's heart went out to Kit. She looked so small, so shocked that he almost got up and went to her. But then she lifted her head and he saw the serene look on her face and marveled at her calm in the face of this betrayal. But this calm could turn deadly at any minute and he had to be ready.

Kit couldn't believe she'd ever trusted this evil woman. How could she have been so gullible, so ignorant?

"So you had an affair with Jacob. How did that lead to this? You've killed people—" She stopped, a low moan choking her throat. "Did you kill Gus?"

Trudy's laugh sounded like brittle glass hitting against stone. "Goodness, no. Gus died of natural causes. I really did care about him but I was in love with Jacob. And he loved me. And we actually owe it all to you, Kit. It happened down in Mexico on one of your tedious mission trips."

Kit closed her eyes, the image of Jacob with her best friend turning her stomach. "No wonder you seemed so excited about going. And you obviously mixed business with pleasure down there. Where does the illegal activity come into play?"

"You always did know how to carry on with witty rapport," Trudy said through a tight smile. "Your husband managed to hook up with a drug cartel down there. You never knew he had a little addiction. He hid it pretty well, but the man was addicted to money and power. It was one of the things I loved about him." She waved a hand in the air. "Anyway, he cut a deal with a drug cartel to make some serious money."

"Drugs?" Kit asked. "Jacob was bringing illegal drugs into the country?"

Trudy shook her head. "Oh, no. He found something worth a lot more than drugs." She grinned then ran a hand through her hair. "Oil, Kit. All rerouted from a big pipeline to a secret pipeline manned by a cartel. We set up a dummy company and backed up the tankers and let it flow. We found a small independent company willing to look the other way and just like that, we were off and running. It was brilliant."

Kit tried to follow Trudy then decided her former friend was quite mad. "You can't be serious."

"Deadly serious," Trudy replied. "We had it all. He was going to leave you. But something went wrong with the cartel and, well, they said we shorted them of a few million. Jacob hid that money. Even from me, the scoundrel. Only, I really need that cash to save myself."

"I don't know what you're talking about," Katherine replied, her gaze sliding toward Shane's still body.

"No, you wouldn't. Too dumb to figure it out. But I watched you, tracked you and almost had you the night of the gala. I picked the hotel and I picked a few select workers to help me." She smiled over at the criminal caterer. "You were supposed to be shot, not killed. And I'd get to the money because I'd have access to you while you recovered. I figured out where the numbers to the safety deposit box were hidden, but I had to make it look like you were in danger."

She got up and with a vicious twist that seared Kit's neck, watched as Kit's glimmering pearls fell to the dirty floor. "The night he gave you these stupid pearls he was supposed to tell you about us. But he couldn't do it." Trudy handed one of the men the empty thread still attached to the heavy oval-shaped gold clasp. "Get the microscope and check the clasp. Look for numbers."

Kit fought at the tears streaming down her cheeks— tears caused by the raw torn skin on her neck and by the horrible truth of what had been going on right before her eyes. Jacob had given her those pearls for one reason. They held the key to all of this. "Did you kill my husband, Trudy?"

"How dare you!"

Trudy slapped her, the force of it snapping Kit's head back. When she straightened, she saw a movement in the shadows where Shane had been lying. He wasn't there anymore. She didn't dare let on that she knew.

She looked up at Trudy. "Tell me the truth."

"I did not kill Jacob!" Trudy shouted, her hand poised in the air. "I loved him. Those pearls were meant for *me*. And he wasn't supposed to get on that helicopter. You were!"

Kit gasped, realization breaking through the haze of horror surrounding her. "I'd scheduled an interview up in Dallas at the end of the week and Jacob had arranged to have a chopper fly me up there. But I never made the trip. Because he was killed that same week."

Trudy nodded, tears in her eyes. "Yes, there was a bad accident on the interstate that morning so Jacob took the chopper to the capital to avoid traffic. He didn't know I'd had it rigged to explode when you took your trip."

"Got the numbers, Trudy," the henchman-caterer said, coming back to give Trudy the gold clasp. She tossed it on the floor.

Grabbing Katherine's shirt, Trudy leaned in, her eyes wild with hatred. "I have what I want and I'm going to kill you and Shane Warwick. Then I'm going to give the cartel the money and I'm leaving the country. The cartel will let me live if I kill both of you. Do you understand now?"

Katherine understood everything now. Trudy's initial

plan had failed. But now, she had Katherine right where she wanted her. She'd probably made sure nothing could be traced back to her, including the tiny numbers engraved on the clasp of those broken pearls.

She'd sent those threats to Katherine as a smoke screen and she'd had someone search Katherine's house for the pearls. Then she tried to isolate Katherine. Hadn't Trudy suggested several times they go together to a remote spa? But Katherine had always been too busy. Thank goodness.

And then Shane had shown up.

"Is this why you want me dead?" she asked, aware that Shane was somewhere nearby. "You hate me because Jacob died in that chopper crash? Or because he still loved me?"

Trudy jerked a finger in her face. "You always had it all. The handsome, powerful man, the beautiful marriage and that blinding celebrity-status that drew people to you. It made me sick because it was all a facade. I had Jacob and the company we created together, until he got greedy. After he died, I tried to figure out a way to get those pearls off your skinny neck. It ends here."

Keeping her eyes on Katherine, Trudy raised a hand toward the man who'd been watching Shane. "Get Warwick and bring him here. I want you to kill him first."

Katherine saw a rising shadow off in the darkness. Shane. She had to protect him.

But it was too late. The guard turned to find an empty spot where Shane had been lying. "He's gone!"

Trudy whirled to stare into the darkness. "You idiot!" Grabbing the gun from the other man, she aimed and fired at the surprised guard, hitting him in the stomach.

And that's when Shane made his move, lunging for

Trudy with a grunt. He knocked her down, rolled and grabbed the gun she'd dropped and took out the other guard before the man even had time to aim his weapon.

"Shane!"

"I'm all right," he said. Winded, he lifted Trudy to a sitting position then reached into her jacket pocket and found her cell phone. "Do you mind? I need to call 911." Shane did so, giving their location while he held the gun on Trudy. Then he called Paco Martinez and gave him the same information.

Trudy looked from Shane to Katherine, terror and madness in her eyes. "I can't let you live. You have to understand. I can't let either of you live. You know everything. They'll kill me."

Shane found some old rope and quickly tied Trudy's hands, holding her firm when she struggled. "You, my dear, talk too much. Too bad for you I have a very good memory."

Shane held the gun on Trudy with one hand while he reached around her and found the other weapon. "If you move, I'll shoot you," he told her as he walked backward toward Kit then went around her chair. Putting the gun on Kit's lap and keeping it aimed toward Trudy, he untied Kit then lifted her up. "How are you?"

"I've been better," she said. Then she reached up and hugged him close. "You're hurt though."

"I've been better," he mimicked, wrapping his working arm around her. "I'll be fine."

"Sit down," Katherine told him, pushing him down in the chair and taking his gun. Off in the distance, the urgent sound of sirens filled the night.

Shane didn't argue. But he smiled up at Katherine while she kept the rifle centered on Trudy Pearson.

"Don't shoot her, luv. She wants to go away, remember? And now, she will, for a very long time."

"Kit?" Trudy looked genuinely scared now. "Kit, you can't let them arrest me. I'll tell them you were in on this, too. You wore those pearls day and night."

Kit walked toward Trudy, the gun centered on her, then bent down to pick up the gleaming gold clasp that lay by her feet. "I don't think that will wash, Trudy. Not when I give the money over to the authorities instead of your cartel."

"She's right," Shane said, his voice gravelly. "We've already found the encrypted files in your home and right about now, someone is probably doing the same at Kit's home, in the senator's study. We have all the evidence we need to put you away for a long time, Mrs. Pearson. We've also checked Katherine's files. They're clean."

"So that's where my files went," Katherine said, her gaze strong on Trudy.

"Sorry, luv. It was for your own protection."

For once, she was so very glad he'd said that.

Two weeks later

"Would you like more tea, dear?"

Katherine looked at Lady Samantha Warwick and shook her head. "No, thank you. Maybe I should go back to my hotel."

"Nonsense," the dark-haired woman said, her serene gray eyes reminding Katherine of her son. "Shane will be here soon. He's usually very prompt."

Katherine didn't respond. Shane was very prompt, and very thorough and very…everything. So why was she in such a panic about seeing him again?

Because after he'd tidied up all the loose ends, he'd taken off for England with a whispered, "I'll be back, if you want me back."

Did he say that to all the women he saved?

"I'm so glad you came across the pond," Lady Samantha said, her gaze moving from the garden to the big stone and brick house on the hill. "Is this your first trip to England?"

"No." Kit admired the woman's manners. Filling time for her wayward son, no doubt. "But it's never looked more beautiful."

"Yes, we're having some good weather." Samantha sipped her tea then put down her cup. "Shane told me about what happened—without giving me the specifics. Horrible."

Kit nodded. "It was horrible."

Trudy had planned the whole scene at the gala, as a scare tactic to get Katherine to leave Austin. She'd hired several men eager to make some extra money and one of those men was supposed to "wound" Kit. Trudy intended to convince Kit to go to a secluded place to recuperate, so Trudy could steal the pearls that rarely left Katherine's neck. But she hadn't planned on Shane being at the gala. Shane, in the meantime, had figured out Trudy was behind everything.

While Kit had continued to defend her.

Was that why he'd left so abruptly? Did he think Kit still blamed him? He had been rather quiet their last day together at Eagle Rock, even when she'd tried to tell him she was sorry.

It didn't matter. Shane Warwick never stayed.

But he'd told her he'd come back one day, if she wanted that. She did. Very much.

So as soon as she'd given a statement and been cleared for travel, she'd come here like a silly school-girl, determined to declare her love for him, no matter the consequences. Because she was not going to let him run away from her love.

"He's changed," Lady Samantha said. "He's more centered and settled. In spite of what you went through, you've been a positive influence on my son."

Katherine decided to be honest about things. "Are you sure? He's known for not making a commitment, or so I've heard."

"Oh, yes, he's known for that but men have a way of changing once they fall in love."

"Is he in love with me?" Katherine asked.

Lady Samantha smiled then glanced over Katherine's shoulder. "Why don't you ask him yourself since he's standing on the terrace looking at you."

Katherine got up and whirled around, her gaze matching his. And without a word, she hurried toward him, her fast walk turning into a headlong run.

He met her in the middle of the garden, his arms opening in a welcoming embrace. "You're here."

Katherine smiled into the tweed of his jacket. "Only because you left me. I had to know why."

He pulled away to give her a relieved stare. "I was afraid."

"You? Afraid?" She could feel the wrapping on his bandaged left arm. "I don't believe that."

"You scare me," he said, crushing her back against him. "I wanted to give you time—"

"No, you wanted to give yourself time," she interrupted, tears in her eyes. "You had to see if this was real, didn't you?"

He looked sheepish. And adorable. "Okay, yes, maybe. But I fully intended to come and fetch you, one way or another."

"Fetch me? You intended to fetch me?"

"Or ask you to run away with me again."

She grinned up at him, her heart joyous. "Hmm. Let me see if I can get this straight. A dashing British secret agent in a precision-cut tweed jacket and a seemingly interested American woman in an overpriced sweater set. Their eyes meet across the country garden, they walk toward each other, smiling and cordial, and the rest is written in the stars."

"Oh, so you've seen that movie, have you?"

"Yes, and I know how it ends."

He reached out and touched a hand to her hair, pulling her toward him. "And tell me, luv, how does it end?"

"Happily ever after, of course."

"I like that ending." He kissed her right there in front of his mother, then lifted his head to gaze down at her. "I love you. I had to be sure though that you love me, so I left—to give you some time to work through your grief and the nightmare you went through."

"I do love you," she said. "I love you so much. And I tried to give *you* some space to work through your aversion to any sort of longtime commitment."

"So you came all this way to tell me that I'm afraid of commitment? And that you love me in spite of that?"

"Yes, I did."

"Did you meet my mother?"

"I did. Lovely woman."

"Do you want to get married in Texas or England, luv?"

Kit sighed and put her arms around him. "We could

start here and work our way back to Texas for another ceremony. I'm sure Lonely Oak is lovely during the fall. And very safe."

He kissed her again. "It shall be doubly safe if you're there, darling. I'll make sure of that. But it won't be lonely anymore. We'll plant another oak—one we can show to our children." Then he took her by the hand and led her toward his mother.

Lady Samantha wiped at her eyes and smiled up at them.

While Katherine smiled up at the Knight who'd come to Texas to save her life. And capture her heart.

* * * * *

Dear Reader,

Have you ever wondered what it would be like to be swept off your feet by a handsome British secret agent? Okay, maybe not everyone thinks about spies the way I do, but it sure is fun to create a spy with a British accent. That's exactly what happened when Shane Warwick popped into my head. Shane, known as the Knight, was charming and cool—traits any good spy needs to have. I had to create a heroine who would match him in every way. Katherine Barton Atkins sure did that and more.

All fun aside, the seriousness of this story took hold of me, too. Katherine had been raised to always be a lady. Proper decorum and impeccable manners were a way of life for this Texas socialite. So it was very hard for her to grieve after her husband's mysterious death. And it was equally hard for her to accept Shane's protection and help. This theme seems a proper metaphor for how we sometimes push God away during times of pain and grief. It's hard to reach out and ask for help when we think we have to put on a good front all the time.

I hope this story entertained you and gave you an adventure and I hope the lessons Shane and Katherine learned showed you that God is always willing to help. It doesn't take a spy to tip us off on that. God is good all the time.

Until next time, may the angels watch over you. Always.

Lenora Worth

THE SOLDIER'S MISSION

But by sorrow of the heart the spirit is broken.
—*Proverbs* 15:13

To my son Kaleb—a true heart hunter.

ONE

He'd had the dream again.

The stifling desert air burned hot, dirty and dry. The acrid smell of charred metal and scorched wires mixed with the metallic, sickly sweet smell of blood all around him. The sound of rapid-fire machine guns mingled with the screams of pain as, one by one, the men in his unit fell. He saw the horror of a landmine exploding against the jagged rocks of the craggy mountainside where they'd been penned down for forty-eight hours. One misstep and three of his men gone in a flash of searing fire and ear-shattering explosions. The others were taken out as the insurgents fought to the finish.

Then, the eerie sound of a deathly silence as the shooting stopped...and even after all of Luke's efforts to save his wounded men, the moans and cries for help eased away…until there was nothing left but scorched dust lifting out over the rocks.

He was the only man left standing. But he wasn't alone on that mountain. And he knew he'd be dead before dusk.

He'd jolted awake, gasping for air, a cold sweat covering his body, his hands shaking, grasping for his machine gun.

Luke "Paco" Martinez sat up and pushed at his damp hair then searched for the glowing green of the digital clock. 6:00 a.m. Old habits died hard. And a good night's sleep was always just beyond his reach.

Barefoot, his cotton pajama bottoms dragging on the cool linoleum of the tiny trailer's floor, Luke went straight to the coffeepot and hit the brew button. And while he waited for the coffee, he stared at the lone bottle of tequila sitting on the window seal.

Stared and remembered the dream, the nightmare, that wouldn't let him find any rest.

Looking away from the tempting bottle of amber liquid, he instead focused on the distant mountains. The desert and mountains here in Arizona were a contrast against the rocky, unforgiving mountains of Afghanistan. Even though this high desert country was harsh and brutal at times, he could find comfort in the tall prickly saguaros and occasional thickets of Joshua trees and pinon pines growing all around his home. Here, he could run toward the mesas and the mountains and find solace, his questioning prayers echoing inside his head while his feet pounded on the dirt, his mind going numb with each step, each beat of his racing heart. *Why was I spared, Lord?*

In the dream, Luke screamed his own rage as he moved headlong into the fray, his M4 carbine popping what seemed like a never-ending round on the insurgents hidden in the hills.

In the dream, he always woke up before they killed him.

And because he did wake up and because he was alive to relive that horrible day over and over, he stared at the liquor bottle while he drank his coffee and told himself he could get through this.

Focus on the mountains, Paco.

That's what his grandfather had told him the day he'd come here to wrestle his soul back from the brink. Focus on the mountains.

He was better now, six months after coming home to Arizona. He was getting better each and every day, in spite of the nightmares. He'd even gone on a few short-term missions for CHAIM, the secret organization he'd been a member of since before he'd joined the army.

He was better now. No more drunken binges, no more fights in restaurants and bars. Not as much pain. The army might not believe that, but his fellow CHAIM agents did, thankfully.

He'd be okay, Luke told himself. He just needed a little more time. And a lot more prayers.

So he drained his coffee and put on his running clothes and headed out into the early morning chill of the ever-changing desert, away from the little trailer that was his home now, away from the nightmares and the memories.

And away from that tempting bottle of golden relief.

She couldn't get his voice out of her head.

Laura Walton thought about the man she'd come to

the desert to find. The man everyone was worried about.
The man who, a few weeks ago, had called the CHAIM
hotline in the middle of the night.

"My father died in Vietnam," the grainy, low voice
said over the phone line. "My brother was wounded in
Desert Storm. He's in a wheelchair now. And I just got
back from Afghanistan. Lost my whole unit. Lost everyone. I think I need to talk to somebody."

Laura had been on call that night, volunteering to
man the hotline that CHAIM held open for all of its
operatives, the world over.

But only one call had come to the Phoenix hotline on
that still fall night. One call from a man who was suffering a tremendous amount of survivor's guilt.

Laura understood this kind of guilt. She didn't have
survivor's guilt, but her own guilt ate away at her just
the same. She'd lost a patient recently. A young patient
who'd taken his own life. She'd failed the teenager.

She didn't want to fail Luke Martinez.

The soldier's tormented words, spoken with such
raw pain, had stayed with her long after the man had
hung up.

Which he did, immediately after confessing that he
needed to talk.

It hadn't been easy convincing her CHAIM supervisors in Phoenix to let her go through case files and
match the man to the words, then come to this remote
spot near the Grand Canyon to find Luke "Paco" Martinez. Nor had it been easy taking time away from the
clinic where she worked as a counselor to Christians
suffering all sorts of crises.

But this crisis trumped all the rest. This man needed
help. Her help. And somehow, in her guilt-laden mind,

Laura had decided this was a sign from God to redeem her. She had to find this man. So she'd traced his cell number to this area.

So here she sat in a dump of a roadside café called The Last Stop, hoping she'd find the illusive Paco Martinez, also known as "The Warrior." Fitting name, Laura thought now as she dared to take another sip of the too-dark, too-strong coffee the stoic old man at the counter had poured for her. While she relied on the tip she'd received about Luke coming here every morning for breakfast, Laura went back over his file.

The army neither confirmed nor denied it, but Luke Martinez was reported to be some sort of Special Forces soldier—a shadow warrior—as they were often called. And while the elite Delta Force didn't put a lot of emphasis on rank, preferring to use code names or nicknames instead of stating rank, from what she could glean Martinez was a hero who'd been the lone survivor of a highly secretive mission to rescue two American soldiers trapped behind enemy lines in Afghanistan.

Everything about the mission had gone bad. Luke's team of men had been dropped by helicopter onto the mountain with orders to find the two soldiers and bring them home. After taking one outpost and locating the two badly beaten soldiers, Luke's team had made it back to the pickup spot to wait on a helicopter out. But the enemy had advanced behind them and taken out all of Luke's men, including the two his team has rescued. Things got fuzzy after that, but according to the rumors swirling around, The Warrior had managed not only to escape the men who tried to take him hostage, but he'd killed all of them in the process. And he refused to leave that mountain until the rescue team had recovered all of his men.

Except the one who'd seen all of them die. Luke Martinez had survived and for that, he was suffering mightily.

So he'd come home an unknown hero—that was the code of Special Forces—but Martinez didn't want to be a hero, didn't care that most would never know what he'd tried to do on that mountaintop. He was still in pain, still reeling from losing his team members. Deep inside, he was having a crisis. Post-traumatic stress over losing his men and for what he considered his failure— not bringing the stranded soldiers back safely.

That had caused a bout of serious drinking and many hours spent in jail cells and later with stress counselors and army specialists.

As well as CHAIM counselors such as Laura. His CHAIM team had stood by Luke, with one stipulation. He had to go to their remote retreat center in Ireland—Whelan Castle—for some serious debriefing and counseling sessions. And hopefully, to find some peace.

Luke had agreed. And he'd improved after his three months in Ireland. Then he'd come home to Arizona to rest. But he'd been called out on a mission in Texas to help Shane Warwick, known as The Knight, guard and protect prominent Texas socialite Katherine Atkins.

According to the official report, Luke had done a good job backing up Warwick and they'd brought down not only the woman who was trying to kill Katherine, but a ruthless oil-smuggling cartel to boot.

But this late night phone call had come *after* Luke had returned from Texas.

Which brought Laura back to the here-and-now. And this stand-on-its-own-legs coffee.

Laura motioned to the old man behind the counter, finding the courage to ask him the one question she'd come here to ask. "Excuse me, sir, do you know a man named Luke Martinez?"

The old man with the silver-black braid going down his back didn't respond to her question. Instead he just stared at her with such opaque eyes, Laura felt as if the man could see into her very soul.

"Sir?"

Finally the man shuffled up to the counter, his tanned, aged skin reminding Laura of one of the craggy mountain faces beyond the desert. He wore a white cotton button-down shirt that hung like a tunic on his body, giving him the look of someone on their way to a fiesta.

Before she could ask the question again, he leaned forward, his frown as stand-up as the coffee. "Would you like some pie with that coffee?"

Surprised, Laura shook her head. "Ah, no thanks. I had a granola bar in the car. About the man I'm looking for—"

"Can't help you there," the old man replied, turning before Laura could finish the sentence.

But the old man didn't need to help her. The rickety screen door flapped open and she felt the hair on the back of her neck rising, felt his eyes on her even before she looked into the aged mirror running along the back wall and saw his reflection there. Completely paralyzed with confusion and doubt, she lowered her gaze then heard that distinctive voice without turning to face him.

"I'll take some pie, Grandfather." He advanced toward Laura. "And while you're getting my pie, I'll ask this pretty lady why she's trying so hard to find me."

Luke stood perfectly still, his senses on edge while he analyzed the woman sitting at the counter. Her brown hair fell around her face and shoulders in soft waves. She wore a sensible beige lightweight sweater, a faded pair of jeans and hiking boots. Interesting. He could smell her perfume, a mixture of sweet flowers and vanilla. Nice.

Then she turned to face him and Luke's gaze caught hers, the deep blue of her eyes reminding him of a mountain sky just before dusk. The look in those eyes amused him even while it destroyed him. She was afraid of him. And she probably had good reason.

"Mr. Martinez?"

Her voice was soft but firm. She quickly recovered from her first glimpse, Luke noted. She got points for that, at least. Most people just ran the other way when he scowled at them.

"Paco," he replied. "That's what everyone around here calls me."

She reached out a dainty hand, her nails clean and painted with a clear sparkle of polish, her fingers devoid of rings. "I'm Laura Walton."

Luke took her hand for a second then let it go, her perfume warming his fingers. "Okay. You already know me and now I know your name. Why are you here?"

She leaned in then glanced around the nearly empty diner. "I'm…from CHAIM."

He liked the way she pronounced it—"Chi-Im", with the *CH* sounding more like a *K* using the Hebrew enunciation. He did not like that she was here.

Luke pushed a hand through his hair and sat down

beside her, the weight of his body causing the old spinning stool to squeak and groan. "Coffee, Grandfather, please. And two pieces of buttermilk pie."

"I don't want pie."

Luke didn't argue with her. "Make that one piece and two forks, Grandfather." He waited for his pretending-not-to-be-interested grandfather to bring the requested food. Then he shoved one fork at her and took his own to attack the creamy yellow-crusted pie. "Eat."

She looked down at the plate then picked up the fork. "I don't eat sweets."

"Try it."

Luke took his time eating his own side of the pie. Then he sipped the dark brew, his gaze hitting at hers in the old, pot-marked mirror running behind the cluttered counter. "Now, why are you here?"

She chewed a nibble of pie then swallowed, her eyes opening big while she slanted a gaze toward him. "One of your friends was concerned."

"I don't have a lot of friends."

"The Knight," she said on a low whisper.

"Just saw him a few weeks ago."

"I know. He wanted to make sure you were okay."

Luke knew she wasn't telling him the whole story. He'd talked to Shane Warwick two days ago. The man was crazy in love and making big plans for his upcoming Texas spring wedding. Shane was going to repeat the vows he'd spoken in England—to the same woman he'd married in England. He'd called Luke to invite him to the wedding but Shane had asked Luke how he was doing. Polite conversation or pointed inquiry?

"Who are you?" he asked, this time all the smile gone out of the question. "And don't lie to me, lady."

Laura swallowed down more coffee, hoping it would give her more courage. "I told you, I'm from CHAIM."

"Who really sent you?"

Laura couldn't hide the truth. "I... I came on my own. I mean, I got clearance to come but I asked to come and see you."

His smile was so quick and full of stealth, she almost missed it. But if he ever did really smile, Laura believed it would do her in for good. The man was an interesting paradox of good-looking coupled with dangerous and scary. His dark hair, longer than army regulations allowed since he was usually undercover, sliced in damp inky lines across his scarred face and around his muscled neck. His eyes were onyx, dark and rich and unreadable. His skin was as aged and marked as tanned leather. It rippled over hard muscle and solid strength each time he moved. He wore a black T-shirt and soft-washed jeans over battered boots. And he smelled fresh and clean, as if he'd just stepped out of a secret waterfall somewhere.

His gaze cut from her to the mirror, watching, always watching the door of the diner.

"Why did you feel you had to come and see me?"

Laura prided herself on being honest. So with a swallow and a prayer, she said, "Because you called me— on the CHAIM hotline—late one night. You said you needed someone to talk to. So I'm here."

Luke lowered his head, the shame of that phone call announcing how weak he'd felt that night. He'd had the dream again, maybe because he had just returned from Texas and more death and dishonesty. Maybe because he would always have the dream and he'd always feel weak and guilty and filled with such a self-loathing that it took his breath away and made him want to drink that whole bottle of tequila sitting on the windowsill.

"I shouldn't have called," he said, the words hurting and tight against his throat muscles. "You didn't have to come here, Ms. Walton. I'm fine now."

She went from being intimidated to being professional with the blink of her long lashes. "You didn't sound fine that night. I called Shane Warwick and he arranged permission for me to come and see you. I live in Phoenix."

Luke whirled on the stool, his face inches from hers. "Then go back to Phoenix and leave me alone."

"But…you…shouldn't be alone. I'm a counselor. You can trust me and you can talk to me about anything. Even if you've slipped up and had a drink—"

"Leave. Now," Luke said, grabbing her by the arm.

"But—"

"I haven't had a drink in four months and I don't need you here. All I need right now is to be left alone."

He saw the concern in her eyes, saw the hesitation in her movements. She wasn't going to leave without a fight.

Luke glanced toward his grandfather. The old man's face was set in stone, as always. But Luke could see the hope shining in the seventy-nine-year-old's black eyes.

He didn't want to disappoint his grandfather, but Luke didn't want this woman hovering over him, trying to get inside his head, either.

"I'll take you back to your car," he said, guiding her with a push toward the door.

Laura Walton shot a look at him over her shoulder. "I have to make sure you're ready to come back to CHAIM full-time now that you're back from the Middle East and out of the army."

"I'm ready," Luke said on a strained breath. Why had he dialed that number that night? Now he had trouble here in the form of a dark-haired female. A pretty, sweet-smelling woman with big blue eyes and an academic, analyzing mind. The worst kind.

"Could we have a talk?" she asked, digging her heels in with dainty force.

"We just had a talk and now we're done."

He had her out the door, the warmth of the morning sun searing them to the dirt-dry parking lot. "Where's your car?"

"Over there." She pointed to a small red economy car. "It's a rental. My car is in the shop."

Luke tugged her forward until they were beside the car. "Then you can be on your way back to the rental counter. Have a nice trip back to Phoenix."

She turned to stare up at him, her eyes so imploring and so blue, he had to blink.

And during that blink, a bullet ricocheted off the windshield of her car, shattering glass all around them in a spray of glittering white-hot slivers.

TWO

Paco shoved Laura down behind the car, his hand covering her head. "Friends of yours?"

"I don't know," she said on a gasp of air, the shock of her words telling him she was being honest. "What's going on?"

"You tell me." He lifted his head an inch. And was rewarded with another round of rifle fire. "Somebody doesn't like you being here, sweetheart."

She tried to peek around the car's bumper, but he held her down. Glaring up at him, she whispered, "I don't know what you're talking about. Are you sure they aren't shooting at you?"

"That is a possibility," he said on a growl. "I've made a lot of enemies lately."

"Anybody in particular?"

Paco thought about the laundry list of sins he'd committed in the name of grief. "We don't have that long. I have to get you out of here."

She seemed to like that idea. "So how do you plan to do that?"

"Good question." Paco pulled his sunglasses out of his T-shirt pocket and shoved them on then slowly lifted so he could scan the surrounding desert and mountains. "If it's a sniper, we're stuck here. If we move, they could take us out in a split second. But if they're just using a twelve-gauge or some other sort of rifle, we might have a chance at making a run for the café."

"My windshield is shattered," she said, her tone sensible. "That means they could do the same to us if we move."

"True. But a moving target is a lot harder to pinpoint than a parked car."

"Maybe they weren't aiming at us."

Paco glanced around the empty parking lot. "We're the only customers right now."

"Your grandfather?"

"Doesn't have an enemy anywhere in the world." Paco held her there, the scent of her perfume merging with the scent of dirt and grim and car fumes. "And if I know my grandfather, he's standing at the door of the café with his Remington." He rolled over to pick up a rock. Then with a quick lift of his arm, he threw it toward the small porch of the rickety restaurant.

His grandfather opened the dark screen door then shouted. "One shooter, Paco. Coming from the west. Want me to cover you?"

Paco took his grandfather's age and agility into consideration. "Only if you don't expose yourself."

"I won't."

"Are you sure he can handle this?" Laura asked, her words breathy and low.

"Oh, yeah." Paco grabbed her, lifting her to face him. "Now listen to me. We're going to make a run for the porch. Grandfather will cover us. You'll hear gunshots but just keep running."

Fright collided with sensibility in her eyes. "What if I get shot?"

"I won't let that happen."

"But you can't protect me and yourself, too."

"Yes, I can," Paco said, images from his time in special ops swirling in slow motion in his head. "I can. But you have to stay to my left and you have to run as fast as you can."

"Okay. I ran track in college."

"Good. That's good. I need you to stay low and sprint toward that door on the count of three."

She did as he said, crouching to a start. Paco counted and prayed. "One, two, three."

And then they took off together while his grandfather stepped out onto the porch and shot a fast round toward the flash in the foothills about a hundred yards away. Paco put himself between her and the shooter and felt the swish of bullets all around his body. Then he pushed her onto the porch and into the door, holding it open for his grandfather to step back inside.

The old man quickly shut the door then turned to stare at Paco and Laura, his rifle held up by his side. "Would either of you care to explain this?"

Laura's gaze moved from the old man to Paco. "I don't know who's out there. As far as I know, no one wants *me* dead." Watching Paco, she could believe the man might have a few enemies—probably several heart-broken women among them. "What about you?" she asked, wondering what was going on inside his head.

His grandfather chuckled at that. "Only about half the population of Arizona, for starters."

"Thanks." Paco replied with a twisted grin. "Grandfather, I forgot my manners, what with being shot at and all. This is Laura Walton. She thinks I need her help."

"Do you?" the old man asked, putting his gun down to reach out a gnarled hand to Laura. "Nice to meet you. Sorry you almost got shot. I'm Wíago—Walter Rainwater."

"Nice to meet you, too," Laura said, her breath settling down to only a semi-rapid intake. The weirdness of the situation wasn't lost on her but she was too timid to shout out her true feelings. Turning back to Paco, she asked, "What do we do now?"

Paco didn't answer. Instead, he went through a door toward the back of the café then returned with a mean-looking rifle. "*You* wait here with Grandfather."

Walter put the Closed sign on the door. "It was a slow morning anyway."

"It's always a slow morning around here," Paco quipped. "Even when we aren't being shot at."

Laura twisted her fingers in Paco's sleeve. "What are you doing?"

"I'm going out there to track that shooter."

"But he might kill you."

"Always a chance, but don't worry about me too much. I think I can handle this."

Laura didn't know why it seemed so important to keep him safe. Maybe because she hadn't had a chance to get inside his head and help him over his grief. Or maybe because while he frightened her, he also intrigued her and she'd like to explore that scenario.

Shocked at her wayward thoughts, she chalked it up to being nearly killed and said, "Well, be careful. I have to give a full report on you."

"I'm used to having full reports done on me," he replied, his dark eyes burning with a death wish kind of disregard. "If I bite the bullet, you can just tell the powers that be that I died fighting."

Laura ventured a glance at his grandfather and saw the worry in the old man's eyes. That same concern strengthened her spine and gave her the courage to reason with him. "But we don't know who you're fighting this time."

"I've never known who I've been fighting." Paco graced her with a long, hard stare before he pivoted and headed toward the back of the building. "Stay put and lock both doors. Don't come out until you hear me calling."

Paco crept through the flat desert, willing himself to blend in with the countryside. The black shirt wasn't very good camouflage but it would have to do. If he could make it around the back way and surprise the gunman, he'd have a chance of figuring out who was out there and why.

So he did a slow belly-crawl through the shrubs and thickets, careful to watch for snakes and scorpions. Stopping to catch his breath underneath a fan palm, he held still and did a scan of the spot where his grandfather had indicated the shooter might be hiding. A cluster of prickly pear cacti stood spreading about four feet high and wide alongside a cropping of Joshua trees centered on the rise of the foothills leading toward a small mesa. But Paco didn't see anything or anyone moving out there.

Thinking maybe the culprit was hiding much in the same way as he, Paco slid another couple of feet, careful to be as silent as possible. The sun had moved up in the sky and even though it was November, the desert's temperature had moved right along with it. Sweat beaded on his forehead and poured down his face. His shirt was now damp and dusty. He could taste the sand, feel it in his eyes. For a minute, he was back on that mountainside, waiting, just waiting for the enemy to make a move.

But fifteen minutes later, Paco hadn't seen any signs of human life in this desolate desert. So he threw a clump of rocks toward the thicket and waited for a hail of bullets to hit him.

Nothing.

Grunting, Paco lifted to a crouch, his gun aimed at the Joshua trees a few feet ahead. He was a trained sniper so he didn't think the other guy would stand a chance. But then, he'd been wrong before.

Laura hated the silence of this place.

Walter Rainwater didn't talk. Not at all. If she asked a question, he'd answer "Yes", "No" or "We'll wait for Paco."

She was tired of waiting for Paco. So she got up to look out the window for the hundredth time. "He should have been back by now."

A hand on her arm caused her to spin around. Tugging Laura toward a booth, Paco said, "We need to talk."

Surprised and wondering more than a little bit how he'd snuck up on her, she pulled a notebook from the shoulder bag she'd managed to hang on to in all the chaos. Maybe the episode outside had triggered something in Paco.

But she was wrong. "Put that away," he said, pushing at the notebook. "We're not talking about me. I need to ask *you* a few questions. We have to figure out who's trying to kill you."

Laura took in his dirty shirt and the sweat beads on his skin. "Did you find someone?"

He shook his head, took the water his grandfather sat on the table. "No. Whoever was there is gone now. I found shell casings and tracks, footprints out toward the highway." Then he handed her a dirty business card. "I did find this."

Laura looked down at the piece of paper then gulped air. "That's one of my cards."

His smirk held a hint of accusation. "Yeah, saw your name right there on it. But nothing after that. I guess once we managed to get inside here, they left. But I don't think they dropped this card by accident. They wanted you to know they were here."

"But why?"

Instead of answering, he drank the water down, giving Laura plenty of time to take in his slinky, spiky bangs and slanted unreadable eyes while she wondered about why the shooter had left *her* business card.

He put the glass down and met her gaze head-on. "I think you know why. Ready to tell me the truth?"

"Me?" Shocked, Laura drew back, her head hitting the vinyl of the booth. "I told you as far as I know, no one's after me."

Paco leaned across the table, his expression as black as his eyes. "Yes, ma'am, someone is after you. Another inch and your rental car's windshield would still be intact. But you'd probably be dead." He sat back, his big hands centered against the aged oak of the table. "Now, think real hard and tell me if you've had any hard-case patients lately."

"None, other than you," she replied, the triumph she should have felt disappearing at the ferocious glare in his eyes.

"Look, lady, I didn't ask you to come here. And up until about an hour ago, no one cared about me or what I'm doing. This place is about as remote as you can get. So I figure someone tailed you here and waited for the right opportunity to shoot at you. And that means you've probably got an unstable client out there with an ax to grind. So quit insulting me and think real hard about some of the people you've counseled lately." He leaned over the table again, his tone soft and daring. "Besides me."

Laura stared across at him, wondering how he could stay so calm when they were sitting here with a possible sniper still on the loose. "I don't have a clue—"

"Think about it," he said in that deep, low voice that sent ripples of awareness down her spine. "How many people have you talked to in say, the last three or four months?"

"Too many to tell," she retorted. "I'd have to have access to my files."

"You mean by computer?"

"Yes." She tapped her big purse. "I didn't bring my laptop with me. Besides, I can't download every case history I have on file."

Paco pulled a slick phone out of his pocket. "What if I get us some help?"

"But no one has access to my patient files. That's confidential."

"I know someone who can break into those files."

She shook her head. "I can't allow that. My clients trust me."

"That won't matter if you're dead."

The man certainly cut right to the chase.

"Who are you going to call?"

"Kissie Pierre. You've probably heard of her. She keeps computer records on all the CHAIM agents and she keeps files on anyone who has any dealings with those agents. And that includes counselors."

"The Woman at the Well. But she can't help us with this type of thing."

"If you give her some names, she'll be able to crack your files and compare notes."

"Confidentially?"

"Yes, completely confidential, I promise."

"Legal?"

"As legal as we can make it. This is an emergency. But if you think you can remember without us going to that extreme then talk to me."

Laura preferred that method to hacking into private files. "Let me make a list of names. Maybe that will bring back some memories."

"Good." Paco grabbed her notebook. "Got a pen?"

She found a pen in her purse then handed it over to him. Walter passed by with phantom quietness, his rifle held at his chest. "Nobody coming to call. I think we're in the clear."

Paco looked at the door. "Keep an eye out, Grandfather. They might try to sneak up on us again."

Walter nodded, his solid presence a comfort to Laura.

Paco and his grandfather were close. She could tell by the respect Paco offered the old man and by the way they teased each other, both serious and stoic but with a trace of mirth in their eyes.

"Are you thinking?" Paco asked, his gaze cutting to the windows and the door. "We don't have much time. They might decide to come back for another visit. And bring friends along."

Laura sank back, terrified of that prospect. "I'm a pastoral counselor. I mostly deal with church members with marriage problems, those who've lost a loved one, or teenagers who are going through angst. Things like that. And CHAIM agents and workers, of course."

"Of course. Anyone who stands out in your mind?"

She put her head down, bringing her right arm up to settle on the table, then leaned her chin against her fist, a dark thought creeping into her mind. In that brief moment, Laura thought of only one possible suspect. "About a month ago, we had a teenager come to the clinic. He was upset about something his father had done."

"Go on."

Not wanting to divulge the particulars, she shook her head. "I can't talk about it—except that the teen was traumatized by what had happened. I counseled him, told him how to get help from the authorities next time it happened. He didn't want to report the incident, but I could tell he was afraid. He was a lot stronger and calmer after our first couple of sessions, though. Then he didn't come back."

"Did he seem angry at you?"

"No, he was angry at the world." And his father. The man had been extremely demanding and controlling. How could she tell Paco this without getting upset or giving away personal information? Or her acute sense of failure. "The young man killed himself about two weeks after he'd talked to me."

Paco scribbled some notes. "What was his name?"

"Is this necessary?"

"We have to assume, yes."

"Kyle Henner. He was sixteen."

She watched as Paco pulled up a number on his phone. "Kissie, it's Paco. Yeah, I'm okay. I need you to run a name for me. See what you can find out about a kid from Phoenix named Kyle Henner." He held the phone away. "Father's name?"

Laura hesitated then said, "Lawrence Henner. He's a big-time developer of some sort. He owns a lot of different companies. Lots of money and lots of power. He was devastated about what happened."

She didn't add that the man was also a walking time bomb who'd verbally abused not only his son but his wife, too. His wife left him after Kyle's suicide. And now that she thought about it, Lawrence Henner was just the kind of man to blame someone else for his son's death.

Someone like her, maybe?

Paco finished his conversation with Kissie then turned to Laura. "She'll get back to us. And if you think about anything else you can tell me about this kid, let me know."

"His father is ruthless," she said, her nerves sparkling with apprehension. "But I don't think he'd try to shoot me. He'd just find a way to ruin my life, probably."

"Or if he's that powerful, he could send someone else to shoot you."

She swallowed back her worries. "Last I heard, Mr. Henner had left the country."

"That could be a red flag."

"Or maybe he needed to get away from everything in the same way you did?"

He gave her a hard stare. "Maybe. Only I'm not the one out there in the hills with a gun, now, am I?"

Laura shivered at his words. No, he wasn't out there trying to shoot people. But if he didn't unload some of his own grief soon, he could be the next one.

How in the world could she help Paco Martinez deal with post-traumatic stress if someone was trying to finish her off before she even got started? That thought caused her to gasp and grab at Paco's hand.

"Did you remember something else?"

"No, but I just realized something."

His dark eyes swirled with questions. "Spit it out."

"What if that person out there was trying to *stop* me from talking to *you?*"

THREE

She had a point there. And she had already suggested he might be the target. But killing her for talking to him—or to keep her from talking to him—that was a different twist. Paco couldn't deny he had people gunning for him on so many levels. But to try and take out a pretty, innocent woman just because she was trying to help him. Who would want to do that? Maybe the shooter *had* been after *him* to begin with. That made more sense.

But he'd gone on a long run early this morning. It would have been easy for someone to spot him and take him out there in the desert. And by the time anybody found him, the vultures and other predators would have finished him off, anyway. No, this shooting had been timed for her arrival, by Paco's way of thinking.

"So maybe I should be asking you all these questions," she said, her expression bordering on smug. "I've read your case file. You've had quite a career in both special ops and with CHAIM. Both classified, of course, but I know things went bad on your last mission in Afghanistan. That's a lot of stress for any one man."

Paco wanted to laugh out loud, except a burning rage kept him from cracking a smile. That and the way she'd changed from timid to tempest by turning the tables on him. "You have no idea, darlin'."

Her expression turned sympathetic, which only made things worse. He could handle anything but pity. "I think I do. That's why you called me that night."

He got up, stomping around the small café, his gaze hitting on an old shelf full of several carved wooden figurines of warriors astride horses his grandfather had created to sell right along refrigerator magnets, greasy hamburgers and ice-cold soft drinks. Grandfather Rainwater was content with his life.

Paco, however, was still struggling with his.

And this perky little counselor lady wasn't helping matters. Neither was being shot at so early in the day.

Remembering his midnight-hour shout-out, he said, "I shouldn't have called the hotline that night. False alarm."

"You called for a reason. Maybe someone else out there thinks you have a problem."

Paco turned to lean over the table, glad when she slid into the corner of the booth. Glad and a little ashamed that he'd stoop to a frowning intimidation to make her go away. "You wanna know why I called that night? Really want to know?" He didn't wait for her to nod. Pushing so close he could see the swirling violet-blue of her eyes, he said, "I wanted to take a drink. I wanted

to get so drunk I could sleep for a week without nightmares or guilt or regret."

He lifted up and sank back down, the shock in her
vivid eyes undoing him. "But I promised that old man
in the kitchen back there that I was done with drunken
brawls and feeling sorry for myself. I respect him and I
didn't want to let him down. You see, he lost his son—
in-law—my father—to the Vietnam War. And you probably know about my brother—he's in a wheelchair,
compliments of Desert Storm. But…it's hard sometimes, in the middle of the night. So I wanted a drink,
okay. But I didn't take that drink. Instead I prayed really hard and in a moment of sheer desperation, I dialed
the number on the card Warwick gave me and blurted
out all of my frustrations to you."

Hitting a finger hard on the table, he said, "I hope
you're satisfied now. All clear?"

"Do you still want to drink?" she asked in a silky-
strong whisper, her wide-eyed expression daring him
to deny it.

Paco looked down at her, saw the strength pushing away the fear in her eyes, the solid concern out-
maneuvering the shock on her face. He had to admire
her spunk. His grandfather was the only person in the
world who never backed down when it came to Paco
and his moods.

Maybe he's finally met someone else worthy of that
kind of status. Someone else he could learn to respect.
And someone else who was willing to go the distance
with him.

"Yes, I still want a drink," he said, surprised at this
whole conversation. "But I won't take another one. I
go to my AA meetings on a regular basis. I'm better

now, I told you. So let's focus on the problem we have here, right now."

The doubtful stare she gave him implied she didn't believe him but she nodded her head in understanding. And right now, Paco couldn't worry about what she thought.

"Are you driving back to Phoenix today?" he asked, pulling her up out of the booth.

The confusion in her eyes slammed head-on into his own conflicting feelings. "No. I have a hotel room at the foot of the Grand Canyon." Looking sheepish, she said, "I thought if I couldn't find you I'd do a little hiking."

He drew in air, thinking it a blessing she'd found him. Just the thought of her alone near the Canyon with a lunatic tracking her sent fingers of dread racing across his spine. "Does anyone know where you are?"

"My parents and my supervisor at the clinic."

"Would they tell anyone else?"

"They might mention I'm at the Canyon. I didn't exactly post what I was doing. Just told them I'd be gone for a few days on a trip to locate a client."

A knock at the restaurant door caused Paco to spin around. His grandfather came out of the kitchen. "It's a delivery man bringing fresh produce," Walter said, waving Paco away. "Sorry. They usually pull around to the back."

Paco watched as Walter headed to open the door, the hair on the back of his neck bristling. His gaze hit Laura's, both of them realizing too late—

"Grandfather!"

Paco went into motion, rushing toward the door. But Walter already had it open, a smile on his face. "Joseph, why didn't you—"

A fist in Walter's face knocked the old man back onto the floor. Walter hit his head on the corner of a bench as he went down. Then he didn't move.

Paco heard Laura's scream even while he rushed the man at the door, taking the intruder by surprise, one hand pressing down on the man's weapon hand and the other one on his throat. With a grunt and heavy pressure on the wrist, Paco forced the man to drop the handgun he was carrying. But his opponent didn't let that stop him. He reached around with his other hand and tried to bring Paco down. Paco countered with an upper-cut to the man's chin. Then they went down with fists popping against skin. The man was big and solid but Paco didn't let up until he had him rolled over faceup. Struggling to hold the man down, Paco memorized his face—scarred and brutal—just before he slammed his fist back into it.

Laura ran to Walter. "Mr. Rainwater? Are you all right?" Paco's grandfather didn't respond. Blood poured out of his nose and his breathing was shallow. Deciding the best thing she could do right now was to help Paco, she searched for a weapon and saw Walter's rifle leaning against the kitchen door. Without thinking, Laura grabbed it, trying to focus on the man who'd managed to get in and knock out Paco's grandfather. When Paco rolled the man over and begin hitting him in the face, she waited, her pulse flat-lining then spurting into overdrive. But the stranger reached up and managed to get his hands around Paco's neck. Paco grunted, working to flip the man over. When that didn't work, he tried hitting at the man again but he couldn't break away.

Pushing at the man's thick arms, Paco finally managed to get his own fingers around the other man's throat.

Then it became a battle of wills as both held tight, each trying to squeeze the life out of the other. She had to do something. If she didn't stop this, Paco might not make it.

Laura raised the gun, her heart beating a prayer for strength. And a prayer for good eyesight. She'd come across the state to save Paco, not watch him die. She would have to shoot the intruder.

Paco knew he wouldn't be able to hold out much longer. Matched in sheer strength by the other man, he fought for control—and his life. With each grunt, each surge of renewed energy, he wrestled and pushed his fingers against the stranger's thick throat muscles. If he could just find the right amount of pressure—

The room shook with a thundering roar and then the man holding Paco in a death grip went limp, his hands loosening and falling away, his expression going from determined and enraged to a surprised tranquility. Paco watched while the intruder's bulging, hate-filled eyes closed and he fell back on the floor with a heavy thud. For a minute, Paco didn't let go of his own frozen grip on the man's throat. But the silence and his own fast-moving breath brought him out of his stupor.

Looking up and around, he caught at a hitched breath. "Laura?"

She stood with the shotgun aimed high, her whole body trembling. "I'm okay."

Paco hopped up and stared down at the blood flowing from the stranger's side. The man wasn't breathing. Then he hurried to her. "Laura?"

"Your grandfather," she said, pointing a shaking hand toward the floor. "Go check on him!"

Paco took the gun, prying it away from her white-knuckled fingers to carefully lower it to a table. Then he went into action.

"Grandfather?" Paco felt for a pulse, relief washing through him when he found a faint beat pumping inside his grandfather's wrinkled neck. "Wíago, talk to me!" Turning Walter's head, he saw blood on the floor then felt around until he found the deep gash on the old man's skull. "He's bleeding from his nose and he hit his head. We need to get him to a doctor."

"I'll call 911."

Paco lifted up, torn between getting the dead man out of the way and taking care of his grandfather. He didn't have a choice. His grandfather could die. They had to call for help.

"I'll do it," he told Laura. Thinking about the implications of the scene, he said, "I'll have to explain this was self-defense." He pulled out his phone and dialed, telling the operator to hurry. "My grandfather was attacked by an intruder and when he fell, he hit his head. He's not responding. Yes, he has a pulse, but it's weak." He hurried to the man lying near the door and felt his pulse. "And the intruder is dead. Yes, from a gunshot wound. Can you please send someone?"

After giving the dispatcher their location, he brought a blanket from the small den in the back and wrapped it around his grandfather, then checked him over again to be sure there were no other injuries. After doing everything he could to make Walter comfortable, Paco left the dead man where he was—afraid to disturb the scene. Then he finally turned to Laura.

And saw that she was about to fall into a heap on the floor.

"Laura," he said, hurrying to her, wishing the nearest hospital wasn't so far away. "Laura, are you sure you're all right?"

She bobbed her head, her arms crossed around her midsection, her gaze locked on the gruesome site of the man by the door. "Is that man dead?"

He pulled her close, leveling his gaze on her until she looked at him. "Yes, he is. You saved my life." He was as amazed by that as she seemed to be.

"I... I didn't know what to do. I had to stop him... and I thought I'd shot you at first. Is your grandfather going to be okay?"

With each word, tears brimmed in her eyes until one lone drop moved down her right cheek. Paco reached up and caught the tear, keeping his gaze locked on her. "I hope so. I think he's got a concussion and he'll need stitches for the gash on his head. I've made him comfortable and the paramedics are on the way. But it'll take them a few minutes. Let me check you over."

She tried to push away and stumbled, her face deadly pale. "I'm okay. I... Paco, I think I'm going to be sick."

Paco hurried her to the tiny bathroom in the back and waited at the door, keeping watch on his grandfather while he paced. When she came out a few minutes later, her skin was whitewashed with shock and she held a damp paper towel to her mouth.

"Better?" he asked, guiding her to a chair.

"I think so." She looked up at him, her eyes as blue as a desert sky at midnight. "I've never killed anyone before. Now I know how you must feel."

That statement punctured Paco's heart. How could

such an innocent woman ever know or understand the way he felt? How could she be so brave, coming here to find him simply because she was worried about him? How could she get herself caught up in something that was probably of his making, put herself on the line like that for him, when she didn't even know him?

Before he could speak, she touched a trembling hand toward his heart. "I know what you were searching for that night, Paco."

Paco swallowed back the lump in his throat, the sound of distant sirens echoing inside his head right along with the rising echo of his pulse. She'd called him Paco. That meant she trusted him now, meant he'd allowed her to get that close already.

"What then?" he asked, unable to stay quiet, unable to comprehend this whole morning.

"You were looking for your heart. You wanted your soul back." She cleared her throat, her delicate hand warm on his chest, her gaze full of understanding and redemption. "I read a poem once where there was this heart hunter. He was searching for his own heart. He wanted to feel that warmth in his soul again. You know, that warmth that comes from faith and love and grace. And forgiveness. And so do you, I think. That's something we can all understand, something everyone longs for."

Paco lifted away, his head down. Grandfather always said there were no coincidences in life. He believed the Father knew all and saw all. Had God seen Paco's pain that night, the struggle for his soul, the struggle he'd battled through between the Bible he'd clutched and the bottle that was trying to clutch him, all night long and well into the early light?

Had God sent Laura to him?

"We have to get you out of here," he said in response, his thoughts too raw and fresh to express right now. He didn't know how to voice his thoughts, even on a good day. "They'll want a statement. Let me do all the talking. If they do ask you questions, just answer as briefly as possible. And be completely honest."

She dropped her hand away. "I have to tell them I shot that man."

Missing her warmth and needing to protect her, Paco said, "We could tell them I did it."

"No, I won't lie to them. And you said to be honest. I shot him because he was trying to kill you. That's the truth."

Paco knew she was right. They couldn't lie. But he had a very bad feeling about this whole situation. And he knew this wasn't over. Someone had sent a killer here two different times this morning. And they would keep coming until they hit their target.

He headed to the door to show the paramedics where to go and to greet the two officers pulling up outside. Then he glanced back at Laura to make sure she was holding up.

She gave him a wobbly half smile, her eyes still moist. Then she pushed at her hair and straightened her clothes, her head lifting as her eyes met his again.

And Paco had to wonder who in the world would want to hurt this woman?

She'd come here to help him, but in doing so she might have put herself in danger. Then she'd somehow managed to shoot a man in order to save Paco, which meant she was stronger than she looked. But that also meant she was now Paco's responsibility.

He had to get his grandfather to a safe place and he had to protect this woman no matter what. Maybe in the process, he just might find that heart she thought he was searching for.

Or lose it completely to the woman who'd come with such an unexpected determination into his life.

FOUR

Paco went into action after the ambulance and the sheriff's deputies left. Good thing the deputies knew his grandfather and him well enough to access the situation and keep it under wraps for now.

"I have to call my brother." Touching a finger to his phone, he waited, his eyes never leaving Laura. "Hey, Buddy. It's me, Paco. There's been a break-in at the café. Grandfather was hurt."

"Hurt? Is he okay?"

His brother's worried question filtered over the line. "He's unconscious. Got knocked on the head. Listen, they took him to the regional hospital near Jacob Lake. I have a situation here, so I need you to go to the hospital and call me with a report."

"What kind of situation?"

Paco huffed a breath. "I can't explain right now." Then he said on an urgent whisper, "I'm on the job."

His brother's silence told Paco Buddy was processing this. His older brother would understand and take action. "Can you talk?"

"Negative."

"Will you call me?"

"Yes. Just go to Wíago and stay with him. Call me when you hear anything from the doctors. Or I'll call you when I get things straight here."

"Got it. I'm on my way to the hospital."

Paco turned toward Laura. "Let's get out of here."

"Where are we going?"

He didn't explain. He had enough to think about without having to report every detail to her. Seeing the distress in her eyes, he gently lifted her up. "You'll be okay. This has become official now."

She followed him without protest. Getting an argument from her would have eased Paco's mind even if he didn't want to hear it. She might be going into shock and that was the last thing he needed right now.

"Do you think the sheriff believed us?" she asked. "I mean, he didn't take me away. I thought he'd take me into custody after I told him what I'd witnessed and what happened." She didn't finish, didn't state the obvious.

Paco did a scan of the road and the desert, careful to shield her by keeping her behind him. "I explained things to the sheriff. Self-defense. He's a good friend of my grandfather's and for that reason he trusted me and he'll keep a lid on this for as long as possible. We both gave a statement and we've been cleared for travel."

"Cleared?"

He shoved her into his truck and closed the door. Once he was inside and feeling confident that they weren't being watched, he turned to her. "CHAIM clearance. For your safety, you're in my custody until we figure this out. The sheriff knows how to reach me if he needs to talk to us. We always alert the locals when we're on a case."

"Oh, of course."

Paco didn't like her quietness but he let it ride for now while he watched the long, flat road and did a couple of quick searches of the desert on either side. When they turned off the dusty lane to his trailer, he slowed the truck.

"I live there," he explained, pointing to the tiny white home on wheels. "I need to get some equipment and then we're going to your hotel room to check it out."

"All right." She studied the travel trailer, her gaze moving between the RV and his face. "That's not very big."

"I don't need much space." Except the emotional kind, he thought, refusing to elaborate out loud.

She went silent again.

"Stay right here while I get some things," he told her. Then he handed her a loaded handgun he kept in the glove compartment, removing the safety before he handed it to her. "Use this if you have to."

Before she could protest, Paco was out the door and running toward the trailer.

Laura sat staring down at the gun. She's just shot and killed a man and now she was holding a gun. What had become of her life, of her plans to help Luke Martinez?

Paco.

The man frightened her as much as he intrigued her. He was all muscle and male, all mad and mysterious. Not the kind of man to whom she was attracted. No, she went more for the button-down, preppy type. But then, that type hadn't exactly been working out for her lately, come to think of it. Her last boyfriend hadn't taken their break-up very well. And why was she even thinking along those lines anyway? She'd come here on a mission of mercy, her faith intact, her concern real.

And now, in the span of less than two hours, she'd been shot at and she'd killed a man. And she still didn't understand who these people wanted to kill—her or Paco.

She looked out across the Painted Desert toward the mountains. They looked misty and solid as they hunched in watercolor shades of orange and mauve like sleeping giants off in the distance, the saguaros and fan palms stark and scattered across the arid vastness.

Who was out there?

Laura felt a chill in spite of the rising heat. She had to get out of this truck. She didn't want Luke to be alone. And she didn't want to be alone. They should stick together. She opened the door and hurried around to the back of the tiny trailer, her gaze taking in the canvas covered tented porch, a small grill and one lonely scarred lawn chair.

He didn't need much space.

Except the desolate emptiness of a desert.

What had she gotten herself into?

Paco whirled when he heard footfalls on the rickety steps, his gun trained on the door.

"I told you to stay in the truck," he shouted, relief

washing over him. Relief followed by remorse. Laura was standing with one foot inside the door and the other one lowered on the steps, her gun shaking in her tiny hand.

"I was worried about you," she said, her gaze sweeping the cramped kitchen. Lowering the gun to the step, she asked, "Are you always this messy?"

"I didn't do this, sweetheart," he replied, disgust making him harsh as he looked over the ruin of his home. Someone had gone through ever nook and cranny, without regard for clothing, dishes or paperwork.

"Apparently, I had a visitor this morning." He touched a hand to something on the counter. "And they left yet another one of your business cards."

She stepped away. "What? But why?"

At least that shocked her out of her fear again. Good. She needed to clear her head because they were just getting started with this thing.

"Good question," he replied as he strapped on knives and guns, tugging weapons in his boots and underneath his shirt. "Either you have a fan, or someone is stalking you."

She looked up at him then, her eyes coloring to a deep blue. "Oh, no. No, it can't be."

She fell back and turned to sit on the metal step. Paco quickly slid out the door and hopped around her then turned to face her. "Talk to me, beautiful."

Laura put her head down in her hands. "I dated a guy for a few months, a while back. On the surface, he was a successful nice guy who said all the right things. But after a few months, things got weird and I broke it off. He started harassing me and I had to take out a restraining order. But he stopped bothering me about a month ago."

Paco leaned down, one hand reaching to lift her head up. "Define 'weird.'"

"After we broke up, he'd still call me and text me all day and night. He got really angry when I didn't call him right back. I got a funny feeling—instincts I guess. I told him to quit pestering me. He didn't take that very well. When he turned violent, I knew I'd made a big mistake. I think he suffered from paranoid delusional disorder."

"Did he hurt you? Hit you?"

She looked away. "He slapped me once."

Paco couldn't tolerate men who hit women. "And?"

"And I reminded him that we were over, he left a note on my apartment door, threatening me, calling me a tease." She looked up at Paco. "I never teased him or led him on about anything. I thought we were having a friendly relationship that might turn into something else. It didn't turn into anything but…creepy. I told him he needed help. I even offered to find him a therapist, since I certainly couldn't deal with him."

"You think this might be the guy?"

"I don't know. He stopped calling me after I took out the restraining order. I live in a secure building with a doorman, so everyone watched out for me. I would have known if he'd come back there."

"What's his name?"

She looked at the phone he'd pulled out of his pocket. "Alex Whitmyer. He came from a prominent family. He was handsome and a bit narcissistic, which I figured out a little too late. I'm still embarrassed about it. I'm supposed to help people like him, but I was too caught up in the relationship to see he was sick. And he was very good at hiding his real personality."

Paco wondered about that. Wasn't she supposed to be able to read people? Maybe not with her heart, but with her head. Had she cared about this guy? "I'll put in a call to Kissie. She can check him out in addition to the father of that kid you mentioned, too."

"Mr. Henner," she said, shaking her head. "I'd put my money on Alex. He was just strange enough to go all ballistic and decide to teach me a lesson."

"But you didn't know our intruder. Why would he send other people to do the deed if he's the one stalking you?"

"He certainly could hire someone to scare me, but then so could Mr. Henner. Maybe it wasn't Alex after all."

He made the call to Kissie, giving her Alex Whitmyer's name. After explaining what had happened, he said, "Looks like I'm on a case, Kissie-girl."

"Paco, you sure you're ready for this?"

"Not you, too," he replied, closing his eyes. "I told Warwick I was doing okay."

"Well, he's so happy he just wants everyone else to feel the same," Kissie said through a chuckle. "Me, I think you find your strength when you need it the most."

"Well, then, we're about to test that theory," Paco replied. "Look, about Alex Whitmyer." He looked at the card. "He dated Laura Walton. Counselor. Works for CHAIM-approved clinic in Phoenix. Except right now, she's with me. I'm sure you've been updated on the shooting here this morning since I had to get clearance from both the sheriff and CHAIM to move the client."

"Heard all about it. We've got your back, Paco. And

I've heard of Laura's work at the Phoenix Rising Counseling Center. But how in the world did she wind up with you?"

"She thinks I need counseling for some strange reason."

"I know Laura," Kissie said. "We've met at some of the company get-togethers. Nice girl. And if anyone can help you, it'd be Laura. Do you need help?"

Paco grunted. "Why is everyone asking me that?"

"We care about you. What about the get-together at Eagle Rock. You gonna be there?"

"Hadn't planned on it," Paco replied. "Since when did CHAIM start having company functions anyway?"

"You've been out of the country too long, my child. We like to get together for some down time now and then. Good for the soul. And just FYI, this is a big to-do coming up next week at Eagle Rock. You know, to remember the fallen on Veteran's Day and to celebrate Thanksgiving. You should come. It's a mandatory callout."

"I'm kinda busy here, Kissie. We'll have to see about that."

"Okay then, but you might want to read the memo. I'll get right on this. You take care of my girl Laura, you hear."

"I hear."

He signed off then turned to Laura. "Kissie seems to think you're a nice girl."

"I am a nice girl," she replied without skipping a beat. "And I'm still wondering how I managed to kill a man."

He hated the tiny bit of little girl in her voice. She was way too nice to be sitting here in this old trailer, in the middle of the desert, with him of all people. She was the good girl who went to church and baked cookies for nursing home residents and planted petunias by the back door. The good girl who actually tried to help warped, scarred, tired souls.

He was the bad boy who shunned crowds, liked his solitude and really never let anyone get too close. He was the loner, the soldier, the warrior who'd fought the good fight and yet, had somehow managed to lose both his soul and his sanity in doing so.

"How *did* you wind up here?" he asked her.

"I wanted to talk to you," she reminded him.

He lifted her up, grabbed the gun she'd laid on the step and pulled her toward the truck. "Well, honey, that's gonna have to wait. 'Cause whoever this is, they seem to be determined to either scare you or kill you. I just don't get why they keep leaving your cards everywhere like a trail. They obviously want us to find these cards."

She grabbed the tattered card out of his hand then gasped. "I didn't notice this before but this isn't my updated business card, Luke. This looks like my old set of cards. I had them changed about two weeks ago. I added my website on the new ones."

"Then where did these come from?"

"I threw them in the recycling bin at my apartment building."

He steadied her hand to stare at the card. "So someone went through that bin and found them. How many did you have left?"

"About twenty-five or so. A little box—almost empty."

"Just enough to spread the word."

"And what is the word?"

"That's the big question," he replied. "That's what we need to find out."

"Do we have to report this to the police?"

"Not yet," he said as he guided her to the truck. "We gave our report this morning about the break-in and the shooting. We might have to go in for more questioning once they identify the man who—"

"The man I killed," she replied, her eyes going all misty. She turned away to stare out into the desert.

Paco didn't press her. Sooner or later, she was going to fall apart and they both knew it. He dreaded it. He'd never been good around hysterical women. But this one was deserving of a little meltdown. He'd see her through it, because *he* wasn't allowed to have any more meltdowns. He had a mission. And he was alone in this until he could figure out what was going on. He couldn't abandon this innocent woman even if he did resent her being here.

"Let's go," he said, tugging her toward the truck.

She wiped her eyes and got in, the big truck making her look even more lost and tiny. Which only made Paco want to protect her even more.

He slipped behind the wheel, shaking his head as he brought the truck to life with a roar. This day had gone from bad to worse. And he had a feeling it wasn't going to get any better anytime soon. His grandfather was in the hospital, probably still in a coma. His brother would want answers. Paco wanted those same answers.

After calling his brother one more time to check on his grandfather, Paco glanced over at the woman huddled in the seat across from him and wondered if he could keep her safe and alive until he figured things out. He had to. He wouldn't lose her. He wouldn't be the last man standing again.

Not this time. Not with Laura Walton. She deserved better than that. Much better.

FIVE

They drove the twenty miles to her hotel near the foot of the South Rim of the Grand Canyon. By now it was midday and a lot warmer in spite of the late fall temperatures. Laura's shirt was sticking to her back, chilling her as she cooled down.

Over the whirl of the faint air-conditioning in the old truck, Paco said, "Here's what we're gonna do. We'll check you out of the hotel and find a safe place to stay for tonight. That way, if you were tracked to the hotel, they'll know you're gone. Or if they've been there, we might find some kind of lead."

"Do you think someone already knows I'm staying there?" she said, glancing up at the stone front of the lobby entrance. This hotel had looked so serene when she'd arrived yesterday afternoon.

"Probably. And they probably couldn't find a way to

get to you before you left this morning. Or they wanted to get you in an isolated situation."

"Which they did."

"Yes. Two attempted hits in as many hours so I can almost guarantee more will follow."

"I don't know why I'm a target," she said, grabbing the door handle. "I wish I could explain this."

He held tightly to the steering wheel, his silence stretching like the long road they'd just traveled. "You might be right about it being aimed toward me. Maybe someone didn't want you to talk to me for a reason."

"Or maybe they wanted to kill both of us for a reason."

"That's what we need to find out," he said as they left the truck and entered the hotel the back way. "Let's check out your room, see if anything looks suspicious."

"What if they're waiting for me?"

"I'll take care of that." He walked her up the empty hallway without making a sound. "Just stay behind me."

Laura wouldn't argue with that. He had a way of going noiseless in and out of places. But then, he was trained to be invisible. Right now, however, he was a very visible presence in her life. And a blessed one, considering she knew nothing about espionage or spying or killing people. She only knew how to help those who did so try and pick up the pieces when things got to be too much.

Was Luke ready to go back into the fray?

Please, Lord, let him be ready. Not for my sake but for his. She had a gut feeling if he failed this time, it would put him over the edge. She also had a feeling he hadn't talked to anyone much since he'd come home from the front. Shane Warwick had warned her Luke

Martinez could be as quiet and stone-faced as a rock when he went into one of his dark moods.

She'd come here on a mission of her own, though. And she'd brought trouble to an already troubled man. So she prayed for guidance and mercy and protection for both of them. She wouldn't abandon him now, no matter the danger.

But when Luke opened her hotel room door and she saw what someone had done to her room, Laura knew this was about more than a jilted boyfriend stalking her or a grieving father seeking revenge. The bedspread and pillows were tossed and scattered, the drawers and closets thrown open and her clothes strewn around the room.

And her laptop was missing.

"I didn't bring it with me this morning," she said. "I had my phone and I'd downloaded your file onto it. I didn't bring the laptop in case I had to do some hiking. I thought it would be safer here than in the car." She turned to Paco, grabbing his hand. "They have my files. Everything is on that laptop."

"Explain *everything*."

"Notes on my patients, my personal files, you name it. My life is on there." She didn't tell him that she'd saved some personal information about him on there, too. "It's all encrypted and backed up on an external hard drive at my office, and I have a password, but still—"

Paco dropped his hands to his hips as he surveyed the damaged room. "And the hits just keep on coming. A password won't stop anyone if they want to get to your files, sweetheart." He gripped her shoulders. "Why would they take your laptop, Laura?"

She stared up at him, her mind racing with confusion. Then she straightened back into business mode. "Maybe they need information on one of my patients? Something damaging? But why would they want to kill me to get that?"

"Well, so you'd be out of the way. Which means this information must be a big deal. Would your stalker guy want any of your files?"

"He might try to use them against me," she said. "I was a mess when Kyle committed suicide and I confided in Alex, without giving out any names."

Paco shook his head. "Doesn't add up. A stalker wouldn't try to kill you without confronting you. He'd want to justify his actions, try to reason with you. But he'd take you somewhere isolated so he could make you listen. And he wouldn't take your private files unless they had something to do with him."

"Do you think it could be Kyle's father then?"

"Could be. Maybe he wants to keep his son's illness and the counseling sessions a secret. But if he killed you, that would only open up a whole new can of worms. Again, doesn't make sense."

"None of this makes sense," she said. "No matter though, I'll have to answer to my supervisors about this. I might even lose my job." She looked down. "Just one more thing."

"You got something else on your mind, something you forgot to tell me?"

Laura didn't have a chance to respond. They heard footsteps in the hallway, causing him to quickly shut the door, lock it, then shoved her into a corner. "Whatever happens, you listen to me, you understand?"

She bobbed her head. "What if something happens to you?"

"Then you go out onto the balcony and jump, run and don't look back."

Laura prayed she wouldn't have to use that plan. Her room was on the fourth floor and she was deathly afraid of heights. She'd been to the Grand Canyon lots of times.

But she'd never once stepped close to the edge.

Paco pulled his handgun out of the holster and held it toward the door. Someone jingled the handle, once, twice. They'd have to either use a card key or break the door down. And if they did either, he'd be waiting for them.

"Maid service," came a feminine call. "Hello?"

He went to the door. "Come back later."

Waiting with the gun drawn, he listened then heard a cart rolling away.

"Was that really the maid?" Laura asked from her corner.

"Can't say, not knowing," he replied. "Let's get out of here." When she rushed for the door, he snagged her arm. "Not that way. We leave by the balcony."

Laura stepped back, shaking her head. Then she started tidying the place, shutting drawers, fluffing pillows. "Isn't there another way?"

Paco counted to ten, taking in her sudden burst of nervous energy. The woman was intelligent so what was she missing here. He pointed to the door. "There is that way where someone could be waiting to ambush us, or there is the balcony—the quickest way to escape."

She straightened the ice bucket, setting it straight. "I vote the stairs."

"Bad choice. Too isolated and too easy for someone to be lurking about. So I vote the balcony." His patience wearing thin, he asked, "Just what is the problem here, Laura?"

She shifted, fidgeted, looked away. "I… I don't like high places."

He frowned, lifting his eyebrows. "Say that again?"

"I don't do high places. I'm afraid of heights, okay?"

"But you're at the Grand Canyon!"

"Yes, but I didn't come to see the canyon. I came to find you."

Putting a finger to his forehead, Paco said, "But you said you planned to do some hiking if you failed at finding me."

"Yes," she said on a frustrated whisper. "Low hiking. As in at the bottom of the canyon or maybe in some part of the canyon but not near the very edge of the high-up canyon."

Tugging her toward the balcony door, he said, "This is only a few floors up, sweetheart. And it's grassy down there. It won't hurt a bit."

"I can't do it." She held back, a solid fear centered in her eyes. "My office is on the second floor of the clinic and my apartment in Phoenix is on the first floor. I usually don't go above level three but this was the only room available. I don't like elevators, either."

"Well, then we're in serious trouble. We can't take the stairs or the elevator here. The only way out is through that balcony door and down."

She ventured a glance out the door. "But we can't just jump."

"I can. And I'm pretty sure you'll be able, too. Since it might mean saving your life."

"But what if they're down there waiting?"

A good point. Paco pushed her away from the door. "I'll check things out." Slowly opening the sliding glass door, he peaked out and looked both ways then glanced down at the parking lot. "I don't see anyone but anything is possible." Then he turned back to her. "I think I see a way to do this."

"What?"

The wash of pure relief in her eyes told him she was serious about being afraid of heights. Another thing he'd have to remember right along with finding out what else she might be hiding from him.

"We can move from balcony to balcony until we reach the outside stairs at the end of the building. Do you think you can deal with that, at least?"

She walked to the open door and peered at the wide wooden-planked balconies. Then she took in a long breath. "I'll try."

Paco heard footsteps out in the hallway. "Good, because I think our visitors are back. And this time I don't think they're concerned about housekeeping."

Before she could panic, he shoved her and her big purse out the door and slid it shut. Holding her away from the open banisters, he said, "Don't think about it. Just act. That's how you survive sticky situations. You just have to take action."

She bobbed her head, her eyes glazing with fear. "I'll try, Paco. I promise."

Good grief, did she have to go all girly on him now? The woman had faced down an intruder and shot him dead. He needed her to stay strong until he could find a safe place to stash her.

"Okay, let's do it then. I'm going to climb over first," he said, dragging her stiff form along. "Then I'll help you over. We do that until we reach the end, okay?"

She strapped her bag across her body as if it were a shield. "Okay."

It was a weak "okay" but he'd have to go with it. "Don't think about it and don't look down. Just focus on getting from balcony to balcony."

She nodded again, her eyes so big and blue he had to look away—or he'd chicken out too just to spare her—and that would be bad for both of them.

He leapt over the first sturdy railing then turned to take her hand. "That's it. I've got you. Just about a half foot between them. Plenty of room."

She scooted across, holding on to him for dear life until he had her over the railing and on solid flooring again, her shoulder bag slung across her body and swinging out as he lifted her.

"See, not so bad. Just three more to go."

"It looks like a lot more to me."

"Just three—then we'll take the outside stairs and be on our way."

If they didn't get assaulted at the corner of the building. He'd have to do a thorough overview before they could advance toward the parking lot and his truck.

"Here we go," he said as he pulled her over the second railing. Glancing inside the room, he noticed an old woman standing there in a jogging suit drinking coffee. Paco waved and kept going. He didn't have time for explanations.

"The last one, Laura," he said, not used to having to

be so nice when giving commands or instructions. It was as foreign to him as holding her hand. Especially since she'd come charging into his safe, secure, quiet world and brought his heart right out its flat-lining existence. Holding her hand, however, was one thing. Keeping her alive was a whole different thing.

"Last one. See, that wasn't as hard as you thought."

She didn't answer. But when he tugged her over the last balcony and settled her on the landing near the hallway door to the inside of the building, she held to his arms with an iron grip. Surprising since she didn't seem to weigh much more than a doll.

"Laura?"

She wasn't listening. Instead, she was staring off over his shoulder. Great. Had she gone into shock again? Or was she about to have that meltdown he'd been dreading.

"Laura, we need to keep moving?"

"Paco," she whispered, her voice low and tight-edged. Then she pointed. "Look at your truck."

He whirled, gun lifting, his gaze moving across the big parking lot. Then with a grunt he dropped his gun down by his side and stomped a boot against the wall. "They slashed my tires!"

"That means they've been watching us. And now we can't leave." She moved near him with an almost automatic need, as if she knew he was her protector now, whether she liked it or not. And whether he wanted to be or not. "What do we do now?"

He let out a breath of pure aggravation then pulled her back against the wall while he scanned the empty parking lot. "Well, beautiful, you did say you wanted to do some hiking. I'd say now's your chance."

SIX

"My other hiking boots are in my car back at the café."

Paco eased her down the stairs, sticking to the wall while he scoped the parking lot. "Your car is no longer at the café. I had someone tow it away—to a safe place."

"Oh." She'd have to remember that this man was trained to be one step ahead of everything and everyone. Including her. "Thanks, I think."

He looked down at her low heeled sturdy boots. "Those should work. You might have to run, though."

"Since I've been shot at and chased already, I can do that," Laura replied, praying she could survive this. "Don't worry about me."

He huffed a chuckle. "Good one."

"Okay, worry about me then. What's the plan?"

"For now, to get around this wall and make sure the parking lot is secure."

Laura didn't push for more. He needed to focus and she wouldn't distract him. She knew this from her years working with CHAIM. She needed to clear her head, too. She'd come here on one quest but now things had changed into a full-fledged CHAIM mission. Now, she was running for her life with the very man she'd come to save.

Funny how the tables had turned on her. Maybe God was giving her a test. She'd been blessed with a good life and two loving parents, siblings to nag her and comfort her. Laura had never been through any kind of test such as this. She'd breezed through school and college, hired on with CHAIM right away and found work at a good clinic in Phoenix. A charmed life, some would say. A blessed life for sure.

Then two things had happened. She'd broken up with Alex not long after Kyle had ended his life, forcing her to wonder what she could have done differently in both situations. She wanted things to be different for Paco. She wanted to help him, had come here to validate her professional skills.

But someone out there had a bone to pick with her. Someone out there wanted her dead. The chill of that ran down her spine with all the pressure of bony fingers. But the injustice of it made her spine stiffen.

She instinctively clung to Paco's shirt but vowed to get herself out of this fix, somehow.

"Looks clear," he said on a low whisper. "We're going to head for those trees to the right. That should give us enough shelter to get us out on the road and away. We can hide behind buildings as we go." He turned, bumping into her, his big body blocking her fears about the outside world, but opening up a whole new set of conflicting emotions inside her heart.

"Stay behind me and hold on to my shirt. If I tell you to run, let go and run behind me, okay? But keep me in your sights."

"Okay."

"On the count of three." Paco counted then took off in a running crouch, his gun drawn. Laura held to his shirt, leaning low as they hurried across the open parking lot.

They made it into the trees then he whirled to tug her behind him while he scanned the area. "So far, so good. Must still be in the building looking for us." Turning to check on her, he said, "Next plan of action—try to find a way out of here."

"We're not going up into the canyon, are we?"

"No. We don't want to get in a ruckus that might injure tourists or attract the park rangers. Not so hot. The idea is to draw our attacker away from this area. He wants to isolate us, but that can work to our advantage."

"But where will we go?"

He rubbed a hand across his brow. "My plan is to either get you back to Phoenix or to get you to Eagle Rock."

"Eagle Rock? That's in Texas."

"Yes, but it's our main safe house. The security is so tight you'd have to bring in an army to get to anyone staying there. Warwick helped update everything recently, since we're all supposed to convene there for some sort of retreat next week. I hadn't planned on attending but maybe that's the best place for you, so I guess we're going to the party."

"You have to attend anyway," she said. "It's mandatory."

"Yeah, only CHAIM would suggest a retreat then make it mandatory. I don't do mandatory very well."

"But if you take me there—"

"I'll have to sign up for the fun stuff. I get that."

That he was willing to do that for her spoke volumes about Paco Martinez. In spite of his tough, gruff exterior he was redeemable. But then, she had believed that since the night she'd heard his voice rasping across the phone line. She'd hold to that belief until they could get past this threat.

"Thank you," she said, determined to stick with him no matter what.

"My job," he replied, obviously just as determined to finish this and get her off his back. He glanced around one more time. "This is a busy area. I don't think they'd try anything but then, they did mess up my truck and trash your room."

"They have my laptop now. Maybe that's all they wanted."

"Maybe. Maybe not. Let's get moving."

He checked his phone. "Hold on. I've got a message from my brother." He pulled up the number and waited. "Buddy, talk to me."

Laura listened as he repeated to her what his brother was saying.

"Wíago's still in a coma. They're doing tests." He waited then said, "But he's in good physical shape." He looked into Laura's eyes. "Something about bleeding in the brain or swelling."

Laura digested the information. "Bleeding in the

brain—a hematoma. That means they might have to do surgery to relieve the pressure."

Paco nodded, repeating what she'd said back to his brother. "Yeah, exactly." He looked at her. "Buddy says that's pretty much what the doctor told him." Then he talked to his brother a couple more minutes. "We're safe for now. No, you stay with Grandfather. The sheriff is investigating the guy who broke into the café. I'll be in touch."

Laura watched as he hung up. "I'm sorry. It sounds as if your grandfather's injury has gone from a concussion to brain trauma. That's serious, Luke."

He looked out over the trees. "Tell me something I don't know."

Laura gulped, thinking one of his black moods was coming. Guilt weighed at her, dragging her down. If she'd stayed in Phoenix, this wouldn't have happened. But then, if she hadn't come here, would someone have come after her in Phoenix? Or worse, come after Paco and killed him? Or did this person want them both dead? Her head hurt from tension and fatigue and shock. She'd like some answers, not constant questions inside her brain. But right now, she'd like to get away from the danger she felt pressing like a heavy fog all around them.

He dragged her along while she mulled over all the variables. Then he stopped so quickly, Laura plowed right into his broad back.

Paco turned to capture her in a long stare. "I don't get the card stuff. Why would they leave your card when they're obviously after *you?*"

"I don't know," she said, gulping back her intimidation. "Disturbed people aren't logical about certain things. They can justify any action with what they think is a good reason. Maybe leaving my card is a way of teasing me, letting me know they can find things that belong to me, even in a Dumpster. It's a tactic to scare me. Which it has, by the way."

Pulling her underneath the eaves of a tourist shop, Paco took out the two cards he'd saved, looking them over. He squinted then held one of the cards closer. "It looks like a watermark or something on the back of both cards."

Laura looked then pulled out her glasses from her purse pocket. "Maybe. Or it could be that they wrote something on a piece of paper that was pressed against the cards—some sort of cryptic message."

"A message to you?"

"Possibly. But why wouldn't they just write it out?"

"Like you said, sweetheart, disturbed people do strange things. And whoever this is must have some sort of plan that he's put into action. Starting with you and me."

He did a visual of the street. "Let's duck into the restaurant on the corner so I can check in. Kissie might be able to give me an update on the two names we sent her."

Aggravated and tired, she followed him. "Shouldn't we stay on the move?"

"We will after I decide where to move to next."

"Do we really have to leave Arizona?"

"Might be best." He nodded then followed the waitress to a booth in the corner. Pulling Laura in beside him, he whispered, "Let's sit together, facing the door."

Laura breathed in the scent of aftershave and sweat, her head reeling with thoughts and feelings best left unexplored right now. Paco practically filled the whole booth with his presence but she did feel safe all tucked in—or rather trapped—between him and the wall.

After they'd ordered sandwiches and coffee, he leaned so close she could see the rich brown around his almost black irises. "We're getting out of here. I have to arrange a few things first. We have a saying in the desert: 'Before you get somewhere, you have to go through a whole lot of nowhere.'"

"Are we going through the desert?"

"If we have to. The desert can hide a person for days."

Laura didn't relish that idea. While she was in pretty good shape, making a trek through the hot, dusty desert wasn't on her list of things to do while she was being chased by bad guys. Nor did she want to spend the night out in the barren hills.

He must have sensed her hesitation. "I know my way around, so don't worry."

"Right. I won't worry—not one little bit. Just like you won't worry about me—not at all. Good one."

"Okay, I get it." He shook his head then got Kissie on the phone. "What do you know?"

While he listened to Kissie's report, Laura kept her eyes on the door of the restaurant. Several other diners were settled into their meals and she sure didn't want anyone else to get hurt on her behalf. Praying that these people would leave them alone now that they had her laptop, she did a mental list of things to do.

Call her assistant to report the laptop missing.

Try to get her hard copy files moved to a safe location.

Have someone check her apartment—not a friend but someone official.

Try to stay alive until this was over.

She didn't realize he'd hung up the phone until she felt his hand touching her arm. "I've got some interesting news."

"What?"

"Kissie says Lawrence Henner has several homes around the world. One in the Cayman Islands, an apartment in New York and…a lake house near Austin, Texas."

"Texas? Why? He can hunt and fish in Arizona."

"Bingo. Why would a man who has everything he needs here in Arizona need a lake house in Texas."

"Maybe he has relatives there. Or maybe he wanted a change of scenery—less desert and canyons and mountains."

"Or maybe he has business there. Business he doesn't want us to know about." He inhaled then added, "Nothing on your stalker boyfriend yet. And that right there should give us pause. He must be keeping a low profile these days."

A shudder of apprehension shimmied down her body. "So what do we do next?"

He was already hitting his apps. "First, I'll let my team know about this. They've been updated on what happened to us today, so they're already on high alert. We've sent people to report to your clinic about your laptop being stolen and we've checked out your apartment. It's been trashed. No surprise there."

Laura's heartbeat increased with each task. He'd just ticked off her to-do list. "I guess you moved my hard copy files to a secure location."

"Yeah, of course we did."

She felt better about the staying alive thing now. And wondered how he'd managed all of that when she'd never noticed him on the phone talking or texting. Well, maybe a couple of times during their drive here. Obviously the man was good at multitasking. "Thank you."

"Quit thanking me." He shrugged. "I don't know what it is, but something isn't right about this whole thing."

A lot wasn't right about this whole thing, Laura thought as she listened while he gave Shane Warwick all the details of this bizarre case. "Since you're in Texas now," he told Shane, "maybe you can do some recon work on this. And keep checking on Alex Whitmyer. I don't like the sound of him, either."

Apparently Shane agreed to that. Paco hung up just as the waitress brought their food. Then he ate his sandwich as if he were starving.

While Laura sat there breaking her food into tiny pieces. Her nerves were rattling and hitting against her insides so furiously, she felt as if she'd been on a roller coaster.

"Eat," he said, a firm tone stiffening his words. "You'll need your strength."

"Pray," she retorted, frustration coloring her suggestion. "*You'll* need your strength."

"Touché," he retorted. "But me and God, we're not talking much these days."

"But you said you prayed to Him."

"Oh, I do. But I'm not sure He's hearing me clearly."

"He listens. You made it through that rough night when you called me."

He took a drink of coffee then sat his cup down. "I

believe the Father always listens. But I also believe that sometimes we're just not worth the fuss."

"You mean you think *you're* not worth the fuss. Luke, you have to know God won't abandon you."

He gave her a hard look. "He wasn't there the day my entire unit was mowed down on that mountain."

Laura had to change his perspective. "You lived for a reason, Luke."

"Oh, yeah. And what is that reason?"

She looked down at her cold food, took a deep breath and looked back up. "Me?" she asked on a squeaky voice. "Maybe I'm the reason you survived. Maybe God knew *I'd* need you one day."

SEVEN

His heart actually started beating faster.

Paco didn't know what to say to that. What did a man say to a woman who looked at him with big dark blue eyes filled to the brim with hope? What did a man who'd up until today been content to be completely alone say to a woman who made all of his protective instincts go into overdrive? A woman who made him think about nice things such as long walks and laughing out loud. Happiness. He didn't even know what happiness meant anymore. And he sure didn't know what God was all about anymore.

"Let's leave God out of this."

She looked disappointed and hurt. She turned away to stare out the window, her fingers twisting a paper napkin against the table. "We need Him now, Paco. I mean, really need Him."

Thinking he was truly lower than a snake's belly, Paco grabbed her hand. "I shouldn't have said that."

Laura glanced down at his hand over hers. "You have a lot of scars. God can heal them."

She was looking at the jagged white scars lining his knuckles. "Yes, I do. Some of them show and some of them don't."

That brought her gaze back up to him. "God can heal all of them. That's why I came to find you. I couldn't stop thinking about that night when you called. I wanted you to know that I can help you, too. That's why God called me to this career, I think. I always wanted to help other Christians, but I'm too chicken to go out into the missionary field or to do the type of things you do. My calling is in counseling and therapy. And I just knew God wanted me to find you. Especially after…"

"After what?" Did she have her own torment? He didn't have the right to ask her about anything. But between the abusive boyfriend and that kid's suicide, she probably had her own guilt weighing her down.

"Never mind," she said. "I came here all self-righteous and determined, wanting to make a difference in your life." She pulled her hand away. "But look at how that turned out. Running for our lives, getting shot at and shooting people." Her words became choppy with emotion. "Your grandfather—"

"Hey, Wíago is tough. He's been through worse. And my brother Buddy is right there with him, guarding him and watching over him. If it makes you feel better, Buddy knows how to pray. He has a pipeline right to God's ear."

She wiped at her eyes. "We all need to pray, for

your grandfather, for whoever is doing this to us, for everything."

"Why don't you pray and I'll plan?"

She pushed her food away. "I'd feel better if we prayed together."

"Here, now?"

She bobbed her head, her eyes full of that glorious hope again.

"I… I'm not good at public displays of praying, Laura. I do my best bargaining with God when I'm faced with a bottle at three o'clock in the morning."

Her eyes widened then and he saw her go from sweet to steely. "Don't you see, Paco? That bottle of liquor represents all your torment and your shame and guilt. All the more reason to learn how to pray without ceasing, no matter the time of day."

"Got it." He looked around, uncomfortable with this whole conversation and stunned by her sharp-edged logic. It wasn't like they didn't have pressing matters to take care of—such as staying alive. But hey, he'd tried everything else. Pray might be their best option right now.

She must have sensed his near-compliance. "Here, take my hand and just close your eyes. Nobody is looking. And so what if they are?"

Paco grunted, but he took her tiny hand, his scarred fingers accepting the lace-delicate touch of her skin.

"Dear Father," she began, her voice going from strained to sure, "we don't know what's going on with us or why we are under siege. We do know that someone wants to do us harm. We ask that You intercede in this warfare, that You show us the right way and guide us through each step we take. And Lord, please help to change our pursuers—whatever their motives. Bless and keep Luke and Wíago and Buddy close, Lord. Protect them and guide them. Amen."

Paco kept her hand when she tried to let go. "Father, don't forget Laura."

When he opened his eyes, she has such a sweet, serene smile on her face Paco knew he was in serious trouble. His heart, so long guarded and lifeless, was pumping new blood through his veins with such intensity, he had to catch his breath.

To waylay that, he said, "Satisfied? We need to get moving."

She didn't answer, and if her smile seemed to fade at his callus treatment, he ignored it. He had to keep his emotions at bay so he could keep her alive.

That was *his* most urgent prayer right now.

Two hours later, they'd hiked out of the tourist-laden foot of the South Rim and were on some dusty back road into the desert. Laura was tired but secure in the knowledge that if anyone could get her across a desert, it would be Paco Martinez. He'd loaded up on gear after taking a quick shopping trip at one of the souvenir stores. He was now fortified with a backpack full of bottled water and power bars slung on his back along with the weapons of various shapes and sizes that's he'd strapped to his body earlier when they'd gone by his trailer, including a nasty-looking knife and a tiny pistol tucked inside his boot. He had compasses and maps and his trusty phone. And he'd made her buy a pair of sturdy hiking boots and good socks, using most of her cash.

While she felt safe knowing he was prepared, Laura

also fretted about how he'd react to whatever came at them next.

Luke Paco Martinez was in full black ops mode from what she could tell. And that "take no prisoners" scowl he wore as they marched through the fall heat didn't bode well for anyone who crossed him. Including her.

"Rest," he said now, his tone curt and no-nonsense. He was the point man, of course, explaining that they would take a five minute rest at the top of every hour. That five-minutes wasn't nearly enough for Laura but she didn't complain. She was at the man's mercy, after all.

He pointed to a big bronzed rock jutting out from a heavy cluster of yuçca plants. Laura gingerly looked around for scorpions, snakes and spiders before she sank down on the warm rock.

"Drink." He handed her a bottle of water.

Laura took it and chugged until the bottle was unceremoniously taken out of her hands.

"Slow, sweetheart. Drink it slow."

Well, at least he was still calling her sweetheart. That endearment coming from any other man would have made her bristle. But Luke seemed to use it almost absentmindedly, making her think he called a lot of people that.

Not just Laura Walton, and not because she was special. She was nobody special, just the woman he was now forced to protect. The woman who'd come here hoping to redeem herself away from the guilt nagging at her, hoping to cure her own ills and insecurities by picking Paco's brain. Fat chance of that. He'd have her talking and confessing everything from stealing a kiss from a boy in the fourth grade to eating too much ice cream while she watched sappy movies, she guessed, before he spoke to her of any of his own pain.

"Thanks," she said, handing the bottle back to him. "I'll save the rest for later."

He drank the rest. Then he halved a power bar and handed her part of it. "Eat."

Laura ate the chewy, nasty-tasting bar with a firm smile on her face.

His next words were, "Let's go."

"Could I ask where we're going?"

"To my brother's house. We can rest there and re-group."

"How far?"

"Another ten miles."

That sounded like a hundred miles in desert time, she decided. Hadn't they already been at least twenty miles? And because she needed to distract herself from the dry heat and the sun and the creepy-crawly things, she said, "I wish I knew why they wanted my laptop."

"To get information," he replied with a "duh" tone.

"But what information? How could they benefit from my patient files?"

"Maybe they wanted your personal stuff."

"That doesn't make any sense either. They apparently know a lot about me already." She shrugged. "And besides, I don't have much personal stuff. My work is my life." A sad admission and one she wished she'd kept to herself.

"Maybe they wanted to get next to you—that thing you said about showing you they could invade your privacy anywhere."

"That worked, then."

Laura decided she'd keep quiet for a while. He didn't

seem in a chatty mood and she'd spill even more of her pathetic personal information if she didn't shut up.

Then out of the blue, he said "Tell me more about the stalker."

"Alex?" Surprise and dread filled her. "Big mistake. We met at a business function. He worked selling alarm systems and seemed to enjoy it. At first, he was so great—kind, considerate, fun to talk to. He asked me a lot of questions."

"Hold it right there. What kind of questions?"

"You know, about my life, my work. The usual."

"Sometimes the usual can be the most obvious."

"You mean, he had an agenda maybe?"

His grunt indicated yes. "How long did you date?"

"A few months. But then he got a little too possessive for me to feel comfortable. He became demanding and paranoid. He even accused me of cheating on him. Things escalated and I got scared. I tried to reason with him, tell him it just wasn't working. I offered to get him help. But he kept at me, telling me he loved me and we were made for each other. After he started showing up at my apartment and my work and sending constant text messages and voice mails, I broke things off. He cornered me in the parking lot and that's the day he slapped me. I was advised to take out a restraining order."

"And he didn't take that too well?"

"No. Not at all. His pleas turned to even more threats. But I never could prove much beyond the text messages I'd saved. He was always careful to leave typed notes or things that couldn't be traced. Little clues—"

She stopped. "Luke, little clues. What if this *is* him

doing all of these horrible things and that's what he's done with my old business cards? Left some sort of clues or threats for me to find—just to scare me."

"Already considered that, sweetheart. I'm going to check those out more when we get to Buddy's place."

Well, of course he'd considered that. "Do you believe it's him then?"

He guided her past a giant saguaro. "I'm liking him for it, yeah. But it's almost too easy."

"Too obvious?"

"Yeah. Like I said, things don't add up. If he's stalking you because he's obsessed with you, he wouldn't try to kill you right away. He'd want to come after you and maybe take you away to convince you to love him the way he loves you. And then he'd kill you if you didn't see things his way."

Laura shivered in spite of the rising heat. "If he was trying to do that, then he might have tried to shoot you, too. If he thought, you know, that you and I—"

"Possibly. But why send another hit man?"

"To keep his hands clean? Or to help him, make it easy for him to take me."

He shrugged, but the look he gave her reassured her. "If we ever get to a safe place, I'll sit down and figure this out." He turned, doing one of his panoramic views, looking behind them.

Laura turned to respond and found herself flat on the sandy desert floor, his hand over her head.

"Don't move," he said, drawing weapons with a swift clarity. "We have company."

Dirt ground like shards of glass against her skin. "Where?"

"On the road behind us to the east. Don't look."

Laura breathed dust, her pulse hitting against the hard desert floor, her mind very much aware of Paco there beside her. "How many?"

"Only one so far. I think I can take him."

She chanced a glance at him and watched as he pulled that mean-looking knife out of his boot. Not wanting to see this, Laura closed her eyes again and prayed with all her might.

Paco held his hand on her neck. "Don't move a muscle. We wait until he's right on us."

"Are you sure it's someone after us?"

"Yeah, since he's packing a high-powered rifle and since I'm pretty sure he has that rifle trained on the spot where he last saw us."

Beads of sweat caught in the center of her back between her shoulder blades and evaporated with each beat of her heart. Her throat was so dry, she couldn't force a swallow. Breathing became impossible. Then she lifted her head an inch and saw something that terrified her every bit as much as the person tracking them.

"Luke?"

"Shh."

"But—"

"Be still. I mean it."

She was going to pass out. Laura knew this but she couldn't voice it. She froze, her gaze fixed, her mind whirling with visions of imminent death.

"Luke, please?"

Had she managed to say that out loud?

She would never know because a gunshot rang out and then in one blur of motion she only caught out of the corner of her eye, she watched as Paco stood and threw the knife at their pursuer, hitting him square in the chest.

And then he whirled and shot in midair the rattle-snake rising up to strike just inches away from Laura's face.

EIGHT

"Are you hurt?"

Paco grabbed Laura, dragging her up with one arm, his gun still aimed on the twitching snake.

"I'm… I'm all right," she said. She buried her head against his chest and closed her eyes. "Is he dead?"

"The snake or the man?"

"Both?"

"Man down and snake giving his last dying twitch. You can open your eyes now."

She lifted away to stare up at him. "I can't take much more of this. I thought snakes went into hibernation this time of year." But obviously, bad guys didn't.

He glanced at the dead snake. "That old-timer was probably on his way to hibernation. Just getting in one last sunning in this warm weather."

The warmth was lost on Laura. A chill went over

her when she thought about the man gunning for her and the snake that had come close to striking her. "I don't like snakes."

"I hear that." Paco checked her over, wiping at the dirt smudges on her cheek. "You have a scrape right there."

His finger stilled on her skin while their eyes locked and held, the awareness between them a brief flare that warred with the sun and sent a new kind of chill down her spine.

Paco stepped back and turned to go to the man. Taking back his knife, he rubbed it through the sand then wiped it on a cactus stalk. Checking the man's pulse, he turned to Laura. "Yes, he's dead." Quickly going through the man's pockets, he pulled out a handgun and a wallet. "Howard Barrow. Do you know him?"

He heard her gasp then turned to see her rushing toward the man. "Howard? Did you say Howard?"

"Yes. Howard P. Barrow. According to his driver's license, he lives in Phoenix."

"He…he was my patient about a year ago."

"Really? No kidding?"

Her eyes burst into blue-tipped flames. "Why would I be kidding about this? Yes, he was a patient. He came to the clinic with a recommendation from…from Lawrence Henner. That was before Mr. Henner's son committed suicide and I got put on his blacklist."

"Okay, this is beginning to make me crazy," Paco said. At her disapproving look, he added, "Sorry. Crazy with *wondering*."

She stared down at the chubby, bleeding man. "Howard was a nice man. He worked for the government but he'd gone through a bad divorce and he had some emotional issues. We spent several sessions trying to get him through those issues. Last time I talked to him, he was dating again and happy."

"So a man who now blames you for his son's death once recommended you as a counselor to this man?"

"Yes." She pushed at her hair. "Poor Howard. This doesn't make any sense. He was a quiet, passive person who worked in records at the courthouse, not exactly someone who'd chase me through the desert."

"Something didn't get all the way cured in Howard, I'm thinking." And Paco also had another bad thought. "Better check his other pockets."

Laura wiped at her eyes while he dug around in Howard's jean pocket. "Just as I figured. He's carrying one of your outdated business cards." He held it up to the sun. "And it looks like the same indentations are on the back of it. Probably planned on leaving it with our dead bodies."

Her low groan brought Paco around. "What?"

"What?" She waved toward the dead man. "We're being stalked by the hour, Luke. You tell me. This man was a patient. What about the others? What about the man I shot?"

"Did you recognize him?"

"No, but it happened so fast I never actually got a good look and people change. They appear rough when I see them—lack of sleep and over or under eating, not to mention other indulgences. That man could have been someone I treated or spoke to in the clinic but he might have changed so much I didn't recognize him."

"When we get to Buddy's, I'll find out," he said. "Right now, we're too exposed. We need to get going."

"What about Howard?"

"What about him? He was going to kill us."

"He's dead now, though. We should do something."

"Look, we can't do anything. We don't have time and if we bury him it won't look so good for us. That whole hiding the body thing and all."

"So we just leave his body here for the vultures?"

"Do you have a better idea?" Cause he sure didn't.

She nodded. "We need to say a prayer over him and then, we need to call someone to come and get him."

Paco let a groan of his own. "Okay. You say a prayer and I'll text in a report to the sheriff."

And so he did. He explained the situation to his friend at the sheriff's department, giving him a location and a promise of a call later for more details. Then he stood silent while Laura said a prayer for the man who'd tried to take them both out.

When she was done, he tugged her along, marveling at her fortitude and her commitment to doing the right thing. "We're not waiting for the sheriff. Too dangerous. Let's go."

She followed him, beating a wide path around the coiled dead snake. "Was that a rattlesnake?"

"Yep. Looked like a western diamondback."

"You saved my life again."

"It's getting to be a habit."

Paco slowed down, thinking this woman had been through a lot for one day so maybe he should cut her some slack. But if they didn't hurry, the sun would go down on them in the desert. He did not want that to happen. He needed to get her to a safe spot so she could rest and digest all of this. And so he could call all the people waiting for him to give updates and reports. Everyone wanted answers. Well, so did he.

"Why would they bother leaving your card if they killed us?"

She pushed at her hair. "Maybe so whoever found us would also find the clues—if there are any clues on those cards."

"I'm guessing there's something on these cards." He did a quick search of the area. "Of course, whoever's behind this might have given the cards to his goons just in case they did get in trouble. That way, it looks like your patients had your business card—which would make sense and that would lead the authorities and CHAIM to think all of your patients were seriously deranged and chasing you all over the state to do you in."

"I'd have to quit work if that's the case. Maybe that's the point—to cause me to lose my license and my job."

He shot her a long hard stare. "We'll figure it out, Laura. While I don't exactly believe in therapy, I can see that you're probably good at your job. You seem to care about people. You went out of your way to find me."

She seemed to bask in that halfhearted compliment but she didn't push him. She was too numb and disturbed to try and break him down right now, Paco reasoned.

They walked in silence a few more miles, with the usual five-minute stops along the way.

"Not much farther now," he said after one of their breaks, hoping to help her along.

She didn't respond, but she got up and started walking again. Paco hated the way she kept looking back at the spot where Howard Barrow had met his demise, even though they were a long way gone from that area.

After they'd walked a while longer, she said, "It doesn't bother you, does it?"

A lot of things bothered him. Especially pretty women in trouble in the middle of the desert. That and the growing body count bothered him a lot. The whole way his day had gone from self-imposed solitary confinement to wide open with visitors bearing guns bothered him. And the fact that his grandfather might be having surgery right now really bothered him. "What *doesn't* bother me?"

She missed the message in the question. "Killing people. It doesn't seem to bother you."

Paco grunted, but her words floored him. "You have no idea how it gets to me, trust me. And I'm not going to discuss that with you since we're not in your office and I'm not lying on the couch."

"But killing has become second nature to you. I saw the way you threw that knife. And killed that snake."

"Instincts, darlin'. I was trained to defend myself when I'm being attacked. I was trained to defend our country and to fight our enemies, both here and abroad. And I'd say we have several enemies on our back right now, right here in my backyard."

"No wonder you can't sleep."

Okay, the woman was tired, shocked and stressed. Paco knew all of those feelings. And in his gut, even though he knew she was being purposely harsh, he also knew she was right. He had become a machine. A killing machine. And her words cut to the quick with a pristine precision that caused him to lower his head and keep walking.

How was he supposed to reconcile that with the big guy in the sky? And how was he supposed to win this woman's respect when she'd witnessed him in action?

"Now I'm just like you," she said on a winded hiss.

"I've killed another human being. And I'm beginning to think I'm responsible for all these people chasing us."

"Okay, enough!" He stopped as they made a turn on the path. "Just because you defended us this morning, doesn't make you like me. You will never be like me, understand? I can't help what happened today. Can't change what I've done in the past in the name of war. But I can save you if you let me—that's my job right now and that means I might have to hurt or kill other people in order to get you to safety. Will that be enough for you?"

She glared up at him, her face dirty and scraped, her eyes full of fury. And despair. "Enough for what?"

"Enough for you to forgive me?" he asked, his words going soft. "Enough for God to forgive me. You said God saved me for a reason and that you might be that reason. But not if you don't trust me and believe in me. And not if you can't forgive me." He held his hands on his hips and gave her a hard look. "I could use a little bit of forgiveness, okay?"

She looked up at him, the emotions boiling over in her misty eyes, a look of utter despair on her face. "It won't be you I'll need to forgive," she said on a raw whisper. "First, I have to forgive myself."

He shook his head. There was no reasoning with this woman. She had a shield of faith wrapped tightly around her true feelings. And now she was shouldering the blame for all of this and taking on his sins, too.

But Paco had a feeling once she let that shield down, let that guilt keep eating at her, she'd sink as low as he'd been at times. When that happened, someone needed to be there for her, the way she'd tried so hard to be there for her patients. And him.

Maybe God did have a plan after all.

Maybe Paco would have to be the one to pick up the pieces when Laura fell apart.

But that particular assignment scared him more than going into battle ever had.

He'd stopped walking just as the sun was setting off over a distant canyon rim. To Laura, it seemed as if they'd trekked over and over in the same circle for hours but Paco kept right on moving, stomping, marching. Did he actually know where they were going or was he as lost as she felt?

"There's my brother's house," he said.

Shocked and relieved, Laura glanced up to see the golden rays of the sunset striking against a small, flat adobe house that looked as if it had been perpetually added onto over the years. It leaned and sagged in places and grew and expanded in other places. And all around the yard, between yucca plants and tall cacti and ironwood and desert willows, parts of cars and parts of motorcycles lay scattered like washed-out bones against the pinks and browns of the desert landscape.

"Interesting," she said on a dry-throated croak.

"Buddy's a mechanic of sorts but he's not known for being neat. Take that as a warning."

She didn't need to be warned. But when they got inside the house, she sure wished she could have stayed at that nice inn they'd left at the South Rim.

Paco must have seen her disgust before she could pull a blank face. "Keep in mind, he's in a wheelchair. He has a cleaning lady, but she only comes once a week. And he wasn't expecting company."

"It's okay. It's shelter." She sidestepped a stack of

newspapers, pretty sure a scorpion ran across the floor when she did.

Paco turned on the kitchen light then stood as if waiting for the night creatures to scatter. "Kitchen looks reasonably safe. I'll find us something to eat."

Laura nodded, so tired she couldn't muster up conversation. In spite of the untidiness of the place, it wasn't dirty. There were clean dishes in the cabinets and the refrigerator was well stocked.

"Found some canned soup," Paco said. "Hope you don't mind another sandwich."

"I never ate my sandwich at lunch, so no, I don't mind."

He pushed past her. "Two bedrooms. I'll find sheets for the bed in that one." He pointed to a little room right off the den. "I'll keep watch here on the couch."

"You'll need to sleep, too."

"I don't sleep."

Then he whirled and turned on the bathroom light. "Towels are in the cabinet. I'll try to find you some clean clothes. I think Buddy's ex-wife left some here."

"He's divorced?"

"Yep. She couldn't deal."

"I'm sorry."

He grunted a response.

She noticed family pictures lining the wall. Men in uniform of various ages. "Your grandfather with your father?"

"Yeah. Wíago is my mother's father. My dad was part Hispanic. That was taken right before he left for Vietnam. He didn't make it home for Christmas. And he never knew about me." He shrugged. "He got killed before she could write and tell him."

"Where's your mother?"

"She died about five years ago."

"Did they live here in this house?"

"We've all lived here in this house at one time or another."

Laura's heart opened so wide she had to hold her rib cage tightly against her hands. What had this man suffered?

What had caused this house to become a sad replica of what it must have been when he'd grown up here with his brother? Had his mother raised them on her own after his father died in Vietnam?

So many questions she needed answering and so much hurt hidden behind smiling faces in faded photographs, in broken fragments of life covering the lonely, desolate yard.

And so much hurt hidden in the dark-as-night eyes of the man watching her now.

NINE

Paco watched Laura gather the clothes he'd found for her. Holding the sweater and jeans close, she went into the bathroom and shut the door.

What did she think of this house? Of him? Did she see the love that still lived here in spite of the shroud of shadows surrounding the rundown, lonely dwelling?

Did *he* still see the love they'd all once known here?

He immediately called Buddy. "How's he doing?"

"You know Wíago. He's tough as nails. Surgery went fine and barring no complications, he should be okay. At least that's what the doctors say."

His brother sounded tired, but Buddy had the same steely countenance of their grandfather. "Thanks for staying with him, Buddy."

"No problem, bro. Everyone's been nice here. I've got what I need and my friend who lives here says I can

stay at his apartment if I want. And I'm even flirting
with this one cute nurse—"

Paco stopped him right there. "Too much information. Just watch over him. And don't come back here
until I give you the all-clear, okay?"

"Got it, but you know I can handle things on my end.
Don't worry about us, Paco. Do what you gotta do and
take care, too."

They talked a few more minutes then Paco shut down
his phone and went to the wide window of the little
den to stare out into the dark night. A lone porch light
was the only glow surrounding the midnight colors of
the desert.

"It's been a while, Lord," he said, closing his eyes as
he rested his forehead on the still warm glass. "I know
I talk to You now and then when I get desperate, but
tonight I hope You're truly listening to me. Wíago is in
the hospital, Lord. He is innocent in this. If I brought
this to our house, I ask forgiveness and guidance. If
You brought Laura to me, I thank You and ask for a
clear understanding. Protect my grandfather, protect
my brother and protect Laura and me, Lord."

He opened his eyes, instincts forcing him to squint
into the night. Was someone out there right now, just
waiting? The desert, as silent and stoic as it seemed at
times, was always alive and teeming with life. It could
be a dangerous place, even when a person wasn't being
tracked or stalked.

What human dangers lay out there?

He heard a crash in the bathroom and hit the floor
running. "Laura, are you all right?"

At first, she didn't answer. He didn't hear the water
running either. "Laura?"

His heart drummed like a warrior's cry against his rib cage. "Laura, I'm coming in—"

"No, don't. I'll be out in a minute. I'm okay."

But she wasn't okay. He could tell by the tremble in her voice she was probably having the meltdown she'd held at bay all day long. Paco respected her privacy while he paced across the expanse of the den.

When the door finally crept open, he hurried toward her. "Laura?"

She looked up at him, her eyes red-rimmed and swollen. "I'm sorry."

"Why? What are you sorry for?"

"For ever coming here in the first place."

Her sobs bubbled over and she put her hands to her face. "I didn't want to cry. I tried not to cry." She was shaking all over. "But I've never killed anybody. I've never even seen anybody killed before today."

Paco grabbed her up and took her to the old couch then found a patterned blanket to put around her. The clothes he'd found were a bit big on her, making her look even that much smaller.

"C'mon," he urged, settling her down on a pillow. "Just rest. The soup's ready and I'll make the sandwiches."

"I can't eat."

"You have to eat."

He started to get up, but she reached out to him. "Don't go yet. Sit here with me for a minute."

Paco sank back down on the far end of the couch. But Laura had other ideas. She scooted toward him then glanced up at him with those big blue eyes.

And he was lost.

With a resigned grunt, he gave in and tugged her close. "Shh. Just rest."

Laura leaned her head into the nook of his arm, forcing him to settle against her. It had been a long time since he'd comforted a woman. A very long time.

"I don't think—"

She shook her head against his chest. "It's all right, Paco. I'm not...we're not... I don't expect anything. I just needed something to hold on to for a little while."

And she'd picked him.

Paco didn't know how to react. She only wanted comfort. And he didn't actually understand how to give anyone comfort. He was rusty in that department. But he knew all about respecting women, so he held her there and let her cry on his shoulder just to prove to her that she could trust him, that she was safe with him.

He had somehow become this strong, brave woman's reluctant protector.

God truly did work in mysterious ways.

Laura woke up, her breath heaving in her chest. She'd dreamed about a snake. Then she remembered everything that had happened, including the snake.

Sitting up on the couch, she looked around and saw Paco watching her from the tiny kitchen table. "Soup's still warm," he said, getting up to ladle her some into a big cup. "It's just tomato soup so you can sip it."

"Thanks," she said on a raspy voice. She'd sobbed every ounce of emotion out of herself and now she felt torn and raw, sore and empty. "How long did I sleep?"

"A couple of hours."

She took a sip of the warm soup. "Have you heard anything from your brother?"

He nodded. "Wíago got through the surgery. The doctor thinks he'll pull through unless we get any surprises such as blood clots, a stroke, or cardiac arrest. My grandfather is tough so I'm counting on that."

Laura could see the worry in his eyes. "And Buddy? Is he coming back here?"

"No. He's staying with a friend near the hospital. I told him it might not be safe to return here by himself." He shrugged. "And he reminded me he was a weapons expert in the army."

Laura sat up and drank more soup. The spicy tomato taste washed over her throat and warmed her insides. "I should call my folks, let them know I'm okay."

"Already done."

"You called them?"

"No, Warwick did. He gave them only the necessary information—that we thought you had a stalker and you're with me until we can get you either back to Phoenix or to Eagle Rock."

"How are they?"

"Upset and concerned, but glad you're okay." He got up to come and sit on the split-log coffee table. "I have information that might explain a lot of this."

"I'm listening." She sat her soup cup down on the side table. "Tell me."

"We've found a pattern regarding the two people who've died today. They were both your patients at one time and they both have connections to Lawrence Henner."

"Even the one I shot?"

"Yes. He came to you about two years ago with post-traumatic stress syndrome. John Rutherford, retired marine. Ring a bell?"

Laura closed her eyes, nodding as she put a hand to her temple. "Yes. He was high maintenance, with major anger management issues. He abused his wife and even after we'd counseled him, he kept right on abusing her. He went to jail."

"And got out about two months ago."

"I can't believe I didn't recognize him."

He gave her a level look. "I'm pretty sure he disguised himself."

"What's going on?" she asked, pushing at her hair. "Is every patient I've ever failed coming after me now?"

"Looks that way on the surface," he replied. "Here's what we know for now—they both had emotional issues of some sort and they both came to your clinic for help. We're pretty sure Rutherford was the first shooter. When he failed the first time, he highjacked the delivery truck. The driver was found unconscious on the road. He can't remember much about his attacker, but he described Rutherford. Rutherford's record fits the mode but his aim was a bit off today. And you probably didn't recognize him because his hair was longer and almost completely gray. He'd lost weight, too."

"I should have realized—"

"Laura, somebody out there doesn't want you to realize anything. They're playing mind games with you. I checked the two cards and rubbed a pencil over the indentions we thought we saw—links to Bible passages in Revelations."

"Revelations? But why?"

"Who knows? The person or people behind this aren't exactly rational. The first one is from chapter one, verse eighteen: 'I have the keys of Hades and Death.'"

"That's the Lord talking through John."

"Not in this case. Some madman is using the Lord's words to taunt us."

"What kind of keys?"

"We don't know. It might not mean anything."

"What about the second one?"

"From the second chapter, verse two: 'And you have tested those who say they are apostles and are not, and have found them liars....'"

Laura's stomach roiled with each word. "Do you think this person is talking about me?"

Paco sat with his hands on his knees. "Again, we don't know. But we do know that these two men recently became employed by Lawrence Henner. You said he's a wealthy businessman? Well, we found out he owns his own security company—listed under some sort of corporation—a shell company. I think you mentioned something about that, too."

She let out a gasp. "No, I mentioned that Alex Whitmyer worked for a security company. What if it's Henner's company?"

"That could be bad. Very bad. Just one more connection though." He tapped into his phone. "I'll put Kissie on it." After explaining a possible connection between Henner and Whitmyer to Kissie, he hung up. "If they're working together, we can stop them."

"Could Alex be in this thing with Henner? That would mean they're both more unstable than I realized. Henner could be fueling Alex's obsession with me so he can come after me for my part in his son's death."

Paco looked grim. "According to data we've found underneath all the corporate logos, Henner does things in a much different way from CHAIM."

Laura could believe that. "He struck me as being

demanding and unyielding, and honestly, I think that's why his son killed himself." She couldn't say anymore. Or maybe she should. "Paco, he verbally abused his son. And now he blames me for Adam's death. I never could prove that he was the one at fault because his son never told me the complete truth. But I believe that in my heart."

"So he's coming after you for justification?"

"Or to ease his own guilt?"

"Then why the card tricks?"

Laura shook her head, fatigue and alarm warring inside her mind. "He could be sending assassins, thinking we'd never trace it back to him. The first one didn't kill me, so he sent another one. Maybe the cards are his way of telling me what I've done wrong. Or his way of sending a message that there'll be more killings and attacks to come."

Paco got up, rolled his shoulders. "Except you didn't do anything wrong. He never demanded any type of settlement? Never came after you or the clinic with lawyers?"

"Lawrence Henner doesn't believe in lawyers. He always told me he liked to handle things his own way. And his son Kyle confirmed that over and over by refusing to open up to me. He was afraid of his own father."

"That's a big clue," Paco said. "He's obviously handling this in his own way. And controlling a possible small army of followers."

"And two men are dead because of it. Not to mention your grandfather almost dying, too."

"It's not your fault. You have to remember that."

"So what do we do now?"

"We keep putting the pieces together. Kissie's got the

whole CHAIM team on this one. They've all gathered early at Eagle Rock for the so-called retreat, so they're brainstorming ways to get to the bottom of this."

"The whole team. I don't merit that, but it's good to know."

"You do merit that, Laura. You've helped countless people find better lives, grow stronger in their faith. This lone black sheep has obviously strayed from the flock, sweetheart." He whirled to stare down at her. "Or he was never part of the flock to begin with."

Then he sat down again and took both her hands in his. "But make no mistake. He brought this to my door and I won't stop until I have him behind bars."

"That could be very dangerous, Paco."

"Nothing for you to worry about."

"Right. Good one."

He touched a hand to her face, his smile sharp-edged. "We can't locate Henner. He's not in Phoenix and he's not in Austin. He must be out of the country, as you said."

"But someone's sending these men after us. Alex, maybe?"

"He might be Henner's right-hand man. It might take a while but if he's hiding something, Kissie will find it."

"*He's* hiding while he sends these killers. His paranoia would certainly fit that mode."

"Killers who aren't very highly trained—bad for them but a blessing for us."

"Or the curse Henner wanted on us," she replied, a shudder gripping her with dread. But underneath that dread, a sense of dignity and integrity took hold of her. And a sense of justice. "They won't get away with this, Paco."

"No, sweetheart, they won't. I promise you that."

Laura took a deep breath then looked across at him. "I'm done with falling apart. I'm done with crying. We have to stop this, you and me. I won't let you hide me behind the gates of Eagle Rock. I want to help find this man. I'm not scared anymore. And I refuse to be a victim."

TEN

The next morning, Paco stood at the window once again, coffee cup in hand as he thought about their next move. And the next move of the apparent madman after Laura.

She'd slept much of the night in the tiny bedroom just off the den while he'd kept watch on the couch, guns all around him, a trip wire set up on the front and back doors.

He'd dosed now and then, but since he was used to surviving on very little sleep, he'd never fallen completely to sleep. Too on edge. Too many images of death all around him. He'd sleep again one day. Maybe.

Right now, he had to map a way out of this desert and on to Texas. His gut told him the only safe place for Laura right now was Eagle Rock. And Warwick and the rest of the team agreed. His four team members—

Devon Malone, Eli Trudeau, Brice Whelan and Shane Warwick had gone ahead of their families to Eagle Rock to go over the annual updates required by CHAIM. They'd also tested the overhaul on the security system, something that happened on an annual basis to protect those who came and went in the big security complex. Everything from iris and fingerprint scanners to updated digital equipment and big-brained computers had been tested and retested. But certain people knew how to overcome all of those things. Was Lawrence Henner one of those certain people?

"She should be safe here, Warrior," Eli had assured him on the phone earlier. "I'm bringing Gena and Scotty here in two days, so that should tell you something."

That did tell him everything. Eli Trudeau wouldn't put his new wife or his child in jeopardy. Nor would Devon, Brice or Shane, all so lovesick they'd protect those they held dear at all costs. Devon's wife, Lydia, was expecting their first child in a few weeks but she'd be at Eagle Rock, too. And Brice and his wife, Selena, would be together at Eagle Rock next week. Selena's father was a superior in CHAIM. Shane Warwick had married Katherine Atkins in England but he'd be remarrying Katherine, the daughter of CHAIM founding member Gerald Barton, again here in the States. They planned to repeat their vows sometime in the spring. But for the next week, they'd all be gathered there in the huge private complex, happy and secure while they celebrated Veteran's Day and Thanksgiving.

It sounded like a good place to leave Laura. Especially since she'd gone from broken and afraid to determined and mad. Not good in a woman even on the best of days.

"I need you to take her in then," he'd told Eli and Shane in a conference call. "I'll get her there but I'm not staying."

"Mandatory," Eli interjected.

That, coming from the original rogue agent.

Paco quickly retorted, "I didn't sign up. I don't have a family so I don't need a retreat or a self-imposed vacation. I need to work. That's what I need to do. I have to get to the bottom of what's going on with Laura Walton. Don't you think that overrides a retreat at Eagle Rock?"

"Hmm. Maybe," Warwick the Brit quipped. "The man does have a point, Eli."

"*Oui,* he does at that, my friend," the Cajun said in a low growl. "We'll protect the woman and let the Warrior do the hard work. Sounds like a solid plan to me."

So that was the plan for now. Paco would get Laura to the safe house and he'd get to the work at hand. Starting with tracking down Lawrence Henner. The man was as slippery as a desert snake. But like any snake in the grass, he'd strike again. And sooner than later, Paco figured.

If they had the right man, of course.

He heard a door opening and turned to find Laura dressed, but bleary eyed. Thinking about how she'd fit so nicely in his arms there on the couch, Paco did a mental shrug to let go of that notion. He didn't get involved. Ever.

Just find out who's after the woman, he reminded himself. All that touchy-feely stuff last night has to be left behind this morning. You offered her some comfort on the worst day of her life.

"Good morning," she said as she headed to the coffee pot. "Have you heard anything from your grandfather this morning?"

"Yes. He had a good night. The doctors believe he'll be okay. Buddy is going to hang around near the hospital to make sure."

She drank a sip of the rich coffee. "This is good."

"Grandfather's special blend. He orders it for the restaurant from a friend in Columbia."

"That explains why the café's coffee is so strong."

"But good for you," he said with a smile.

"Right now, I agree." She sipped it again, her hands clutching the heavy brown mug. "I'll need the jolt."

"You need to eat," he said, moving toward the tiny kitchen, the scent of the spicy shampoo she'd used to wash her hair surrounding him. "I made toast and bacon."

She watched him, her gaze weary and almost shy. Was she thinking about last night, too? Did she regret turning to him?

"Thanks." She picked up a crispy strip of bacon and nibbled at it. "What do we do now?"

Paco managed to look at her, trying to gauge whether she was travel-ready or not. "We're going to hike out of here and find the vehicle CHAIM is leaving for us at a gas station near a back road out of the state."

"Hike? But why?"

"Well, for starters, we don't have a car. Besides, our pursuers might be able to track us easier in a vehicle. And because I can track them better if they try following us through the desert."

"Won't that be dangerous?"

"Not any more dangerous than driving out of here.

The desert protects its own. And I was born and raised here."

She shot him a look that indicated he was just that wild, too. "If you say so."

"I do." He had to be curt with her to regain control of oh-so-many emotions. "You need to follow my directions, no matter what."

"Even if I don't agree with your directions?"

"Even so. You're still alive, right?"

She shuddered, her fingers tightening on her coffee mug. "Yes, thank you."

Paco hated the hurt in her expression but he had to protect her, not make nice with her. Today would be hard on both of them. But he had to keep her enclosed in the landscape so they could get out of here alive.

"They found us yesterday," she said by way of an argument.

"Yes, but we were on a familiar trail. And the man they sent didn't succeed in killing either of us, in spite of that."

"Good point."

"Are you up to this then?"

"You mean walking around in the hot, dry, scary desert? I guess I don't have a choice."

"We can sit here and get caught or we leave," he retorted, grumpy with trying to focus on the work and not her pretty eyes. "My mission is to get you to Texas, sweetheart." He held up a hand. "I know you don't like that idea, but we're going there first."

"And then what?"

He took her mug and put it in the sink. "And then, I go to work to put a stop to this, one way or another."

* * *

Laura wondered about that one-way-or-another stuff.

She knew how CHAIM operated. The secretive security organization had agents scattered all over the world and for the most part, the agency went by its own code. Try to keep people alive, if possible. Don't break the law. Report to and hand over information, informants or suspects to the local, national or world authorities as needed. And always, always protect the subject, no matter what.

She'd never dreamed she'd be one of those subjects. She'd helped heal agents, victims, family members and innocent bystanders. Now she could wind up trying to heal herself instead of Luke Martinez. What a strange twist on her mission of mercy.

She didn't want him to be her protector.

But she sure felt safe knowing that he was.

Even if her protector was in one of his bad moods. Maybe he wasn't a morning person. Or maybe he was distancing himself after witnessing her humiliation as she fell apart right there in his arms last night.

The ugly truth looked so harsh in the glaring light of morning. And Luke Martinez was a harsh, tormented man. He'd only been kind to her so she could get through her own terrors from the day before. This was a new day and the man was on a new mission. She'd become his unwelcome burden. Now he had to deal with her and get on with things.

"I can help you with that," she said now as he moved with lightning fast efficiency around the house, gathering supplies for another trek through the heat and dust and prickly bushes and crawling critters of the unforgiving desert.

"Good. Look in that tall cabinet by the stove. That's the pantry. Look for disinfecting wipes, bandages and a box of energy bars. There should be a bottle of water purification tablets in there. Buddy keeps hiking supplies."

"Buddy? I thought he was in a wheelchair."

"He is. But he has a fancy motorized contraption. Takes it out for day hikes." He shrugged. "He'd need supplies if something happened."

"Oh." Laura rummaged through the overstuffed pantry, finding most of what he'd asked for. "Do you want me to put these in one of the backpacks?"

"Set it all on the counter. I'll have to pack tight."

"I can carry my own."

"You'll have a smaller one." He must have seen her frown. "Look, you're not acclimated to this type of hike. We'll have to keep moving as much as possible."

She couldn't argue with that. "You're right. I've only gone on casual day hikes with friends. And usually on well-traveled paths." She fully expected him to take her off the beaten path. In oh-so-many ways.

Wanting to get to know him better, she asked, "Are you and your brother close?"

"Not every day."

She smiled at that. "I used to fight with my brother and sister all the time."

He grunted a reply of sorts.

"What do you do around here? I mean, since you got home?"

Another grunt, then a direct stare. "Well, up until yesterday, I didn't do much of anything. Just helped Grandfather around the café and stayed to myself."

Laura could almost feel the pointed emphasis of that statement. "I guess I messed up your sabbatical from CHAIM."

"I guess you did."

"How far do we have to go today?"

He stopped packing, his expression as blank as the rocks and dirt outside the door. "As far as we need to, sweetheart, to keep you alive."

Laura fell silent, wondering when this would end. Wondering why it was happening in the first place. Did Lawrence Henner have her on some sort of hit list? Thinking back to her counseling sessions with his son Kyle, Laura wished she could have done more for the boy. But then, Kyle was so afraid of his father he refused to open up to her no matter how much she pushed. Did she push too far?

Her guilt regarding Kyle Henner had tripled since coming here. And so had her feelings of stupidity regarding Alex Whitmyer. How could she have believed his pretty lies? She should have seen the truth sooner. So much for trying to heal herself. Had her actions brought this on Luke?

Lost in her dark thoughts, she didn't notice Luke standing there beside her until his hand touched hers. "Let me get you packed so we can go."

She looked up at him, all of her questions hushed for now. For just a minute, he looked so primal and hard-edged in his camo pants and green T-shirt, she almost stepped back.

"Here, put this on," he said, handing her a green canvas hat and a dark khaki long-sleeved shirt. "To hide you and to keep you from getting sunburned."

Laura took the garments, her breath hitching against her rib cage.

Luke Paco Martinez was in full combat mode.

And she pitied anyone who tried to get in his way.

ELEVEN

The man was loaded for bear.

Laura stumbled but regained her footing as they moved over the rocky terrain, her sturdy boots no match for the red sand and craggy rocks of the desert. Luke didn't seem to have the same problem. He moved like a shadow through the shrub brush and cacti, at times blending in so well with the land she found it hard to see him a foot ahead of her. And all of this with a heavy pack on his back.

"Need a break?" he asked, lifting his binoculars to take yet another panoramic scan of the land. They'd hiked up onto an outcropping of jagged rock that formed a wide mesa, giving them a clear view of the surrounding desert.

"I could use a drink of water," Laura replied, thinking silence with this man was just about as uncomfortable as a shouting match with her siblings. His silence shouted out at her with every twist and turn.

Taking a long swig of water from the canteen he shoved at her, Laura decided he had gone all noncommunicative today because she'd gone all dramatic and hysterical last night. So much for finding a chink in his solid armor. Some men couldn't handle feminine theatrics.

Or maybe that was the problem. Maybe she had found the chink and he didn't like her seeing that side of him. If that was true, then at least she was on the right path. She'd just have to keep trying to get him to open up.

But how? It was like talking to a stone-faced mountain. This desert was easier to read than the man standing like an ancient chief in front of her.

"Are we still alone?" she asked then quickly amended. "I mean, besides the lizards, buzzards, chipmunks, snakes, spiders and scorpions?"

"No other humans," he said, dropping the binoculars back around his neck. Reaching for the canteen, he took a long drink.

That allowed Laura time to have a concentrated look at him. He lived up to his code name. He was a warrior, so fierce and so focused, she was afraid to sneeze.

"How far do we have to go?"

"About fifteen miles. It's not a long hike."

"Maybe not for you," she said, her tone mustering up an attitude. "Haven't we gone that far already?"

Paco turned to give her a once-over. "Are you faint? Do you feel light-headed?"

Only when I look at you, she wanted to retort.

"No, I'm fine. Just hot. You'd think with the temperatures in the sixties, it would be nice and pleasant."

"Not when you're moving and not with the sun shining on this dry land. So let me know if you feel a heat stroke coming on."

Did she detect a bit of condescension in that tone?

"I'm fine. Let's go," she shot back, determined to show him she could handle a mere fifteen more miles.

A few saguaros later, Laura decided to pass the time analysis style. "So you've lived here all your life?"

"Yep."

"Tell me about your dad?"

She saw him stiffen. "He died in Vietnam. My mom was pregnant with me."

"So you never even knew him."

"No. Just from pictures and memories. Only, she didn't like to talk about him much."

Laura let that soak in. "But you and Buddy, you seem to be close. I mean, do you two talk about things?"

He pivoted, his dark eyes hitting her like a sandstorm, all brittle and biting. "If you mean, do we share war stories, the answer is no. Soldiers don't like to talk about such things."

"Really," she said on a sarcastic note that she instantly regretted. "I know it's difficult, Paco. But since we don't have anything else to do—"

"I have something to do. I'm trying to get you to safety."

"Oh, so that means you can't be distracted, right?"

"That's right."

His dark frown ended that conversation.

They stomped on for a while. Laura scooted around another scorpion, groaning as the spindly creature lifted up from the dark shade of a prickly pear cactus and hurried across the desert floor.

"What?" Paco said, glancing over at her. He's insisted she try to stay beside him instead of behind him.

"A scorpion. He went the other way."

"Maybe he's afraid you'd analyze him, too."

Laura shot him a glaring look then saw the tilt of his lips. "Are you actually making a joke at my expense?"

"I guess I am at that."

"Well, don't bust a gut laughing."

"I'm not laughing—on the outside."

This time, he actually smiled. It was such a pretty sight, Laura wanted to grab him and hug him tight. Or at least grab on to something as that light-headedness he's mentioned seemed to hit her. But she refrained from that since everything out here in the desert was prickly. Including the man.

"I'm glad I can at least make you smile," she said.

"I don't have anything better to do."

"Except protect me as you've reminded me over and over. I mean, that is why you're being so surly, right? I interrupted your quiet self-imposed isolation and you're not very happy about that. And I guess you're not happy about getting shot at and about your truck getting messed up and especially about your grandfather being hurt."

"Nope. Not happy about any of that." He stopped, put his hands on his hips and leveled her with one of his fierce looks. "But I am happy that scorpion went the other way because I don't have time to nurse you if you get bitten."

"I'm so touched by your consideration."

"Don't mention it."

"How do you know which way to go?" she asked, fascinated by how he would take a turn without even missing a step.

"I do have a compass," he pointed out, showing her one of many cords around his neck. "And I watch the barrel cactus. If you notice, they tend to tilt toward the south."

She hadn't noticed. Now Laura had something to concentrate on, at least. So she started watching for any barrel cacti, noting that some of them grew to four feet tall. "So we're going south?"

"Bingo."

She let out a sigh, wishing the man liked to chatter as much as she did. Then something up in the sky caught her attention. "Oh, look."

Paco glanced up to where she pointed. A lone hawk spiraled through the clouds like a dancing warrior.

"He's so beautiful," Laura said, shading her eyes even though her hat provided a little shade.

Paco didn't say anything. He nodded and moved on.

And then the hawk swooped down and went in for the kill. When he lifted up, he had a fat desert rat in his talons.

"Beautiful and deadly," Laura said, her enthusiasm and interest taking a dark turn. "I need to remember it's survival of the fittest out here."

Paco didn't respond. But she did see him glance over at her, a look of apology on his face.

"We're here," Paco told Laura a couple of hours later. Thankfully, she'd become quiet the last few miles of this trek. She had to be exhausted, but she'd been a trooper. He admired her determination.

"I see civilization," she said, happiness shining in her eyes. "I can't wait to have a nice long shower."

"That might be a while. This is just the first part of our journey."

He ignored her groan and instead concentrated on scoping the tiny village where Shane told him a used pickup from a local dealer would be waiting. Shane had arranged that over the Internet and phone, so Paco trusted their mode of transportation would indeed be here.

He stopped Laura before they emerged onto the lonely road cutting a patchy gray ribbon through the craggy hills.

"Okay, here's the deal. See that gas station over there."

She nodded. "The one with the red stripes."

"The only one in town, sweetheart."

"Got it. Gas station."

"See the blue truck parked by the road?"

"Yes. Is that our truck?"

"Should be. Let me see if I can get a line out to Eagle Rock." He pulled out his phone and hit an app. "Signal looks good."

While he waited for Shane to answer, he said, "Drink," and shoved the canteen at her. Then he motioned toward her small backpack. "Eat a power bar."

Laura rolled her eyes, but did as he asked.

The Knight answered on the first ring. "Warwick."

"We've made it. Blue truck?"

"That's the one. The keys are under the seat."

"How high-tech of you."

"It's the middle of nowhere, old boy. And it was the best deal I could make over the net."

"Looks like a keeper."

"Did anyone follow you?"

"Not that I can tell. Everything's cool right now."

"Good. But, Warrior, I need to tell you something. You might want to keep this information from Laura. I'll let you decide."

"Shoot."

"We think we've located Laura's missing laptop. Kissie zoomed in on the tracking device."

"You can do that?"

"Kissie can, yes. She found a weak signal. And that's the odd part."

"Keep talking."

"The signal is nowhere near the desert, Paco. The laptop seems to be in Texas now."

Paco glanced over at Laura. She was stubbornly chewing on her power bar. "I understand."

"Didn't you say Henner owns an estate in Texas?"

"Affirmative."

"Interesting, don't you think?"

"Extremely. I'll bear that in mind."

"Right. And we'll keep trying to get to the bottom of this, maybe scout out his property here. The signal comes and goes which means he's still on the move. If he tries to break into any files, Kissie might be able to check the IP addresses to get the local network topology. She can encrypt the data, possibly."

"That Kissie is amazing."

"That she is. You take care. 'The eyes of the Lord are in every place, keeping watch on the evil and the good.'"

"Proverbs," Paco said, understanding his friend wanted him to use his own eyes for Laura's safety. "I hear you, Knight." Then he asked, low, so Laura wouldn't pick up on it, "And what about Alex Whitmyer?"

"Interesting about that one," Warwick replied. "We got a hit on his fingerprints because he works in security, and possibly because he was booked a few years ago for harassment charges. They were dropped, apparently. He does indeed work for Lawrence Henner. He's one of Henner's top men. In fact, he's the one in charge while Henner is out of the country. Did subject happen to mention that?"

"I don't think subject knows that."

He heard Warwick let out a long sigh. "This is a very odd case, Paco. Too many variables and way too much coincidence."

"There are no coincidences," Paco retorted.

He put the phone away and wondered if he should tell Laura about this latest development. Why was her laptop coming onto the radar in Texas? And exactly when did the man who'd stalked her start working for Lawrence Henner?

What was so important about her files that someone would take her laptop across the Southwest and into another state?

And was the threat to her now over?

So many questions and each one holding some sort of danger for Laura.

"Is everything all right?" Laura asked, her eyes holding his.

"Everything is just fine," Paco retorted. He'd get her in the truck and on the road and then maybe he'd tell her about the missing laptop's whereabouts.

And about her ex-boyfriend's brush with the law and his interesting employment record.

TWELVE

The truck was loud and without air or heat.

Unless Laura counted the heat in Paco's gaze each time he glanced in the rearview mirror or looked over at her.

The weather was mild so she wasn't too miserable. But she was pretty sure the man driving was full of misery. He didn't want to be here, but his sense of duty obviously trumped any personal feelings he might have. Including how he might feel about her, she decided.

"Are we being followed?" she asked after an hour of his famous silence.

"No."

"Are you mad at me?"

"No."

"So you're just not a big talker, right?"

"Right."

This didn't set well with Laura. She needed him to talk to her, and not just so she could find out information about him. She needed to hear his voice to keep calm, to keep from screaming in sheer terror, to keep the memory of that man she'd killed out of her mind. If she talked, she could forget how the man's eyes opened in a vacant stare or how the touch of his death still stained her with guilt and grief.

"I need you to talk to me," she said. Putting a hand to her mouth, she added, "I didn't mean to say that out loud."

"What do you want to talk about?" he asked through what sounded remarkably like a snarl.

"I don't know. What kind of movies do you like?"

"Don't go to the movies very much."

"If you did go, what kind of movie would you want to see?"

He sat so silent, she wondered if he'd even heard her. Then he finally said, "Film noir."

Laura did not see that coming. "So you like classic movies better than modern-day ones?"

"I guess I do. Used to watch them with Wíago a lot. He liked movies with Humphrey Bogart and Cary Grant and all the John Wayne Westerns, but I think he loved Lauren Bacall and Grace Kelly—pretty women in pretty clothes. He also read a lot of detective novels and passed them on to me. We didn't have a lot of money to buy new books."

Laura catalogued the remark about pretty women. She didn't fit into that sophisticated category but she wondered if that was the type Paco liked, too. He didn't seem to be all that urbane but then that was why she was asking questions. "What about music?"

He shifted the gears as he made a turn. "I guess I can tolerate country music—the good old-fashioned country music. And I like classical music, too."

"Classical? I wouldn't have pegged you for that." Another surprise. Next he'd tell her he had a tuxedo tailor made and as fine as any Shane Warwick would wear.

He gave her a slanted look. "What? I don't fit the bill?"

"Not exactly."

"Wíago traded some of his sculptures once for a whole batch of Bach, Beethoven and Mozart records. We used to crank it up and sit out on the porch and look at the stars. That music would drift out over the desert and soothe the lizards and snakes, even the coyotes, I think."

"Did it soothe you?"

"It did. It used to."

She noted that. "I love classical music, too. I use it a lot at the clinic. But I also love rock and roll."

"Wouldn't have pegged your for that," he retorted, mimicking her earlier words. "You're full of surprises."

"So are you."

"Me?" He slanted a look toward her. "What you see is what you get."

Was that a warning to her? Laura figured he wasn't interested in her in any way, so she let that one slide.

"Can you tell me what Shane Warwick said to you on the phone?"

He shifted in his seat. What did he know? What was he not telling her? Laura tried to reassure him. "I can handle it, Paco."

Another hard glance told her he did have information he wasn't sharing with her. "Are you sure?"

"Of course. This is my life, after all. And we have a lot of hours left to get to Austin, by my calculations."

Taking another scan in the mirrors, he let out a sigh. "Your laptop has surfaced in Texas."

"Texas? How…when?"

"Kissie Pierre has ways of tracking just about anything issued by CHAIM. And that includes stolen laptops, cell phones, anything electronic. She did some finagling and got a hit. We think Henner might be back in the States and on his way to his home in Austin. Or someone working for him has it. It's all speculation right now, but it's the only lead we have."

"He probably had someone steal the laptop while he distracted us with all those attempts on our lives."

"Good point. Whoever took it messed up your room, maybe to make it look like a random robbery or to scare you."

"It worked. I don't have anything to offer these people."

"They took your laptop for a reason, though. If we can track the laptop, we might find our culprits. Or one of the culprits."

"Do you think they'll keep coming after me?"

"They could. If they only wanted information, well, they have that. If they come after us again, well, that means they want to make sure you don't talk."

"I don't have anything to talk about," she said, dread and frustration warring in her mind. "I can't imagine what they think I know."

"You know everything about your patients."

That stunned Laura. "You think they're going after my patients, too?"

"All I know for sure is this—two of your patients

have tracked you and tried to kill you. They both worked for Henner and they're both dead now. And in spite of the fact that they were amateurs, it was either them or us, sweetheart. And the other thing I know for sure—your stolen laptop has all of your patient information on it." He stopped, his hesitation telling.

"What else did Warwick tell you?" she asked.

"You don't need to know everything, okay?"

"Yes, I do. I need you to be honest with me so I can deal with this. I'm not good with surprises."

He glanced in the mirrors, scanning each one in his own dear time. Finally, he looked at her. "Your ex-boyfriend Whitmyer works for Henner. Did you know that?"

Laura's breath caught while her heart raced ahead. "No. I wondered about that, remember? He was always vague about it because it was a security company. I even suspected he might work for CHAIM."

"He's never been with CHAIM, I can tell you that. Warwick thinks he must have signed on with Henner recently."

"Like—after we broke up?"

"Could be. Or maybe before he started dating you. We'll keep researching that angle."

"This goes from bad to worse."

"That's usually how criminals work."

Laura stared out as the landscape changed to more stark rocky mesas. They were nearing Albuquerque, New Mexico, and making record time since he was driving at full speed. He had somehow managed to avoid any state troopers.

"They might be after a specific person, but then that doesn't explain why they keep coming after us. If

Henner and Alex are working together, this could go way beyond me, Paco."

"If they want patient information, they'd also want to kill you so you can't stop them from getting it. Or so you can't stop them from whatever it is they're trying to do."

Laura leaned her head against the cracked leather of the old truck seat. "I wish I could understand this."

"You and me both. But for now, we keep driving and we keep playing with any scenario you can think of. Any memories that trigger something, you let me know."

She wanted to say she'd do that for him if he'd do the same for her. The distraction of getting to the bottom of his torment would sure help her in trying not to think of her own. "I will," she said, wondering if she could come up with anything concrete.

Her eyes still closed, she thought back to the two men who'd been killed. What else about those two that could be a common thread? They were both in their early thirties, both had failed at other jobs and they'd both failed at relationships. What had become of them in between the time she'd treated them till yesterday when they'd died?

"Did Kissie happen to find anything on what our two shooters were doing recently?" she said, looking over at Paco. "Any employment issues or status changes, things such as that?"

"I can find out," he said, grabbing his phone out of the cup holder on the dash.

"Hey, Kissie. Yeah, we're okay for now. Question for you." He repeated what Laura had just asked. "I'll wait.

"She's checking," he reported to Laura. Then "Really? That's interesting, isn't it? Thanks. I'll tell Laura that."

"What?" Laura asked, hoping Kissie could help her.

"This is starting to make more sense, at least," he replied, his eyes on the road. "Both of these men *were* hired by a Central Security Network a few weeks after Kyle Henner died. But Alex Whitmyer has worked there for several years. He worked his way up to a top-dog and he's been in charge since Henner left the country. He's very knowledgeable regarding electronics and high-tech security systems."

Laura felt sick to her stomach. Her nerves roiled as the truck kept moving up the back road. "If Henner is trying to get even with me, Alex would be the perfect man to do it."

"Yes. So we can surmise that Lawrence Henner has hired former patients of yours, apparently to come after you and leave you calling cards with cryptic verses on them. And that he is also in cahoots with your former boyfriend, too."

Laura put her head in her hands. "He must really hate me. He does blame me for his son's suicide—that much I knew. I just didn't know he'd want revenge enough to kill me."

"Or take your private files. We still have to figure out why he's doing that."

"He might think he can find other patient cases where I failed."

"Are there others?"

"Not many. I can only do so much, but unless the patient is willing to follow our suggestions and recommendations regarding treatment and medication, I can't completely cure them."

"So do you think there might be others?"

Laura thought back over the few years she'd been at the clinic. "We have a strong success rate, but we aren't one hundred percent as far as curing patients. I don't recall any other cases, though."

"Anything else about these two that might connect them even more?"

"If I had my files, I could check," she replied. "It's hard to say from memory alone."

"Think, Laura. There must be something we can use to keep putting the pieces together."

Laura sat silent for a few minutes. "I'm sorry. My mind has gone numb from all of this." Pushing at her hair, she let out a breath. "I'm tired, Paco. So tired."

"Sleep," he ordered. "Don't think about it anymore for now. Rest."

His orders didn't help matters but since she didn't know what else to do, Laura closed her eyes again and put her head back against the seat. The warmth from the winter afternoon was waning as sunset began to take over.

Paco tossed a jacket toward her. "Cover up."

He had such a way with words, she thought as she grabbed the camo jacket to wrap it against her arms and shoulders. When she immediately recognized his scent of sweat mixed with the spicy shampoo they'd both used back at his brother's house, Laura inhaled and tried to relax.

She didn't know when it had happened, but she felt safe with Paco Martinez. In spite of his gruffness and his unwillingness to talk about his own feelings and emotions, she knew he was a good man.

And that's all she needed to know. He'd protect her

because he was a trained soldier. A reluctant hero. A man searching for his own heart.

Laura decided to pray for Paco while she tried to relax. And so she began, asking God to guide him and help him, to heal him and nurture him. Laura wanted Paco back in the fold. He might seem like a black sheep, but he was really just hurting and disillusioned by all the death and destruction he'd had to witness in the war.

If I can't help him, Lord, I know You can. Please guide Paco as he tries to protect me. Help him to find out who these terrible people are and what they want from us.

Laura kept going, her prayers changing as she thought about every detail of Luke Paco Martinez. She thought back over his life, over his army career and his time with CHAIM. He'd wanted to serve both his country in the military and CHAIM in the private security sector. And working for CHAIM meant Paco wanted to serve the Lord, too.

She'd learned a lot about him before coming to find him. She'd even downloaded some very high-security files on him, with CHAIM's permission since his case was active and highly sensitive. At least, she had somewhat of a handle on him even if he didn't want to talk to her.

That brought Laura even more comfort.

She was drifting off to sleep, her prayers on a perpetual spin inside her head, when she suddenly realized something very important about her two former patients.

"Paco," she said, lifting up so fast the big jacket fell to her waist. "I remembered something. Something so obvious I don't know why I didn't think of it before."

THIRTEEN

He pulled the truck off the road at a deserted farmhouse then after doing a quick surveillance of the area, shut down the engine. If she'd figured out something significant he wanted to be sitting still when he heard it. "Go ahead. Tell me what you remembered?"

Laura inhaled then shook her head. "It might not mean anything but... Howard Barrow and John Rutherford had both applied to become CHAIM operatives when they were younger. And they both got turned down. I'm surprised Kissie didn't find that in her background check."

Paco rubbed a hand over the beard stubble on his chin. "Applied? Most of us were invited to join or were nominated by an older member. Rarely does a person ask to join CHAIM because so few people know about the organization. Are you sure about this?"

She bobbed her head. "It's in their files. I can't believe I didn't make the connection sooner."

If anyone could understand repressed memories, it was Paco. He was running from his own. "That's okay. Stress can do that to a person and you certainly had no way of knowing this would come up again. But you're remembering things now, so keep talking."

She closed her eyes for a minute then looked at him. "We might be able to pull more information from my office hard copy if I can get to someone and explain why I need the information. Those files are confidential but this is an emergency situation." Then she put a hand to her mouth. "Unless of course, whoever took my laptop has erased that information."

"Good point, and possibly why Kissie didn't spot it." He held a hand on her arm. "Tell me more about these two. Why weren't they accepted?"

"Howard Barrow had a drug problem in his teens so he didn't past muster for what he called the 'elite, holier-than-thou group.' He was kind of bitter about it, but he only mentioned it once and in passing. And that's strange since he had no way of knowing I work with CHAIM employees. They're usually referred by church counselors."

"Is that how *he* came to you—from a church referral?"

"No. He was a walk-in."

"And what about John Rutherford?"

"He was a member of CHAIM for a year, right after he graduated from college. But he told me he didn't like the work." She shrugged. "That's all I can remember about him."

Paco thought back on the two men who'd come gunning for them. "Neither of them were pros, that's for sure. We're talking about late thirties, paunchy and, well, downright foolish if you ask me. If Henner sent them, he sure was asking for failure. But why would he want their CHAIM records erased?"

Laura tugged at the jacket in her lap. "And why in the world would either of them do his bidding in the first place?"

Paco had to remind himself of how innocent this woman was. Innocent and naïve and too good to be caught up in this kind of mess. "Laura, some people will do just about anything for the right amount of money."

"Henner has lots of that."

"Yes, the man has money, power, several locations to hide out, and he runs a security company—that on the surface is somewhat like CHAIM."

"But *not* on the surface?"

"Not on the surface, something isn't right. I don't think our man Henner is using his powers for good."

"He's evil. I can believe that from talking to his son, and from seeing the way he blamed me for Kyle's death. If the man only knew. I do blame myself, but I also think Lawrence Henner pushed his son to the breaking point. And from what Kyle told me, he pushed his employees in much the same way. Kind of a vigilante tactic."

Paco reached over to push a strand of hair off her cheek. "Yes, he's got some kind of agenda—maybe a vendetta against you. He's after you for a reason, Laura. Maybe because of his son's death or maybe for another reason all together. You can't blame yourself for some whacked-out man's idea of justice."

"I'll always blame myself," she replied, looking away.

Paco understood a lot about her now. Had she come

here to help him, hoping he wouldn't end up like Kyle Henner? "Look," he said, "if Henner is behind this, we'll get him. And this information is just another link. I have to call Kissie and the others. They can research away while we try to get you there."

"And what about you?" she asked. "You keep telling me you're taking me to Eagle Rock, but you don't say anything about staying there yourself."

"I'm not planning on staying," he said while he waited for Kissie to answer. "I intend to find Lawrence Henner and ask him a few questions."

He heard Laura gasp, saw the denial in her eyes. Holding up a finger to quiet her, he said, "Kissie, how's everything?"

"The gang's all here. All except you, of course."

"I'm on the way to drop off the package."

He looked over at the package and saw that Laura was perplexed and a bit perturbed at him. It would have to do.

"Kissie, I have some new information." He reported what Laura had told him. "You might do another search to connect any of Laura's patients to both CHAIM and Henner's security company. See how many hits you get. We think Henner somehow erased that bit of information from Laura's files—possibly her laptop and any hard copy or backup files, too."

"I'm on it," Kissie said. "This is getting downright weird, Warrior."

"Yep. Where is the team today?"

"Where else? In the war room, trying to figure this thing out. You've handed us a fascinating case and it's rare these days that we're all in one place to solve it.

Feels like the good old days when we all worked together."

"I can use the help, that's for sure."

"We'll be here. The family members are arriving today. My son Andre will be here. He's so ready to start training to become an operative."

"Andre's that old?"

"Yes, sir, almost twenty-three. You know, you could stay here with Laura. I'm sure she'd feel better if you did. We'll solve this together, Paco. It's safe here."

Paco heard the undercurrent in her words. *Are you sure you're ready for this? Should you go out there on your own? Will you crack under the pressure?*

He didn't intend to crack and he prayed he wouldn't. He had to keep it together for Laura's sake.

"Nice try, Kissie. But I need to find out what Henner is up to. My first stop after Eagle Rock will be his estate in Texas. Any more on the laptop?"

"The signal comes and goes. But it's still in Texas."

"Okay. We've got to get a bite to eat and keep moving. I should have her there by midnight."

"We'll keep a light on for you."

Paco put his phone away then looked at Laura. "I know what you're thinking but I can't hide out at Eagle Rock. These people came after us, Laura. And my grandfather could have been killed. They put this at my doorstep so it's up to me to get to the bottom of things."

She sat up to glare at him. "And I'm the reason for that. I brought this to your door, Paco. I can't have your death on my conscience, too. Let one of the others go after him. Or take them all with you to find him."

"Not a bad idea," Paco said. "Just might work."

"Are you serious?"

He saw the hope in her eyes. And something else he didn't want to see. But he had to ask anyway. "Worried about me, sweetheart?"

She got all fidgety, her fingers working the frayed flap of his old camo jacket. She wouldn't look at him. "I told you, I don't want anyone else to die."

Of course she didn't. She was a good girl caught up in a bad situation. Nothing to do with pining for him. "No one else is going to die if I can help it. I'm not going to die and neither are you. That's the plan."

"But you will consider taking help—some backup? I mean you're part of a five-man team. It doesn't make sense to let four of them stand around doing nothing while you go in alone with guns blazing."

He put his hands on the steering wheels. "It *has* been a long time since we all went out as a team. Not since South America when we tried to bring that girl out of the jungle."

"And Eli's grandfather was behind her death and everything that happened to Eli. That was horrible. You were all betrayed. I don't want this to turn out that way."

"Neither do I," he said. "And if I know my team, they won't let me go alone. Unless I give 'em the slip, of course."

"No." She grabbed his arm, her gaze flaring hot. "Promise me you won't go without one of them at least."

Because he didn't want to think about the gentle tug of her touch or the tug inside his heart, Paco shook her away and cranked the truck. "You don't think I can do it alone, do you, Counselor?"

Shock colored her face. "I didn't mean it that way, but now that you mention it—are you ready for this?"

He hit the steering wheel. "Why can't anyone believe I'm okay?"

"Okay is one thing, Paco. But being sound in both body and mind is another. That's why I came to talk to you in the first place."

He shut his eyes, saying his own prayer of patience. "I don't need to spill my guts to anyone else. I went over everything with debriefing and army therapists. And I had a nice long stay in Ireland at Whelan Castle. I'm a soldier. This kind of thing comes with the territory."

"This kind of thing can push you over the edge, too. It's called post-traumatic stress and survivor's guilt and you have—had—a classic case of it."

Anger colored his next words but it felt good to be angry. "Yes, maybe I did but I'm good to go now. I've been to the edge, sweetheart. I won't go back there."

"Then don't take a chance on having to face that kind of pain again. Ask for help, Paco. There's no shame in that. That's why CHAIM has teams to begin with."

He couldn't argue with that. And he didn't want to go rogue and mess up the delicate balance of the CHAIM team he'd been a part of for years. He could be a hothead or he could keep a cool head. The difference could mean saving lives.

"I'll think about it," he said. Then he surprised himself. "I'll make you a promise. Once I get you safely inside the gates of Eagle Rock, we'll find a quiet spot and you can ask me anything you want. How's that?"

She didn't look as pleased as he'd hoped. "I don't need that kind of promise from you. I need you to be ready to deal with what happened to you in Afghanistan." Her shoulders lifted in a shrug. "Maybe now is not the time. You're already under a lot of pressure."

"What do you really want from me, Laura?"

Her eyes brightened with unspoken words. "I want you to heal. That's all. I want you to heal."

"Then give me time and let me do what I have to do. The only way I can function right now is by getting you to a safe place and figuring out what Henner is up to. That's what gives me strength. That's my job."

"Okay." She bobbed her head. "Okay. You're right. I came to see you for one reason and now, we have other things to consider. I haven't been fair in trying to make you open up to me in the midst of all of this."

If she only knew. He'd like nothing more than to turn this truck around and find some pretty spot so he could just talk to her, get to know her. But he couldn't do that tonight.

"Are you hungry, thirsty? Do you need a break?"

"I'm okay for now," she replied, quieting back into her corner as if she didn't want to provoke him. "I just want this to be over."

"You and me both," he replied.

Because if this didn't end soon, he would be in too deep to turn back. He might actually start caring about this woman. And that could be his downfall.

Midnight inked its way through the ribbon of winding back road. Laura woke up with a start to stare out the window, her disoriented mind searching for a reason why she might be sleeping in a moving truck. Then she turned and saw the hawkish features of the man driving her across the Texas Hill Country.

"Where are we?" she asked, her voice raspy and low.

He shot a glance toward her then turned back face

forward to stare at the road. "Almost to Austin. We should be at Eagle Rock in about an hour."

"We'll wake everyone up."

"Nah, they never sleep."

"Good point, since I've never actually seen you sleep."

For just a flashing second, Laura imagined what it would be like to have this man in her life in a normal way. A way where she fixed him breakfast and sent him off to a safe day job. A way where he came home to dinner and kissed her on the cheek.

She turned toward him and thought she saw an awareness rushing like a fast rain inside his mysterious eyes. Did he feel it, too? Did he feel the tug, the pull, of wondering what it would be like to have one normal day together?

Laura reminded herself that this man was a loner who lived a hard, dangerous life. He was broken and bitter and she couldn't hope to fix all of him. The counselor part of her could try to help heal his wounds, but her woman's heart urged her to fix the rest of him, to try and get inside his heart and not just his head.

But that was dangerous territory.

He gave her another glance. "Look, Laura—"

And then a piercing sound shot through the old truck and it started spinning out of control, air hissing out of a tire.

Paco grunted in surprise then pushed her down with one hand while he maneuvered the truck into the spin with the other hand. "Stay down and hold on!"

Laura's heart fell to her feet, the heavy pace of her pulse booming in her ears while her world spun like a top, memories and feelings flowing over her as the truck whirled and careened. In her mind, she was still waiting for him to finish his sentence. But he didn't.

She heard more shots, felt Paco's hand on her arm. He held the truck steady, cycling around and around, ducking his head now and then, then lifting up to glare into the mirrors. Rising up, Laura tried to see behind them.

"Don't move, Laura. Stay down!"

How could she possibly move now? Laura became frozen in a numb kind of panic. But inside that panic, her heart beat with a fierce need to stay alive. She wouldn't let this happen. She wouldn't let Paco give his life for her here on this dark road out in the middle of nowhere. And so she fought to hold on, fought through silent, screaming prayers, the touch of his hand guiding her.

It was only seconds, but in Laura's mind, this dizzying trip into the dark night went on and on. She could hear Paco's gruff complaints, see the control in his stoic face, and feel his fingers gripping her, holding her as the windshield shattered. Then she felt a piercing pain as the truck jolted up into the air, causing her to bounce up and right into the windshield, even while Paco managed to hold on to her arm.

Finally the groaning truck came to a shuddering stop, the sound of tires grinding into dirt and rock and shrubs sliding over Laura's ragged nerve endings with a hissing protest.

The shots had stopped. The truck rattled to a loud stillness. Her heart pumped and pushed inside her body, her breath came fast and furious and mingled with Paco's rapid breathing next to her. While the pain tried to pull her deeper and deeper into the darkness.

And still, his hand had never left her arm.

Through it all, Paco had held on to her.

FOURTEEN

Paco tugged at her. "Laura? Laura, are you all right?"

She nodded then lifted the jacket. "Paco?"

He saw the blood, a bright red stain moving over her sweater. Then he saw the hole in the jacket. He looked up, his gaze slamming into hers. Her face was pale in the moonlight, her eyes whitewashed with fear. And pain.

She'd been hit.

Still holding her, he reached into the bucket seat behind his seat and grabbed his gun, placing it on the dash. Then he felt around for the first aid kit.

"Hang on. Laura, do you hear me? Hang on." He touched two fingers to her neck, prayers screaming in silence inside his head. He had to do something. He had lots of supplies, but nothing to stop this kind of bleeding. Throwing the kit back behind the seat, he pulled on her sweater and saw the tiny bullet hole piercing her left upper shoulder.

"I'm okay," she said, grabbing at her sweater. "It's just a little cut or something—probably from the glass. Let's go. Just go."

"I can't go until I know how bad you are." He pulled a T-shirt out of his duffel. "Can you hold this tight against your wound?"

She gave him a feeble nod. "Uh-huh."

"Where does it hurt?"

"Everywhere. Mostly my left arm."

Paco did a quick scan of her body, touching on her head, neck and shoulders and working his fingers on her legs. "No other injuries that I can find."

"Nope. Just a bump on my head and a hole in my arm." She swallowed, her eyes closing in a squint of pain.

"I'm going to lift you," he said, gently reaching behind her. "So I can see if the bullet went through."

She nodded, gritted her teeth.

Paco reached behind her, his arms around her shoulders. "Hold on."

She moaned as he lifted her forward and let her fall against his chest. "There's no tear in the seat and you're not bleeding on your back." He might have to dig the bullet out. "Okay, I'm gonna lay you back against the seat."

Slowly, he leaned her down. Her head loped back and she closed her eyes again. "Laura, try to stay awake. Stay with me, sweetheart."

"Tired."

"I know. But I need your help."

She opened her eyes. Her pupils were dilated and

she would go into shock soon. Meanwhile, the hit man might be approaching them right now.

"I need you to hold this shirt and press it against the wound. Okay. Pressure, lots of pressure. You hold on to that while I see if it's safe."

She didn't respond but she let out a moan as he carefully shifted her head against the seat and put his jacket over her. Moving away to grab his gun, he opened his door and jumped out, taking a fast glance around the deserted road and nearby woods.

"Laura, I'm going to call Eagle Rock and then I'll make sure the shooter is gone. Eagle Rock can send the chopper to get us."

She moaned but he felt her hand move and watched as she pressed the wadded up shirt against her shoulder.

Paco looked down and saw blood covering his shirt. Laura's blood. For just a minute, he felt a buzz inside his head, could hear the drone of helicopters, the shout of soldiers, while he remembered holding a man in his arms, watching him die.

Shaking off the flashback, Paco made a vow. "I won't let you die, Laura. Do you hear me?"

She moaned again.

Hurrying, he grabbed his night vision binoculars then crouching low, moved around the wheelbase to view the damage and their location.

The truck had landed in a ditch just off the road near a big hilly pasture. They'd cut a path through the bramble and bushes, but he didn't see or hear anyone coming. Not a sound of footsteps or motors running. Whoever had shot them must have thought he'd finished the job when the truck careened off the road. Or was hiding out there, waiting to see if Paco and Laura were still alive.

Paco looked at the left back deflated tire, remembering the sound of gunshots and tires squealing. At least he'd managed to avoid hitting a tree head-on.

He had a few cuts and bruises. But Laura had been shot. He did a quick scan with the binoculars and seeing nothing, prayed their attacker was long gone.

Grabbing his cell, he hit buttons and waited, his breath coming in great huffs, until he heard Kissie on the line. "I need help. We've been hit and Laura's injured."

"Got it," Kissie said. "Give me your coordinates."

Paco rattled off the location, remembering the nearest mile marker and the road number. "Hurry, Kissie."

"We're firing up the chopper right now. Eli and Shane will be there soon. And we'll get a doctor out here to meet y'all when you land."

Checking the area once more, Paco made sure no one was lurking in the woods. He couldn't leave the truck so he got back in and slid close to Laura, lifting her head with his hands. "How you doing?"

"I'm alive," she said, her words weak and slurred. "I want to go to sleep."

"Soon, baby, soon. Help is on the way." Frantic to keep her awake, he said, "But let's talk while we wait."

"You don't like to talk."

That was a fact but right now, nervous energy had him more than willing to spill his guts.

"I don't mind talking to you, Laura. Not now anyway."

Paco tried to make her comfortable. As long as he could hear her soft breath, he knew there was hope. So he clung to that hope as tightly as he clung to her hand in his. And then, he started talking.

"You know, up on that mountain in Afghanistan, I held a young soldier's hand just like this." He stopped, swallowed the bile of grief. "It was his first mission. He was twenty-one years old. Just starting life, Laura. So young and so confident. He died right there in my arms and there was nothing I could do for him. Nothing."

"You did your best," she said on a ragged whisper.

Shocked that he'd blurted that out, Paco prayed for the chopper to come before he said too much. But the dark night and her ragged breathing kept him talking. "They all died, Laura. All of them but me. I don't understand that."

"I know," she replied in a tightly held breath. "I know, Paco. All in your files. Can't explain. God has a plan for you."

"And what is that plan?" he said, his words harsh in the still truck. "What kind of plan allows for everyone I cared about to die and leave me like that?"

Including her? Did God intend to take Laura from him, too?

"You have more missions," she said, her words drifting off as her eyelids fluttered. "Important missions."

"But what about all those young men? Why didn't they get to live for one more mission? Why didn't they get to come home?"

She lifted her hand toward him then dropped it away, the look in her eyes full of longing and hope. "Look not to your own understanding...."

"Laura, Laura, don't go to sleep." He listened then let out a breath. "Laura, I hear the helicopter. Eli and Shane are here."

But Laura didn't hear him. She'd passed out.

* * *

"What's taking that doctor so long?"

Paco paced the confines of what they called the war room then turned to stare out the window, his gaze scanning the many outbuildings and fences around the secluded, sprawling compound. "We should have heard something by now."

Shane Warwick walked up to him, putting a hand on his back. "Relax, Warrior. Dr. Haines is one of the best and we have a complete medical wing in this compound. He'll do everything he can to help her and right now, he's probably thinking about what's best for Laura. She might need surgery."

Paco whirled to grab Shane's lapels. "We can't take her to a hospital. They'll come after her."

"No hospital, old boy," Shane said, gracefully lifting Paco's hands from his jacket. "We have the equipment here, if need be. And Dr. Haines served in Iraq. He knows all about triage and operating in a field hospital."

Paco stared down at his hands, realizing he'd almost attacked his best friend. "I messed up, Warwick."

Devon Malone, Brice Whelan and Eli Trudeau were all in the room. Devon stepped toward them. "You didn't mess up, Paco. You were on your way here and you did everything you could to save her."

"We were so close," Paco said, reliving the nightmare of seeing that blood flowing out of her body. "So close."

"You're here now for sure," Eli said. "You're safe, *mon ami.*"

"I don't care about being safe," Paco retorted. "I want Laura safe and healthy again. I don't get why anyone would come after that woman."

Brice shot a look at Devon. "Man, just how deep are you into this mission?"

Paco stared across at them, taking in the worried looks on their faces. "How deep do you expect me to be?" he asked, his hands on his hips.

Brice's smile was tight-lipped. "'Consider beauty a sufficient end'," he quoted.

"And what does that mean?" Paco shot back, in the mood for a fight, not Whelan's sappy poetry.

"It's Yeats, actually," Brice said, his eyes solemn.

"I don't care who it is," Paco said. "You never make any sense, Whelan."

Eli clapped Paco on the back. "I think what this moonstruck poet is trying to say is that you're fighting for more than good over evil. You have never been one for theatrics or skittishness, Warrior. But you're obviously highly wired right now."

"Meaning?"

Devon shot Brice and Eli a warning look. "Meaning, you're either not ready for this mission or you've become emotionally involved with the subject. Or both."

Paco's pulse raged inside his body. "The *subject* is a nice woman who only wanted to help *me*. And now look at her. She's been shot!" He crossed his arms at his chest. "And as for me, I'm ready and willing since I was forced to take this on in order to protect her. We've had a couple of really bad days, so yes, I'm wired to the gill, boys. And I failed at protecting her, in spite of my best efforts. That tends to make a man skittish and *involved*."

"These people would have found her one way or another, Paco," Shane said. "They obviously want something from her. And the way I see it, she came to you at precisely the right time. If you hadn't been there to help her, she indeed might be dead already."

Kissie came into the room, followed by a young man. "Paco, this is my son, Andre. I sent Andre back to the wreck sight to look for evidence and clean things up." She turned to the tall, muscular youth. "Andre, tell them what you found."

Andre, his head shaved and his smile full of apology, handed Paco a card. "It's a business card, sir. It has Ms. Walton's information on it. Found it a few yards from where the truck landed."

Paco grabbed it. "And let me guess. It has another verse from Revelations etched invisibly on the back?"

Kissie nodded. "It does indeed. From chapter eleven, verse seven, just part of the verse: 'The beast that ascends out of the bottomless pit will make war against them, overcome them, and kill them.'"

Kissie touched Andre on the arm. "Go on back, son. Stand by and watch out for Miss Walton."

He gave Paco a shy stare then left the room.

Paco's brain buzzed with all that he'd been through and the implications of the verses he'd read. His gaze swept the room. "I think someone is declaring war on CHAIM. And they're using Laura to do it. How deep do you think I need to be into this mess now, gentlemen?"

Shane stared at the card. "We're all in it now, Warrior. In too deep to turn back."

Paco nodded. "Thank goodness I at least got Laura here alive."

Dr. Haines came into the room. "And she should stay very much alive because of your efforts."

Paco pushed toward the doctor. "How is she?"

Dr. Haines took off his glasses and cleaned them

on his lab coat. "Well, she's resting now. I cleaned and debrided the wound and did a thorough search for any internal damage. Based on the X-ray, I found bullet fragments in the wound but the bullet didn't go all the way through. She probably got hit when the bullet shattered the windshield—I'd say a high-powered rifle did the job. I think I got it all, but I've given her antibiotics for infection and a pain pill to keep her quiet through the night. And I wrapped the wound to staunch the bleeding." He held up a hand. "However, if she runs a fever or presents any other signs of infection, I suggest you get her to a hospital as soon as possible."

Kissie touched Paco's arm. "I could take her into Austin and have her checked out and back in no time."

"I don't want her to leave Eagle Rock," he replied, warring with himself on how to handle this. "Doc, are you sure she's gonna be okay?"

"As long as infection doesn't set in, I think so. But again, I can't predict that. She's blessed it was a clean wound. But she'll be weak and sore for a couple of days since she got a bump on the head and she was tossed around, too."

"Can I see her?"

The doctor nodded. "Just briefly. She's exhausted and she needs to rest so her body can heal."

Sally Mae Barton entered the room, her eyes gleaming. Married to CHAIM founder Gerald Barton, Sally Mae has once worked for CHAIM. And the woman didn't pull any punches. "Mercy, let the man see her. We've dressed more wounds around here than a Civil War widow, I reckon. And we've got Selena Whelan here. She's a nurse. We'll watch over Laura, Dr. Haines.

You have my word on that and we won't hold you accountable if anything does go wrong. Which it won't."

The doctor looked skeptical. But he didn't protest. "Okay then, I guess I'm done here."

"I'll show you out, Dr. Haines," Sally Mae replied with a sweet smile. Then she turned to the others. "Kissie, take Luke to see Laura. And the rest of you, get back to work on solving this case. We have a celebration coming up."

Paco looked at Kissie, hoping she'd let him stay with Laura longer than just a few minutes.

She nodded toward him. "I'll take you to her."

Devon followed them. "I'm going to check on Lydia."

Devon and Lydia had fallen in love a few years ago in spite of his secret identity and his cover as a mild-mannered minister. Now they were expecting their first child.

Paco shut his mind to the thought of bringing children into the world and concentrated instead on his work. "What next?"

Brice, Shane and Eli stood like a solid wall over the long conference table. "We'll be here," Brice said. "Hey, Dev, can you check on our ladies, too?"

Eli's wife—Devon's sister, Gena Malone Trudeau—was here with their son, Scotty. Eli had come back from the brink just to save the son he never knew he had. And he'd fallen in love with the woman raising that son.

Just one big happy family.

And that cool, calm Brit Shane Warwick had fallen for Gerald and Sally Mae's daughter, Katherine Atkins. They'd gotten married in England but planned a second service in the spring here in Texas.

Devon smiled at Brice's request. "Of course. I'm

sure they're not happy about this lockdown we're under now."

"Better safe than sorry," Eli said, his tone grim.

Paco gave them all one last look, his heart twisted with feelings he didn't want to explore right now, then followed Kissie to another wing of the house.

As they snaked through hallways and doors that required scanners and key cards in order to unlock, he asked, "Is she being guarded?"

"She is," Kissie replied. "Andre volunteered for the first shift."

"I'll take a shift, too," Paco replied.

Because he wasn't going anywhere until he knew Laura was going to pull out of this. And once he was sure she was safe and well, he was going to find Lawrence Henner and have a long talk with the man.

If talking didn't work, Paco would go into action mode and get the truth, no matter what.

He had a new mission now.

And if God had brought him to this mission then Paco aimed to finish it to the bitter end. For Laura's sake.

FIFTEEN

Paco entered the sterile room hidden in the back of the big, rambling complex, nodding to Andre as he opened the door. Lydia Malone smiled up at him. She sat next to Laura's bed, reading what looked like a devotional book.

"Luke," she said, struggling to get up. Pregnancy agreed with the pretty blond-haired woman. In spite of her rounded stomach, she was glowing, her soft smile full of understanding and compassion.

"Hello, Lydia." He didn't waste time with the niceties. He went straight to the bed and took Laura's hand. She was as pale as the crisp white sheet and blanket covering her. "How is she?"

Lydia came to stand beside him. "I think she's gonna be just fine. She's sleeping now. The doctor gave her something to help her relax and the antibiotics are probably making her drowsy, too." Then she glanced at him. "How're you doing?"

Paco found it hard to look into Lydia's vivid, all-knowing eyes. The woman had a direct link to the Almighty and she used it with all the precision of a hunter with a bow. "I've been better."

Lydia nodded then touched a hand to her stomach. "I've prayed for both of you."

"I have no doubt of that," he replied. "Thank you."

Lydia looked down at Laura. "She was asking for you earlier."

His heart did a funny little thing that made him think of a tank roaring across rocks. "She was?"

Lydia looked from Laura's pale face back to him, a silent stealth message passing between them. "Talk to her. It might help her."

He nodded, the knot in his throat choking him with misery. "I'm not good at talking."

"You don't have to be good at it," Lydia replied. "Just speak with honesty. Laura, like most women, probably values honesty above all else."

Paco stood silent as Lydia discreetly left the room. How could he be honest with this sweet woman? How could he tell her that he wasn't worth her trouble? That he *was* trouble.

He went to the door. "Andre, you can go now. I'll take the next shift."

"Yes, sir." Andre's big brown eyes held a thousand questions. None of which Paco wanted to answer right now. He wasn't a hero and he didn't want the kid staring at him with admiration or anticipation. But he didn't want to discourage the kid either. Andre was about to become a man and life was hard. That was all Paco could really tell him.

But he couldn't talk to the kid right now. He only wanted to sit here with Laura and will her to wake up and fuss at him. It was pretty amazing that he'd only known her for a few days and yet, she'd come bursting into his life full of fire and determination and just like that, she'd changed him. He wished they could have met under different circumstances but then he probably would have pushed her away. Even on a good day, he was so good at alienating anyone who cared about him.

But just knowing that she'd cared enough to find him based on a desperate midnight call, touched Paco deep inside his burned, battered, scarred heart.

And scared him more than anything he'd ever encountered.

So he sat down in the middle of the night and he talked in soft tones to the woman sleeping in the bed. He took her hand and he told her all about the horrors of being trapped on that mountain, the agony of watching his men die, and the relief that he hated each time he took another breath. He told her about the dreams and how they'd come all during the night. About how, in the dreams, he was left standing in a white-hot desert, the silence so telling it made him want to scream out in agony, the intense loneliness he experienced so bitter and cutting, he felt as if he truly was the last man left on earth.

He told her about when he was young and how his family had struggled, so Paco decided to follow in the family tradition and join the military to see the world and learn more about life. Then after his first tour, he was asked to join CHAIM. And even though he re-upped with the military, he did join CHAIM because he wanted to fight the good fight and be a good man like his own father—the father he'd never really known. He also wanted to honor God, both on and off the battlefield.

But he'd done so many things that didn't honor God. And he's seen so much that didn't honor God. He'd felt thoughts that didn't honor God. So why would God honor any of his prayers now?

"I shouldn't be here, Laura. I don't have any right to be here."

When he tired of talking, he stopped to pray, leaning forward so that his forehead touched her hand, his prayers asking for some of her softness, for some of her strength and integrity and faith. She has such soft, pretty hands. So soft and so pretty that he yanked his calloused, scarred fingers away for fear he'd damage her in some way.

By the time he was finished, the sun was rising toward the east and he could hear birds chirping just outside the high, secure windows.

The room became flooded with a brilliant creamy yellow glow that hurt Paco's tired eyes. The silence of that light sent shivers down his spine but he could still hear the birds fussing and playing in the courtyard. How he wished he could see God's touch in that brilliant light, hear the Lord's words in the song of the birds.

Then he heard *her*. He heard Laura's gentle voice.

"*I'm* glad you're here, Paco. You're not on that mountain alone now. You have God and you have me."

And right then and there, Luke Paco Martinez knew God had brought him to this very moment, the moment when he'd accepted God back into his heart and the moment when he'd finally fallen in love.

Laura tried to smile but the effort hurt too much. Paco reached for her hand, his gaze holding her in a tender way that seemed different from his usual cynical, abrupt nature. She'd heard his confession, her mind drifting between sleep and being awake. She'd wondered at times if she was just in a long dream where he trusted her and wanted to talk to her. At other times, she knew she was fully coherent and this troubled, honorable man was pouring his heart out to her because he thought she was asleep. So she didn't speak and she didn't dare move and she ignored the creeping pain in her body to listen to his quiet voice.

That voice had carried her through till morning.

That and her silent prayers to God each time Paco let go of another nightmare memory.

"Hi," she said, remembering his hands covering hers, his head bowed near her. Did he know she'd prayed right along with him?

"Hi." He didn't say anything else. He didn't have to. And she didn't have to tell him that she'd heard him off and on during the long night, his words blurring out the pain ebbing and flowing with each heartbeat. Laura had focused on his monotone words, her heart aching in a different way than her bones and tissue.

So now, she stared up at him while she thanked God for allowing her to find Paco Martinez. *Lord, this good man is hurting. He needs Your love now more than ever. I don't know why he lived when others died, but I do know You hold all the answers. I'm willing to trust all of that to You, if You'll trust me with him.*

"I'm okay," she told Paco. "You don't need to worry about me."

He nodded, his hand tight over hers. "I have to finish what we started, sweetheart."

"I know. I don't want you to and I don't understand why these people are coming after me, but I understand why you need to do this."

He opened his mouth to say something else, but the door swung open and Eli Trudeau stepped in. "Sorry, Paco, but we need you in the war room."

Laura didn't miss the urgency in his words or the hesitation his expression held when he glanced toward her.

Paco reluctantly let go of her hand then nodded. Looking down at her, he said "I'll be back soon. Rest."

Laura gave him a weak thumbs-up.

Then Sally Mae and Selena entered the room and started fussing over her, so she didn't get a chance to tell him goodbye.

"What is it?" Paco asked as he hurried up the long hallway with Eli, both waiting as the scanners and ID cards gave them access to the next wing.

"Bad stuff, man," Eli said, glancing around. "A report of a dead body out near where you ran off the road."

"And?"

"And the body was identified by some of the locals. Kissie got a hit on the report just minutes ago. It's the same MO, Paco. Shooter was Kevin Booker from Flagstaff, Arizona. Worked for CHAIM for a year as an officer manager who mainly served as a liaison between field agents and supervisors. Was fired three months ago for giving out highly sensitive information to certain factions."

Paco let out a tired sigh. "Was he a former patient of Laura's?"

Eli shot him a hard stare. "Bingo. Saw her right after he lost his job."

They'd reached the door to the conference room.

Eli stepped aside and let Paco go ahead of him.

The big room was full to the brim with CHAIM people.

Starting with the team and ending with the founding members—Gerald Barton, John Simpson and Alfred Anderson. And the father of Brice's wife Selena, Delton Carter.

They were all staring at Paco.

"I'm Selena," the golden-haired nurse told Laura as she checked her vitals and readjusted the drip bag. "I helped Dr. Haines clean and treat your wound last night."

"You're Brice's wife, right?" Laura asked, her voice sounding hollow and raw to her ears.

Selena nodded then smiled. "Yes, for about six months now."

"You went through your own ordeal."

Selena nodded. "I sure did. I have an idea how you might feel, being chased by people you tried to help. The doctor I worked for was corrupt and I almost let him get away with it out of respect and fear. Won't make that mistake again."

Laura took a breath then grimaced as pain shot through her. "Sometimes we do things for all the wrong reasons, thinking we're doing them for the right reasons."

"Exactly." Selena finished her work then patted Laura's arm. "You didn't cause this, Laura. Someone somewhere wants to come after all of us. And he would have done it, with or without you."

"But why me?" Laura asked, sick with frustration. "Why me and why now?"

"He was probably waiting for the perfect time to strike," Selena said. "My father thinks this person wants a lot of power and he's trying to obtain it through CHAIM."

"But we're all here now," Laura said. "How can he hurt anyone else?"

Selena didn't answer. But Laura saw the apprehension moving through Selena's blue eyes. And felt that same apprehension building inside her booming heart.

"You don't think…"

Selena shook her head. "The entire team is working on this, including my father and the other founding members. You need to rest right now. Try not to think about all of this."

After asking if she needed anything else, Selena left the room. But Laura couldn't rest. Not when it seemed as if she'd be putting everyone here in danger just by being at Eagle Rock. Paco had believed this to be the safest place for her right now.

But what if it wasn't?

Paco held his stance, his expression never changing. He knew all about Eagle Rock. Agents were brought here for training, for fellowship and workshops, and for reprimands. He figured he was about to get the latter, big time.

"Talk to me, gentlemen," he said. "Let me have it. All of it."

Shane stepped forward. "We have a theory, Paco."

"I'm listening."

Gerald Barton motioned to the conference table. "Let's sit down. We might be here a while."

"What about Laura?" Paco asked, looking at the door.

"Selena is with her and Andre's back guarding her door," Gerald replied.

Paco didn't miss the look passing amongst the men. He needed to get his head back on straight and focus on this mission. He sat down and waited.

Delton Carter nodded toward Shane. "Go ahead, Warwick."

Shane went to the big board on one wall. "We've established a connection to Laura Walton with each of the three men who've come after her—Howard Barrow at the café, John Rutherford in the desert and Kevin Booker out on the road last night. They were all former patients of Laura's and they all currently worked for CSN—Central Security Network, which happens to be owned by one Lawrence Henner. They each also either tried to work for CHAIM or have worked for CHAIM briefly at various times.

"Lawrence Henner's son Kyle was also a patient of Laura Walton's. Sixteen years old. He committed suicide a few months ago. Meantime, Laura dated Alex Whitmyer but when things became uncomfortable for her, she broke it off and had to get a restraining order when Whitmyer started stalking her. And Whitmyer also works for Lawrence Henner.

"So we have this connection between Laura Walton and Lawrence Henner…and CHAIM."

Shane stopped, letting that statement soak in.

Brice got up and took over.

"Three of the above mentioned men are dead now— Barrows shot by Laura at the café, Rutherford killed by Paco in the desert and the third one—Booker—killed by someone else out on the road last night."

"Which means whoever is doing this means business," Brice said. "He killed his own man last night—"

"Because that man failed," Paco finished. "Shane, that's what happened this summer with you and Katherine. They killed their own people to keep 'em silent."

"We've noted that similarity," Shane replied. "But the people responsible for that are accounted for and serving jail time now. We can't trace anything back to that incident."

Devon leaned forward. "We don't know yet who killed Kevin Booker, Paco. But we'll find out. The point is—it's all connected to Henner and it's all connected to Laura."

"Which brings us to our theory—because they're all also connected to CHAIM. We believe you're right— Henner is coming after CHAIM and he used Laura to do it. And you brought her here to protect her, thus exposing all of us to this danger."

The implication of that statement hit Paco with lightning swift clarity. "You're not thinking—"

Gerald Barton lifted a hand. "We have to consider every angle, Warrior. We could all very well be in danger, but we can't be sure at this point. But, son, it doesn't look good."

Paco stood up. "You keep working on all the angles, but I'm going after Lawrence Henner. The man hired all of these people to do his dirty work—we have that connection, too, right?"

"You're right, bro," Eli said. "Henner hired all three men to work at Central Security Network. And we have the other connection."

"They all worked for CHAIM at one time or another," Paco finished. "And failed."

"And that's the sticking point," Eli replied.

Shane pointed to the names. "Barrow, Rutherford and Booker were not CHAIM material. And let's be honest here, based on their clumsy attempts to harm Laura, they weren't trained operatives under CSN, either. So the big question is why would Lawrence Henner hire men he knew would fail?"

"And why did he come after Laura?" Paco asked, that question foremost in his mind. "She thinks he blames her for his son's death but it sounds like the man himself might be responsible."

"We have a theory on that, too," Shane replied. "We think he was watching Laura, maybe had someone on the inside keeping tabs on her work, her whereabouts. He was just waiting—"

"For her to come to me?" Paco asked, jumping up. "Warwick, are you saying all of this was to get to me?"

"We think maybe he waited to get to one of us, yes," Shane said. "But there's more. As we said, we also believe he's not only targeting you and Laura. He wants to come after all of CHAIM, taking us out one by one. When Laura found you, he went into action."

"But why?" Paco asked, his mind whirling.

Gerald Barton stood up and glanced around the room. "We believe he's trying to form his own undercover team. But we also believe his team will be much different from ours. Lawrence Henner is forming a vigilante group."

"For what purpose?" Paco asked, his heart aching with apprehension and concern. And rage.

"That's what we have to figure out," Shane said. "And it will take all of us working together to do so."

SIXTEEN

P_{aco} wasn't so sure about that together part. But he had promised Laura he'd ask for help. Could he do that?

Devon shifted in his chair. "You can't do this alone, Paco. We won't let you."

"You won't let me?" Paco took his dear sweet time eyeing each of them. They'd all been together for years, so it was only natural that they could read each other so easily. "Is this some sort of intervention?"

Eli huffed a chuckle. "*Non,* bro. It's not like that. Listen to one who knows—this is bigger than you. Now, you can be a hotshot and take off like a lone wolf into the wild or you can let this team—*your team*—help you out."

Paco sank down on a chair, his mind whirling with what he could do and what he should do. Were they right about this? Laura had seen this coming and she'd only known him a few days. These men knew his soul and his flaws. But did he dare reach out for help? Wasn't that a sign of weakness?

"There's no shame in having a team to back you," Devon said. "Especially now when we could all be in danger."

Paco looked up at Devon. "Do you think Henner will come after us here?"

"It could happen," Devon said. "In spite of our precautions and our security measures, if someone wants to get to us badly enough, they can find a way. Especially someone who also runs a security company."

Paco couldn't let that happen. "I brought Laura here to protect her. Maybe that's what Henner expected and wanted since we think he's in the vicinity."

"That's all the more reason to do some recon, old boy," Warwick said with an eloquent shrug.

But Paco saw the shade of worry in Warwick's cold-steel eyes. He couldn't let these men down. And he wouldn't put their loves ones—or Laura—in harm's way. Maybe if he hadn't been so determined to win at all costs on that mountainside in the Middle East, his men might be alive today. And maybe Laura was right. Maybe God did have one more mission in mind for Paco Martinez.

"All right," he said, tapping his hands on the table. "I need help on this. Where do we start?"

Warwick nodded his approval, admiration in his eyes. "We start at the beginning, going back over everything. But first, we decide who goes out there with you and who stays here to protect everyone else."

The founding members argued amongst themselves

and finally all agreed they were too old to do field work, so they'd stay here and monitor the situation.

"With the women and children," Gerald said with a cowboy twang. "Just like the good old days even if we can't go out into the fray."

"Your wife would tell you she can handle that part," Delton Carter said with a smile.

"She probably could," Gerald agreed. "But I ain't going anywhere. Time for these young cowboys to take over."

Shane looked at Devon. "Dev, you should stay here with Lydia."

Paco watched Devon's face, saw the battle of duty toward CHAIM warring with duty toward his wife and unborn child. "I don't think—"

"Then I'll think for you, bro," Eli said. "Do not leave her and that babe here alone. Trust me, it's not worth it."

Eli should know, Paco thought. He'd gone on a mission only to return to find his pregnant wife had been taken. He believed she'd died but she'd survived in a coma long enough for her child to be born. And Devon had protected that child from everyone, even an unstable Eli, up until a year or so ago.

Devon shot Eli a long look. "You're right. Gena won't like it if you go and I stay, but I can watch over Scotty for you if I stay behind."

"Just as you did before," Eli reminded him.

Brice stepped forward. "I'm more than willing to go out with you, Paco."

Delton Carter shook his head. "Brice, I'd feel better if you stayed here to help Kissie with the technical details. And besides, you're good with hostage situations and interrogation."

Brice frowned then nodded. "Just in case?"

"Just in case," Delton replied, his expression grim.

Warwick glanced around the room. "So it's settled. Paco, Eli and I will try to track down Lawrence Henner, first to observe and report, then to get proof of what we think he's trying to do. If we find proof, we call in the authorities and make sure we stop this before anyone else gets hurt."

Paco got up. "That just leaves one detail. Who's going to tell the women about this?"

Laura had expected him to come back. She looked up when Paco walked through the door to her room, her heart jolting her pulse into a heavy cadence she could feel beating against her temple.

"Hi," she said, trying to smile.

"Hi," he replied back, without a smile.

"You're going after him, aren't you?"

He didn't even seem surprised at her words. "I have to. We've connected some of the dots and—"

"And Lawrence Henner has several people working for him, people who tried to or either became CHAIM agents but wound up being my patients, not to mention my stalker ex-boyfriend, who also works for Henner. And Mr. Henner is bitter about his son's suicide. Something else I was involved in. Did I miss any of the dots?"

He almost smiled at that. "No. You've pretty much put it all together. But, we also hit on something else, sweetheart. Something you said early on."

She shifted, grimaced with pain. "What?"

"Me," he replied. "We're beginning to think he used you to get to me, somehow. If he wanted either of us dead, we'd be gone by now. But he knew I'd protect you."

She shook her head. "That can't be. Henner had no idea you'd call me that night or that I'd go out and try to find you."

"But he could have pinned his hopes on you becoming my counselor sooner or later. We gave him the sooner the night I called you. He could have been waiting for a CHAIM operative to call for help. And I guess I got the short straw."

"Do you think he tapped the hotline?"

"Wouldn't put it past him. Especially if he wanted to monitor the whereabouts of what people consider an unstable CHAIM agent. He obviously did his homework on that one."

Realization colored her expression. "It does seem each CSN person he sent after us was unstable, doesn't it? Surely he doesn't think you'd turn on CHAIM and join up with him?"

He shrugged, looking uncomfortable. "Hard to rationalize a madman's plan. Everyone thinks I'm on the brink. Why not Henner, too?"

"You're not like those men, Paco."

He stood there, looking down at her for a long minute then he reached out and took her hand, his gaze dancing around the room. "I talked to you last night. I told you everything."

"I know," she said, watching for his reaction.

His gaze slammed into hers. "You heard me?"

"I heard most of it." She smiled. "I heard what God wanted me to hear, I think."

He let go of her hand and backed away. "I thought—"

"You thought no one was listening." Laura reached

out for him again. "Paco, you have to remember something about God and me. When it comes to you, we're both willing to listen."

His expression went from hard-edged and unyielding to open-faced disbelief and finally, a quiet awe. "Why me, Laura?"

"Why not you, Paco?" She held tightly to the edge of her blanket. "Maybe the only way you could truly confide in someone was exactly the way it happened, while you thought no one was listening. But I heard you and I'm telling you, we can get you through this. You have to forgive yourself and you have to let go. But that's easier said than done. I should listen to my own advice."

He took her hand back in his. "You amaze me, you know."

Laura felt the heat of that gentle praise warming her all the way to her toes. "I take my job very seriously," she said to hide that heat.

"So do I," he retorted. "And I want the world—your world—to be safe again."

That shattered the delicate emotions floating like crystal inside her head. "So you have to finish this, right?"

"Right. Henner's either after me or he wants to bring down CHAIM."

"Why would he do that?"

"Power, vengeance, greed. Your guess is as good as mine, sweetheart." He leaned down close. "But I intend to find out."

Laura stared up at him, her heart hammering so fast she thought it might burst out of her chest. "Could you do me one favor before you leave me?"

He leaned in a little farther, his dark eyes burning with a brilliant fire. "Anything."

"Kiss me goodbye."

The look on his face wasn't very encouraging. Laura's warmth turned to an outright blush of shame. She turned her head away, mortified. "I'm sorry. Just go."

The next thing she knew, Paco was lifting her head back around, his hands pulling through her tangled hair as he lowered his head to hers. The kiss started out as a fast and furious peck and ended up as a slow and caressing, very real kiss.

This is how it is with us, Laura thought as her mind filled with the essence of Paco Martinez. This is how it will be with us. This guessing, wishing, needing, finding.

She didn't want it to end.

But he pulled away just as quickly as he'd come close.

"You didn't have to give me a mercy kiss," she said, tears forming in her eyes in spite of her intake of breath.

He touched a hand back to her hair, his eyes locking with hers. "Sweetheart, that was not a mercy kiss. That was a promise that I don't have the right to make to you."

Hope lifted her. "What kind of promise, Paco?"

He kissed her again, his lips feathering over her tears. "A promise that I will be back. For you."

And then, he was gone, just like that, the imprint of his hard-edged touch and his hard-fought promise lingering like a distant mountain vista just beyond her mind.

Paco did one last check of the wing where Laura was recovering, making sure Andre was standing guard and

Devon and Brice would take shifts, too. Selena had assured him all of Laura's vitals were good and she had no signs of fever or infection. Dr. Haines was scheduled to return later to check on her again, but Paco trusted Selena until then.

Brice met him outside the secure wing. "Things are about as tight as we can get them, Warrior. You have my word I'll take care of everyone here."

"Laura," Paco replied, the memories of her satin-sweet touch lingering in his mind. "I need you to protect Laura."

"Granted," Brice replied, his expression questioning.

Paco wasn't ready to answer any questions right now. These new feelings were too bittersweet with their intensity and too raw and fresh for him to make any kind of declarations. He'd get through this task and then he'd step back and examine these new sensations rushing through him like a gully-wash over a dry creek bed.

"You okay, friend?" Brice asked as they headed back toward the war room.

"As okay as a man can be," Paco replied.

Kissie and Eli met them at the door. "I've isolated the signal from Laura's laptop," Kissie said.

"Where?" Paco asked.

"Just as we thought," Eli replied. "The laptop is at Lawrence Henner's estate about an hour outside of Austin."

She gave them the coordinates. "He doesn't know we're onto him."

"Or he wants us to find him," Eli warned.

"Either way, I'm gonna pay the man a visit," Paco retorted.

"And Shane and I are going with you," Eli countered.

Paco saw Shane coming up the hall. "Gear's all packed. Ready, gentlemen?"

Eli nodded. "I've explained to Gena and she's good. Well, as good as Gena can be—stubborn woman that she is. And Scotty's mad he can't go with us."

Shane's grin didn't reach his eyes. "Same here. Katherine is with her mother, putting on a brave front. No, that's not quite true. She is brave, very brave." He frowned. "Too brave. I'll have to remind Brice of that."

They both looked at Paco. "How's Laura?" Shane asked.

"Laura knew this was coming," Paco said, rather than getting all sappy like these two lovesick cods. "Let's get out of here."

He saw the lift of Kissie's dark eyebrows but thankfully, she didn't say anything. Except her call as they went down the hallway.

"Stay safe. You have my prayers."

They all needed that, Paco decided. And inside his head, no, inside his heart, he felt that same tug that his buddies must be feeling. He didn't want to leave Laura.

But he had to do this in order to come back to her, whole and healed and ready to kiss her one more time.

Laura had visitors in the hours after Paco, Eli and Shane left. She figured these strong, supportive women were not only trying to distract and comfort her, but were also trying to keep themselves centered and calm, too. They had to be used to this kind of scene where their loved ones left to save the world, but she sure wasn't.

Now several women huddled around her bedchamber, some sitting on the edge of her bed and some settled into the comfortable chairs that had appeared in her room.

"This reminds me of that scene in *Gone With the Wind*," Lydia, a Georgia girl, said with a drawl. "You know when the men go out to protect Scarlett's honor after she was accosted near her mill by Shantytown. They're all sitting around knitting and stitching, their nerves on edge, while their men are out there about to get in a big fight."

"I've never seen that movie," dark-haired Gena Malone Trudeau said. "And I don't knit. I'm sure my nerves will be shot before this is over. At least Brice is entertaining Scotty for me."

"You should read the book," Selena, also born and raised in Georgia, replied as she filled Laura's water glass. "It's better than the movie. Brice has read it several times to 'understand the southern female mindset,' or so he tells me. That's my Irish poet, always trying to maintain his sensitive side."

"I've practically memorized it," Lydia replied with a smile. "My favorite book ever. I have the movie poster in our bedroom even though Devon frowns every time he walks by it."

Katherine Barton Warwick, the cool Texas blonde now married to Shane Warwick, patted her smooth bob, her gaze moving over Laura. "How do you feel?"

Laura looked up in surprise. "About *Gone With the Wind*? I can take it or leave it."

They all laughed. "She's asking how *you* feel," Selena said with an indulging smile. "Are you in pain? Do you want us to leave so you can rest better?"

"I'm fine," Laura said. "Just sore. And no, I don't

want you to leave. I can't rest. But y'all have taken good care of me. I appreciate that."

"I made mother and the others go to their rooms," Katherine replied. "She has a tendency to hover. They all love it when we're gathered here. They try to spoil us."

"Your mother is nice," Laura said, wondering how she could keep this constant fear at bay. "And scary at times, too."

"She is one of the strongest women I've ever met," Selena replied. "And so are her friends, Mrs. Simpson and Mrs. Anderson, and my own mother, for that matter. In fact, we're all pretty amazing." She grinned then winked at Laura. "It's nice to have a circle of friends to get us through the stress of being involved with men who work in such high-risk jobs."

"How do you do that?" Laura asked. "How do women live with sending their men into battle?"

Katherine shook her head. "There are all kinds of battles out there and our husbands fight them each and every day. All men have battles to fight, whether they work for some sort of secret organization or they work at the local bank or grocery store. It's part of life. And yes, it takes some adjustment, trying to make it balance. And trying to understand it."

"It's hard," Selena said. "But we have to trust in God and in those we love. It took me a long time to figure that out."

The silence and the glances passing between the four other women forced Laura to ask her next question. "What if the one you love is trying hard not to love you back?"

Selena leaned forward. "Oh, we all have a story to tell about that, don't we, girls?"

"Oh, yes," Gena said, shaking her head. "That's something I do know a lot about—even though I lived in isolation in Maine most of my adult years."

"I've got some time on my hands," Laura replied. "And I'd really like to hear all of your stories."

Lydia held up her hand. "It all started with Pastor Dev and me...and you won't believe what happened."

He couldn't believe this.

Paco stood with Shane and Eli inside a big, cozy den centered in the massive hill country hunting lodge owned by Lawrence Henner. Stood and looked at Laura's laptop sitting on a pristine oak desk nestled by the big bay window of the grand room.

"He's not here," Eli said, stating the obvious.

"But the laptop is, of course," Paco replied while he searched the desk drawers. And found nothing much to help them. Hitting a hand on the desk, he said, "I don't get the man. He leaves clues and a wide-open trail. What's he trying to prove?"

They'd searched the whole house and that covered a lot of square feet in this creepy, dark, depressing place. Lawrence Henner wasn't here. In fact, no one was here.

Paco touched the mouse pad on the laptop and the screen came to life. "Look, another scripture passage. Revelations Six, Verse Two: 'And I looked, and behold, a white horse. And he who sat on it had a bow; and a crown was given to him, and he went out conquering and to conquer.'"

"We saw a white horse out in the pasture here," Shane said on a low whisper. Then he put a hand on the leather chair behind the desk. "Obviously, he *did* know we were on to him and he set us up. Seems he's also setting himself up to be some sort of hero."

Paco whirled, headed for the door. "Yeah, which means he could be on his way to Eagle Rock right now."

Shane grabbed the laptop then hurried to follow Paco and Eli. They made it out into the hallway.

Then Paco heard a chuckle coming from the dark shadows on the other side of the wide planked hall.

"Finally, some company. I was getting downright lonely, waiting for the famous Paco Martinez to come and visit. What a bonus that you have most of the CHAIM team with you, too."

"Henner?" Paco said, his gun drawn.

"Not even close," the voice replied.

Then a man stepped out of the shadows, his own gun raised toward Paco and the others. "I suggest you lower your weapons, gentlemen. You're surrounded, even if we didn't extend a nice welcome when you broke in—I mean—arrived earlier."

"Who are you?" Shane asked, his tone conversational and almost lighthearted.

The slender blond-haired man stepped even closer. "Me? I'm Laura's heartbroken boyfriend—the one she put a restraining order on. I'm Alex Whitmyer. And I've been waiting a long time to meet all of you. Now, tell me, how's my dear sweet Laura doing these days?"

SEVENTEEN

Late afternoon sunshine filtered through the windows of Laura's room. All of the women had left except Lydia. She was in the comfortable blue armchair by the bed, reading out loud to Laura from a humorous devotional book.

Laura laughed as Lydia finished yet another comical story with an inspirational point. "Thank you," she said. "I appreciate everyone sharing your stories. It's so amazing how you all met CHAIM agents and fell in love."

"Add one more to that list," Lydia said, patting her rounded tummy. "Paco was the last holdout."

"He might still be the last holdout," Laura replied, wondering where he was right now. "I wish we'd hear something."

Lydia shook her head. "They only tell us things on a

need-to-know basis. I'm sure Brice and Devon are getting hourly updates."

"Eagle Rock does make me feel safe," Laura said, hoping to hold off the sense of dread coursing through her heart. "I wonder what will happen between Paco and me, when this is over."

Lydia looked down at her book. "He still has a lot of healing to do. I'd be cautious if I were you."

"I've always been that," Laura said, glancing at the clock. "But my one mistake has come back to haunt me. Alex Whitmyer. I think he's involved in this whole mess."

"He's on the radar screen," Lydia said. "I've heard his name mentioned but no one can locate him."

And that was the source of Laura's dread.

They heard footsteps outside then the door opened.

"Dr. Haines," Lydia said, getting up. "We thought you'd be here at noon."

The doctor looked haggard, his eyes rimmed with fatigue, a frown pulling on his face. "I…uh…had a conflict."

"Well, you're here now," Lydia said. "I'll get Selena so you can examine Laura."

Another man stepped around the door behind Dr. Haines. "That won't be necessary, Mrs. Malone. No one will be examining Laura Walton today."

Laura gasped, her worst fears shining inside the man's demented eyes.

Lydia glanced from the man to Laura, realization coloring her skin. "Who are you?"

Laura reached out toward Lydia. "He's the man we were just talking about. Lydia, this is Alex Whitmyer."

Alex grinned. "The stalker ex-boyfriend, come to fetch little Laura home."

He hurt all over, but Paco was alive. And mad.

And sitting in some dark smelly dungeon.

"Paco?"

Shane's voice was like a hollow echo.

"I'm here. What's left of me, that is."

"Eli?"

"*Oui*, John-boy," Eli retorted with a snarl. "Enough with the roll call. We need to get out of here."

"Got a plan, old boy?" Shane asked, his tone now back to drawing room pitch.

Paco grunted against the ropes holding his arms and legs tied. "He didn't gag us. His mistake. We can scream, at least."

"No need to silence us," Shane said. "Who would hear us out here on this lonely stretch of land?"

"Why didn't he kill us?" Eli asked, the echo of his surprise hitting the rafters. "I reckon beating us to a pulp was a bit more fun for him."

"He wants us alive, remember?" Paco replied. "The man actually thinks he can form his own vigilante team. But if he's trying to convince us to join up, this wasn't the smartest way to do it."

"Not with us," Eli said. "He might think he can brainwash us into becoming his puppets, or maybe he plans to drug us to the point we'll do anything he says. Apparently, he tried to do that with the other poor saps. Ain't gonna happen. Not as long as I have breath in my body."

Paco heard Shane moving around. "While we're figuring out how the man managed to hide a whole half dozen men and how those men managed to overpower us and dump us here, let's also figure out how to get out of here."

"To get back to Eagle Rock," Paco said, his fingers twisting against the ropes. "He wants Laura. We thought Henner was behind this but all along it's been Whitmyer."

"I fear Henner is long dead," Shane said, a grunt of exertion coloring his words. "And probably buried somewhere here on his own property. Whitmyer has obviously taken his place. Wonder how that'll go over at the Christmas party?"

"He's gone not only rogue, but psycho-rogue," Eli said on a snort. "The worst kind. I feel better about my past bad habits now, for true."

"Enough chitchat," Shane said, the rustling of ropes around him. "We need to move on while we can still stand."

Paco let out one last grunt as he managed to tug at the circle of knots around his wrist. "I'm out," he said, quickly untying his feet.

"Me, too," Shane replied, his grin flashing in the dark, dank room.

"Eli?"

Paco felt a nudge from behind. "What are we waiting for?" Eli asked. "Whitmyer might have Henner's white horse, but we have something else on our side."

"What's that?" Paco asked.

"People we love," Eli replied. "And that can make a man mean with honor, understand?"

"I hear that," Paco said. Because sitting here in

this gloomy cold basement had brought a clear light to his eyes.

He loved Laura.

And he was going back to her, just as he'd promised. *Please, Lord, don't let me be too late.*

She wasn't going to let this happen.

Laura looked at the man holding a gun on Dr. Haines. "How did you get in, Alex?"

His glassy gaze held her. "Well, it wasn't easy, little darling, that's for sure. First, I had to take your laptop so I could scan all the files and find some vital passwords and information. Then I had figure out where that brooding has-been soldier was taking you and get the right people to follow you. Only, that didn't work out the way I'd planned." He let out an exaggerated sigh. "And then, I had to wait until I could find a way in the back door to this fort. A few security codes jammed and changed and the doctor was more than happy to oblige—"

"He threatened my wife," Dr. Haines said, pointing a finger at Alex. "And he knocked out that young man out there and moved him to another part of the building. Held a gun on me while I tied him up. He's—"

"Shut up," Whitmyer said, poking at the doctor with his gun. "We're here now but if you keep whining, old man, I can put you out of your misery. And *then* go after your wife. So I suggest you don't say a word, not about what I've done with that kid or anything else you've seen here."

The doctor's shocked silence ended that conversation.

Laura tried to reason with him. "You might have

us locked inside this room, Alex, but there are others here." She saw Lydia's warning glance. "There is an agent on sight."

"Oh, you mean a powerful CHAIM agent? Right. I get that, Laura. I came prepared, of course. They won't bother us." He pointed the gun toward Lydia. "Not if they want little mama here to live."

Laura glanced at Lydia. Whitmyer had forced Lydia back in her chair. They were trapped in this room with a madman and a shaking doctor. And she had no idea where Andre was. Or Brice, Devon and the others for that matter. So she did the best thing she could do. She went into therapist mode, hoping her questions would distract him.

"Did you hire those men to come after me?"

Alex grinned. "Oh, you mean those losers who wanted to be super agents? Yeah, I kind of set them up. I told them if they'd prove themselves I'd let them join one of Henner's special teams." He laughed. "I learned a lot of inside information, dating you. Found out so many fascinating things from hacking into your files, too. Those wannabes fell for it and did precisely what I thought they'd do. They messed up. Oops. But hey, got everyone's attention, didn't it?"

He laughed, glancing over to where Dr. Haines sat patting Lydia's arm more to calm himself than Lydia, Laura thought, her heart going out to the doctor.

"Where is Mr. Henner?" Lydia asked, her tone calm and guarded, a fierce determination in her eyes.

Whitmyer shook his head. "Out of the country for a while."

"Did you hurt Kyle's father?" Laura shouted. "Alex,

why would you do that? Why are you doing any of this?"

"The old man was depressed," he retorted with a shrug. "He'd lost focus on our plans. I had to do something to save the company, to save his empire. And to prove to you that I'm worthy, of course."

"It wasn't your place to do that," Laura said, her prayers bringing calm over her now that she saw him face-to-face and knew he was behind all of this. Maybe she could talk him through this. "And you don't have to prove anything to me."

But Alex wasn't having any of that. "It was my place. I worked hard for that man for years, jumping like a dog every time he wanted things done. And he never saw it. He wanted his stupid son to man up and get with the program. Why? He had me right there all the time. I tried to show him we could take his company to the next level. But after you messed things up and his weak son offed himself, Henner went from blaming you to blaming himself. He wouldn't listen to reason so I had to act fast."

"Is that why you dated me?" Laura asked, stalling, praying Brice, Devon and Kissie would figure things out.

He pushed off the locked door. "No, no. I dated you because I loved you…and I needed access to your file of reject-CHAIM agents and crazy rogue agents. I had this grand plan to take you with me into CSN, to create an organization better than CHAIM. After reading your files, I figured that whacked-out Martinez would jump at the chance. So when I heard you were going to find him, I set things into motion. And here we are."

"There is no better organization than CHAIM,"

Lydia said, rising off her chair. "And you need to understand what a mistake you've made here today."

Whitmyer pushed the gun at her. "Sit down. The only mistake I made was wasting my time with Martinez and his merry band of followers."

"You've seen Paco?" Laura tried to sit up straight. It was hard to breathe. And her calm was fast disappearing.

Whitmyer shot her a cold stare. "Saw him, made him an offer—which he refused—and then made sure none of them will be returning here tonight."

Laura gasped. "What did you do to them?"

Whitmyer walked over to her bed. "Ah, now, I never heard you worry like that for me. What happened? You go and fall for that worthless burned out soldier?"

Laura swallowed a retort, her mind centered on the one hope that Paco and the others were still alive. "I was trying to help him when all of this started."

"Yeah, I saw some of those tender moments," Whitmyer replied, his face inches from hers. "You've betrayed me, Laura. Just like everyone else I depended on."

"So why are you here then?" she asked, anger giving her strength. "Why didn't you kill me yourself, instead of sending those men? They died because of you, Alex."

"Actually, I should have done that but I needed you to help me, or so I thought. I decided I'd give you one more chance," he retorted. "Either you agreed to leave here with me, or—" He pointed the gun toward Lydia and Dr. Haines. "Bang, bang."

"He's posted guards all around us," Paco said on a frustrated hiss. "That's why he wasn't too worried about us escaping."

"How many?" Eli asked from his crouch behind Paco. They'd centered themselves near the lone window of the basement but it was hard to see anything in the growing dusk.

"I count six at least," Shane replied from somewhere in the darkness. "But I only figure that from the ones we've been able to see moving by. Could be more."

"That's only two each, *mon ami*," Eli replied. "We've been in worse jams."

Shane let out a breath. "Yes, that's true. But we have only our wits and our fists to help us in this jam."

Paco couldn't argue with that. Whitmyer had stripped them of their weapons and their phones. "Let's just do this thing so I can get to Laura."

Eli rolled over to stare at him. "What's the plan?"

Paco closed his eyes, said a prayer then forced all the ugly scenarios involving Whitmyer and what he might do to Laura out of his head. "Get their attention, bring 'em in here and then, confuse 'em by gaining control over this situation."

"*Oui*, and how do you propose we do that?" Eli asked.

Paco motioned to them to come close. "There's this black ops tactic we can use and I'm pretty sure it's one Whitmyer failed to mention to his henchmen out there. Listen and learn, boys."

The phone on Laura's bedside table rang.

She glanced at the phone then up at Alex Whitmyer.

"Answer it," he said. "But keep in mind, anything you say can be used against those two." He pointed toward Lydia and the doctor. "I don't have anything to lose if I shoot one or two more people."

Laura put the image of him shooting Paco or any of the others out of her mind, willing herself to be calm. "Hello," she said into the phone, her voice low and shaky.

"Laura, it's Kissie. The system is jammed and we can't gain access to your wing. Talk to me, baby."

Laura swallowed, trying desperately to show no reaction to the thread of distress in Kissie's words. "Kissie, it's okay. Dr. Haines and Lydia are with me. We're fine."

"Is someone there, honey?"

"Yeah, we were wondering where Selena went. The doctor wants to examine me."

"Selena is across from you in another room. She alerted us when she realized the security code went red."

"Oh, I see. We can wait for her then."

Alex grabbed the phone away then put it to his ear. "Listen to me, and listen good. I've got your patient and the pregnant lady in my gun sight, understand? And if anyone tries to come into this wing, I will shoot the pregnant woman first."

He stood silent then responded to whatever Kissie had said. "Laura? Laura's just fine. She's enjoyed her stay but she'll be leaving with me soon. Goodbye."

He hung up then glanced around. "I think it's time for a change of scenery, Laura. I want you by my side when I take over CSN. I had hoped to make this easy and bring a few CHAIM agents with me, but they don't want to play nice. So we do it the hard way. We start over, you and me."

He tilted his head toward Lydia. "Help her get

dressed. And Doc, make sure she's bandaged up. We won't be stopping to dress wounds."

Lydia glared at him. "Where are you taking her?"

He cackled and aimed the gun toward Lydia. "I could tell you, but then I'd have to kill you."

Laura pushed up. "It's okay, Lydia. I'll go with him. Just do as he says." She sent Lydia a pleading look. "I'll be okay."

"I can't let him take you," Lydia said, her voice rising.

"You don't have a choice," Whitmyer retorted, pressing the gun toward Lydia. "If you want to live to deliver that kid, you'd better do as I say, woman."

Laura shook her head. "Lydia, it's all right."

Then Lydia's face went pale as she grabbed her stomach. "It's not all right." A grimace of pain colored her expression. "I think I'm going into labor."

EIGHTEEN

"Divide and conquer," Eli said. "It's been a while since I've had so much fun." Then he rubbed his face. "Except for my sore jaw and black eye, of course."

"Let's hope that's the last of them," Shane retorted, holding the flashlight they'd found so Paco could finish tying up the men who'd been guarding them. "They're down to four now at least. Two of them are no longer breathing."

Eli grunted. "Hey, they came at us first. Strictly self-defense."

"These four aren't going anywhere for a while," Paco said, making sure the knots he tied couldn't be untied. He'd also put tape over the unconscious men's mouths and tape around their legs, too. "Once I tie them all together, it'll take hours for 'em to figure out how to get loose."

"Now to find a phone," Shane said.

"Let's get out of here," Paco retorted, finished with securing the unconscious men.

He waited for Shane and Eli to go out the big steel door then he shut it and wedged a crowbar against it. Just as another precaution.

They did one more search of the estate then found their guns and phones in a pile in the office where they'd been attacked.

Paco immediately dialed Devon's number.

"Paco? We've been trying to reach you."

He didn't like the tone of Devon's voice. "We ran into some trouble, but that's been taken care of. Is everyone safe and accounted for?"

Devon's hesitation seemed to last a lifetime. "Negative on that. An intruder blocked off the wing where Laura is quartered. We've lost communication and we can't get any visuals. And Lydia's in there with her. They're being held hostage. Selena's hiding in the room next to Laura's but she has her cell with her. She's keeping us updated through text messages. Everyone else is safe for now."

Paco's heart pulsed and pitched then settled into shell shock. "What's the situation?"

"Based on what Selena can glean, one armed man. He apparently jammed the security long enough to force his way inside with Dr. Haines. No news on Andre's condition or his whereabouts. Brice saw the breach and tried to get back in, but the security code blocked access and then the computers went down. Kissie's working to get surveillance back on line. Meantime, we're waiting for another update from Selena. It's too dangerous for us to storm in there." Silence again. "I'm worried about Lydia."

Paco relayed this to Eli and Shane. "We're on our way."

He forced himself to focus on the here and now. He quickly told Devon what had happened with Whitmyer. "It has to be him, Dev. Alex Whitmyer has Laura. He lured me away so he could get to her."

He put away his phone, his blood boiling with anger. "Why didn't I see this coming?"

Eli pushed a hand in his face. "We move forward and stick to the plan, bro, okay?"

"The plan has changed now," Paco said, shoving him away. "The plan was to get her to safety then find Henner. Well, Henner is nowhere to be found and he's probably dead. We focused on him instead of Whitmyer and so now, the plan has changed."

Shane glanced at Eli then back to Paco. "What *is* the plan now, Warrior?"

Paco grabbed his gun. "To get to Whitmyer before he hurts Laura or anybody else. And to finish this."

"I'm not falling for that one," Whitmyer said, lifting his gun in the air. "I mean it, lady. Don't play games with me."

Laura looked from him to Lydia. "I don't think she's faking. Her baby's due in a couple of weeks."

"Then she needs to hold off on that," Whitmyer retorted. "Check her, Doc. And don't make any stupid moves."

The doctor got up to help Lydia back into her chair. After taking her pulse and asking her a few questions, he held her while another spasm hit her stomach. "This baby is about to be born whether you like it or not."

"Now isn't that just peachy," Whitmyer shouted. Then he smiled. "Well, okay then. I'll take Laura and you can deliver the brat right here in this room. Case closed."

"We can't leave her," Laura said, shaking her head. "I can help."

"She has a doctor for that."

Dr. Haines stood up, reaching a hand to his chest, his flushed face lined with pain. "It's too dangerous. He has a—"

"Stop," Whitmyer shouted, his gun lifting toward the doctor. Laura screamed but it didn't matter. The gun popped, the sound shattering and final.

And then the doctor looked down at the blood spurting from his chest and fell to the floor.

Laura screamed again and got out of bed, her head swimming, her heart pumping as she pulled at her IV drip. She reached toward Lydia, taking her hand. "Hang on, Lydia."

Whitmyer looked as shocked as Laura felt. "There. That's one down and two to go."

"You shot an innocent old man," Laura said, anger giving her the courage to scream. Then she yanked her IV out and got between him and Lydia. "You want me? Well, take me. But stop killing people."

Whitmyer reached toward her but a loud knock at the door stopped him. "Go away," he shouted. "Leave or I shoot another one."

"Let me in there right now. I'm a nurse."

Laura and Lydia glanced at each other. Selena.

Whitmyer shook his head then opened the door and

dragged Selena inside. "Just what I need, another aggravating woman." Then he stood still, his harsh gazing moving over the three women. "But, if my notes are correct, two of you are married to CHAIM agents." He glared at Laura. "And one of you obviously has a thing for the mighty Paco Martinez."

Selena took in the scene but didn't say anything. She bent to examine Dr. Haines then looked up, shaking her head. Then she whirled toward Whitmyer. "You made a fatal mistake, taking them hostage. If you think they'll let you get out of this alive, you're wrong." She glanced at Laura. "I need to bandage her arm. It's bleeding."

Whitmyer looked at the spot where Laura's IV had been positioned. "Do it." He held the gun on them while Selena grabbed some gauze and bandages and went to work on Laura's wound.

Selena leaned down close to Laura. "There's blood in the hallway and Andre's missing."

Laura didn't dare react. She stared up at Whitmyer. "She's right. You can't win, Alex."

Whitmyer shrugged, but Laura saw the flash of fear in his eyes. His grand plan was falling apart around him. "I came here for you, Laura. I don't care about the rest."

The phone rang and Laura scrambled to reach it, ignoring Whitmyer's fidgeting. "Hello?" She looked over at him, daring him to shoot her.

"Laura?"

Paco. She didn't dare say his name. "Yes?"

"Are you all right?"

"Yes, but Lydia's going into labor and Dr. Haines is dead. We don't know where Andre is."

Whitmyer stomped toward Selena and Lydia. "Hang up or I'll shoot one of them."

"I have to go," Laura said. "You need to know..."

"I know, sweetheart. You don't have to say anything. I know. You stay strong, you hear me, Laura. I'm coming for you, just like I promised."

Then she heard Brice's clipped words. "Let me speak to him, Laura."

Laura handed the cordless phone toward Whitmyer. "They want to talk to you."

"I'm not making any deals," he said, refusing to take the phone.

"Please?" Laura asked, hoping there was some bit of decency left in the demented man's soul. "For me, Alex. We need to understand why you're doing this. I'll go with you, but at least help me to understand."

Alex hesitated then took the phone, his expression full of rage. "You want to know why I'm holding three women and a dead doctor hostage? I'll tell you. Because I can. Because I've been trained just like all of you, because I gave my life to CSN and Lawrence Henner but he ignored me and focused on his whiny son instead. Then when I offered the deal of a lifetime to all of you, you turned on me, too. So now, it's payback time. Laura is my only hope. Laura understands me. I'm taking her out of here."

He waited, and Laura watched his face, wondering what she'd ever seen in this man. He wasn't rational. She'd dated him when she should have been counseling him. It was way too late to change that. What was Brice saying to him?

"I see. Well, that won't cut it, Mr. Whelan. I can't surrender—and your negotiation tactics won't work.

But I do have a request. I want a helicopter out of here. I'm taking Laura Walton with me and if anyone tries to stop me, I'll kill the woman who's in labor and the cute nurse—your wife, I believe—then I'll kill Laura and myself. How's that for negotiations?"

Brice turned to the other men in the room, his hands on his hips. "You heard the man. This could go on for hours."

Devon pushed at his hair and paced. "Lydia's in labor? That is what he indicated, right?"

"Aye," Brice replied, his expression grim. "And now Selena's gone and got herself into the mix, too. We need to alert Kissie that Andre's still missing. That can't be good."

Paco thought about Laura's words to him earlier. Just hearing her voice made him so crazy he wanted to storm the house and tear down that door barring him from her. He understood her message even if she couldn't voice her feelings for him. And he wanted to give her the same message.

He loved her.

Brice went into the computer room next door then came back. "Kissie is trying to get the cameras back online to that section of the house. She's concerned for her son's safety, of course." Brice looked as haggard as Paco felt. "So here's what we have: Security system breached and jammed on south side of the compound due to forced entry using one hostage as cover. That hostage is now dead. Three hostages taken alive. One person missing. Intruder has demands. He wants a helicopter out and he's taking Laura with him."

"Over my dead body," Paco said, slapping his fists together.

"Careful, bro," Eli warned. "We don't need that."

"I can't let him take her," Paco said, staring at his friend. "Do you hear me? I can't let that madman take Laura out of here. You know what that could mean."

Brice nodded. "We understand, Paco. But we have to consider he's also holding Selena and Lydia, too." He glanced toward Devon. "He confirmed that. And Lydia's apparently in labor."

Devon pushed toward the double doors of the war room then turned back around. "I can't take this."

"Selena is with her," Brice said. "In his need to impress, that idiot spilled enough information to help us evaluate the situation and form a plan." He closed his eyes and breathed deep. "We have to focus on that, gentlemen. A plan to get our loved ones out of harm's way."

"Lydia," Devon said. "The baby." He looked at Eli. "I can't let anything happen to them, Eli."

"Nothing will, bro," Eli said. "We're gonna fix this and you'll be a proud papa before sunrise."

Devon didn't look so sure. "Where's Scotty and Gena?"

Eli pointed across the hallway. "They're safe right where we left them—in this wing in the big dining hall with everyone else. Trust me, I've checked on them about three times since we got back."

Shane nodded. "Kit's in there with her parents and the others. Our superiors are well armed and waiting. Meantime, they're all praying and trying to stay calm. Now we need to decide a plan of action. The sooner the better."

Paco whirled around. "We don't have much time before he calls again about the helicopter. Let's get in there and get them out." He looked past the door. "And let's take that psychopath out so he can't hurt anyone else."

"Laura, you need to change clothes."

Laura turned from helping Lydia onto the bed. "I told you, Alex, I'm not leaving her like this. I'll go with you but I don't want to leave Lydia."

He pointed the gun toward Lydia. "And I told you, I don't care about her or that brat."

Lydia grimaced as another round of contractions gripped her stomach. Selena held her hand, talking her through her breathing. "It won't be long now, Lydia. You're doing great."

Lydia used all her angst and agony to stare down Alex Whitmyer. "What kind of man are you?" she shouted between breaths, her knuckles white as she held on to Lydia.

"The kind who takes charge." Whitmyer shot back, grabbing Laura by the arm. "Call Martinez back and tell him we want that helicopter in ten minutes. And don't stall. I know there's at least two choppers on the premises."

Selena shook her head. "Laura can't travel. She's been shot—by someone you sent to harm her."

"I'll get her help as soon as we're out of here."

"You could cause the bleeding to start again or she might go into shock or get an infection."

"I'll take care of her."

Laura glanced from Selena to Whitmyer. She knew what both Selena and Lydia were thinking. If this man took her, her chances of surviving were slim to none. Alex wanted revenge against her and against CHAIM.

It was unreasonable and unbelievable, but he wasn't a rational man.

"I'll make the call," she said. She'd convince Paco to give them a helicopter and hope he'd put his sniper skills to good use once they were out in the open.

"Do it." Whitmyer pointed the gun at Lydia. "One wrong word and I'll take mother and baby out of their misery."

God, help me, she prayed. *What should I do?*

Then a thought rushed through her mind. *You're trained to help people like him, Laura. Use that training.*

Somehow, she had to make this look good and then figure out a way to stall him. So she dialed the number to the conference room, her prayers keeping beat with her pulse. She didn't like flying but she had to keep moving, keep hoping that she could find some courage. Blocking nausea, she swallowed back her fears.

Brice answered on the second ring. "Hello?"

"I need to talk to Paco," she said.

"I'll put him on," Brice replied. "I have you on speaker, Laura. So anything you can tell us…"

"Laura, sweetheart, talk to me."

She heard the worry and fear in his words. But she knew this man. He was stronger than he realized. "We need the helicopter. You have ten minutes to get it ready."

"Got it. But you won't be on that chopper. How's Lydia?"

"In labor. Selena's coaching her."

Whitmyer stepped forward. "Enough. Hang up."

Laura glanced at Selena then back to Whitmyer, her fingers touching the button to end the call. Then she put the phone down behind the water pitcher on the table by the bed. And left it on.

Please, Lord, don't let him notice.

"Alex, I promise I'll go with you as soon as the baby is born. Then we can talk. I think I misjudged you."

He shook his head. "It might take all night for that baby to be born. We don't have time, Laura. You have to go with me if you want them to live, understand?"

Laura didn't have a choice. "Okay. The helicopter should be ready soon. But before we go, you need to understand about Paco and me. This isn't his fault."

Whitmyer's gaze darted here and there. "Then why were you traipsing all over Arizona with him? You love me, Laura. You don't love him."

"You're right. I don't love him. I barely know him, but I'm his therapist and I found him so I could talk to him. I can do the same for you. We can get you the help you need."

"I don't need anything, except you to come with me," he shouted, his gun bobbing. "I had this big plan to make CSN into the best—better than CHAIM could ever be. But, I'll give that up just to be with you."

Laura could see the desperation in his eyes. He believed he was in control but he wasn't. And now his misguided delusional scheme had collapsed. She had to make him listen to reason.

"Why did you do all of this, Alex? Why did you send out those inexperienced men to kill me? Why the cryptic messages on my business cards?"

His chuckle sent chills up her spine. "You don't get it, do you, Laura? You belong to me but you wouldn't see me anymore. I had to find a way back to you. I followed you that day, the day you met with Martinez. And I saw you with him. I couldn't take it."

Laura's heart pumped so fast she felt disoriented. "You were at the café in the desert?"

He laughed again, his eyes wild with determination and madness. "I was the first shooter. I wanted to talk to Martinez but when I saw him with you I just wanted to kill him." He shook his head. "Things got crazy after that."

Slanting a look toward Selena and Lydia, Laura took advantage of the precious time. "But what about those other men? Why did they come after me?"

He scoffed, swung the gun around. "Those idiots? It started out with me getting information from your patients since you refused to talk to me. Then I used them as distractions. They wanted to be *somebody*, Laura. They thought if they worked for CSN, they could become security agents. I needed them to believe that so I could keep an eye on you. I brought them with me. They thought it was a training mission.

"But *I* followed you to your hotel and I broke in and got your laptop so I can find out why you were after that loser Martinez. I left the first card for you in the desert but you didn't take the hint. So I fixed up another one and gave it to good ol' Howard and found him a delivery truck. Same with Rutherford—sent him into the desert with promises of a big promotion if he did the job. I knew Martinez would take them out. I knew because I was watching the whole time." He shrugged, his smile smug, his eyes glassy. "I set up the shooter out on the road, too. And I tracked the chopper that brought you to Eagle Rock."

Lydia cried out then, her hand flailing toward the

table as another contraction moved through her body. She hit the water pitcher and sent it flying.

Whitmyer whirled toward Lydia, his gaze hitting on the phone's flashing light. Grabbing it, he stared at Laura. "You forgot to hang up?" His expression etched in rage, he held the phone to his ear then pulled her close. "You can never get away from me, Laura. And Paco Martinez will never have you." He shouted into the receiver. "Hear that, Martinez. You will never have her. Never."

NINETEEN

Paco couldn't breathe.

Never.

That one word followed by a dial tone shouted at him with a laughing glee that seemed to sum up his entire miserable life.

"He's going to kill her," he said, the words dropping out him like rocks hitting concrete.

"We won't let it go that far," Devon replied, his cell phone in his hand. "Mr. Barton is releasing the chopper to you, Paco, because he trusts you to do the right thing. Laura was very brave in risking the open phone line, but she's a counselor. She's trying to talk this man down and give us information at the same time."

"And she's trying to save Lydia and my child," Devon said, a hand on Paco's arm. "I need to get to my wife. I'm just thankful she's still alive."

Paco was thankful for all of that and more. But his heart, once so hard and closed, was now open and raw, exposed to the incredible power of love. He turned to Devon. "He said *never,* Dev. You heard him. This was his plan all along. If he can't have Laura, then no one ever will."

Devon's gaze moved over the others then back to Paco. "He's a very sick man, Warrior. But we have might on our side. We stay the course."

Eli grunted, his arms crossed over his chest. "There's him and then there's us. I don't think he's gonna make it out of this, *mon ami.* Dev's right. We go by the book on this one."

Paco stared over at his friend. "You tell me how to do that? Tell me how to focus, how to go on faith." He sank down on a chair. "I don't think I can do this. I don't think I can take losing another person I care about. Especially Laura. You don't understand the thing about Laura."

Shane sat down beside him. "We all understand, Paco. We've all fought the good fight for CHAIM. We've worked to save innocents all over the world and sometimes, we've failed at that or worse, we've been forced to take the lives of others. We did that for years, thinking we understood the true meaning of love and faith." He rapped his fingers on the table. "And then, we each got handed these special assignments that changed our whole way of thinking. We love Christ and we believe. But falling in love with someone you want to spend your life with and knowing that very person is in danger—well, that puts a new wrinkle into the whole equation."

"And makes this job unbearable at times," Eli said from his spot against the wall.

Paco's eyes stung. The unfamiliarity of his tears floored him. He'd held these tears for so long and now they burned their way down his face. If he let go now, he'd never make it back. Fighting the pain, he closed his eyes, memories of dust and blood and gunfire covering him. And in those horrid murky memories he could hear a keening, a kind of wailing that shattered his resolve. He fought against that wailing, against what it meant for him now, on this mission.

Then he opened his eyes and looked at Devon, the pastor. "It was me, man. I was the last one standing and… I saw that kid laying there, dying and I fell down and held him in my arms and…every time I relive that nightmare, I hear this horrible wailing." He put his hands to his face, the tears flowing now. "It was me, Dev. I was wailing at God for doing this. For taking their lives and sparing mine." He grabbed Devon's lapel, his heartbeat bursting through his temples. "I can't take that kind of pain again, man. I can't. What do I do? How do I do this? If I lose Laura—"

"You won't lose Laura," Devon said. "Paco, do you hear me? God is with us even when we fail. Look around you. Look at us. Me, I hid the truth from Eli for years and I almost got Lydia and Eli both killed. Eli— he came back from his own nightmare to find out he had a son in danger because of mistakes from *his* past. He has a reason to live now. Brice was so in love with Selena, he failed to see her worst flaw—her misplaced loyalty to a man who was a criminal. And Shane—he had to fall long and hard before he could get over his fear of a true commitment, not to mention he had to tell the woman he loved her best friend had betrayed her. And that brings me to you, friend. Laura sought you out to help you overcome your post-traumatic stress and survivor's guilt and now you're being tested because of her concern and generosity. Laura believes in you, Paco. We believe in you. And God will see you through—no matter the outcome."

Paco looked around at his friends, memories of all their times together, memories of their trials and failures, rushing through his mind like an old movie.

"We've done good, haven't we, though?" He waited for Devon to respond.

Eli, Shane and Brice all stepped forward. "Yes, we've done good," Devon replied in a quiet voice. "This can be one of those times, Paco. We're all here with you to make sure of that."

Did he have the power to bring about a hopeful outcome instead of yet another tragedy in his life?

"Laura told me I might have one last mission," he said, wiping at his face. "But she didn't tell me I might fail at that mission. Or that it would be this hard."

"You aren't going to fail," Shane said, grabbing Paco up out of the chair. "You have something to fight for now, Paco. And that means you aren't allowed to fail." He blinked back his own tears, then straightened Paco's jacket. "Now, we're going to get things in order. While you sit here and have a quick talk to the Lord. Understand me?"

Paco nodded. "I don't have much time, do I?"

Devon slapped a hand on his back. "Just enough for the Lord to hear you. Then we take care of this so I can enjoy becoming a father."

Paco waited for the others to leave then took a long

breath. Normally in a situation such as this, he'd be the first one out the door—hot dog, hothead, whatever you wanted to call it, he lived for the chase. But that old adrenaline rush had turned into a dreaded beating pulse that lived to torment him.

So he looked up at the intricately woven iron cross centered on the wall, his heart warring between the need for battle and the need for peace. He stared at the cross, taking in the way the iron twisted and turned and merged into itself to form a crossbar of strength.

And in his head, beyond all the tormented memories and the twisted guilt he'd carried for so long, he at last saw the strength forged in fire and steel and blood and tears. The strength of Christ's love guiding him and holding him, even when he'd believed himself to be alone.

"Are You there, Lord?" he asked now, his hands folded in prayer. "I'm not worth it but I need You now. I need You for Laura's sake, Lord. Spare her and I will gladly hand my life over to You. Not a bargain but a promise that I've failed to honor. I love her, Lord. I don't yet understand this love, but I love this woman. And I can't lose her."

He stopped, hitched a breath. "One last mission, Lord. A mission to make up for all the others, to make up for all the loss and the pain and the guilt of my failures."

Paco reached for the Bible that was always on the table, his fingers flipping through the pages. He settled on the book of Psalms, chapter fifty-five, verses four through six:

"'My heart is severely pained within me, and the terrors of death have fallen upon me. Fearfulness and trembling have come upon me, and horror has overwhelmed me. And I said: "Oh, that I had wings like a dove! For then, I would fly away and be at rest."'

He finished the entire chapter, amazed that some of the very things he felt inside his soul were written here in the Word.

Paco put the Bible down and closed his eyes, his prayers centered and concentrated, his wails of despair changing to silent and steady pleas for God's grace and intervention. Then he opened his eyes and put on the mantle of the Lord so he could join his friends in this fight to save all that they held dear.

Shane and Eli stood back out of sight, watching as Paco went about doing a safety check on the whirling helicopter centered on the landing pad near the back of the big compound. Brice was inside helping Kissie to regain visual surveillance, hoping to make a last-ditch effort to rescue Laura and the others. And Devon was waiting for the go-ahead to break the door down so he could get to his wife before she gave birth.

Paco left the helicopter idling, then hopped out, his thoughts clear now, his on-edge nerve endings humming with purpose. The adrenaline was back, allowing him to keep the dark dread at bay. He had a new hope. And his friends were right. He had a reason to fight one more battle.

Running toward Shane and Eli, Paco did one more scan of the surrounding buildings. "He should be watching," Paco said. "The man has to know I'm going to take him out once he clears the entry door."

They were all geared up for warfare, each wearing a bulletproof vest and loaded with weapons. Shane rubbed his chin. "Of course he's factored that in, but he'll use Laura as a shield. He'll lock Selena and Lydia in the room then bring Laura out the passageway to the same door he entered with Dr. Haines. Still can't figure how he beat the system."

"He's obviously an expert at security," Eli retorted. "He's gone overboard with this obsessive need to take over the world and get the girl."

"It might be different if the man actually knew the difference between right and wrong," Shane said, his tone murderous. "But a jilted stalker who has grandiose ideas about how to run a company is an unstable person to begin with, so this could be tricky to the bitter end."

Paco checked the high-powered sniper rifle he'd taken from the weapons closet. "I only need one shot."

"Better make it a good one, bro," Eli said.

Paco intended to do that. It would be a kill shot.

Laura held Lydia's hand on one side while Selena spoke to Lydia with soothing words on the other.

"You're doing great," Selena said. "Your breathing is right on target."

"The baby?" Lydia asked, her voice raw, tears of frustration streaming down her face. "Selena, what about my baby?"

Selena's smile was practiced and serene. "As far as I can tell, the baby is right on target, too. You're not quite there yet, though. You need to dilate a few more centimeters."

Lydia nodded. "I'm trying to hold off. I want Devon to be here."

Laura sent Alex Whitmyer a hard look. "Devon will be here soon, honey."

Alex rolled his eyes and flexed his gun. "He won't if they don't call about that chopper."

The phone rang a second later, jarring all of them into a nervous twitter. Laura picked it up, her heart doing laps against her ribs. "Yes?"

"The helicopter is ready," Paco told her. "Laura, listen very carefully. I'm going to be watching. We're all watching. And I'm going to get you out of this."

"I understand," she said. She wanted to say so much more, but she didn't. She couldn't. Her one prayer shouted for God to watch over these people. And to help Alex, too.

And then Alex motioned for her to hand him the phone.

"Martinez? You don't want to make that shot, understand?"

Laura met Selena's knowing gaze as they listened. Had he heard what Paco had said?

"I'm not stupid," Alex shouted into the phone. "You're trained to do this so I expected it. But I've left one little surprise for everyone here at Eagle Rock. And if you kill me, that surprise will blow up in your face, understand? I'm taking her out of here and there's nothing you can do to stop me."

He hung up the phone then went into action. Motioning to Selena and Lydia, he said, "You two will have to stay in here and birth that baby, I'm afraid. I'm going to lock the door. They know where you are, but they might not make it in here to help you."

He didn't elaborate but Laura got a sick feeling inside her stomach as he urged her toward the door. Alex Whitmyer wasn't through with CHAIM yet.

* * *

Paco hung up the phone then looked at the group. "He's planted a bomb."

Kissie rushed out the side door and hurried to where they were hiding behind a garage fence, her eyes wild, tears streaming down her face. "It's Andre, Paco. He made Dr. Haines strap a bomb on my baby boy." She grabbed Paco's arm then turned toward Eli. "Eli…"

Eli took her into a hug, looking over her shoulder at Paco. "He probably set it to go off after he's up in the air."

Paco looked at the chopper then back to Eli. "Or to go off if he's shot. He could have the detonator centered somewhere on his body."

Kissie lifted away from Eli, wiping her eyes. "You can't shoot him, Paco. This whole place will go up."

"How did you discover the bomb?" Shane asked Kissie.

"I got the cameras back up," Kissie said, then she shook her head. "No, *I* didn't. He must have a remote jamming the system covering that wing of the compound. He brought the surveillance back online so I'd see my baby strapped to a chair with a bomb ticking on his chest."

Eli took Kissie by the shoulders. "Where is Andre?"

"In the chapel," Kissie replied. "Inside the wing where he's been holding the others. I reckon no one thought to go in there to pray today."

"Here they come," Devon said, turning toward the chopper.

Paco watched Whitmyer and Laura moving toward the helicopter. He had Laura on his left side, using her as a shield. She looked scared but even from this distance Paco could see the resolve in her expression.

Then the house phone he'd brought out here rang again.

"Can you see us?" Whitmyer asked, flashing a grin.

"I see you."

"Good. Now here's your dilemma, Martinez. By now, you know where that kid Andre is and you also know that he has a bomb ticking right along with his heart. I can deactivate the bomb at anytime by hitting a button on my watch, but I'm giving you a choice here. You can take me out and save Laura, but everyone inside that big house will die. Or you can let me take her and save Andre and the rest of your band of brothers. It's your choice. I'll give you exactly one minute to decide what kind of hero you want to be."

TWENTY

Laura gasped, her stomach roiling with nausea. Her prayers skidded and careened inside her head. Andre had a bomb strapped on him? And Alex was asking Paco to make a choice.

There was no choice. Paco had to save the others.

"Alex," she said, trying to turn so she could see his face. "You don't have to do this. I'm going with you."

He yanked her arm, causing her to cry out. "You don't want to be with me though, do you? You'd rather be with that renegade soldier. I hear he's just about as crazy as I am but I guess I'm not as charming as him, huh?"

Laura knew all the correct answers but nothing in her training had prepared her for this. How many would die here today if she didn't stop this? She thought about Gerald and Sally Mae Barton and Mr. and Mrs. Simpson and the Andersons. She thought about Shane and Katherine happily planning their second wedding just so they could repeat their vows. And Eli laughing as he tossed his son Scotty up into his arms and dangled him by his feet until the boy cackled with laughter. She thought about how Brice loved to recite sonnets to Selena and how she smiled each time he walked by. Then she thought about Devon, waiting to hear word on Lydia and his child. Their love was so strong, so secure.

Then she thought about Paco. This would destroy him. He would have a breakdown. And this time, he might not recover.

"Alex, we can start over. Just you and me. I promise I'll listen to you. We had a good thing. I just didn't see how much you loved me before."

"Oh, so you get that now!" His harsh laughter indicated he really didn't care. "Time's up. Your man Martinez didn't want to join up with me at CSN so now he has to make a choice."

Laura touched a hand to Alex's face. "No, Alex, you don't understand. You have a choice to do what's right. *You* have to show me you can be the kind of man I'll respect and admire by letting these people live. And in return, I'll willingly go with you and we'll figure this out."

He stared down at her, then put his hand over hers, his expression softening. "I do love you, Laura."

"And I love you," she replied, asking God to keep her calm. "It'll be all right, Alex. I promise."

Paco had them in his sights. He could get this over with and done right now but he couldn't take the shot. Sweat poured down his forehead and pooled between his shoulder blades. His fingers felt sticky against the metal of the rifle. He watched as Laura reached up to touch Whitmyer's cheek, watched as the man looked down at her.

What was she doing?

Brice called from the house. Shane held his phone so Paco could hear. "Eli and I both think we can get to Andre. The bomb's ticking but the timer's not set. If we can get in there, I'm pretty sure I could deactivate the bomb before he hits the remote timer."

"We don't have time to deactivate the bomb, Whelan," Paco said, wiping sweat with his sleeve. "*My* minute's up."

The house phone rang again. Paco dropped his rifle. "Whitmyer—"

"It's me, Paco."

Laura.

He swallowed, took another breath. "Are you all right?"

"I will be," she said, her words low, her voice strained. "Paco, I'm going with him. I'm going with him and as soon as we're in the air, he's going to deactivate the bomb and you'll all be safe."

"No, Laura. No. He told *me* I had to decide. We can figure this out, sweetheart. Just give me some time."

"There is no time. I'm going with Alex and everything will be fine."

"Laura, it won't be fine. He'll kill you. He's insane and he won't let you go. Ever. Do you understand?"

"Yes," she said. "But Paco, God and I, we believe in you. Remember that. I have to go now."

The line went dead. Paco picked up the gun, rage filling his soul. That lunatic had used her guilt and her generosity to seal the deal. And Paco was helpless to do anything about it. All he could do was watch through his rifle scope while Laura ducked low under the chopper's rudders and waited as Whitmyer lifted her up into the chopper.

And then, Paco saw it. He knew what he had to do to save Laura. He turned to Shane. "I have a new plan. And this one won't fail."

Laura hurt all over. Her breath hit at her ribs, reminding her that she still had a wound in her shoulder. Her insides roiled, not so much from the pain radiating across her body. But mostly from the sheer terror she felt about getting into this helicopter. She'd been blissfully unconscious when they brought her in.

She wouldn't look down. She'd never gotten close to the edge of any cliff or any high windows. She'd always taken the aisle seat on airplanes and that, only after she'd run out of other travel options. But she could do this. Her prayers asked for courage and protection, her heart hurt for the agony of leaving Paco behind.

"Dear God, give us all strength, show us Your grace, allow us Your redemption."

"You think prayers will solve everything, don't you?"

Laura opened her eyes to find Alex staring over at her, a smug look on her face. "Yes, I do. You should try it sometime."

He laughed, his hands working the controls. "I learned a long time ago I can't rely on God for anything."

Hoping to understand, Laura pushed. "What happened to you, Alex?"

He shook his head. "Too late for therapy now."

He lifted the bird into the air, the process shaky.

"Do you know how to fly this thing?" Laura asked in a loud voice, a new fear surfacing. If they crashed, the bomb might still go off.

"Like riding a bike, baby," Alex shouted. Then he motioned for her to put on her headphones. "Mr. Henner trained me to fly both choppers and light planes."

"What happened to Mr. Henner?" she asked to distract herself, the drone of the chopper muffled for now.

"He and I had a disagreement," Alex replied through the static in her ears. "He lost."

"I think he was a good man but he never got over his son's death."

Alex gave her a thumbs-up. "No, he didn't. But you see, Laura. He had *two* sons. Nobody knew it but him and me—happened before he married and had Kyle. After my mother died, he reluctantly took care of me and later, brought me into the company. But he could never see my potential. He ignored me all of my life. But not anymore. Not this time."

Shocked and appalled but understanding his motives at last, Laura braced herself as the chopper whirled through the air. Taking deep breaths, she held to her prayers and her training. "Alex, you promised you'd deactivate the bomb, remember?"

He checked several gauges and buttons. "What if I lied about that?"

Laura cried out, trembles moving through her body. "You promised, Alex. Don't be like your father. You can't hurt those people."

"Watch me."

And then, she caught a movement out of the corner of her eye, behind them.

Paco swept a hand around to Whitmyer's throat, a thick nasty-looking knife centered on his Adam's apple. Yanking off the headphones, he shouted, "He's not going to hurt anyone, ever again, sweetheart."

Whitmyer pointed toward his watch, but Paco pushed the knife close enough to draw blood. "One move and you die, Whitmyer. Now take off the watch very slowly and hand it to Laura."

Whitmyer shook his head. The chopper spiraled and whirled.

Dizziness hit Laura. She gritted her teeth against it.

"We'll all die together," Whitmyer shouted above the deafening noise, his eyes wild. "How about that?"

Paco let out a grunt, twisted his hand around the man's neck and watched as Whitmyer passed out. Then he went into action, dragging Whitmyer out of the pilot's seat. "Laura, undo his watch while I land this chopper."

"What about the bomb?" she asked, frantically trying to unbuckle the black band.

"If I know Brice, he's already subdued the bomb but we have to make sure we turn off that detonator to be sure. And that's what I need you to do right now."

Laura slid the watch off of Alex's limp wrist. "Which button?"

Paco held on to the controls, steadying the big bird, his gaze moving over the dial. "The red button on the left should do the trick."

Laura prayed he was right. She pushed at the button, her hands trembling and shaking with each jolt of the chopper. Then she heard a beep, beep, beep and held her breath as she finally looked out the window toward Eagle Rock.

The beeps stopped. Laura closed her eyes, terrified she'd hear an explosion from below.

Then Paco touched her hand. "You can open your eyes now, sweetheart. We're headed for solid ground."

Laura looked down and cried out with delight. Kissie stood waving to them, Andre by her side.

"He's in custody," Paco told Laura two hours later. "And we're to head into Austin tomorrow to give a full report." He reached for her hand. "You don't have to go. The authorities will get your statement when you're feeling better."

Laura didn't know if she'd ever feel better. But having him alive and nearby did help. She still couldn't believe he'd hitched a ride on a chopper leg and crawled through the open door into the back of the chopper undetected to stop Whitmyer.

"And everyone else?"

"They're all relieved and celebrating their blessings. I think Mrs. Barton and the other ladies are cooking up a feast."

"*Our* blessings," she corrected.

He looked confused.

"We're all counting our blessings, Paco. And you're the number one blessing on my list."

He let go of her hand then walked over to the window. She was now in a plush bedroom in the main part of the house. "I don't consider myself a blessing to anyone."

"Your grandfather thinks you're a blessing. He wasn't even surprised when we called to tell him the news that we were both safe. He knew you'd take care of business."

Now that his business was finished, would he leave her here? He was already putting distance between them.

He turned to stare down at her, his expression caught between acceptance and resistance. "I have a long way to go, Laura. It won't be easy. I'm not an easy man."

"I have a whole lifetime to wait for you, Paco."

He came over to her and lifted her into his arms. "Would you wait that long for me?"

"I think I might," she said, snuggling against him. Maybe it was the pain meds, or maybe it was the warmth of his arms, but she felt drowsy with happiness.

"We've got a lot to sort through," he said. "Whitmyer left a long trail of dead bodies and it'll take months to clean up this case."

Laura nodded. "I can't believe he killed Mr. Henner—his own father—and buried him on his ranch. And I can't imagine what kind of warped relationship those two had. It's so sad, so horrible."

"Whitmyer is a very sick man, Laura. He hid it well. But he's going to be locked away a long, long time. Seeking revenge, he took advantage of Henner's grief and your guilt in an attempt to change CSN into a killing machine. He might have compared himself to CHAIM but I pray none of us are like him."

Laura looked up at him. "No, you're not like him. And that's why I won't ever give up on you, Paco."

There was a knock on the door. "Come in," Laura called. Paco got up to see who it was.

Devon wheeled in Lydia. And she was holding their little girl.

Tears sprang to Laura's eyes as she looked at the tiny bundle Lydia held in her arms. "Oh, she's so beautiful."

Devon grinned. "Yes, she is. I think she looks like her mother."

Laura smiled up at him. "I hear you made it just in time."

"Yes. Just in time," Devon said, nodding toward Paco.

Lydia shot Laura a thankful look. "You were so brave today, Laura. You and Selena got me through this."

Laura looked over at Paco. "It's been a long day, and I'm so thankful it's over."

Devon glanced at his friend. "It's almost dinner time. You two coming or do you want a tray here in your room?"

"We'll be there in a few minutes," Paco said.

Laura grinned at Lydia. "Oh, what did you name the baby?"

Lydia smiled up at Devon. "I had planned on naming her Scarlett, but we came up with a better name. Lana. It's a cross between Laura and Selena."

"And it has an *L* to remind us of Luke," Devon added with a wink.

Paco actually grinned back at them. "That's kind of cool."

After they left, he came and sat down in the chair by Laura, took her hand then lowered his head. "I want you to know...today when I thought I was going to lose you, I prayed, Laura. I prayed so hard and I turned my life over to Christ. I mean, really turned my life over to Christ. I promised Him I'd serve Him if He only let you live."

Laura touched a hand to his head. "Paco, God knew you had already been serving him. He knew your heart and your pain when you were holding that soldier on that mountaintop. It's all right. You're going to be all right now."

He looked up at her. "How did you get so wise?"

She smiled. "I'm not that wise. But I believe in the power of God's love and healing."

He tugged her close and kissed her. "This won't be our last kiss, you know."

"I sure hope not."

"It might take a while, but I believe I can make you happy."

"I'm already happy," she said. "I love you."

He stared at her as if he'd never heard those words before. "I love you, too." Then he kissed her again. "If I were to ask you to maybe marry me one day, what would you say?"

Tears streamed down her face. "I'd probably say yes."

He kissed her again. "And if I were to ask you where you'd like to go on our honeymoon, what would you say?"

She touched her hands to his face and smiled. "I'd say, let's go to the Grand Canyon."

"You're kidding, right?"

"No," she replied. "I think I'm finally ready to get close to the edge."

He pulled her up and held her, his gaze moving over her face. "You are an amazing woman, Laura Walton."

"Don't you forget it, Paco Martinez."

A few minutes later, Gerald Barton stood at the head of a long table, his smile proud, his eyes misty. "We started CHAIM all those years ago to do good in this world, to serve the Lord in battle and to protect Christians who needed our help. We've made mistakes and lost a few fights, but we're still here and we're still kicking. And tonight, after all the hoopla and excitement, and now that we have our own Laura back safe and sound, we raise our voices in thanks to five brave men—Devon Malone, the pastor, Eli Trudeau, the disciple, Brice Whelan, the shepherd, Shane Warwick, the knight, and Paco Martinez, the warrior. We thank each of you for your service."

Then Delton Carter stood. "And in light of the events that brought us all here tonight and in light of how these young warriors have changed into strong family men, we'd like to announce a new venture. We want the five of you to run a brand-new branch of CHAIM."

"I'm retired," Devon reminded him with a smile.

"I'm thinking about opening a fishing charter in Grand Isle," Eli said.

"I'm going back to Whelan Castle," Brice shouted out.

"And I'm going to remarry the woman I love," Shane reminded them.

They all looked at Paco. He took Laura's hand and glanced around the room. "I'm going to show this woman that I can be a good husband and... I haven't thought much beyond that."

Everyone clapped, but Delton raised a hand for quiet. "This venture will be different. We'll still be security, but we'll mainly market and sell a line of security products for business and homes. Safe, honest work, but with a bit of challenge now and then."

The agents all stared at each other then Eli shrugged. "*Oui,* and how long do you think that will last, Delton?"

Delton grinned and reached for the carving knife. Looking at the big turkey waiting to be cut, he said,

"Oh, it was worth a try, right, fellows! And anyway, my wife suggested it."

Everyone started laughing at once. Then the food was blessed and passed around the table.

Laura looked over at Paco and smiled. Then she reached up to touch his chest. "You've found your heart, Paco."

He nodded, kissed her fingers then leaned over to kiss her. "Yes, and I'm looking at it."

Shane raised his water glass then winked at Paco. "Mission accomplished."

* * * * *

Dear Reader,

This is a bittersweet book for many reasons. It's the last in my CHAIM series of secret agents. Who knew that one workshop at a conference would bring about five different stories! I'll miss these characters but...maybe one day I can revisit CHAIM and see how things are going.

I actually got the idea for this book from a dream where a soldier came to me and told me his father died in Vietnam, his brother was wounded in Desert Storm and he'd just returned from Iraq. He said he needed someone to talk to. I woke up crying and jotted down his request. And this is his story. This is a story of every soldier who is hurting or afraid. Luke needed someone to talk with, but he was so afraid of letting go of all the horror of war. Laura Walton wanted to help Luke but she learned a few valuable lessons along the way. And she slowed him how to love again. When I researched this story, I found a poem about a heart hunter. It talked about a man who went around searching for a true heart—he wanted to understand why things happen and he wanted to find love so he could feel his heart beating again. I think Luke was such a man. And I'm so glad that he found his heart again.

Thank you for going on this adventure with me. Let me know what you think by visiting my website at www.lenoraworth.com. I love hearing from readers.

Until next time, may the angels watch over you. Always.

Lenora Worth